KU-779-019

Minette Walters is the critically acclaimed and internationally bestselling author of suspense novels, including *The Devil's Feather*, *The Sculptress* and *Acid Row*. She is the recipient of an Edgar Award and two Crime Writers' Association Gold Dagger awards, among other accolades. Minette is also the author of two bestselling historical novels set during the time of the Black Death in fourteenth-century England, *The Last Hours* and *The Turn of Midnight*. She lives in Dorset with her husband.

OTHER BOOKS BY

Minette Walters

The Ice House (1992)
The Sculptress (1993)
The Scold's Bridle (1994)
The Dark Room (1995)
The Echo (1997)
The Breaker (1998)
The Shape of Snakes (2000)
Acid Row (2001)
Fox Evil (2002)
Disordered Minds (2003)
The Devil's Feather (2005)
The Tinder Box (2006)
Chickenfeed (2006)
The Chameleon's Shadow (2007)
Innocent Victims (2012)
A Dreadful Murder (2013)
The Cellar (2015)
The Last Hours (2017)
The Turn of Midnight (2018)

MINETTE WALTERS

THE
SWIFT
AND THE
HARRIER

ALLEN&UNWIN

First published in Australia in 2021 by Allen & Unwin
First published in in Great Britain in 2021 by Allen & Unwin,
an imprint of Atlantic Books Ltd.

This paperback edition first published in Great Britain in 2022 by
Allen & Unwin, an imprint of Atlantic Books Ltd.

Copyright © Minette Walters, 2021

The moral right of Minette Walters to be identified as the author of this work
has been asserted by her in accordance with the Copyright, Designs and
Patents Act of 1988.

All rights reserved. No part of this publication may be reproduced, stored in
a retrieval system, or transmitted in any form or by any means, electronic,
mechanical, photocopying, recording, or otherwise, without the prior
permission of both the copyright owner and the above publisher of this book.

This novel is entirely a work of fiction. The names, characters and incidents
portrayed in it are the work of the author's imagination. Any resemblance to
actual persons, living or dead, events or localities, is entirely coincidental.

10 9 8 7 6 5 4 3 2 1

A CIP catalogue record for this book is available from the British Library.

Paperback ISBN: 978 1 83895 455 0
E-book ISBN: 978 1 83895 454 3

Printed and bound in Great Britain by Clays Ltd, Elcograf S.p.A.

Allen & Unwin
An imprint of Atlantic Books Ltd
Ormond House
26–27 Boswell Street
London
WC1N 3JZ

www.allenandunwin.com/uk

For Hermione

And my three closest friends during Covid lockdown:
Lambert, Butler and Mr Rooster

THE ENGLISH CIVIL WAR

THE FIRST PHASE OF THE civil war was fought in England and Wales from 1642 to 1646 and was sparked by Parliament's questioning of King Charles I's belief that, since his authority came from God, he could not be held accountable by an earthly power. This doctrine, known as the Divine Right of Kings, caused both political and religious division. Adherents to the Protestant Church of England, of which the King was the head, tended towards the Royalist cause; while non-conformists—Puritans, Presbyterians and Independents, who believed the Church of England was modelled too closely on the Catholic Church and needed further reformation to rid itself of governance by bishops and priests—tended to side with Parliament.

Parliament's aim was to pressure Charles into relinquishing absolute power in favour of shared power, and, to that end, several attempts were made to negotiate the terms on which he could keep his throne. The King refused them all, including those presented to him after his surrender to a Scottish army in June 1646. Knowing he still had support in Scotland, he made a treaty with the Scottish Parliament to impose Presbyterianism on England in return for being restored to absolute power by a Scottish army. This led to a war between Scotland and England in 1648, which was of short duration and finished in victory for England's New Model Army. The King's treason against his English subjects resulted in his execution on 30 January 1649.

An uneasy ten-year republic followed, with Oliver Cromwell emerging as its leader under the title of Lord Protector. However, his early death in 1658 left Parliament divided over who should replace him, and the decision was taken to invite Charles II to accede to his father's throne. Known as 'the merry monarch', Charles II ruled wisely for twenty-five years and was greatly loved by his subjects. Nevertheless, Parliament's victories in the English Civil War established the precedent that a monarch could not rule without the consent of his people through Parliament, and this set the nation on the path to universal suffrage and true democracy.

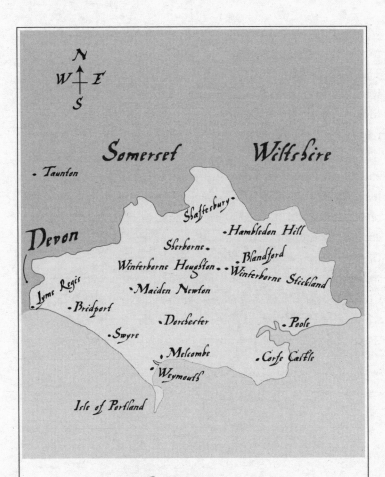

The County of

Dorsetshire

1642–1649

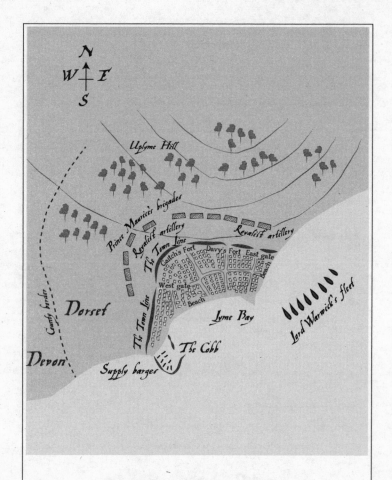

The Siege of

Lyme Regis

1644

Swift: a fast-flying, medium-sized brown bird with a white throat and forked tail that can outdistance most birds of prey.

Harrier: a large sharp-sighted hawk which hunts by gliding low and silently over open ground with its wings held in a shallow V-shape.

No bird soars too high when he soars with his own wings.

WILLIAM BLAKE

THE
SWIFT
AND THE
HARRIER

1642

The English Civil War begins on 22 August when King Charles raises his standard at Nottingham. Three days earlier, a Catholic priest is executed in Dorset for treason.

ONE

Dorchester, Dorset, 19 August 1642

As THE HOUR FOR THE priests' execution approached, the press of people heading for Gallows Hill grew denser and more impatient. Jayne Swift had expected crowds, but not such a multitude as this. It seemed every Puritan in Dorset had come to gloat at the spectacle of Catholics being hanged, drawn and quartered, because there wasn't a road or street in Dorchester that wasn't thronged with hard-faced men and women, their eyes aglitter in anticipation of papist blood being spilt.

Jayne's only means of making headway against the tide was to stay close to the fronts of houses and try to move forward each time there was a gap, but she was attracting unwelcome attention by doing so. She made the decision to retreat into a doorway and wait for the crush to subside after a man rounded on her angrily for knocking against him. She raised her hands in apology, but the suspicion in his eyes as he studied her gown alarmed her. She lowered her head submissively to prevent confrontation, and sighed with relief when his wife and the flow of humanity carried him on towards Gallows Hill.

The embrasure was deep enough for her to withdraw into the corner where the door was hinged to the wall, allowing her to avoid further curiosity by facing the way the people were walking. All were dressed in the drab uniform of Puritanism—simple dark clothes with plain white collars and, in the case of women, tight-fitting bonnets and starched aprons—and Jayne wondered whether it was fear of being thought less righteous than their neighbours or sincere belief that Catholicism was evil that had brought them to the executions. She hoped it was fear, for she struggled to accept that tolerance of other religions was entirely dead in Dorset.

The two priests slated for evisceration that day had been arrested by a customs officer five months earlier when they boarded a ship for France in Lyme harbour. Since then, they had languished in Dorchester gaol, awaiting trial and inevitable sentencing. Yet their crime was not that they were Catholic. Rather, they had been convicted of treason for taking a ship too late to obey the King's edict that all priests must leave the country by the tenth of April, and it mattered not that neither had seen the writ or knew the required date of departure.

Had Jayne felt any animosity towards Ruth, she would have cursed her cousin for summoning her at such an inopportune time; but since she did not, she pressed herself deeper into the embrasure and prepared to wait for the crowd to thin. All might have been well had the door not opened behind her to reveal a thin-lipped matriarch of some sixty years, clad in unforgiving black, who was clearly affronted to find a young woman loitering

4

on her step, particularly one as tall as Jayne, who overtopped her by a good four inches.

She ran a critical gaze over Jayne's apparel, lingering on the lace trim around her bonnet and apron, and the slashes in her sleeves which revealed pale green silk beneath the dark blue of her tailored gown. It was hard to say if she was being taken for a trollop or a Royalist sympathiser because, under close inspection, none of Jayne's garments could pass as 'plain' and 'unadorned', in the Puritan style; though glimpsed at a distance in the streets of Dorchester they usually escaped notice. With a smile of apology, she adjusted the strap of her heavy leather satchel, which she wore across her shoulders, and made ready to set off again.

She was prevented from leaving by a surprisingly firm hand gripping her right wrist. 'You have a crest embossed on the flap of your bag. Name it for me, please.'

'Swift, ma'am. I am daughter to Sir Henry and Lady Margaret Swift of Swyre.'

'What brought you to my door?'

'Nothing, ma'am. I have urgent business in High East Street and sought shelter inside this embrasure when it became impossible to move against the press of people.'

'Which house in High East Street?'

'Samuel Morecott's.'

'I know Samuel. What business do you have with him?'

Jayne smiled slightly. 'With respect, ma'am, that is none of your affair.' She tried to pull away. 'May I leave now? I have no wish to cause you further inconvenience.'

'You'll inconvenience me more if you're suspected of having sympathy with priests. I was sitting at my window and saw the anger in the face of the man you jostled.' She drew Jayne inside and closed the door. 'It will be another hour before you can continue safely. Only servants with tasks to perform will be out on the streets once the executions begin.' She led the way into a chamber to the left. 'You may wait in here.'

Jayne followed, wondering who the woman was. Her austere dress suggested an allegiance to the more extreme forms of Protestantism, as did her acquaintanceship with Samuel Morecott, and neither gave Jayne confidence that her reasons for rescuing a stranger off the street were benign. Perhaps loneliness was the cause. The house seemed deathly quiet after the noise outside, with nothing to suggest that anyone else lived there. Not even servants.

She dropped a respectful curtsey. 'I thank you most sincerely for your kindness, ma'am, but I spoke honestly when I said my business was urgent. If you have a door at the rear of your house which opens onto a less travelled street, I would choose that.'

'There's no hurry. I saw Samuel and his disciples pass this window some thirty minutes ago. If he knew of your meeting with him, he has forgotten it in the excitement of the executions.'

Disciples? What a strange word to use, Jayne thought, while being grateful to learn that Samuel was already absent from home. 'You asked which house I was visiting—not which person.'

'I recall Samuel's wife was a Swift before they married. Do you have kinship with her?'

'Ruth is my cousin, ma'am.'

'Through marriage or blood?'

'Blood.' Jayne shook her head before another question could be put, finding the woman's curiosity ill-mannered. 'Time is passing, ma'am. May I ask again if you have another exit?'

'I do, but you will find the same press of people on that side also. Every road leads to Gallows Hill eventually.' With a slight wince, the woman lowered herself into a chair and nodded towards another at its side. 'Sit and talk with me awhile. Am I right to think you're Jayne Swift, the physician, and that your cousin has called on you to help her son?'

The question discomfited Jayne because Ruth had been most insistent that the reason for her visit be kept secret. And how could someone she'd never met guess her name and profession so easily? Jayne had some small celebrity in country areas but none at all in Dorchester, where only men were accepted as medical practitioners. 'No woman would claim such a title, ma'am. To do so would be fraudulent since she cannot be granted a licence by a university or college.'

'Few men are so honest. The town is full of quacksalvers who pretend learning and licences they don't have. My brother praises you most highly. You treated his gout some six months back, and he's not had a recurrence since.' She canted her head to one side and studied Jayne closely. 'He described you very well. He said you were unusually tall for a woman, had yet to reach twenty-seven and carried yourself with confidence.'

The mask of confidence was a trick Jayne had acquired from her tutor, Doctor Theale of Bridport. *You'll never win a patient's trust by looking nervous*, he'd told her. *School yourself to appear calm at all times, look a person in the eye when you speak to him and do not fidget whatever the circumstances.* The lesson had been learnt through five long years of training and was now second nature to her. 'Does your brother have a name, ma'am?'

'John Bankes of Corfe.'

Jayne made a play of lifting her heavy satchel from across her shoulders to give herself an excuse to lower her head and avoid the other woman's all-too-penetrating gaze. She could hardly accuse an elderly matriarch of lying, but her disbelieving expression would have made her scepticism clear. Sir John was the King's Chief Justice, owner of Corfe Castle and a Royalist to his core. His booming voice could often be heard condemning Parliament for inciting discontent, and he pledged his castle and his household to the King's cause as soon as war became inevitable. How could he be brother to this pale Puritan who looked as if strong meat and intoxicating liquor never touched her lips?

The reason for Sir John's gout had been obvious in his huge girth and the broken veins in his bulbous nose and fat cheeks, and he hadn't taken kindly to Jayne's removal of the tankard of brandy that he hugged against his chest. As for praise, there had been none. Sir John had had only insults for Jayne throughout the time she'd ministered to him. When she wasn't an 'imperious despot' for forcing him to drink water in 'hideous' quantities, and a 'vile torturer' for holding his throbbing foot in a bucket of costly imported ice, she was a 'two-faced shrew' for teaching his wife to prolong his persecution. Every other physician bled him with leeches. Where were hers? And how dare his friend Richard Theale send a woman in his place?

The first lesson Richard had taught Jayne when she began her studies with him was never to betray a patient's confidence. If she couldn't earn a reputation as a physician through the success of her healing methods, she'd not do so by naming her clients and their ailments. Leave that to the quacks, he'd said. Men of little ability had no other way to attract business than by listing which members of the gentry they'd tended.

'Forgive me, ma'am, but I doubt your brother would want you discussing him with a stranger. I know mine would not.' To divert the woman's attention, she gestured towards the portrait of a handsome man, hanging on the wall behind the chairs. 'Is that your husband?'

The matriarch's mouth twitched. 'My husband had a cast in his eye and would never allow me to paint him. That's John when he was a struggling young lawyer. He was quite beautiful before the King's patronage turned him rubicund and fleshy. I've caught his image several times during his life.'

Jayne could see the likeness now that it was pointed out. The shape of the face might have changed but not the eyes. 'You're a fine artist, ma'am.'

'Some say so.'

Jayne moved closer and made out a signature in the bottom right-hand corner of the painting. It was a name of some renown, Gilbert Jackson, and she wondered if the woman had lied about being the artist or had forged the signature to add spurious value to her work. Either way, Jayne decided she'd rather take her chances on the street than remain in this house. Neither solitude nor religious fervour was healthy, and it was a strange lunacy that adopted the manner and dress of Puritanism while claiming close connections with artists and prominent Royalists.

She reached for her bag again. 'You must forgive me, ma'am, but I truly must leave. My cousin begged me to make haste and I am pledged to honour her wish.'

The matriarch nodded. 'No doubt requesting that you come during the executions when she knew Samuel would be away?' When Jayne made no answer she went on: 'It won't help you. Ruth will have no more authority to admit you in her husband's absence than when he's there, so you must be forceful in demanding entry.' She pushed herself to her feet, wincing again at the effort. 'Allow me and my footman to escort you. Three will make better progress than one, and William has the strength to push against the door if the need arises.'

There was no gainsaying her. She led Jayne through an interlocking room, magnificently furnished and with several more portraits on the walls, and thence down a corridor to the kitchen. Several startled maids dropped deep curtseys and a footman rose from his seat at a table and bent his neck in a bow. 'You should have rung, milady.'

'I'm saving time, William. My young friend is in a hurry to reach High East Street, and I believe she'll have a better chance from this exit than from the front.'

'You wish me to accompany her, milady?'

'We will both accompany her. The house she seeks is Samuel Morecott's and I doubt she'll gain entry without assistance, since I'm told all visitors are refused.' She turned to the oldest of the maids, a woman of some fifty years. 'Mistress Swift needs to cover her gown, Molly. Will you fetch her a cloak and one for me also? Perhaps a plain bonnet as well? The one she's wearing has far too much lace and does little to hide her curls.'

As the maid hurried away, the footman pulled on a plain dark jacket and brushed imaginary dust from a pointed hat. 'I would prefer you to remain here, milady,' he said with unusual firmness. 'The Sheriff fears rioting if anything goes amiss with the executions, and I can't be responsible for two if that happens. My duty is to you, which means Mistress Swift will have to fend for herself. Do you wish to put her in such danger?'

'You're a tiresome person, William.'

His eyes creased in an affectionate smile. 'There's a powerful crowd out there, milady. You'll not keep your feet if they push against us. Humour me and stay inside.'

She sighed. 'I humour you every day, even though your single aim in life is to spoil my fun. My desire is to observe, not engage.'

'You'll not observe anything if you fall, milady. Does the window at the front not serve the purpose?' He gestured behind him. 'We see faces well enough through this one.'

'But do you feel what they feel, William?'

'Thankfully not, milady, since I don't have their thirst for Catholic blood. The problem will be if the priests recant. There'll be no holding the mob if they're cheated out of their pleasure.'

The maid reappeared with cloaks and a bonnet. 'May I help you dress, milady?'

'Not this time, Molly. William refuses to take me.'

The woman gave the footman an approving nod. 'As he should, milady. Your leg hasn't mended from the last time you were caught in a crowd. To risk such a press again would be madness.' She turned to Jayne. 'If you give your bag to William, ma'am, I can better ensure your head and gown are properly covered.'

Jayne did as she was bidden, since she doubted she'd have better luck opposing the stern-faced maid than the mistress. She handed her satchel to the footman before allowing Molly to thrust her smoky brown curls beneath a second bonnet and use pins to stitch her into a brown woollen cloak. Once properly covered, she turned with a grateful smile to her rescuer.

'You've been most kind, ma'am. Please remember me to your brother.'

The woman nodded. 'I will,' she said. 'If what he tells me about you is true, you're better qualified to help Ruth's son than the ignorant quacksalver Samuel has been employing.'

'May I ask which physician it is, ma'am?'

'Robert Spencer. Do you know him?'

'Only by name and reputation. I'm told his cure for gout is to plunge the foot into near-boiling water while instructing the sufferer to drink vinegar.'

The matriarch's eyes lit with amusement, but she delivered a warning nonetheless. 'Even so, he's an elder of Samuel's church and highly respected in the town. Ruth must have summoned you without Samuel's knowledge, for I cannot imagine a single circumstance where he would permit another physician to question Robert Spencer's ability. Samuel's too ambitious to improve his status to make enemies unnecessarily.'

Jayne thought this a perceptive description of Samuel, who had distanced himself from his family rather than admit his humble origins. 'Ruth says their son is dying. Surely any father would seek a second opinion in those circumstances?'

'You would hope so.'

'But not Samuel?'

'I fear not.' The matriarch urged Jayne towards the door. 'With William's help, you've a better chance of forcing your way inside. I wish you luck in saving the little boy's life, but know that Samuel will give the plaudits to Robert Spencer if you do. He guards his future prospects too carefully to give credit to a woman.'

Jayne followed William's instruction to walk in his shadow and hold firmly to the strap of her satchel, which he wore across his shoulder. He was some thirty years of age, strongly built and of a good height, and seemed to have little trouble forging a path between the oncoming crowd and the houses which fronted the road. Several times, he nodded to individual passers-by and received an answering nod in return, but none questioned his purpose in taking the opposite direction to them. When they reached High East Street, he turned to the left instead of attempting to push through the press of people to their right, and drew Jayne into an alcove formed by the narrow projecting porchway of a bakery. The doors were closed, but there was enough room for them both to shelter from the teeming mass that thronged the road.

'They're waiting for the priests to be brought from the gaol,' he murmured. 'It won't be long before the cart appears, so I suggest we do the same. The crowd will follow or disperse once they've hurled their insults.'

'I'm sorry to have put you to this trouble, William. I should have accepted your mistress's invitation to remain with her for an hour.'

'Why didn't you?'

Jayne gave a wry smile. 'I found her a little alarming. She assumed I knew who she was, but I don't.'

'Lady Alice Stickland, widow of Sir Francis Stickland. She took up residence in Dorchester when her son inherited his father's estates and title two years ago. Young Sir Francis is even less tolerant of her waywardness than her husband was.'

Jayne longed to ask what form the waywardness took, but didn't choose to show the same ill-mannered curiosity as his mistress. 'Is her brother as tolerant?'

'When he's in Dorset. He wouldn't embrace her so readily if she lived in London.'

'Why not?'

The question seemed to amuse him. 'He'd lose the King's patronage if he acknowledged a sister as outspoken as Lady Alice. She makes no secret of her support for Parliament.'

Jayne kept her voice low. 'Yet she spoke critically of Samuel Morecott, and there's no more ardent supporter of Parliament than he.'

'It's the only belief they have in common. Nothing else about him attracts her.' He looked above the heads of the people in front of them. 'The priests approach. You should turn away if you don't wish to see their anguish.'

Jayne questioned afterwards if it was stubbornness that made her reject his advice. He was overfamiliar for a servant, towards both his mistress and herself, and she was inclined to recite her own lineage in order to put him in his place; but the opportunity never arose, for her voice would have been drowned by the raucous shouts of the crowd. There was no slur too bad to cast at the thin, frail-looking men who stood with their hands tied in front of them in the back of a horse-drawn cart. Children chanted 'papist pigs' and flung cow dung; adults favoured 'spies', 'traitors' or 'Devil's spawn' and stepped forward to launch mouthfuls of spittle.

One of the priests, the younger, was so frightened he was visibly shaking, and the other took his tethered hands in his own to give him strength. Jayne guessed the older to be close to sixty and wondered if it was age or faith that was allowing him to face his execution so calmly. She saw his mouth move and fancied he was urging his friend to trust in God's love and mercy, but, if so, his words fell on deaf ears. The younger man shook his head and gave way to sobbing.

William spoke into her ear. 'He'll recant at the foot of the gallows. The Sheriff must hope Hugh Green remains steadfast or the crowd will become ungovernable.'

'Is that the name of the older priest?'

'It is. He was confessor to Lady Arundell before his arrest. She wrote to my mistress, begging her to go to the prison and assure Father Green of her continued prayers and devotion, because she wasn't strong enough to make the journey herself. Lady Alice visited him several times during the months he was held.'

Jayne thought of how anti-Catholic feeling in the country had grown with the rise of the Puritan faction in Parliament, and wondered that Lady Alice was so willing to show kindness to a priest. 'Was she criticised for it?'

'If she was, she paid no heed. She cares nothing for what others think as long as she believes that what she is doing is right.'

Jayne watched the cart turn onto High East Street and head towards Icen Way. 'Will she fight against her brother if war comes?'

'In as much as they'll be on opposing sides.'

'And her son?'

'The same. He, too, is for the King.'

'I find that sad.'

'Do you not have the same dilemma in your own family, Mistress Swift? Your cousin's husband is for Parliament, but I've heard that your father, Sir Henry, is for the King.'

His prediction that the crowd would thin once the priests were out of sight was correct. Some crept back to their homes or shops, but most followed the cart, their jeers echoing back along

Icen Way as Jayne said, 'You and your mistress seem to know a lot about me, William. How so?'

'Sir John spoke of you at length. The conversation piqued Lady Alice's interest and she asked me to discover what I could about you.' He gave a low laugh. 'I doubt she expected to make your acquaintance so easily, however. One of my tasks was to try to arrange a meeting.'

'To what end?'

'You refused to align yourself with Sir John and the Royalist cause, and you treat the rural poor for free. Milady hopes that means you're on the side of Parliament and the people.'

Jayne gave a surprised laugh. 'Then I'll disappoint her as badly as I disappointed her brother. I support men and women who seek an end to division, not those who look to make it worse.'

'Do any such exist?'

'I know of one: the doctor who trained me. He makes no distinction between political or religious beliefs, and requires all who learn with him to sign a pledge to treat the sick to the best of their ability regardless of circumstance, status or conviction. Were the King and Parliament as tolerant of difference, there would be no talk of war.'

William eyed her cynically. 'You're a dreamer, Mistress Swift. War will come whether you desire it or not, and neither side will accept pleas of neutrality to let you pass. Even to reach your cousin's house today, you've had to accept my help and dress as a Puritan. What would you have said if someone had challenged you?'

'The same as I told your mistress: I have urgent business at Samuel Morecott's house.' She held out her hand for her satchel. 'I'm quite able to gain entry on my own, William, and you will serve Lady Alice better if you follow the cart and bear witness to Hugh Green's martyrdom. She must have sympathy for him or she wouldn't have visited him several times. He will die well, I think, and she will want to hear that from someone she trusts.'

He passed her the bag. 'Indeed. When your business at Mister Morecott's house is concluded—with good health for the child, I hope—will you do Milady the kindness of returning her cloak and bonnet? Her son starves her of money and she is not so rich that she can afford to replace them.'

'I can give them to you now. The road is almost bare of people and it will take me but half a minute to reach Samuel's house.'

But he was already several paces away, his ears firmly closed, seemingly intent on obliging her to return for a second visit with his formidable mistress.

As Jayne approached the Morecott house, she saw that every shutter was closed, even those at the upstairs windows. On another day, she would have assumed the house to be empty, but she knew from Ruth's letter that this couldn't be the case. Her cousin wouldn't have begged her on paper stained with tears to hasten to High East Street if she and her son were in residence elsewhere.

Jayne halted before the door, wondering what to do. It was two months since Samuel had banished her permanently from his house after she'd questioned one of his more foolish interpretations of a biblical text, and the servants would refuse to admit her on that basis alone, with or without orders to keep all visitors away. Preferring guile over force, she moved three houses down. 'Doctor Spencer has sent me with a delivery of medicine for Mister Morecott's son,' she told the footman who answered her knock. 'My instructions are to go to the rear of the building and place it in the hands of a servant so that the little master isn't disturbed by noise. Can you tell me how to find the entrance to the kitchen quarters?'

He pointed to an alleyway some fifty yards farther on. 'Walk to the cross path, turn left and count off six doors,' he said. 'Give the medicine to the cook. She's the only one with the courage to hand it to Mistress Morecott of her own accord. The rest are too afeared of their master to act without his instruction.'

Jayne produced a shy smile. 'Would it be possible for you to accompany me, sir? I'm sure the cook will answer more willingly to you than a stranger. Doctor Spencer was most insistent that the child start his medicine this morning. He would have come himself were it not for the executions.'

The footman eyed her for a moment, perhaps trying to assess how truthful she was being, and then, with an abrupt nod, closed the door behind him and led her towards the alleyway. Mention of the executions had loosened his tongue, and he regaled Jayne with complaints that service to another meant he was unable to attend. How was this fair, he asked, when high days and holidays were so few that all men should be allowed to enjoy them?

Jayne was relieved that he didn't expect anything more than sympathetic noises by way of answer, and that his impatient steps brought them quickly to the house they wanted. He knocked loudly, calling out his name, and the door cracked open a couple of feet to reveal a timorous maid holding a finger to her lips. With the shutters at the window closed, the entire kitchen was in darkness, although light from the doorway reflected off the white aprons and bonnets of other women in the room. All were whispering 'shush' as if their lives depended on it.

With a murmured thank you to the footman, Jayne stepped around him and pushed her way inside before the maid could close the door again. 'Don't be alarmed,' she said, picking out faces in the gloom. 'Some of you know me from previous visits. I am Jayne Swift, cousin to your mistress, and have come at her request. Only she and I will be blamed for my presence here.'

'The master banned you, ma'am.'

'He did indeed,' said Jayne, shooing the barely seen women aside and moving firmly towards the door that led from the kitchen to the rest of the house. 'And when he returns, you may tell him I used deceit to gain entry.'

'Have you come to help little Isaac, mistress?' asked another voice.

'I have.'

'Then you'll need our prayers, ma'am.'

Jayne opened the door to the corridor. 'I'd rather have your assistance than your prayers,' she answered. 'Will one of you show me to Isaac's chamber?'

It seemed not. The request was met with silence, as if the household felt they'd already transgressed enough.

TWO

WILLIAM STOOD TO THE REAR of the crowd when he reached Gallows Hill, having too much liking for Hugh Green to witness his death at close quarters. He'd come to know the man well through escorting Lady Alice on her visits to the gaol, and it grieved him that Dorchester Puritans had commandeered his execution to demonstrate their hatred of the monarchy. For every shout of 'papist traitors', there were louder cries of 'traitor King'.

The scaffold was built on raised ground, so it mattered little where a man stood. All were meant to see it easily, for punishment of the guilty served as a warning to others to keep to a righteous path. Both priests had been dragged from the cart by the time William arrived, and he watched the younger recant beside a table which bore the butchery knives for the drawing of entrails and the quartering of limbs. Deathly pale, he admitted his fault, forswore the Pope and begged forgiveness from the crowd, and so great was his terror that his body shook from head to toe and urine seeped down his legs onto the dusty ground at his feet.

The mob, whipped to a fury by men at the front, roared their disapproval of his cowardice, and only the steadying hand of Hugh

Green beneath his elbow kept him upright. Perhaps fearing the trembling creature would be ripped limb from limb by bare hands, the Sheriff ordered five watchmen to drag him away, and the last William saw of him was when he was carried, half swooning, into a side street to be returned to Dorchester gaol.

As Mistress Swift had predicted, Hugh Green's commitment to his faith never wavered. He drew the sign of the cross on the young priest's forehead as the terrified wretch was torn from his grasp and then, with enviable composure given his situation, lowered himself to his knees beneath the scaffold and bent his head in prayer. Nothing disturbed or upset his meditation. He might have been alone in his church for all the attention he paid to the jeers that came from behind him.

The foremost rabble-rouser was Samuel Morecott. William had no trouble spotting him because he was taller than his neighbours and had placed himself on the incline leading up to the gallows. Every so often he turned to incite the crowd to greater excess by raising his arms, and the easily persuaded responded with shouts of 'papist filth' and 'papist scum'. Yet even Morecott fell silent when the Sheriff nodded to four women and an elderly man who stood at his side. Showing the same indifference to the mob as the priest, they moved forward to kneel around him and share his prayers, courageously identifying their faith with his.

William judged some quarter-hour passed before Hugh Green blessed his companions and rose to his feet, saying he was ready. Assisted by the hangman, he mounted the ladder to the scaffold platform and then, as custom allowed, he addressed the crowd. He began with a sincere profession of his faith, speaking strongly and clearly so that all might hear, and went on to declare his sadness to see his country so troubled by disagreements between the King and his subjects. He prayed daily that solutions might be found and begged his listeners to do the same, saying God would hear them.

Samuel Morecott stepped forward to challenge him. 'Enough!' he shouted. 'The views of a Catholic traitor have no place here.'

Green paid him no heed, and went on to speak of God's love for all men. 'If war should come, pray for those who oppose you as earnestly as you pray for your friends,' he urged. 'Our Lord's words should be your guide. "Love your enemies, bless them that curse you and pray for those who persecute you."'

Morecott turned to the crowd with a scornful laugh. 'This blasphemer makes himself the equal of Christ. Is this not the heresy we fight? That priests believe they're closer to God than every righteous man who reads his Bible?'

The hangman intervened. 'All convicted men are entitled to speak, Mister Morecott. Allow him to continue.'

'I will not,' Morecott countered, turning to face the priest again. 'He forced us to endure his interminable prayers and now seeks a further delay through the preaching of deceit. How do you answer that, Mister Green? You've been tried and found wanting, yet you still have the arrogance to pretend you know the mind of your Maker.'

'You've chosen an unseasonable time to engage with me in these matters, my son,' the priest said gently. 'Could you not have visited me during the five months I was in prison? I had more leisure then and would have answered your questions willingly. I fear time is too short to do them justice now.'

A murmur of laughter rose from behind Morecott, as if some in the crowd wanted to applaud the condemned man's attempt at humour. If nothing else, it spoke to his bravery in face of the torment that awaited him.

Morecott shook his head angrily. 'I have no need of a priest. God answers my questions.'

'Then I envy you, my friend. I wish every man, myself included, heard Him as easily as you do. There would be no talk of war if His pleas for us to love each other sounded clearly in our ears.'

Morecott stared at him for a moment and then pointed at the hangman. 'Do your job, sir. He's a traitor and a blasphemer. Stop his mouth. Put the noose about his neck and throw him off the ladder.'

Shouts of approval came from those around him and, whether from boredom or agreement, many others took up their cries. Hugh Green raised his bound hands and spoke further, but his words went unheard, drowned out by the clamour of sound that beat against him. William saw a smile of acceptance lift the corners of his mouth and then, without a flicker of fear, he stooped towards the hangman, offering his neck for the noose. He was lifting his hands to make the sign of the cross on his chest even as he was thrust from the platform, and William looked away rather than watch the frantic movement of his legs and his desperate attempts to claw at the rope. It seemed a foolish custom to tie a man's hands in front of him in order that he might pray for his soul, since even the most courageous fought to save themselves when the noose began to bite. But perhaps that was the intention. To show that all men, even priests, gave way to fear at the end.

William could have left then, and often wished later that he had, for he was never able to blot out the memory of Hugh Green's subsequent suffering. The poor man should have been insensible when he was lowered from the scaffold on the end of the rope, but whether through being released too soon or incompetence on the part of the hangman, the noose loosened about his throat and he was able to sit upright in front of the crowd. All could see he still had his wits about him. Perhaps he thought he'd been given a reprieve, because a look of surprise appeared on his face, softening to something like gratitude as his executioner descended the ladder to squat in the dust beside him. But the oaf whispered something in his ear—an apology?—and the smile faded. Green closed his eyes.

Such chaos followed that William struggled to understand what was happening. While the priest continued to sit on the ground, an argument broke out between Samuel Morecott and a person near him. So heated was the exchange that the two came to blows, and it was only when the second man attempted to escape that William recognised him as Matthew Barfoot, a barber. Morecott's companions caught Barfoot and pinioned his arms at his side, but he still put up a mighty fight to tear himself free.

'What troubles him?' William asked the person next to him.

The man gave a grunt of laughter. 'He was told the priest would be dead when he performed the butchery, not awake and sitting up.'

'The barber's been tasked with the quartering?'

The man nodded. 'And taken the fee in advance so he could pay off his debts. He'll be labelled a thief if he doesn't honour the obligation.'

William watched Samuel Morecott sink a fist into Barfoot's gut. 'Perhaps he'd rather be a thief than a murderer,' he murmured.

'Without doubt, but he shouldn't have spent the money if he wasn't prepared to follow through. He's making it harder on himself by resisting.' The man glanced at Hugh Green. 'If he doesn't set to with some haste, the priest will be on his feet preaching again, and he'll have to plunge his knife into a standing victim.'

The same thought had clearly occurred to Samuel Morecott, because he sent four of his companions to throw Green onto his back in the dust. Seizing a knife from the table, Morecott sliced through the ties that bound Green's hands before rolling him onto his front and commanding his companions to strip him of his clothes. The garments were so threadbare and thin they came away in tatters and, when the priest was naked, Morecott used his boot to turn him once more onto his back, laughing to see that Green's first instinct was to cover his genitals. Remarking that the traitor had nothing to hide, for his rod had shrivelled through lack of use, he thrust the knife into Barfoot's hands and forced him to his knees beside the priest. 'Proceed,' he ordered, 'or suffer the same fate.' It was as treasonable to make deceitful promises in return for thirty pieces of silver, he told the barber, as it was to be a papist.

Barfoot began forcefully enough, slicing into the man's belly, pulling back flaps of skin on both sides and spilling entrails onto the ground, but fear and nervousness took over when Green, still in full possession of his wits, made the sign of the cross upon his chest. Thereafter, inhuman savagery reigned. Ordered by Morecott to cut out the traitor's heart, the ignorant barber hacked at anything he thought resembled it, near swooning with terror each time he removed a bloody piece of flesh, while the priest, far from breathing his last, begged Jesus to have mercy on him.

If there was anything fine about the terrible scene, it was the courage and devotion shown by a woman who defied Morecott and knelt in the dust at Father Green's head. She was one of the five who'd prayed with him at the foot of the scaffold, and William knew from meeting her in the prison with Lady Stickland that her name was Mistress Elizabeth Willoughby. She cradled the priest's face in her hands throughout his ordeal, offering love and kindness through prayers and sweet smiles, although her fortitude wavered when Barfoot, imagining he'd finally found Green's heart, cut out a piece of his liver and exposed it to the crowd.

She raised her head to look at the Sheriff. 'Honoured sir, you have the authority to end this barbarity. Please use it. Father Green has suffered more than enough to assuage this assembly's thirst for blood.'

The Sheriff needed little persuasion. He beckoned the hangman forward and ordered him to end the priest's pain by cutting his throat. Pausing only to take a second knife from the table, the hangman did so, but not before Hugh Green raised his hand one last time to draw a trembling cross in the air. To William's eyes, the blessing was a general one. To others, including Samuel Morecott, it seemed to be directed at his executioners, and this so enraged him he turned to address the spectators.

'What greater evidence do you need of this traitor's blasphemy than that he takes it upon himself to forgive those who carried out his just and righteous punishment?' he shouted.

It may have been the cries of approval from the mob that sent Morecott into a frenzy, although William thought the more likely cause was Mistress Willoughby's careful laying of her cloak over the dead priest's body. With a face full of anger, he ripped the cloak away and hauled the woman to her feet, bundling the now-bloodied garment into her hands. 'Begone,' he ordered, pushing her roughly towards the Sheriff before wresting the knife from Barfoot's hands. 'Our work here is barely begun.'

Work? What a false word this was for the desecration and atrocity that followed. 'Fun' or 'amusement' would have been more accurate, since Morecott was incapable of hiding his pleasure as he chopped and tore at the priest's ribs to expose his heart. He laughed aloud to grasp it in his hand and slice through the sinews that held it in place before tossing it towards the crowd. Even as someone caught it and lobbed it to another, Morecott was sawing at the priest's neck. By then, his hands were so bloodied they kept slipping on the handle of the knife, and he tugged the scarf from around Barfoot's neck to wrap around the haft to give himself a better grip.

Once the neck was fully severed, he left the barber to quarter the body and leapt to his feet to display the head, grinning and prancing like an ape with his hands, clothes and face smeared with the priest's blood. Egged on by his companions, he dropped the gory object at his feet and began kicking it about like a football. Not every spectator shared his contempt for the priest, however, because murmurs of revulsion began at the back of the crowd. A woman called out that a brave man should not be treated in such a way; another that even papists deserved respect and dignity in death. Their cries were taken up amongst the throng, and the Sheriff, perhaps relieved to be given an excuse to end the unwhole-some affair, sent men forward to gather the head and quartered torso into a hessian sack. Morecott argued that the head should be placed on a spike at the town gates, but with only the voices of his companions supporting the idea, the Sheriff paid him no heed. Instead, he turned towards the alleyway down which the younger priest had been taken and commanded the next to be hanged to be brought forth.

'The rest are women,' murmured William's neighbour, 'and Morecott will insult them as vilely as he did the priest.'

'Why?'

'Green reconciled them to the Catholic faith during the time he spent with them in the gaol and then used his priestly authority to absolve them of their sins. Such things don't sit well with the likes of Samuel Morecott.'

'What crimes have the women committed?'

'The usual.'

William stayed long enough to watch the first reach the foot of the scaffold. She was some forty years of age and so thin that her bones showed through her skin. 'The usual' meant theft of food to feed a starving family, more often because the husband was a drunkard or absent than because the mother was lost to moral behaviour. Inevitably, her death would result in more suffering for her children, though such concerns counted for nothing in her sentencing, since thievery was considered as pernicious a crime as murder and deserving of the same punishment.

William took note of the peaceful expression upon the woman's face, and the cross she drew upon her chest as she was led past the red-stained earth where Hugh Green had been butchered, and he found himself hoping she would remain steadfast to the end. When the events of this day were recorded, the priest's loving forgiveness would be far worthier of memory than Morecott's hate-filled vengeance.

THREE

JAYNE WOULD HAVE STRUGGLED TO find the stairs in the darkness that engulfed Samuel's house had she not known where they were from previous visits. She wondered by what absurd logic Samuel had ordered every shutter closed. Did he think his ailing two-year-old would find comfort in eternal night?

As she felt her way up the wooden treads, she wished for the hundredth time that Ruth had never set eyes on Samuel Morecott, or he on her. There was no mystery about why either had wanted the marriage. At twenty-six, Ruth had despaired of ever finding a husband and couldn't believe her good fortune when handsome Samuel found reasons to visit her father's house and waylay her in the garden. Three years her junior, he had flattered her shamelessly, calling her plain face 'beautiful' and her lank hair 'lustrous'. To all who loved her for her sweetness and kindness, his compliments had sounded false and insincere, and few doubted he had an eye to her fortune. There was no quicker way for a man of humble origins to improve his station in life than to marry the only child of a wealthy landowner.

Once on the landing, Jayne listened for noises, hoping to discover which room to enter. Surely Ruth would be talking to her son? It seemed not, and Jayne was obliged to open two or three doors before she found the one she wanted. Without bothering to announce herself, she moved to the window and flung back the shutters to let in light and air, and then turned to look at the wooden crib on the floor. Ruth knelt rigidly beside it, palms pressed together, lips moving in supplication, and her single acknowledgement of Jayne's arrival was a whispered warning that Samuel would be angry if he came home to find the shutters open.

Jayne removed the pins from the cloak and discarded it on the floor. 'Is he so careless of his son's distress that he'd rather not see it?'

'Doctor Spencer has persuaded him that darkness is the best aid to recovery.'

Jayne shook her head in disbelief as she stooped to examine the child. 'What other remedies has he offered?'

Ruth nodded to a stoppered bottle of murky-looking liquid on the table beside the crib. 'An infusion of white wine and crushed woodlice. Isaac retches it up each time I try to give it to him.'

Jayne wasn't surprised. Even adults gagged on the evil concoction so favoured by quacksalvers as a cure for respiratory problems. Ruth had written that the town's physician had diagnosed chincough—a dread disease that led to death when breathing stopped—but, since none of his cures was working, Ruth had turned to her cousin in a last desperate attempt to save Isaac's life.

Seeing how weak the little boy was, Jayne feared it was already too late. Had his cheeks not been flushed with fever, she would have thought him dead already, since his crib resembled nothing so much as a coffin without a lid. He lay on a thin, straw-filled mattress atop hard, unforgiving wood, without a blanket to warm his body or pillows to support his head. Stifling a sigh of impatience, she scooped him into her arms and moved to the window, cradling him in an upright position. The fresh air and change of stance brought on a burst of coughing, and Ruth pleaded with her to return him to the crib.

'The physician advised against holding him,' she said. 'He told us Isaac would have fewer spasms if he was left to lie on his back.'

Jayne ignored her to listen to the coughs. To her practised ear they sounded more like the gravelly barks of croup than the whooping wheezes of chincough, but in either case, his breathing required assistance. With reassuring smiles, she stroked his cheek and hummed a lullaby to soothe him, and when the convulsions subsided, she turned to Ruth.

'If you wish my help, you must summon the cook and instruct her to obey each of my directions. I'm told by your neighbour's footman that she has the courage to act independently of Samuel.'

'Will Isaac live if I do?'

'Only God knows that, Ruth. Have Doctor Spencer's methods brought relief?'

'No.'

'Then you risk nothing by letting me try something different. The executions should keep Samuel away for two or three hours, and that's time enough to see if Isaac fares better with other treatments. You have but to go downstairs and fetch the cook.'

A tired smile crossed Ruth's face as she rose to her feet. 'I wish it were that simple,' she said.

The cook, who gave her name as Mary, listened closely as Jayne listed what she needed—a nursing chair, kettles of boiling water, a flagon of ice-cold water from the well, bowls, napkins and some sweet, warm custard for Isaac—but she shook her head when Jayne asked if she and the maids could bring them immediately. There were no chairs in the house, Mary explained, only wooden stools; the fire in the kitchen had gone unlit since Wednesday through lack of wood; and she had no eggs, sugar or milk to make custard because her larder was empty. His son's illness, coupled with preparations for the priests' executions, had caused Mister Morecott to overlook the need for food and logs.

'You haven't eaten for two days?'

'We have not, ma'am, and little Isaac and Mistress Morecott have been without food for even longer. The master gives me an allowance of three shillings each Monday to buy what is necessary, but this week I've received nothing.'

Jayne cupped her palm around Isaac's head where it nestled against her shoulder. 'No wonder he's ailing,' she observed. 'There's no fighting disease when the body is weakened by starvation.' She nodded towards her satchel, which lay on the floor by the crib. 'You will find a leather purse in the front pocket, Mary. Take five shillings and make haste to the grocer and log merchant. We women need meat, cheese and bread, while this little man'—she touched a finger to Isaac's nose—'needs as much healthy broth and sweet custard as he can manage.'

Mary glanced at Ruth. 'Am I permitted, mistress?'

Ruth nodded. 'If the master challenges you when he returns, tell him the instruction came from me. I will not have you punished for something I have done.'

Jayne shook her head. 'You will tell him the truth, Mary: that it was Jayne Swift who gave the orders. I am without position in this house so have nothing to lose by courting Mister Morecott's disfavour.' She gave a small laugh. 'Nonetheless, since the household will be eating at my expense, I shall demand hard work in return. Take two maids to help you with your purchases and send others to me now with the flagon of cold water, stools, bowls and napkins. I require the first kettle in this chamber within an hour. Can you manage that?'

Mary bobbed a curtsey. 'Yes, ma'am, but it will mean opening the shutters in the kitchen and at the top of the stairs if we're to handle boiling water safely. Will you take the blame for that also?'

'Gladly.'

Mary located the purse and removed two half-crowns before scurrying for the door. 'God bless you for your generosity, and Mistress Morecott for summoning you,' she said over her shoulder.

Jayne offered Isaac to Ruth in order to free her hands to take what she needed from her bag, but Ruth shook her head. 'I've broken too many pledges already,' she said. 'You must let me return to my prayers. I can better withstand Samuel's anger if I can be truthful about those at least.'

After that, she refused to speak and Jayne had to rely on the maids to give her what she needed. Three arrived with stools, bowls of cold water and napkins, and she asked the eldest to remain behind to answer some questions. The girl, who said her name was Sarah, shook her head in terror. 'It's not permitted to talk of the young master, ma'am.'

'Your mistress gives you permission. Please nod to say I'm right, Ruth, for I cannot help Isaac without knowing his symptoms.'

Ruth's nod was firm enough to loosen Sarah's tongue, and, once started, she answered intelligently. Jayne learnt that Isaac had had the sniffles and sneezes for several days before the coughing began. Sarah likened it to the barking of a dog and said Doctor Spencer had thought it was croup until his remedies failed. Now he believed it to be chincough because the barking had continued for two weeks. Jayne asked which remedies had been tried, and Sarah gestured to a number of bottles on the table, which included sour whey and lungwort tincture. In addition, the master had ordered the household to pray, and the servants had done so diligently, taking to their knees between tasks, while Mistress Morecott had remained steadfast beside her son's crib for five days.

As she listened, Jayne used her finger to moisten Isaac's lips with water from the flagon. She was sitting on a stool, supporting him in an upright position on her lap and cooling his burning forehead with a cold, damp napkin.

Sarah wrung her hands and begged her to stop. 'You should be using one of the infusions, ma'am. Doctor Spencer impressed upon us all that water would reduce the effectiveness of the cures.'

Jayne smiled. 'But you've just told me how *ineffective* they are,' she murmured. 'Shall we put our faith in pure well water instead? Isaac must be thirsty if all he's been given is curdled whey, acrid wine and woodlice. Oblige me by opening my bag and bringing me one of the small spoons from the beechwood box inside.'

Sarah marvelled at how greedily the child sucked water from the spoon, and how comfortable he seemed, sitting with his cheek resting against Mistress Swift's shoulder.

When the kettle arrived, Jayne passed the boy to Sarah's care in order to prepare her own cure. She removed jars of mint and rosemary oil from her bag and added drops of each to a bowl of steaming water before selecting the largest of the napkins and draping it across her arm. Once ready, she took Isaac back into her arms, lowered herself to the stool and held the bowl beneath his chin. To show him there was nothing to fear, she placed her cheek next to his, and asked Sarah to cover both their heads with the napkin so that they might breathe the scented steam together.

The toddler was easily persuaded to copy her long, deep breaths instead of taking the hesitant, shallow gasps that had become his custom. Yet the vapour seemed to make his coughing worse, causing his little chest to heave through every spasm. Unalarmed, Jayne stroked his back and whispered words of encouragement, and her calmness passed to the child because, as the minutes slipped by, the bouts grew shorter. Once the water began to cool, she carried him to the open window and allowed him to breathe fresh, dry air.

'I see no evidence of chincough,' she told Ruth. 'Steam loosens mucus, and he would have brought up green phlegm if that was what afflicts him. I believe Doctor Spencer's first diagnosis was correct and Isaac is suffering from croup.'

She didn't expect an answer, and was surprised to receive one. Perhaps Ruth had needed but a diagnosis of croup, so much less severe than chincough, to abandon every pledge she'd made to her bully of a husband.

'But why have the cures not worked? Why has the malady persisted for so long?'

'Because Isaac's too weak and anxious to fight it. We must cajole him into taking as much water and liquid nourishment as we can and soothe his fears while we do it. He needs to see your face and feel the comfort of your arms, Ruth, not stare into darkness and listen to prayers.'

'You wish me to go against everything Doctor Spencer advised.'

'I do.'

'It will be seen by all as a criticism of his methods.'

'They deserve to be criticised.'

'Samuel will not be happy about it.'

Jayne gave an involuntary laugh. 'Then nothing will change, cousin. Samuel and happiness have always been strangers to each other.'

$\sim$

The women in the kitchen were agog for news when Sarah descended to ask for a second kettle, more cold water and a bowl of warm custard. Was the little master improving? How could that be? What was Mistress Swift doing?

Sarah rolled her eyes. 'Storing up trouble for us all,' she said. 'She has the window wide open, allows the wee one to drink as much water as he wants, and has persuaded Mistress Morecott to hold him in her arms, drop kisses on his head and sing lullabies to soothe his fretting.'

Mary, the cook, chuckled as she added hot milk to sweetened egg yolks and stirred until the mixture thickened. 'Thank God for someone sensible,' she declared.

'Mister Morecott will be angry with us for letting her in,' another maid warned. 'We'll be on our knees for eight hours tomorrow while he sermonises on the sin of disobedience.'

'He'll answer to Mistress Swift if he does,' said Mary, giving the custard a last stir and handing it to Sarah. 'She gave me her word she'd court the master's disfavour before she let it fall on us.'

$\sim$

The sun was well down in the west before Samuel returned. Jayne was alerted to his approach by the youngest of the maids, whom she'd stationed at an upstairs window. The girl ran down the corridor, calling out that Mister Morecott was a hundred paces from the door and that Mistress Swift must hurry if she wanted to waylay him in the hall. By then, Jayne's simple cures—ten minutes of medicinal steam followed by a longer period of dry breathing at the window, cool water, warm broth and custard—had relieved Isaac's symptoms enough to allow him to fall into a deep, restful sleep in his mother's arms.

With a smile of encouragement to Ruth, and a whispered assurance that she would not allow Samuel to disturb them, she instructed the maid to remain with Mistress Morecott and then made her way down the stairs.

The light from the unshuttered window on the landing and the open door of the kitchen at the end of the downstairs corridor were immediately visible to Samuel as he entered through the front door, and, mistaking Jayne's silhouetted figure for his wife's, he chastised her angrily.

'Why do you persist in disobeying me, woman? Did I not order the shutters to remain closed? It is written in Timothy that a wife may not usurp her husband's authority but must subject herself to his will without complaint. What is it about that instruction you find so hard to understand?'

'I'm sure Ruth understands it perfectly well, Samuel,' Jayne answered. 'It's acceptance she finds difficult. She prefers the verses in Proverbs Thirty-One that urge husbands to value their wives. I heard her father recite them to her many times before her marriage, and the one that best describes her is the twenty-sixth.

"She opens her mouth with wisdom and speaks always with kindness." You might do well to listen to her from time to time.'

Her voice sparked him to fury. 'Out!' he roared, kicking the door wide and gesturing towards the street. 'I ordered your shunning eight weeks ago and that order has not been rescinded.'

Jayne remained where she was, for there would be no protecting Ruth and Isaac if Samuel thought he could intimidate her. Nevertheless, she had to draw deeply on her self-training in composure to appear unconcerned at his violent agitation and the blood on his hands. 'I was summoned by Ruth,' she answered calmly, 'and since this house belongs to her father, she has as much right as you to say who may enter it.'

He clenched a fist. 'The rights of a husband take precedence. You will discover that for yourself if you ever persuade a man to offer for you.'

She shrugged. 'I've yet to meet one who's worth persuading. It's not my ambition to marry a fortune-hunter who seeks to advance himself at my family's expense. Does my uncle know you allow but three shillings per week out of Ruth's allowance to feed eight people? What do you do with the rest of the money? Purchase influence with men such as Robert Spencer?'

His eyes narrowed angrily. 'My affairs are not your business.'

'They are when I find your household starving. I was obliged to give your cook five shillings to buy logs and food, for no one here has eaten since Wednesday.'

This seemed to unsettle him. 'Be done with your nagging,' he said irritably. 'It was an oversight. Why does she not have stores in her kitchen?'

'You keep her too short of money to stock her larder with reserves.'

'The running of the house is Ruth's responsibility. She should have reminded me the payment hadn't been made.'

'She tried, but you ordered her to silence.'

'I had other matters on my mind.'

'As did she,' Jayne murmured, 'though not the same as yours, I imagine. There's no thrill in anticipating the execution of priests when your only child is dying. Were their deaths as painful as you hoped, Samuel? You must have been close because you seem to have their blood on your hands . . . and on your face and boots as well. Shall I fetch water so that you may clean yourself?'

He made for a room to his left. 'Send a servant.'

'As you wish,' she said, moving to close the front door, 'but it will have to be the cook. The younger four are so afeared of you already, they'll likely swoon to see you in such a state.'

He spoke from inside the room. 'Send Ruth.'

'She's nursing Isaac. You must choose between me and Mary.'

She heard the thump of a fist against a wall. '*You* then, but speak no more. Your hideous whining grates on my ears.'

What a child he was, Jayne thought, throwing tantrums one minute and sulking the next. She wondered how Ruth had ever tolerated him, for his undeniable beauty could never compensate for the selfishness of his nature nor the paucity of his intellect.

It had been no surprise to Jayne when he'd declared himself a Puritan six months into his marriage and banned the parish rector from his house. Weak men invariably saw advantage to themselves in ridding their households of priestly influence, or indeed any other male influences, since it was no accident that Samuel employed only female servants, in the belief they could be more easily intimidated. He'd told Ruth the reason for the change was to advance his ambition to enter Parliament, saying a man must gain the trust of the people if he wanted their votes. Ruth, wishing only the best for him, had agreed to espouse Puritanism, not realising that, once free to inflict his own interpretation of the Bible on his wife, child and servants, Samuel would impose a domestic tyranny that brooked neither criticism nor complaint. Jayne had learnt that his preferred method of gaining compliance was to separate Ruth from her son whenever she dared challenge him, and the last of these separations had endured a week, until Ruth, driven to despair by Isaac's plaintive crying, had gone to Samuel on bended knee to beg his forgiveness. And now that she'd broken every promise she'd made to him, she was fearful he would banish her from the house, never to see her child again.

When Jayne returned with a napkin and a bowl of warm water, Samuel demanded to know what she had meant when she said Ruth was 'nursing Isaac'. Like every other room, this, too, had been kept in darkness, but enough light filtered down from the window on the landing for Jayne to make out his tall figure beside the chimney breast. Without speaking, she placed the bowl on the floor at his feet and walked away. He ordered her to answer and, when she paid him no heed, he followed her into the hall, grasping at her sleeve.

'She is forbidden from holding the child.'

'It's but ten minutes since you ordered me to silence, sir, and I have pledged myself to obey.' She pulled herself free with a look of withering contempt. 'Henceforth, there will be no conversation between us.'

Sarah and the youngest maid crept down to the kitchen some quarter hour later and instructed Mary and the other two servants to take all the food Mistress Swift had purchased to Isaac's chamber, along with a tinderbox and as many candles as they could find. They were to move as soundlessly as they could to avoid disturbing Mister Morecott and, once delivered of the food, they should return to help Sarah and Rose fill buckets of water from the well and carry those upstairs also.

'And afterwards?' Mary asked. 'Does she mean for us to stay in the chamber with her?'

Sarah nodded. 'I believe so, though she doesn't want Mister Morecott to know about it. She was most insistent we do everything quietly.'

'Then so we shall,' said Mary, setting them to work. 'For myself, I'd rather be upstairs with the two mistresses than at the master's mercy down here. He came home with blood all over him and looked quite mad to my eyes.'

The servants were further convinced of Mister Morecott's madness when he began pounding on Isaac's door and demanding entry. On Mistress Swift's instruction, they remained silent, leaving the master to roar at thin air. By then, a heavy oak cabinet used for storing clothes had been pushed in front of the door, and his attempts to shoulder his way inside came to nought. In frustration, he issued a stream of commands to his wife, followed by threats of banishment when she made no answer. Next, he turned his anger on Mistress Swift, calling her all manner of beastly names, but her only response was to smile and hold a finger to her lips to remind all in the room to hold their peace.

Women had strength and power when they acted together, she'd told the servants, but almost none when they had to face their oppressors alone. They knew this, for they had seen how their mistress had suffered each time she'd tried to speak out in defence of them or her son. This day she had disobeyed her husband in the hope of saving Isaac's life, knowing that if her punishment for defiance was to be barred from this house, she might never see her beloved child again. Each servant must decide for herself whether she wanted to support her mistress or her master, but Jayne promised employment in her father's house at Swyre to any who lost her position for choosing her mistress.

Mary, who was holding a kettle over five lit candles, shook her head. 'We don't need bribes, ma'am. We'd have stood with the mistress long ago if she'd allowed it. She wasn't the only one who grieved each time little Isaac was taken from her and left to cry in his crib.'

'We were never allowed to comfort him,' said Sarah. 'The master believes he'll grow up weak and sinful if he's given hugs and kisses.'

Rose nodded. 'We know the verse in Proverbs off by heart, for we've heard it often enough. "He that spares the rod hates his son, but he that loves his son chastises him often."' She looked shyly towards Ruth. 'The poor mistress refused to smack Isaac for laughing when he shouldn't, and he was taken from her for seven days.'

Mary eyed Jayne curiously. 'You seem to view silence as a weapon, Mistress Swift. Has it worked for you before?'

'Only against my father when he denied me permission to train as a physician. My mother joined me and, with both of us refusing to speak to him, we were most effective in persuading him to change his mind.'

'Will it succeed against Mister Morecott?'

'Providing we don't allow him to frighten us into opening the door. The longer we keep him out, the better Isaac's chances of recovery.'

A wiser man might have questioned how seven women closeted inside a room would view his intemperate threats and name-calling, but Samuel appeared to assume their only reaction would be fear. He certainly hadn't bargained for amusement. Emboldened by the laughter in Jayne's eyes to hear herself and Ruth described as 'heathens' and 'harlots', the maids allowed themselves to smile also, for they knew both words to be silly descriptions of Mistress Morecott. None broke the code of silence. Indeed, they embraced it more resolutely, understanding for the first time how quickly a man was reduced to absurdity when his authority was challenged.

Samuel's parting threat before he stormed down the stairs was to bring elders from his church to force the door and give every woman inside a horsewhipping for disobedience. Jayne shook her head when Rose asked if that might happen. 'He seeks only to make you anxious,' she said. 'Puritans take their instructions from the Bible, and I don't recall any verses about whipping another man's wife and servants.'

Ruth stirred. 'He'll fetch Doctor Spencer. The man is power-fully persuasive and will put forward arguments about why he should be allowed to examine Isaac.' She dropped a kiss on the child's head. 'He's as quick-witted as you, Jayne, so you'll not find him easy to resist. One way or another, Samuel will make his way through that door.'

'But not until Isaac has regained his strength,' said Jayne firmly, 'and that will take another twenty-four hours.' She used a napkin to lift the lid of the kettle to see how close the water was to boiling. 'A few minutes yet, I think, Mary. If your arm grows tired, let Sarah take over from you.'

'It's only heavy when it's full, ma'am.' She glanced at Ruth. 'Would this be a chance for the mistress to eat? She's been without food for days and will likely fall from the stool if she abstains much longer.'

Blessing the cook for her common sense, Jayne urged everyone to take some nourishment. For herself, she knelt at Ruth's side with a platter of bread, cheese and stewed mutton, and fed her cousin titbits in between taking some herself. In truth, Jayne thought Ruth would have fasted forever as long as she could sit as she was now, with Isaac asleep and breathing more easily in her arms, and Jayne's heart hardened further against Samuel for his cruelty to them. Her tutor, Richard Theale, would counsel her against allowing personal feelings to sway her judgement, but in this instance she would tell Richard he was wrong. She needed to be fired by anger if she was to keep this child, his mother and their servants safe.

FOUR

As Ruth had predicted, the next voice at the door was Robert Spencer's. He began with bluster, demanding to see his patient, but turned to honeyed cajolery when he received no response.

'Allow me to introduce myself, Mistress Swift. I am the physician, Doctor Spencer. You have no reason to shun me, for it's not I who ordered you to silence. In addition, I've heard only good about your nursing skills and am willing to receive your report on young Isaac's condition.'

Jayne had already warned her companions that she would have to answer the doctor if he questioned her on medical matters. 'I'm happy to do that, sir, for, as you say, my pledge of silence relates only to Mister Morecott. I have been treating Isaac for croup, and, through the alternation of steam inhalations and cool fresh air from the window, his breathing has improved enough for him to take broth, custard and all the water he needs. The worst of the symptoms have already calmed and I expect him to be back to health by this time tomorrow evening. I trust that sets your mind at rest.'

'It does not, Mistress Swift. The child has chincough, and the methods you are using will repress his symptoms rather than cure them. You must revert immediately to the remedies I recommended.'

'With respect, sir, if Isaac were suffering from chincough, his phlegm would be thick and green, his coughing fits less frequent but of longer duration, and the rasp would be on his indrawn breath, not on the air he expels. Mistress Morecott tells me the only reason you changed your diagnosis from croup to chincough was because Isaac failed to recover in the time you expected. Dare I suggest you should have questioned your methods before offering a different disease?'

The women inside the room heard a brief discussion outside before Robert Spencer spoke again. 'Allow me to enter so that I may examine the child for myself, Mistress Swift. As his physician, I have that right.'

'You've had that right for two weeks, sir, yet Mistress Morecott tells me you've been to this chamber only twice in all that time. What do you hope to find this evening that you couldn't have discovered on those previous occasions?'

'Whether you're speaking the truth, Mistress Swift.'

'Be assured I am, sir. If you doubt me, I will allow a woman into this room to verify what I say. In view of the horsewhipping Mister Morecott promised his wife and servants one hour ago, I'm unwilling to admit a man. My suggestion would be Lady Alice Stickland of Church Street. I met her by chance this morning and I'm sure we can agree she will make an honest judge.'

Jayne didn't think for one moment that he or Samuel would consent to such an idea, and it worried her when they did. Certainly, neither seemed aware of the disdain in which the matriarch held them, and Jayne feared she'd put too much faith in her second impression of the woman instead of holding to the first: that Lady Alice was a stranger to truth. Nonetheless, she hid her concerns through the wait that followed, since there was nothing to be gained by spreading alarm.

They heard Lady Alice's complaints all the way up the stairs and along the corridor. Why was the house in darkness? Where were the servants? Why hadn't they lit the candles in the sconces? What did Samuel mean, 'They were all in his son's chamber'?

She rapped sharply on Isaac's door. 'Do you hear me, Mistress Morecott? I am Lady Alice Stickland, summoned from my bed to verify whether Mistress Swift speaks the truth about your son. Do I have your permission to enter?'

Ruth placed her arms protectively about Isaac and stared in anguish at Jayne. 'I cannot deny her, for she is here by your request.'

'Indeed, but you have the right to say she must enter alone.'

Ruth ran her tongue across her lips. 'I hear you, milady. May I have your pledge that no man will accompany you inside? We are seven frightened women, caring for one sickly child, and are wearied of the threats that are being made against us.'

'You have my word, Mistress Morecott. My footman William is with me, and he will guard the door for as long as is necessary.'

Jayne gestured to Mary and Sarah to join her in easing one end of the cabinet aside, then raised the latch to allow Lady Alice to squeeze through the gap. She seized the matriarch's arm and spun her none too gently into the room. 'Forgive me, milady,' she said, putting her shoulder to the chest and shoving it back into place with the help of the servants, 'but I have more faith in this cabinet than in William.'

Lady Alice glanced around the sparsely furnished room, taking in the crib, the bottles of murky liquid that Jayne had placed on the floor, the table which held the lit candles and platters of food, the queue of maids taking it in turns to hold a kettle over the flames and, lastly, Ruth, sitting on a stool beside the window, her back supported by the wall and Isaac awake on her lap.

'You look tired, Mistress Morecott,' Lady Alice said gently. 'Would you not be more comfortable on a chair?'

'I would, milady, but there are no chairs in this house. My husband prefers stools.'

'Feather pillows on the floor would do as well. Does Mister Morecott disapprove of those also?'

Ruth nodded. 'We live simply, milady.'

'So it would seem.' The matriarch stooped to look at Isaac, who stared solemnly back at her while sipping broth from a spoon. 'I worried your closed shutters meant this beautiful boy wasn't long for this world. Are Mistress Swift's remedies helping him?'

'They are, milady. This morning Isaac could barely raise his head from his mattress to cough, and now he holds himself strongly in my lap to eat and drink. Are you able to persuade my husband and Doctor Spencer of this? It would be foolish to return him to the previous regimen when he's doing so well under my cousin's care.'

'What form did the previous regimen take?'

'Lying in his crib in darkness with only a white wine tincture to soothe his coughing. Water was forbidden, as was physical comfort and soothing words. He weakened as each day passed.'

Lady Alice gave a snort of derision. 'There's more nonsense spoken in the name of medicine than there is in religion.' She turned to Jayne. 'What do you hope to gain by shutting yourselves in here and making an enemy of Samuel?'

'Time, milady. The longer we can prevent him separating Isaac from his mother, the better the child's recovery will be.' She nodded towards the door. 'In truth, all the enmity is coming from the corridor. Samuel seems to find our silence frustrating, even though it's a bare two hours since he ordered me to keep a still tongue in my head. I shall count it a good reward if, by buying another twelve hours, common sense can prevail.'

Lady Alice unbuttoned her cloak. 'Then you must allow me to stay and be your spokesman. My presence will serve two purposes. First, you will have protection against the door being forced, since William will remain on guard as long as I'm inside; and second, Samuel and Robert Spencer will be obliged to put forward reasoned arguments for their behaviour.' She turned back to Ruth. 'Does that meet with your approval, Mistress Morecott? Please believe my single wish is to help you.'

Tears glittered along Ruth's eyelashes. 'You're very kind, milady.'

'You may think otherwise when you hear me give credit for Isaac's recovery to Robert Spencer.' She folded her cloak and laid it in the crib to form a second, softer mattress before nodding to the cloak Jayne had discarded. 'I suggest we use that for a pillow when the child's sleep is deep enough to put him back to bed. You're too weary to support him all night on a stool, my dear, and he'll take comfort from the wool.'

'Thank you, milady,' Ruth said, 'but may I know why you think Robert Spencer should take credit for this day's happenings?'

Lady Alice chuckled. 'He shouldn't, but I'll not win agreement from him on Isaac's future care unless I flatter him. The same applies to Samuel, I'm afraid. You should close your ears if my smoothing of their ruffled feathers offends you.'

'It will, milady, for it's my cousin who deserves your praise. She's worked harder on our behalf than anyone.'

'Indeed, and I shall extol her virtues when the time comes. But not tonight. Tonight must be dedicated to keeping you and Isaac together. You understand that, don't you, Jayne?'

'I do, milady, and will not take umbrage however outrageous your arguments.'

It was easier to hold to that promise than Jayne had feared, for the matriarch's favourable comments invariably carried a sting in the tail. The last exchange remained in Jayne's memory because it was amusing enough to make the maids giggle, although she questioned whether Samuel or the physician understood they were being mocked.

After spending several minutes honouring Doctor Spencer's well-earned reputation as a healer and assuring him that his remedies seemed to be working, Lady Alice asked his advice on how to proceed. 'Mistress Swift advocates taking him from his crib and allowing him to sit on his mother's lap in order to sip broth and water. Do you concur, sir?'

'I do not, milady, and have already instructed Mistress Swift to revert to the wine infusion. To dilute a medicine through the ingestion of other liquids is to reduce its efficacy. The child should continue without food or water for another two days at least.'

'How wisely you speak,' she said, stooping to lift the infusion from the floor. She winked at her companions as she pulled the stopper and poured the liquid out of the window. The maids clapped their hands to their mouths to stifle their laughter. 'You can be sure that Mistress Swift has followed your instructions, but she wonders how vital it is to leave the child in his crib. Will he suffer harm if he sits on his mother's lap?'

'I wouldn't advise it, milady. Children never benefit from pampering.'

'What does Mister Morecott say?'

Samuel's voice answered. 'The same, milady. The Bible teaches us to be strict with our sons if we wish them to tread the path of righteousness.'

'Do you speak from experience, sir? Were you so cosseted as a child that you find it difficult to tell right from wrong?'

'I was not, milady. My father was a harsh taskmaster, which is why I have no confusion over which path to follow.'

'I envy you your certainty, sir. My own parents were so loving that I can rarely decide whether it's better to chastise or forgive.' Lady Alice smiled at Ruth and Isaac. 'Nevertheless, you can be assured no pledges have been broken and your son is in his crib.'

The falsehood was so blatant that the maids pressed their hands to their mouths again, only to widen their eyes in fear at Samuel's reply.

'With respect, milady, I would prefer to see that for myself. Please order your footman to stand aside and instruct Mistress Swift to remove her barricade.'

'I doubt that's wise, Mister Morecott. Women and children are easily frightened, and it's not so dark in here that the stains on your clothes and boots won't be visible. I observed them clearly when you met me on your doorstep.'

There was a short hesitation before Samuel spoke again. 'The day's events were bloody, milady.'

'Indeed, and William tells me you won praise from the crowd for taking such an active part in the proceedings. You must hope that those who hear the story at second hand will applaud you as eagerly. Distance has a habit of shining a different light on events, I find.'

'They will know we did what had to be done, milady.'

'For your sake, I hope that's true, Mister Morecott. However, I would urge you to consult with Doctor Spencer before you inflict yourself on those with tenderer consciences. Not everyone shares your appetite for gore.'

There was a whispered conversation before the women heard footsteps receding down the corridor, followed a few minutes later by the slam of the front door. William tapped lightly on the panels. 'The physician has persuaded Mister Morecott to sleep under his roof this night, milady. It seems he shares your concerns about his friend's appearance, and since Mister Morecott believes his chest of clothes is blocking the door to this chamber, he must borrow attire from the doctor.'

'He's correct,' said Jayne, lifting the lid of the cabinet. 'Samuel reserves the best and heaviest pieces of furniture to himself. It required all of the maids to move it along the corridor.'

Lady Alice bent forward to inspect the contents. 'He certainly doesn't stint himself on finery,' she said tartly. 'Can we rely on his remaining with the doctor, William?'

'I wouldn't wager on it, milady. I've never seen a man so atremble with emotion or so unable to stand still. My guess is he'll return before midnight, if only to command the same respect here that he received on Gallows Hill.'

Lady Alice pondered for a moment. 'We should leave,' she told Jayne abruptly. 'The servants also. Will it damage Isaac's recovery if his mother wraps him up warmly and carries him to my house?'

'I wouldn't think so, milady, for the journey's a short one. Are you sure it's necessary?'

'I don't know, my dear, but I wouldn't want even a modicum of the brutality shown on Gallows Hill to be exercised inside this house.'

FIVE

JAYNE CAME TO UNDERSTAND WHAT Lady Alice had meant by her reference to 'brutality' from her conversations with William during the dark hours. He and she were alone in staying awake, since even Ruth was lulled into slumber by the softness of the pillows that supported her and Isaac on a feather bed in an upstairs chamber of Lady Alice's house. With the help of Mary and Sarah, Jayne moistened and scented the air of the room with steam, though when it became clear that the child was as deeply asleep as his mother, she ushered the weary servants to the chamber appointed to them and went to sit with William in the kitchen. His task was to guard the front and back doors in case Samuel was foolish enough to come hammering upon them; hers was to tiptoe upstairs every hour to check on her little patient. In between whiles, they talked.

Jayne found him easy company, and considerably more confident than her father's younger and shyer footmen. She asked him first about Lady Alice's difficulty with walking. The matriarch had retired to bed within minutes of entering her house, excusing herself on grounds of age; but Jayne had seen how laboured her steps had been from High East Street, how heavily she'd leant on William and how deeply pain had been etched in her face by the time she reached her door. Jayne could guess at the explanation, for she'd heard enough that morning to tell her the probable cause, but she was interested to hear the details of Lady Alice's fall and which doctor she'd consulted.

William told her Milady had lost her footing in the middle of a boisterous crowd on the twelfth day of Christmas and tumbled against a low wall, cracking the bone in her thigh. He held himself to blame for becoming detached from her when a surge of young men pushed past them, and even more for placing her at the mercy of Robert Spencer. William should have engaged help to take her back to her house and search out the most competent bonesetter in Dorchester; instead, and seeing how close they were to the physician's house, he'd carried her the fifty yards to Robert Spencer's infirmary.

'It was a mistake. Spencer summoned a colleague to help him and neither was comfortable dealing with a fracture so far up Milady's thigh. She pulled up her skirts and told them not to be so foolish, but they were too timorous to do the job properly.'

Jayne was sure he was right. The setting of a thigh bone required strength and force to pull against the muscles in order to return the bone to its natural position, and there would be little left to the imagination if the patient was a woman. 'The pain would have been intense,' she said. 'Perhaps they were as reluctant to see that as anything Milady keeps hidden.'

'She'd rather have endured the agony then than now. She spent near on three months in bed before the uneven healing was discovered. Her leg withered from lack of use and she hasn't been free of pain since.'

'What further treatments has Doctor Spencer suggested?' Jayne asked.

'Only hot poultices and more time in bed.' William gave a gruff laugh. 'He might as well have ordered the sun to stop shining. Milady was barely able to tolerate the first period of staying still; she couldn't have borne a second. She says she'd rather live with the pain of walking than become a prisoner in her own chamber.'

Jayne smiled. 'Her instincts serve her well. She needs to use her leg if it's to grow strong again. You'll help her greatly if you and a maid support her while she places her weight on it. The exercise should be done for an increasing number of minutes each day, and, when she feels confident enough, you must encourage her to bend her knee and push upright again. My tutor, Doctor Theale of Bridport, has used such methods to treat soldiers returning from the European wars with legs so crooked you can see where the break was.'

William was doubtful. 'Does it work?'

'A great deal better than allowing limbs to waste in bed.'

Thereafter, Jayne turned the subject to Gallows Hill. She wanted to know what had happened there and why Lady Alice had been so keen to remove the women from Samuel's house. She assured William that nothing he said would shock her, but she knew by the end of the story she'd been wrong. Whatever dislike she'd had for Samuel in the past was nothing compared to the revulsion she felt for him now.

Samuel Morecott presented himself at the front door shortly before midnight, demanding to know where his family and servants were. He began quietly enough, but when William refused him entry, his tone grew strident and harsh. Jayne, drawn by curiosity, slipped through the interlocking room to the parlour and watched Samuel from the shadows at the side of the window. He stood in borrowed clothes on Lady Alice's doorstep, a lantern clasped in one hand, lambasting a man he judged to be his inferior.

William ignored the slurs. 'You'd do well to speak quietly if you don't want the street to learn of your troubles, Mister Morecott.'

Samuel scowled. 'Are you lecturing me?'

'I prefer to call it advice, Mister Morecott. You'll not escape gossip if you rouse the town in search of your wife.'

'Then let me in.'

'I can't. Milady's door is closed to you. I suggest you return to your bed.'

Jayne saw a candle flicker to life in a window opposite. Perhaps the same was happening in houses on Milady's side of the street, because Samuel grew cautious suddenly. 'Bring Jayne Swift to the door,' he muttered. 'I'll hear what she has to say.'

'That's not in my power, sir, and even if it were, I understood from Doctor Spencer that Mistress Swift is pledged to silence in your presence. She impresses me as a lady of firm resolve, so why would she speak to you now?'

Samuel clenched his right fist and shook it at the footman. 'Your mistress will hear of your insolence.'

'Not until the day is well advanced, Mister Morecott. Milady never receives visitors before noon. I wish you goodnight.'

Jayne heard the sound of the door closing, followed by the soft pad of William's feet as he crossed the floor to join her at the window. Together, they watched Samuel stand irresolute in the street, clearly undecided about whether to pound upon the panels once more or return home with his tail between his legs. After a minute or two, he departed—realising, perhaps, that further knocking would draw more attention from Lady Stickland's neighbours.

William urged Jayne towards the hall, taking a candle from one of the sconces to light the way. 'Why did your cousin's father allow her to marry him?' he asked curiously. 'He wouldn't be my choice of husband for her. She's too gentle a lady for one so coarse and ignorant.'

Jayne could hear her father's voice in her ear, warning her against discussing Swift business with servants, but she and William had shared so many thoughts already, it seemed foolish to deny him an answer. In any case, she found his easy manner difficult to resist. 'Ruth's only other suitors were elderly widowers with adult children. She longed for someone younger and lost her heart to Samuel the first time he came to her father's house. He offered his services as a bookkeeper, and she was so entranced by his looks and manner she persuaded my uncle to give him a position.'

'And then her hand?'

Jayne nodded. 'Samuel has a great ability to present himself well when the situation demands it.'

'What does your uncle think of him now?'

'The same as before. Ruth tells me Samuel never behaves better than when my aunt and uncle make their twice-yearly visits. Those are the only times Ruth is allowed to speak without deferring to Samuel first.'

'But not to complain about her lot, presumably.'

'Indeed.'

William accompanied Jayne to the kitchen and pulled out a chair for her. 'Would her father agree to take her back if he knew how Morecott treated her and the child?'

Jayne sat down. 'You mean if Ruth chooses to estrange herself from him?'

'Yes,' said William, placing the candle in a holder on the table.

'It won't happen. Samuel will never allow Ruth to leave with Isaac, and Ruth won't leave without him. She told me this afternoon she's willing to endure anything as long as she doesn't lose her son.'

Jayne watched Samuel's arrival at noon the next day from the window of Ruth and Isaac's chamber. He was so full of swagger and importance she expected him to appear at their door within minutes, ordering their return, and was surprised when he didn't. She was even more surprised when he slunk away again some half-hour later, head down and shoulders slumped. Shortly afterwards, Molly, the maid, brought a spinning top to the room for Isaac to play with, and asked Jayne if she was willing to speak with William downstairs.

He stood in the hallway and gave a small bow as she approached. 'Mister Morecott has given permission for his wife and son to reside at Mistress Morecott's father's house in Weymouth, ma'am. His servants, too, should they wish to accompany her. I hope this meets with your approval.'

Jayne made a conscious effort to close her mouth. 'Amazement, rather,' she declared. 'How was such a miracle achieved?'

'It seems he's more amenable to reason than we thought, ma'am,' he murmured, rubbing the knuckles of one hand.

Jayne gave an involuntary laugh. 'Did you strike him?'

'Not through choice, ma'am. I merely countered the punch he threw at me.' Attractive creases formed about his eyes. 'I can't say how long he'll tolerate the separation, but I trust Mistress Morecott will be less fearful of confronting him in Weymouth.'

'Without a doubt,' said Jayne. 'But how am I to get her there? Will Milady allow her to stay another night while I ride to Weymouth and beg the use of my uncle's carriage?'

'Where would you find a horse, ma'am?'

'My mare is stabled at the King's Head Inn on the Bridport road. I left her there yesterday morning and came into town on foot. It will take an hour to return and another two to ride to Weymouth, which won't allow time for the carriage to make the journey here and back before nightfall.'

William found her estimate of two hours to Weymouth overly confident. 'You must be an accomplished rider, ma'am. A man could take that highway at a gallop, but not a lady, sitting side-saddle.'

Jayne saw no reason to lie. 'It's a long time since I've travelled side-saddle, William. I leave my mare at the King's Head to avoid Dorchester Puritans seeing the britches beneath my gown. The innkeeper and his wife call on my services from time to time and are unshocked that their physician rides astride.'

And so, it seemed, was William. 'You're a woman of many surprises, ma'am, but perhaps a simpler solution would be for me to drive Mistress Morecott in Milady's carriage. I can have it ready within the hour, if you think that's time enough to consult with her servants and prepare Isaac for the journey.'

'Is the carriage large enough for so many?'

'It will help if you retrieve your mare and ride on horseback, ma'am. There's a crossroad south of the King's Head that will bring you to the Weymouth road, and I can wait there until you join us. The maids may have to take it in turns to follow behind on foot, but we won't be travelling so fast that they can't keep up.'

Jayne thought for a moment. 'It might be wiser for me to ride ahead in order to warn my aunt and uncle of Ruth's arrival,' she suggested. 'They're more likely to take her side if they hear the truth before they see her.'

'Are you worried they'll turn her away?'

'A little,' she admitted. 'They're followers of tradition and find it shameful enough that their niece purports to be a physician. I dread to imagine what they'll make of their daughter leaving her husband.'

'There's no compulsion on her, ma'am,' said William. 'If she chooses to remain with her husband, she may.'

'She'll suffer worse consequences if she does.'

'Indeed, but the decision must be hers.' He nodded towards the stairs. 'Will you consult with her on the matter? I'll wait in the kitchen to hear whether she wishes me to ready the carriage.'

Jayne returned upstairs. The door to the first room off the landing opened as she passed, and a maid came out with a jug in her hand. Beyond her, Jayne caught a glimpse of Lady Alice, still in night attire, seated in front of a mirror. Molly stood behind her, brushing and twisting her long grey hair into a bun at the base of her neck, and any ideas Jayne had had that Milady might have been present when William 'reasoned' with Samuel quickly vanished. However wayward Lady Alice was, she wouldn't appear unclothed before a male visitor.

All in all, it was quite a puzzle. Jayne had little difficulty imagining Samuel striking a footman—it was the nature of weak men to ill-treat inferiors—but she found it hard indeed to conceive of a footman daring to return the blow. It left her thoroughly curious about William's real status, for only a man of similar or better standing than Samuel could have dismissed him so easily.

Whatever the truth, Ruth's tearful relief to learn she needn't go home to Samuel was cause to be grateful. Never doubting that Lady Alice was their saviour, she and her household dropped deep curtseys and blessed the matriarch for her many kindnesses as they bade her farewell. By dint of the two youngest maids sitting on Mary's and Sarah's laps, there was room for all inside the carriage and, with four horses to draw it, William was confident they could reach Weymouth by late afternoon.

Lady Alice and Jayne watched the conveyance move away, but when Jayne attempted a curtsey of her own before leaving to fetch her mare, Lady Alice prevented her. 'We're both too contrary to pay lip service to convention,' she said with a smile, taking Jayne's hand. 'You need to make haste to reach Ruth's father ahead of her or she'll take the blame for this failed marriage upon herself. She's been subject to Samuel's will too long to plead her case as forcefully as she should.'

Jayne nodded, for she had the same fear. She eased her satchel across her shoulders. 'I wish you well, milady. Should you ever have need of my services, you have but to ask.'

Lady Alice released her hand. 'Be sure I shall,' she said. 'Godspeed, my dear.'

⌐⌐

Jayne gained two hours on the carriage by taking a cross-country route to her uncle's estate on the outskirts of Weymouth. Her usual mode of arrival was to gallop up their driveway, her skirts folded across her thighs, but this time she dismounted out of sight of the windows and made sure her britches and boots were properly hidden beneath her gown before walking her mare towards the forecourt. Now was not the time to tease her aunt and uncle with her refusals to conform; instead she must persuade them she was an honest broker for Ruth.

The task proved easier than she'd expected, for it seemed they'd had word of Isaac's illness from friends in Dorchester and had been waiting on news ever since. Her uncle told Jayne he'd written twice to Samuel this last week but had received no reply, while his letters to Ruth always went unanswered. To hear that Ruth was forbidden to write privately to anyone, and had chosen silence over having her words corrected by Samuel, both shocked and angered him—though not so much as learning that Ruth had only been able to send her plea for help to Jayne through the generosity of her cook, Mary, who had used her own meagre savings to pay a traveller to carry the message to Swyre.

Even Ruth's mother, the most placid of women, became incensed when Jayne described the conditions in which she'd found Ruth and Isaac. Jayne explained that Samuel apportioned three shillings a week out of Ruth's allowance to feed himself, his wife, son and five servants, and said her best guess was that Samuel was using the rest of Ruth's money to buy influence with Parliamentarians. Since Jayne knew her uncle favoured the King, it was hardly necessary to besmirch Samuel further by repeating the story of the priest's death, but she did so anyway. She was conscious that Samuel had the right to present himself here at any time and insist that Ruth and Isaac be returned to him, and when he did, she wanted Ruth's parents to remember that his glib tongue and handsome looks belied a cruel nature.

The carriage appeared on the driveway shortly after five o'clock, and Jayne, who'd been watching from a window, stepped out onto the forecourt to meet it. William acknowledged her with a respectful bow from his place on the driver's seat and held the horses steady while two grooms hurried forward to assist Ruth and her household to alight.

'I trust all is well, ma'am,' he said.

She took hold of the lead horse's chinstrap. 'It is,' she assured him. 'My uncle's indebted to you for the help you've given his daughter. Will you come into the house and allow him to thank you in person?'

William watched maids hasten from the door to escort a tired-looking Ruth, her sleeping toddler and weary servants inside. 'It's not necessary, ma'am. He and his wife have more pressing matters to occupy their minds, and I promised Milady I wouldn't tarry.'

'Then allow me to bring you some refreshment. You've attended me so well these last two days that it would please me to repay your thoughtfulness.'

His eyes creased in a smile. 'There's no need, Mistress Swift. I was happy to be of service.' He gathered up the reins. 'You'll be in high demand as a physician when war comes, ma'am. Should we find ourselves on opposing sides, know that I wish you good fortune anyway.'

She smiled back. 'Thank you, William, but I spoke the truth when I said I would remain neutral. You can be confident I shall ride to Dorchester to tend your wounded as surely as I will to Corfe Castle if Sir John Bankes makes a similar request.'

'You'll be taken for a spy if you do, ma'am. The crossing of enemy lines rarely inspires trust.'

'You seem very knowledgeable about war, William. How so? Were you a soldier before you became a footman?'

There was the briefest of hesitations before he answered. 'Nothing so grand, ma'am. The men in my family have had charge of the hounds and hawks on the Stickland estate for three generations, and I practised the skills for several years before I accompanied Milady to Dorchester.' He saw her disbelief. 'You shouldn't doubt me, Mistress Swift. My patronym is Harrier, which refers to both the hunting dog and the bird of prey.'

Her smile widened. 'I don't doubt you for a moment, William. I'm merely trying to imagine my father's keeper of hounds abandoning his much-loved charges to live the life of a footman.'

'I had no choice in the matter, Mistress Swift. The present Sir Francis dismissed me when he learnt of my support for Parliament. I took it as a kindness when Milady invited me to work for her instead.' He nodded to Jayne's fingers, which still grasped the chinstrap. 'You need to release the horse if I'm to reach home by nightfall.'

Jayne ignored the request. Instead, she lifted her other palm to fondle the animal's muzzle. 'My uncle had business with Sir Francis Stickland three months ago,' she said idly, 'and he sounds quite unlike your description of him. My uncle described him as "a timid little fellow who wouldn't say boo to a goose". I wonder he found the courage to expel his headstrong mother and powerfully built servant from his property.'

The smile flickered around William's eyes again. 'We live in confusing times, ma'am.'

Jayne laughed as she dropped her hands and stepped back. 'We can agree on that at least. Farewell, William. You can always reach me at Swyre if you think my skills preferable to those of the quacks and butchers of Dorchester.' Her eyes danced with mischief. 'As long as the message is signed "Harrier", I shall know it comes from you. A swift never forgets a meeting with a hawk.'

He hid his own amusement behind another respectful bow. 'Good day to you, ma'am,' he said, clicking his tongue to set the horses in motion again. 'It's been an education to meet you.'

1643

After a year of war, the Royalists are in the ascendancy across England.

Dorset, previously under Parliamentary control, surrenders to the Earl of Carnarvon and Prince Maurice of the Palatinate in the first week of August.

SIX

Dorchester, Dorset, 1 September 1643

JAYNE NEVER TRAVELLED THE HIGHWAYS these days. Her encounter with a dozen Parliamentary soldiers on the Bridport to Weymouth road in the early days of the war had shown her how dangerous it was for a woman to ride alone, and she still blessed her good fortune that one of the men had recognised her as the physician who had treated his mother. She was in little doubt as to what her fate would have been had he not waded in with boots and fists after his companions pulled her from her saddle and flung her to the ground. Even so, he'd had to draw his sword to keep them at bay while she remounted, and his angry warning as he ordered her back to her father's house remained with her. Women who flaunted themselves were fair game in war.

Thereafter, she took cross-country routes, always keeping a good distance between herself and the highways, and dismounting to make the final leg of her journey on foot. A woman leading a horse on a halter attracted little attention, particularly one dressed in the style of a poor farmer's wife, as Jayne was. Parliamentary soldiers seemed to have more sympathy than desire for a humble woman whose poverty showed in her heavily patched and darned brown bodice, threadbare ankle-length grey skirt, workman's boots and dirty coif, tied in a bow on the nape of her neck to cover her tightly braided hair. She always kept her head lowered to avoid meeting anyone's gaze, and was helped in this by carrying her medicine satchel inside a coarse hessian sack, clasped by its neck across one shoulder, which obliged her to walk with a stoop.

She hadn't spoken of the incident on the highway to anyone, least of all her family, but it had left her deeply shaken. At night, she relived the terror of hands tearing at her clothes; by day, she became paralysed with fear if a man came too close. All the while, she berated herself for thinking a column of marching soldiers would have no interest in her and, worse, drawing to a halt to allow them to pass instead of spurring her mount to a gallop. She never doubted that her own idiocy had brought the trouble upon her, or that her father would confine her to the house if he learnt of it. She excused her sudden preference for dressing in peasant clothes and taking only bridleways on the increased number of people on the roads, any of whom might be desperate enough to rob her of her horse and medicines. And Sir Henry, who had never had cause to doubt his daughter's word and had long since given up trying to stop her riding alone, accepted this reason, having heard from friends in other counties that war was turning even the most honest to thievery.

While Jayne may have regained the confidence to ride alone, her fear of men in groups remained strong, whichever side of the divide they were on, and she felt immediate anxiety when she came in sight of the King's Head and saw upwards of twenty armed soldiers milling drunkenly about the door. She knew them to be Royalists by the red sashes they wore across their chests, but this only exacerbated her dread. Dorset had been rife with rumours of indiscipline in the King's army since the Parliamentary garrisons of Dorchester, Weymouth and Portland had surrendered to the Earl of Carnarvon a month ago, and to Jayne's eyes the behaviour of these twenty seemed to prove the stories true. It was barely nine o'clock in the morning, but some were so inebriated they were staggering in circles about the fore-court, while others upended tankards of ale over two who were brawling on the ground.

She would have retreated had the innkeeper not emerged from a wooden barn at the side of the main building and hastened to meet her. Perhaps he saw the tremor in her hands, for he took the mare's halter and positioned himself between her and the men. 'Pay them no mind, Mistress Swift,' he murmured. 'They're so drunk they don't know which day it is. You'll be safe if you walk between me and the horse.'

Jayne forced a smile. 'Thank you, Timothy. I admit I find them alarming.'

'As did I when they first arrived. Now I have only contempt for them.' He shepherded her towards the barn, which served as a stable for his customers. 'They're worse thieves than Parliamentarians, and that's not something I ever thought I'd say.'

'How long have they been here?'

'Four days. They rode in from the west. Their captain commandeered the inn without so much as a by-your-leave and then ordered me and the wife to give up our bed to him. I sent her and the children to her parents' house in Frampton and have been sleeping in here with the horses.' He led her inside and nodded with annoyance towards the numerous chargers that were tied to halter rails along the walls. 'I'm expected to feed everyone for free, even the animals.'

Jayne followed him to the far end of the building, where he tied her mare to the same rail as his shire horse. 'Have you tried refusing?'

Timothy gave a sour laugh. 'I did, and got a bloody nose for my efforts. They're Prince Maurice's troops and don't give two farthings for the promises Carnarvon made. It was a bad day when Dorchester gave up without a fight.'

Jayne had heard the surrender described in worse terms. 'Abject cowardice' and 'inglorious capitulation' were the phrases her father had used, and when word arrived that Weymouth and Portland had surrendered similarly, Sir Henry was so confident the war was nearly won that he took to tying a red scarf about his neck to show he was a King's man. It pleased him to draw comparisons between Parliament's gutless troops—in Dorchester's case, it was said that six hundred musketeers ran away rather than engage with the enemy—and Carnarvon's fine Royalist army. Carnarvon was a man of decency and honour who had pledged there would be no arrests, punishments or pillaging in return for the Parliamentarians laying down their weapons, and he and his men had upheld those terms for all of five days, until Prince Maurice arrived with reinforcements.

Prince Maurice, fourth son of the deceased King of Bohemia and nephew to King Charles of England, cared nothing for gentlemanly promises, and he allowed his troops to pillage and plunder at will. Having learnt his soldiering in Germany, where the spoils of war were considered legitimate payment for fighting men, he saw no reason to leave anything of value to a treacherous county which had lent its support to the enemy for upwards of a year. Sheep and cattle were as highly prized as gold and silver, and few landowners escaped having their flocks and herds raided to feed Prince Maurice's rapacious regiments. Even Sir Henry, despite his professed allegiance to the King, was ordered to send twenty head of cattle to the Royalist camp outside Weymouth without reimbursement, being advised by an officer speaking in heavily accented English that failure to do so would risk the forfeiture of his house and estate. In a small act of rebellion, Sir Henry had removed his red scarf and tied it about the horns of one of his cows as his farmhands mustered the herd for the drive, saying the King's colours looked as well on a beast as on a man.

'Do you know when they'll leave?' Jayne asked Timothy.

He shook his head. 'Whenever they get orders to move on, I imagine. I pray each morning this will be the day, though I worry they'll set fire to the inn when they do. They're spiteful enough. The captain considers me a traitor because I served Parliamentary troops when they had dominance in Dorchester.'

'Even though you had no more choice then than you do now?'

Timothy nodded. 'Prince Maurice is better able to excuse his stealing by branding all in Dorset as enemies. The captain delighted in telling me he'll take whatever's left of my stores when he goes.'

'How will you feed yourselves?'

A smile flickered across Timothy's lips. 'Purchase more. Our money's safely hidden. I buried it deep in the woods some five months back. We've worked too long and hard to have mercenaries steal it . . . whichever side they support.'

Jayne laughed. 'My father and his neighbours have done the same. I warrant there's more silver buried under Dorset's turf than ever graced the King's treasury.' She untied the hessian sack from the pommel of her saddle and hoisted it across her shoulder, nodding to the small door in the rear wall. 'Will I encounter soldiers if I leave through there? I'd rather walk across the fields than have those at the front see me set out along the highway alone.'

'May I ask who summoned you, Mistress Swift?'

'Lady Alice Stickland of Church Street.'

Timothy gave a nod of relief. 'Then her man awaits you by the stream. He said Lady Alice had sent him, but I take so little on trust these days that I wasn't sure whether to believe him.' He opened the door. 'I'll escort you to him now.'

'There's no need,' Jayne answered. 'I'm sure I'll be able to find him.'

'There's every need,' the innkeeper retorted severely. 'He doesn't look like anyone's "man" to me, and I'll not leave you in his company unless I'm satisfied he is who he says he is.'

The last time Jayne had seen William, he'd been dressed as a coach driver with cropped hair and a clean-shaven face. Now, his dark hair had lengthened, a moustache covered his upper lip and he wore the attire of a well-to-do merchant—a buff coat, knee-length britches, white stockings and black shoes. He bent his head as she and Timothy approached. 'I trust you're well, Mistress Swift.'

She expected to feel her customary alarm at being in the presence of a stranger, but she found more to recognise than fear. 'I am, William. Thank you for asking. You seem to have risen in the world since last we spoke.'

'Lady Alice thought I could better protect you from Royalist soldiers if I wore her dead husband's clothes, ma'am.'

Jayne recalled her uncle saying that Lady Alice's son took after his father—short and slight—and she doubted tall, well-built William could have squeezed himself into such a man's garments. 'They look made for you,' she said lightly, 'though we're ill-matched to be in each other's company. You're dressed too finely to be escorting a poor countrywoman.'

'I expected to find you as handsomely gowned as you were last year, Mistress Swift.'

She shrugged. 'Times have changed. I learnt within days of the war starting that the poor travel more safely than the rich.'

He nodded gravely. 'Indeed, but we'll not see anyone until we enter the town and, once there, I'll walk a few steps behind you.' He held out his hand. 'Allow me to carry your bag until then.'

Jayne relinquished it and turned to Timothy. 'I'll be safe with William,' she assured him. 'You were most kind to be concerned, but he is indeed in the employ of Lady Alice.'

Timothy's expression suggested he thought otherwise but, with a small bow of his own and a promise to watch over her mare until she returned, he took the path back to the inn.

William waited until he was out of sight and earshot before asking, 'How many of Prince Maurice's troops are billeted on him?'

'I can't say.'

'Can't or won't?'

Jayne smiled slightly. 'Both,' she said. 'I neither ask such questions nor answer them for fear of being taken for a spy. In any case, you'll have counted them yourself when you went to the inn to tell Timothy to expect me.'

He laughed before gesturing to the path beside the stream. 'Shall we go, ma'am? Milady is impatient to see you again.'

Lady Alice's letter had been brief, asking only that Doctor Swift attend upon her that morning. It was the first communication Jayne had received from her since leaving her house the previous year, and she was intrigued by the summons. William refused to enlighten her, however, being as reticent on the subject of his mistress as Jayne had been on the number of soldiers at the inn.

She picked her way across stepping stones to reach a path on the other side of the stream. 'Life was pleasanter before the war turned friends into enemies,' she said over her shoulder. 'Now the only people I speak to with any ease are my patients. The sick have no interest in politics or fighting.'

'Do you share your thoughts with your father?'

'Not often. Like you, he thinks me naive to favour reconciliation over conflict. He says the bad blood in the country will only be drained by the victory of one side over the other, regardless of how many die in the process.'

William joined her on the path. 'Some would say death is a price worth paying if the cause is a good one.'

'But not the fighting men of Dorchester,' she said dryly. 'I'm told they had no appetite for battle when they saw Carnarvon's army.'

'You shouldn't believe every story you hear,' he said, matching his stride with hers. 'There are more lies than truths told in war. It was anger at unpaid wages that caused the surrender, not fear of Carnarvon. The men would have fought readily enough if they knew they'd be recompensed for their bravery.'

Jayne wondered whether this was a truth or a lie. 'It's a poor cause that has to buy its soldiers' courage with wages.'

He didn't take umbrage. 'How else do you expect them to feed their families? The only other choice is to allow them to seize what they want by force, as Prince Maurice's troops do, but that makes them greatly disliked by the populace. Which method would you advocate?'

'Wages,' she said. 'How long had they gone unpaid?'

'Several weeks.'

He fell silent for a moment or two, clearly debating with himself how much more to reveal, but it seemed his irritation with the people of Dorchester was greater than his distrust of Jayne. The war was being fought at such a remove, he told her, that the town had become complacent. After six months without attack, arguments began over whether the garrison's levy was necessary. The wealthy were the first to withhold their share, and others quickly followed. Some, such as Milady, continued to donate, but by the beginning of July, the fund was so depleted that no wages were paid.

News came soon after that the Parliamentary stronghold of Bristol had fallen to Prince Maurice's brother Prince Rupert, and the city had been plundered of everything of value. Prince Maurice was given command of the King's Western Army, and he sent the Earl of Carnarvon to subdue Dorset with two thousand horsemen. Hearing this, sensible men would have reinstated the levy—even better, increased it to attract more recruits—but instead the rich of Dorchester had chosen to remove themselves and their fortunes from the town. This made a poor impression on the soldiers of the garrison, who saw little hope of their arrears being paid if the wealthy fled, so they laid down their arms rather than sacrifice their lives for nothing.

'Do you blame them?' Jayne asked when William finished.

'Not at all. My quarrel is with those who argued against the levy, and then left as Carnarvon approached. Your cousin's husband, Samuel Morecott, was amongst them. I had word a week ago that he's now in London.'

Jayne looked at him in surprise. '*London?* Why would he go there?'

'To further his ambitions, I imagine. I'm told he's residing with Denzil Holles, who was one of the first to bolt.'

'Denzil Holles? The Member of Parliament for Dorchester?'

'The same. Morecott's been courting his friendship diligently these last few months.'

'How?'

'By tempering his religious opinions and saying what Holles wants to hear. You gave a true description of Morecott when you said he has a great ability to present himself well when the situation demands. He now favours moderate Presbyterianism and argues for a negotiated peace with concessions made on both sides.'

Jayne knew these were Denzil Holles's views, for her father had spoken often of the Member's desire for compromise, but information had reached Swyre recently that Holles had been threatened with arrest for promoting dialogue with the King. 'Could Samuel have chosen unwisely in his patron?' she asked. 'I'm told Holles and his peace-making ideas are thought treacherous in Parliament.'

'At the moment, perhaps, but there are as many warring opinions in the House as there are in the country. The militant Puritans have the upper hand for now, but they'll lose credibility if Prince Rupert and Prince Maurice succeed in capturing ports along the south coast. Holles's time will come again, which is why Morecott has pinned his colours to his mast.'

Jayne kicked irritably at a hummock of grass. 'That doesn't please me at all. I've wished Samuel only bad fortune these last twelve months. Ruth's heard nothing from him since October. He bedevilled her with letters at the beginning of their estrangement, threatening to brand Isaac as illegitimate if she didn't return, but once my uncle agreed to continue paying him her allowance, all communication ceased. There could be no stronger evidence that he married her for money and not for love.'

'Was there ever a doubt?'

'Ruth hoped so and, had he offered apologies instead of menaces, she would have gone back to him. It will break her heart to know he's in London, quite uncaring that he has a wife and child in Dorset.'

'Don't tell her.'

'I have to. She'll hear it from someone less kind if I don't. Are you sure the information is true?'

William nodded.

'Then my uncle should know also, since one of the conditions for Samuel continuing to receive the allowance was that he maintains the house in Dorchester. Do you know if anyone's living in it?'

'Carnarvon commandeered every empty property when he first arrived. There are upwards of two dozen Royalist troops billeted in Morecott's house, and they're as badly behaved as those you saw at the inn.'

Jayne shook her head in disbelief. 'I can't tell my uncle that. He'll die of apoplexy.'

'Perhaps you can persuade him it's a privilege,' William murmured. 'He's such a strong supporter of the King, he should be glad to lend his home to drunken soldiers.' He paused. 'Unless, of course, your father's persuaded him otherwise. I'm told Sir Henry resents having twenty of his cattle confiscated by Germans.'

Jayne studied him for a moment, wondering where he'd heard that story. 'There are more lies than truths told in war,' she said, lengthening her stride to move ahead of him. 'I learnt that from a footman who claimed to come from a long line of harriers.'

Dorchester was strangely unchanged despite the presence of Royalist soldiers on her walls. No hindrance was placed in the way of people entering or leaving through the gates, and business continued as it always had. Wagons laden with grain and drovers herding livestock made their ponderous way to market; shops and taverns stood open, displaying their wares; and the inhabitants performed their daily tasks without apparent care that their town was now under the command of the King. They might have felt otherwise had Prince Maurice broken Carnarvon's pledge not to arrest or punish any of their number, but, since he hadn't, Jayne was left thinking that ordinary folk had more sense than their political masters, preferring to get on with their lives rather than fret about matters they couldn't control.

Before entering the town, William returned her sack and assured her he would follow ten paces behind to guarantee her safety. Once or twice, Jayne saw groups of uniformed men loitering on street corners ahead of her, and she crossed the road each time to avoid them. In doing so, she acted no differently from anyone else, for none seemed willing to contest the soldiers' right to hog the pavements. Swaggering cavaliers walked in pairs, forcing women to step into the gutters; infantrymen sat on stools outside their billets, cleaning their muskets and grinning at the wide berth they and their weapons were given. To Jayne's eyes, they were cut from the same cloth as her attackers on the highway, and she formed the same low opinion of the King's army as she had of Parliament's.

Because of her dress, William had suggested she enter Milady's house through the kitchen quarters at the back, so she left the main thoroughfare and took the side street that would lead her there. Once arrived at the door, she turned, expecting to see him, but he wasn't there. She waited a moment to give him time to turn the corner and then tapped on the panels, announcing herself as Mistress Swift when a woman's voice asked who was there. The door was opened by Molly, and at her side stood a Royalist soldier, smartly dressed in dark jacket and britches, with a red sash about his waist and a sword in his hand, the tip resting on the floor.

It was clear to Jayne that Molly was frightened and distressed, for her appearance had none of the neatness of the last time she'd seen her. Greying tendrils of hair hung from beneath the maid's bonnet, her collar sat askew atop her bodice and her apron strings were trailing on the ground. Nevertheless, whatever concern Jayne might have for Molly's strained look was nothing to the alarm in Molly's eyes as she took in Jayne's apparel.

The dragoon raised his sword tip twelve inches. 'Did she give her name as Swift?' he demanded in a German accent.

Molly ran her tongue across her lips. 'No, sir,' she managed. 'This is Mistress Smith, Milady's laundress. She comes each Tuesday to collect our most soiled items.'

The man ran his gaze over Jayne's dirty coif and patched bodice. 'She gives herself airs by calling herself mistress. What's your given name, woman?'

Jayne took her cue from Molly's answer. 'Y'am Peg, sir,' she said in a broad Dorset lilt, dropping a curtsey. 'I be 'ere for 'e maëdes' bloodied napkins.'

He frowned. 'I don't understand her. What's she saying?'

'She speaks of the towels the maids use for their monthly bleeds, sir. Milady prefers them to be cleaned away from the house so that no clots are left in the washbowls.' Molly nodded to Jayne's sack. 'Peg collects them from all the houses hereabouts.'

Jayne swung the sack from her shoulder. 'Do 'e wish to see?' she asked, stooping to loosen the string that tied it.

The dragoon had no trouble understanding that. 'God forbid!' he declared in disgust, stepping back. 'Be on your way, woman.'

Molly intervened. 'With respect, sir, it would be better to let me bring her this week's items. Four girls are bleeding this week, and it's not wise to keep their towels inside the house. The stench becomes unpleasant and some believe the blood is cursed.'

The officer viewed her with alarm. 'Where are they kept?'

'Upstairs, sir. It will take me but a moment to fetch them, though you may wish to leave this room before Peg opens her sack to receive them.' She gestured towards the corridor. 'You can guard these quarters as well on the other side of that door as you can on this, and Peg knows she's not allowed to cross the threshold.'

The officer needed no persuading, being as fearful and ignorant of female bleeding as every other man. He crossed himself hastily, clearly hoping to ward off a curse from Jayne's sack, and then scurried for the corridor ahead of Molly. The maid stared hard at Jayne, mouthing, 'Wait for my return,' before closing the door behind them both.

Jayne held her breath for several moments, listening for anything that would tell her why a Royalist soldier had been in Lady Alice's kitchen. Were there more? she wondered. And why had William made no mention of them? Thoroughly bemused, and fighting against her own fears, she remained unmoving at the open door, head down and hands clasped in front of her.

A good five minutes passed before Molly came back with a linen laundry bag. 'The youngest maid has soiled her nightshift and bedsheets,' she said crossly as she entered the room. 'If you can't find space for them in your sack, you'll have to carry this bag as well.' She blocked Jayne from the dragoon's sight but shook her head to warn her against speaking. 'Milady will pay you an extra three pence for the added work,' she said loudly, pulling a scrap of paper from her pocket and passing it to Jayne, 'but you must be sure to return the bag when you return the laundry.'

Jayne read what was written on the paper. *William awaits you outside the bakery in High East Street.* She raised her head. 'Is Milady all right?' she whispered.

Molly shook her head again. 'Make haste,' she mouthed, as she handed Jayne the linen bag and forced her onto the street by closing and latching the outside door.

SEVEN

JAYNE, UNABLE TO MAKE HEAD nor tail of what had just happened, worked up a considerable anger against William as she walked towards High East Street. Why hadn't he warned her she would be met by an armed officer? And why had he abandoned her? She might have been tempted to ignore Molly's request to meet him had her concern for Lady Alice not persuaded her otherwise. She found him outside the bakery where they'd stood on the day of the priest's execution, but he was showing more interest in a young girl than in searching the crowd for Jayne. He had to crouch to catch her words, and only became aware of Jayne's presence when she dropped the linen bag at his feet.

He dismissed the girl immediately. 'I wasn't expecting you, Mistress Swift.'

'Clearly not.' She studied him for a moment. 'An explanation on our walk from the inn would have been helpful. I'd have played the role of laundress rather better had I known what to expect.'

William hid his reaction to this by stooping to lift the linen bag. 'There's a private room upstairs where we can speak more freely,' he said, gesturing to the interior of the bakery. 'Will you allow me to take you there?'

Jayne turned to look into the shop, which was full of servants buying bread. 'Is it necessary?'

'It is if I'm to tell you why Lady Alice summoned you, ma'am. You'll do her a great service if you're prepared to listen.'

Jayne assented reluctantly. 'How do we reach it?'

'Through the door at the back of the shop,' said William, ushering her around the interior wall. He raised the latch and stood aside to let Jayne through, and she found herself in a narrow hallway with a flight of stairs leading upwards. 'It's the first room at the top on the right, ma'am,' he said, removing the hessian sack from her shoulder and motioning for her to go ahead of him. He felt her sudden stiffening at the brush of his hand against her arm and, when she didn't move, he eased past her and took the treads himself. 'The steps are uneven. You'll feel safer if you take your time and keep hold of the rail.'

Jayne steadied herself against the door. There was no logic to these bouts of sudden paralysis. They'd become mercifully rare in the last four months, but even her father could induce panic if he came too close in a confined space. Yet William was no more likely to attack her than Sir Henry was. If he'd meant her harm, he'd have taken advantage of her on the walk from the inn, not waited until they were in a building full of people. Even so, it was a minute or two before she felt able to mount the stairs.

The chamber was larger than she'd been expecting, mirroring the size of the shop and bakery downstairs. It had the appearance of a dining or drinking hall, with a long table running down its centre, and shelves carrying pewter tankards lining the wooden panelling at one end. Three windows evenly placed in the wall overlooking High East Street admitted light and air, and the room was so open and bright that Jayne's anxiety began to dissipate. She took a single pace inside, noting that William had placed her medicine sack and the linen bag on the floor beside the door.

He stood at the central window, watching the comings and goings in the road outside. 'I was wrong not to wait for Molly, ma'am,' he said quietly. 'Will you accept my apologies? It was most inappropriate to invite you inside without a chaperone.'

'Is Molly coming?'

He continued to watch the road. 'I believe so. She asked me to meet her here.'

'When did you speak with her? Were you inside the house when I was at the back?'

He shook his head. 'I can't gain entry either. The girl you saw me speaking with is our parlourmaid. She came with messages from Molly.'

'What did she tell you?'

William turned with a sigh. 'Very little. All I know is that six of Prince Maurice's dragoons are in the house, five in good health and one unwell. They'll not accept help from the Dorchester physicians because they don't trust them, so Milady sent for you.'

'How did it become her business?'

'She's related to the only Englishman in the party. He came asking for help yesterday, and she didn't feel she could deny him. The sick man was taken to her house last night when all were asleep, and a messenger was dispatched to Swyre as soon as it was light.'

Jayne stared at him in puzzlement. 'Then why did Molly send me away? Why am I not in the house caring for this person?'

'I imagine because you're not what the Royalists are expecting, ma'am. It seems Milady promised them her brother's physician, and they assumed that meant a man.' He paused. 'I was away yesterday and last night and only learnt something was amiss when I returned this morning, and by then the messenger had left for Swyre. Had it been otherwise, I would have urged Lady Alice to refuse her relative's request, and we would not be in this unhappy situation.'

'Through your fault,' Jayne admonished William sharply. 'Had you given me this information at the inn, I could have ridden to Bridport for my tutor, Doctor Theale. He was Sir John's physician long before I was and would not have refused a request from Lady Alice.'

She turned at the sound of footsteps on the stairs and saw Molly, red-faced from exertion, struggling up them.

'You mustn't blame William, Mistress Swift,' Molly said breathlessly, inching past Jayne to place a covered bread basket on the table. 'The only message I could give him this morning was a written request similar to the one I gave you. First to waylay you and send you to the kitchen quarters, and then to wait for me at the bakery. All is at sixes and sevens. Milady is confined to her chamber, the maids to the scullery, and decisions have fallen on me.' She shifted her attention to William. 'Did little Jenny find you? She's so tiny I hoped she might squeeze through the scullery window. I told her you'd be here if she could find a way to escape.'

'She found me,' he said gently. 'Now breathe and be calm. Mistress Swift is as eager as I to hear what you have to say.'

Molly paused to gather her thoughts and then told her story in short, clipped sentences. Lady Alice had agreed to give Sir Walter Hoare, the son of her cousin, a bed for the night. He claimed to have business in town and was gone two hours. By the time he returned, night had fallen, and all were asleep except Molly. When she opened the door to admit him, he caught her about the waist and clamped a hand over her mouth. Other men came in behind him, one barely able to stand.

Lady Alice had been called from her bed in her nightclothes and then subjected to threats and menaces. Her Parliamentary sympathies were well known, but so was her brother's allegiance to the King. She must summon Sir John Bankes's physician, whose competence and loyalty could be relied upon. Discretion should be her watchword. If news of the sick man's presence in her house became public, she would forfeit everything she owned.

Jayne raised a hand to stop her. 'Who is this person and what ails him?'

'I don't know, ma'am. We were ordered to make up a bed for him in the salon and have been barred from that room ever since. Even Milady hasn't spoken with him. She wrote the summons to you under instruction from Sir Walter and was then returned to her chamber. No one's allowed to enter and she cannot leave.'

'Why did she address me as Doctor Swift rather than Mistress Swift? Sir Walter was bound to think me male with such a title.'

'It was he who gave her your name, ma'am, or an approximation at least. Send for Doctor James Swift, he said, of whom Lady Bankes speaks highly. He became angry when Milady tried to point out his mistake, and I believe he may have struck her, for the door to the parlour was slammed shut. He was insistent that his friend have a competent doctor and not an ignorant army butcher or a Dorchester Puritan quack.'

She went on to explain that, before she was returned to her chamber, Lady Alice had whispered to Molly that William must prevent Mistress Swift from coming. There was danger for her if she presented herself as a physician. But Milady's instruction was easier given than obeyed. Once a guard was placed in the kitchen to stop anyone entering through the rear of the house, Molly was obliged to send everyone away—including William.

'I told the dragoon he was Milady's silversmith, come to collect a bonbon dish for melting down,' she said. 'I passed him the note when I handed him the dish.'

William stirred. 'Why did you not write that I should prevent Mistress Swift coming at all?' he asked.

'I was frightened for Milady. Sir Walter has a powerful temper and is very set on his friend being cured. It seemed to me that a female physician was better than none.' She turned apologetically to Jayne. 'Or it did until I saw how you were dressed, ma'am. I doubted Sir Walter would accept a poor countrywoman as Sir John's physician, however hard I tried to persuade him that's what you were. You were so pretty the last time I saw you that I was sure the ugly creature would be charmed by you.'

Jayne stared at her in consternation. 'I'm not in the habit of selling my skills through charm, Molly,' she protested, 'and certainly not to men as unpleasant-sounding as Sir Walter Hoare. Nor do I wish to enter a house full of soldiers. In any case, these are the only clothes I have, so there's little we can do to rectify the matter.'

Molly nodded to the linen bag that lay beside Jayne's hessian sack. 'One of Milady's gowns is hidden beneath the sheets, Mistress Swift. There's so little flesh on her bones these days it no longer fits, but I believe it will hang well on you. Will you allow me to show it to you?'

She didn't wait for an answer but opened the bag and removed a carefully folded garment from beneath a crumpled sheet, turning to place it on the table and spread it across the surface. The fabric was pale green silk, and the style of tailoring—fluted sleeves, square-necked bodice and wide skirt—still fashionable. When Jayne made no comment, Molly took another garment from the bag, this time in a darker shade of green. 'Milady always wore this fine wool cloak atop the gown,' she said, holding it up to allow the fabric to fall to the floor. 'It has a high collar and is attached to the dress by hooks at the shoulders. The drape at the back will hide any gaps there might be in the laces that hold the bodice together.'

'Which there will be,' said Jayne. 'Even when she was fleshier, Lady Alice was clearly slenderer than I.' She pointed to her workman's boots. 'And what of these? I have a good four inches on your mistress, so they're bound to show.'

Molly pulled back the cover on the woven bread basket to reveal hairbrushes and a pair of green silk mules to match the gown. 'Your heel may hang over the end, ma'am, but I believe they will serve the purpose. I do most earnestly beseech you to try. Milady's too frail to take any more threats.'

William shook his head. 'You're being unfair, Molly. Whatever the situation inside the house, we can't endanger Mistress Swift. We must find a way for me to enter. Am I right that only one dragoon is guarding the kitchen quarters?'

Molly nodded. 'But he keeps his sword drawn and will recognise you from your earlier visit. You'll not get past him easily and, even if you do, four more are guarding the hall, the stairs and the salon.'

'What do you know about the man who's sick?'

'Nothing . . . except that his companions are afraid he's dying. They look scared every time he cries out, and Sir Walter's never so angry as when he leaves the salon and demands to know if the doctor's arrived.'

William pondered for a moment. 'You should have told the dragoon *I* was Doctor Swift,' he said. 'It may still be possible if Mistress Swift's willing to lend me her satchel. I need but to gain admission.'

Jayne joined Molly at the table and ran her hand across the gown. 'You'll not help Lady Alice by killing these men, William. The town is under Royalist control and she'll be held as responsible as you for six dead soldiers in her house.' She pinched the silk between her fingers. 'If I'm dressed as a lady, Sir Walter will expect me to be chaperoned by a gentleman. Can you pass for one of my Swift relatives? That would allow us both to gain entry.'

'Are you sure that's what you want to do, Mistress Swift? You're under no obligation to any of us.'

'I'm aware of that,' she told him, 'so I require your promise to offer me the same protection you afford Lady Alice.'

A smile touched his eyes. 'You have it. How long can you give me, Molly?'

'Thirty minutes at most,' she said. 'I must return an hour before noon with bread and meat.'

William walked around the table. 'When the time comes, you must greet me as a stranger.'

'Sir Walter knows your face, William.'

'He may think he does,' he murmured before departing down the stairs.

Molly led Jayne into the far corner of the hall, where she was hidden from the windows, and asked if she needed help unfastening her bodice and skirt. Jayne shook her head. 'The task isn't difficult, since clothes such as these are worn by women who don't have maids.'

Molly watched her release the hooks at the front of her bodice. 'Why do you feel the need for a disguise, Mistress Swift?'

'The poor travel more safely than the rich.'

'Will your father not pay for a groom to accompany you?'

'He'd pay for two or three if I allowed him, but the stories they'd take back would give rise to too many lectures. I'd rather dress as a countrywoman and ride alone.' Jayne slipped the bodice from her arms and handed it to Molly. 'Take good care of this. I'll need it for my return journey.'

'What sort of lectures?'

'Angry ones on matters such as this.' She loosened the ties at the side of her skirt and allowed it to drop to the ground before smoothing the creases in her shift. 'Sir Henry would not approve of his daughter removing her clothes in a Dorchester drinking hall.'

Molly smiled as she retrieved the skirt from the floor and carried the two garments to the table. 'Lady Alice's husband was the same. They had more arguments about the way she dressed than they ever did about her beliefs.' She returned with the gown and lifted it over Jayne's head, assisting her to feed her arms into the sleeves.

'What did he object to?' Jayne asked, as Molly eased the waisted bodice to sit above her hips.

'Milady wearing men's apparel, ma'am. Sir Francis thought it immoral, and scolded her constantly about the impropriety of pretending to be something she wasn't. It was my job to dress her and she always looked the part.' She moved behind Jayne to begin tightening the laces at the back.

'Is that what she wanted? To be taken for a man?'

'Indeed, but not one who spoke or had a position of authority. Most normally, she played the part of bag carrier.'

'To what end?'

'I shouldn't tell you, Mistress Swift. It's been a well-kept secret for a long time.'

'You will if you want me to charm Sir Walter Hoare,' Jayne said firmly. 'I see no reason why I should humour you if you're not prepared to humour me.'

Molly told the tale as she laced the bodice as tightly as Jayne could bear. Had Lady Alice been male, she would have earned her living through painting portraits; being female, she'd been obliged to wed. During the early days of her marriage, Sir Francis had been a kindly but absent husband, and Milady, driven to distraction by the dreariness of wifely duties, had devoted her time to painting her servants. Visitors had remarked on the excellence of her talent, while Sir Francis had merely congratulated her on finding an amusing way to entertain herself.

He was foolish to belittle her in such a way, for she became more determined than ever to prove herself worthy of being paid for her skills. Unwittingly, Sir Francis gave her the opportunity. He had a fondness for the theatres in London, hence his many absences, and he offered charity to an actor, a particular favourite of his, who had fallen on hard times through his inability to remember lines. The actor, a handsome but lazy man, accepted a small stipend and a cottage on the Stickland estate in return for the occasional reading aloud of a play by Shakespeare whenever Sir Francis was at home.

'The master tired of him within six months and urged him to return to London,' said Molly, draping the cloak about Jayne's shoulders and hooking it to the shoulders of the gown, 'but Milady had found another use for him and wouldn't hear of his going. She increased his stipend and gave him the cottage for life.'

'Where is he now?'

'He died of a fever a few days after Sir Francis. It was very sad. Milady had no reason to remain in Winterborne Stickland with both of them gone.'

'What was his name?'

'Gilbert Jackson.' Molly stepped back. 'The gown looks very well on you, Mistress Swift. You're fuller-breasted than Lady Alice, so I haven't been able to draw the laces tight at the top of the bodice, but as long as you wear the cloak the gaps won't show.' She pulled a chair from the table and pressed Jayne into it before removing the dirty coif and tut-tutting at the tightly coiled braids Jayne's maid had fashioned that morning. 'You must let me loosen these, ma'am. They do nothing to flatter you.'

'They're not intended to,' said Jayne. However, she allowed Molly to remove the pins and shake out the braids. 'Am I right to think Gilbert Jackson posed as an artist and Lady Alice as his paint and brush carrier?'

Molly nodded. 'He was a poor actor of Shakespeare but most persuasive at pretending to work at an easel. He had a flair for attracting attention to himself through the telling of amusing stories, so no one took notice of what his manservant was doing.'

She described how Mister Jackson would position himself and his subjects in such a way that they were in light and he was in shadow. In addition, he would never allow anyone to pose for more than an hour, or see how the work had progressed in that time. This allowed Milady to sit unnoticed behind him, making colour matches and sketches of her own which she could then transfer to the canvas when they were alone. The partnership had lasted thirty years and, as Gilbert Jackson's renown grew, the two had travelled farther afield than Dorset. At her husband's request, Milady never accepted invitations from London, since Sir Francis believed the pretence was more likely to be discovered there than in the provinces. It was one thing to hoodwink the gullible rural gentry, quite another to attempt the same with the worldly-wise of London. In this, Sir Francis was supported by his brother-in-law, Sir John Bankes, who was nervous of his sister's rebellious ideas becoming known at court.

'Yet he was happy to have her sign his portrait as Gilbert Jackson,' said Jayne.

'Better that than Alice Stickland,' said Molly, using her fingers to coax Jayne's hair into graceful ringlets. 'She's painted him several times and one of her early portraits hangs in his office in London. He tells her it's much admired, but he always claimed Gilbert Jackson was dead if anyone showed an interest in having their own likeness captured.'

'That must have annoyed her.'

'No more than it annoys you that you can't call yourself a doctor, Mistress Swift.'

Jayne gave a low laugh. 'I'm driven to distraction and beyond because I haven't that right, Molly. My sympathies are with Lady Alice.'

Molly departed to purchase food, and Jayne was left alone to consider the folly of what they were about to do. The plan had too many flaws to succeed, not least her own reluctance to play the coquette with Sir Walter Hoare. She found herself wishing Molly had thought to dress her as a man, for she was more confident that she could lower her voice than simper and pout like an empty-headed girl. And what if Sir Walter responded to such behaviour? Molly had described him in the most unflattering terms, and the idea of such a person pressing himself against her appalled Jayne.

A knock came on the door before she could alarm herself further. She asked who it was, and when William announced himself, she moved behind the table and called, 'Enter.'

She wouldn't have known him. He was transformed by a long dark wig, an embroidered black doublet with a half-cloak over one shoulder, dark britches gathered at the knee, fine leather boots and a gold-hilted sword at his side. She wondered how he had come by such finery, since Lady Alice's house was closed to him.

'You look most elegant, Mistress Swift.'

'As do you, William. Whose appearance is the more fraudulent, I wonder?'

He smiled. 'There's nothing fraudulent about yours, ma'am. Sir Henry would be proud to present you as his daughter. As for mine, I thought you'd be more comfortable with a brother as your chaperone. Will I pass for Andrew, whom I believe dresses most fashionably?'

I believe . . . Where had he come by these details about her family? 'Not to anyone who knows him,' she said, picturing her shorter and stouter older brother.

'Then we must hope he and Sir Walter have never met.' He removed a folded piece of paper from inside his doublet and passed it across the table. 'I'm conscious that we first have to persuade Sir Walter you're qualified to tend his friend, so I've taken the liberty of writing a letter of accreditation from Sir John Bankes. Sir Walter has the same relationship with Sir John as he does with Lady Alice, but not so close that he's in regular communication with either of them and knows their style of writing. I've kept the letter short and used the dry language a lawyer might employ.'

Jayne unfolded the page and read the words inscribed on it.

Honoured Mistress Swift,

Please accept my gratitude. Your services have been most beneficial to me. Be assured I shall recommend you as an able physician to any who ask. You may use this letter as a testimonial.

Your obedient servant,
Bankes (Lord Chief Justice)

She raised her head. 'I doubt it's in Sir John's nature to be so generous,' she said. 'He never expressed gratitude when I was treating him.'

William stooped to remove her satchel from the hessian sack. 'He praised you highly enough to Lady Alice, so the sentiments are true even if the words are mine.' He retrieved the letter and placed it atop her medicines. 'You must insist on seeing Milady when you arrive. It was she who summoned you; it is therefore she whom you're expecting to treat.'

'Will Sir Walter agree to such a request?'

William passed the strap over his head and settled the satchel on his hip. 'It matters not. Forget everything Molly's told you and pretend ignorance of Sir Walter and anyone else in the house. You must express the same surprise to see him as he to see you. Can you do that?'

'Rather better than trying to charm him,' she answered dryly.

On William's advice, it was he who knocked on the front door and gave the name of Doctor Swift. Believing him to be the physician, the guards admitted him readily, and by the simple expedient of thrusting his boot against the door, he was able to usher Jayne past him. She made no further progress, however, for the dragoons raised their swords to prevent her. With an angry expletive, William drew his own sword and stepped in front of her.

'What effrontery is this?' he demanded. 'My sister is here by invitation of Lady Alice. Through what brazen impudence do you threaten her?'

'Who are you, sir?'

'Captain Andrew Swift of the King's Regiment of Horse, son to Sir Henry Swift of Swyre and brother to the physician Mistress Jayne Swift. Lower your swords and explain yourselves. Begin with the name of your commander.'

A man appeared from the front parlour. 'They're Germans in Prince Maurice's regiment,' he said. 'You speak too fast for them to understand. State your business to me.'

Jayne had little doubt this was Sir Walter Hoare, though he was considerably younger than she was expecting. His skin was pitted with pockmarks and he chewed on a piece of bread as William repeated what he'd said. She felt a flutter of nervousness when he moved past the dragoons and studied William closely.

'We've met before,' he said. 'I remember your face.'

'And I yours, sir, though I don't recall your name. Were you part of Hopton's army at Roundway Down? Or perhaps we encountered each other during the siege of Bristol?'

'Not Roundway Down, sadly, but Bristol for sure. Glorious victories both.' He held out his hand. 'Sir Walter Hoare, aide-de-camp to Prince Maurice of the Palatinate.'

William sheathed his sword and clasped the hand warmly. 'An honour, sir. Allow me to present my sister, Jayne Swift. Lady Alice sent word this morning that she has need of her.'

Sir Walter frowned. 'For what purpose?'

'The relief of pain,' said Jayne. 'Lady Alice calls on my services when the aches in her hip and head are unbearable.' She turned to William. 'My satchel, brother. I can make my own way upstairs.'

Sir Walter blocked her path. 'There seems to be some mistake, ma'am. A nurse is of no use to us. Lady Alice assured me she'd summoned her brother's physician.'

'And so she has. I have been physician to Sir John Bankes and Lady Alice for nigh on eighteen months.' She took the satchel. 'Now, order your men to lower their swords and allow me through. I don't pretend to understand your presence here, but my business is with Lady Alice.'

'You're wrong, ma'am. Allow me to see inside your bag.'

Jayne handed it to him with a shrug. 'You will find only medicines and instruments, sir.'

He lifted the flap. 'What is this?' he asked, removing the folded paper.

'You may read it if you choose.' She watched him scan the page. 'If you need further proof of my learning, there is another document at the bottom. I trained under Doctor Theale of Oxford and Bridport and he signed a list of my attainments, which match his own.' She tapped her foot impatiently as he fumbled through the satchel. 'You're being criminally clumsy, sir. I shall expect compensation if any of my medicines are spilt.'

Sir Walter frowned at her for a moment and then turned away, ordering the dragoons to keep their swords raised before disappearing through the door to the parlour with her satchel still in his hands.

Unhurriedly, William drew a pair of leather gloves from his doublet and pulled them over his hands. '*Es ist nicht höflich eine Dame zu bedrohen*,' he murmured to the dragoons.

'*Wir haben unsere Bestellungen.*'

William smiled. 'Don't say you weren't warned,' he said mildly. 'It's not my habit to tolerate threats against women.'

His disarming smile and reversion to English caused them to hesitate, unsure what he was saying. Certainly, neither expected him to step between them and knock their heads together. One dropped his sword of his own volition, the other had it chopped from his hand, and then both were hauled by their collars into the street and flung to the ground.

William retreated inside again and closed the door. 'Make haste to Milady's chamber and remain there until you're sent for,' he murmured, taking Jayne's arm and walking her none too gently towards the stairs. 'Leave me to manage affairs down here.'

EIGHT

LADY ALICE WAS SITTING BEFORE her mirror with a box of combs and pins on her lap, attempting to fashion her hair into a coil. An unlaced gown gaped open across her back and two more lay discarded on the floor. She lowered her hands as she watched the door open behind her, and Jayne, failing to see recognition in her eyes, held a finger to her lips as she eased through the gap on stockinged feet. She placed Milady's mules on the bed and then moved to crouch at her side.

'It's Jayne Swift, ma'am. You wrote to me on Sir Walter's instructions.'

'I know who you are, my dear, it's what you're doing in my house that worries me. Did William not find you and tell you not to come?'

'He did, ma'am, and accompanied me here on the pretext of being my brother Captain Andrew Swift of Swyre. We both feel we can end your imprisonment more quickly if Sir Walter accepts me as Sir John's physician and allows me to treat his friend.' She described the morning's events as briefly as she could, including William's explanation for why Sir Walter recognised him and his expulsion of the two dragoons from the house. 'I believe his intention was to secure me safe passage to the stairs, but I'm doubtful he should have done it in that way. Sir Walter had already accepted him as a fellow Royalist, so he should have looked to foster the friendship rather than create unnecessary antagonism.'

Lady Alice shook her head. 'Walter will admire him for it. He's always impressed by men who seek redress for real or imagined offence.'

'Does William know that?'

'Most certainly, or he wouldn't have acted as he did, though I doubt he was wise to pretend he was at Bristol.'

'Sir Walter knows him from the visits he's made here, ma'am. He had to say something.'

'Indeed, but a single error will set Walter questioning, and his memory's as likely to conjure up a footman as a soldier.'

Jayne rose to her feet. 'The two dragoons will swear that William's a soldier,' she said, moving behind Lady Alice. 'He disarmed them too easily to be a footman.' She smiled at the woman's reflection. 'If I were to guess, I'd say his fluency in the German language means he fought as a mercenary in the war that has ravaged Europe these last thirty years.'

Lady Alice's expression was unreadable. 'You have a grand imagination, Jayne.'

'So I'm told . . . usually by patients who'd rather have a different diagnosis from the one I give them.' She bent to lace the matriarch's gown. 'Allow me to help you. I can't claim to be as capable as Molly, but I have passable skills in the tying of bows and the pinning of hair.'

'Thank you, my dear. I was greatly disadvantaged last night having to speak with Walter in my nightshift. He felt he had the upper hand and will believe so again if I'm forced to present myself with my hair in disarray and my dress undone. What a nonsense it is that the fixings for women's garments are at the back while those for men are at the front. I've struggled all morning with these beastly gowns.'

Jayne nodded solemnly. 'Our lives would be a great deal easier if we were allowed to wear britches,' she said, gathering Lady Alice's tresses into her hands and coiling them into a bun.

Molly came with a guard to summon Mistress Swift downstairs. She curtseyed to Lady Alice and then addressed Jayne. 'Your presence is requested in the salon, ma'am.'

Jayne stood back to allow Lady Alice to precede her, but the guard shook his head. 'Not you, milady,' he said.

He might not have spoken for all the notice Lady Alice took of him. With a smile for Molly, she took Jayne's hand and, together, they walked out onto the landing and began their descent of the stairs. Sir Walter and William waited at the bottom, the one scowling, the other impassive. Behind them, restored to their positions on either side of the front door, were the two dragoons.

'You seem irritated, Walter,' said Lady Alice as she reached the last step. 'Why so?'

'I ordered you to remain in your chamber.'

'You did indeed.' She turned her attention to William. 'Are you Captain Swift, sir? If so, I'm pleased to make your acquaintance. My brother and I value your sister's services most highly.'

William bent his head. 'The pleasure is mine, ma'am.'

Sir Walter placed a restraining hand on Lady Alice's arm, and she fixed him with a withering gaze. 'Do you intend to use violence against me before witnesses, Walter? Be sure I shall neither forgive nor forget the exchange between us at three o'clock this morning.'

'You had no reason to deny my request, Alice.'

She pulled her arm free. 'You've lost the right to address me by my given name, sir. Any small affection I had for you is gone and, once this sorry episode is over, I shall cease to acknowledge a relationship with you. Your stupidity and boorish manners offend me, for it was my attempt to correct your assumption that Sir John's physician was a man that earned your ire.' She stepped from the stairs and drew Jayne down beside her. 'You've shown Mistress Swift only drawn swords and discourtesy since she arrived, and if she decides it's wiser to refuse her services out of fear of further threats, she will have my support. I shall ask Captain Swift to escort her, my servants and myself from this house, and the problem of what to do next will be yours.'

'There will be no further threats. Mistress Swift is acceptable to us.'

William stirred. 'I believe Lady Alice and my sister require rather more persuasion than that, sir. You ask a lot of both to take what you say on trust.'

'What better pledge can I give?'

'That you will release Milady's servants and leave her house as soon as my sister has done what she can for your friend.' He turned to Jayne. 'Sir Walter has described the man's symptoms to me, and it's my belief his need for attention is urgent, Jayne. If you and Lady Alice leave now, he may die before another physician is found.'

Jayne addressed Sir Walter. 'What ails him? Is he feverish?'

'He suffered a sword wound to his chest two days ago, and it shows no sign of healing. His breathing is fast and his forehead hot to the touch.'

Jayne released Lady Alice's hand and urged her towards the kitchen quarters. 'Prepare your servants for hard work, ma'am. If Sir Walter has described this man's condition correctly, he's most certainly in need of urgent treatment.'

—

'Man' was hardly the word to describe the sweating, panting boy who lay, naked from the waist up, on the makeshift bed in the salon. Indeed, were it not for the smattering of hairs on his chest and the pencil-thin moustache on his upper lip, Jayne would have doubted he'd even reached shaving age. A dragoon sat at his side, dabbing at the wound with a pus-filled rag, and she ordered him away, telling him to take his filthy cloth with him, before bending to examine the gaping cut some two inches wide in the fleshy part beneath the boy's left shoulder.

'How old are you?' she asked him.

'*Zweiundzwanzig.*'

'In English, please.'

'Twenty-two.'

'You look younger.'

She brushed the damp dark hair from his face and rested her hand on his brow before taking his wrist and counting the beats of his pulse. 'You have a fever and your heart is beating too fast, but your skin is a good colour and you have youth on your side,' she told him. 'An older man would be in worse condition with a wound that is festering as badly as yours. The only mercy is it isn't gangrenous. What is your name?'

'None of your business.'

Jayne smiled. 'Then I shall call you by the King's name, for, though you lack his beard, you have his long hair and moustache.'

She sat on the bed beside him. 'I need to see if the sword ran you through, Charles, so I must pull you into a sitting position.'

'It did not.'

'Nevertheless, I would still like to see.' She linked her arm through his and leant back, using her own weight as a counterbalance. 'Maintain that position while I look. It will take but a moment.' She rose to run light fingers over the inflamed but unbroken skin around his shoulder, which was clearly tender to the touch, for he winced when she pressed a little harder.

'Are you satisfied?'

She lowered him again. 'I'm satisfied you're in a great deal of pain, Charles. The blood is poisoned around the wound, which is why you have a fever, and if nothing is done the poison will spread. I believe I can help you, but the cure will not be pleasant.'

'Do you plan to cover me in leeches?'

She shook her head. 'Something worse, I'm afraid. Salt.'

It was a treatment Richard Theale had used successfully on a farmhand who had slashed his calf with his scythe. The man's wife had bound the wound, but within a day his body was overheating and the wound suppurating badly. Another doctor would have used cautery to burn the ulcerating flesh, but it was a drastic method that rarely prevented the infection spreading. Instead, Richard had chosen to lower the man's fever and cleanse the purulence from his wound by immersing him in a tub of cold brine for fifteen minutes in every hour. The healing properties of salt had been understood since the time of Hippocrates, as was the value of using cold water to reduce inflammation and fever, but by combining them, Richard had effected a quicker cure than he could have hoped. Even so, it had taken two days and nights to break the fever and cleanse the wound, and forever after he instructed his students to introduce salted water to an open cut at the earliest opportunity. Better to cleanse the poison before it spread than allow it to take hold.

Lady Alice possessed a bathtub constructed from teak, but it was situated in a small room on the second floor at the back of the house. Jayne instructed Sir Walter and his men to bring it down to the kitchen, which was closest to the public well in the street outside, but he refused. It wasn't fitting for 'Charles' to be treated in the servants' quarters, or for low-born women to see him naked.

Jayne shrugged. 'Then you and your men must help the maids fill and empty the tub,' she said. 'The work of raising water from the well and then carrying the buckets upstairs without respite will be too arduous for women on their own. As to your friend's nakedness, do you not think he's too sick to worry about the status of those who are helping him?'

'If strangers come to the door, he'll be seen. There'll be no guarding it with maids trooping in and out with buckets of water.'

'Station one of your men outside.'

'Tongues will wag if dragoons are seen carrying water.'

'No one will know they're dragoons if they remove their jackets and work in their shirts.' She shrugged again when he didn't answer. 'There are other physicians in Dorchester,' she said. 'Perhaps you should consult one of them.'

William broke the silence that followed. 'I suggest you ask Charles to make the decision,' he said to Sir Walter. 'I imagine he'd rather be treated in the kitchen than have no treatment at all.'

And so it proved. Whoever 'Charles' was, his only care was relief from pain, and he seemed to prefer the soft voices of women to the rough chords of soldiers. The younger maids fell in love with his handsome looks while the older ones wanted to mother him. Even Lady Alice acknowledged his charms, referring to him sotto voce as a 'heartbreaker'. For herself, Jayne saw only a patient to whom she administered fifteen minutes of cold brine per hour, followed by forty-five minutes of drying warmth in front of the kitchen fire, during which she allowed him to cover his naked-ness with a blanket over his lap. Throughout, she urged him to drink as much fluid as he could, infusing elderflower tea with a tincture of willow bark to ease his pain.

She permitted him only two immersions in the same water before she ordered the tub emptied and refilled with clear, cold water to which she added fresh salt. However, since salt was an expensive commodity, she sent Sir Walter to buy it. He was accom-panied each time by Molly, who took him to different parts of the town so that the purchases were never made in the same shop. Upon his return, Sir Walter invariably took Jayne to task for some perceived fault, most often her refusal to allow Charles to wear a blanket around his shoulders. It wasn't seemly for a young man to sit unclothed in front of women.

Charles's injury was small compared with the curved slash of a sickle, and Jayne hoped this meant the poison would be defeated faster. If not, she had little doubt Sir Walter would end the treat-ment and label her a charlatan. Everything about her seemed to incense him, not least her insistence that he raise his complaints away from his friend's hearing.

'Why do you keep trying to force your opinions on him?' she asked. 'He may be young but he's not foolish. If my methods aren't working, he'll tell me himself.'

He eyed her with dislike. 'Do you look to win favours by keeping him to yourself?'

She thought she detected a note of jealousy in his voice. 'If by favours you mean payment, then yes, I expect to be rewarded for my services. Shall I present my account to you or to Charles?'

'You'll not present anything unless he's cured.'

She studied him for a moment. 'Be grateful I'm an honest physician, Sir Walter. A fraudulent quack would charge double for a cure.' She turned away. 'Now cease bothering us. Charles will recover faster if he's spared your needy presence every thirty minutes.'

Come midnight, Jayne instructed the maids to bring the mattress from the salon and lay it on the floor in front of the hearth along with some pillows. Then she dispatched them to their beds, including Molly, who was so tired she could barely stand. Lady Alice had taken herself to her chamber some two hours previously, and Molly expressed her intention of sleeping on the floor beside her. Should Mistress Swift need her, she would find her there.

The kitchen was ablaze with candlelight. Jayne, satisfied that the wound had dried and the swelling around it diminished exactly as Richard had said they should, assisted Charles from the tub and lowered him to the mattress. 'You're the sort of patient every doctor yearns for,' she said with a smile, kneeling to settle his head on the pillows and draw the blanket over his legs and lower torso. 'You take your medicine without protest, respond as you should to the treatments you're given and never once question your physician's advice.'

His short, panting breaths had long since subsided and he spoke fluently. 'Why would I want to? To lie in a bath, even one filled with cold water, is a pleasure. You English should do it more often.'

'You're fortunate to come from a wealthy family, Charles. In this country few are rich enough to own a bath.' She pressed her fingers into the previously inflamed flesh about the cut. 'Does that hurt?'

He shook his head.

'Then I think it's safe to let you sleep.' She rose to her feet and prepared a cup of chamomile tea, to which she added some drops from a bottle of valerian root infusion. 'This will help,' she told him, kneeling again to hold the cup to his lips. 'Untroubled rest is the best of all remedies. I need to keep one candle alight, but do you wish me to extinguish the others?'

'Are you staying?' His tone was curt.

'I must,' she told him. 'If your sleep is disturbed, it will tell me the poison has yet to be defeated, and we shall have to resume the treatment.'

He closed his eyes. 'Then keep the candles burning for yourself. The light will not bother me.'

Jayne sat on a chair at the table, writing her record of which remedies she'd applied and how the patient had responded to them. She noted the proportion of salt to water she'd used, the number of immersions it had taken before she began to see a reduction in the swelling around the wound, and her own belief that leaving the wound to dry in the air, rather than bind and cover it, had achieved quicker results. Her custom for the entries in her register was to describe her patients only by their forenames and occupations in order to preserve an element of anonymity should anyone else read the notes. 'Charles', by accepting a false name, was anonymous enough, although Jayne had discovered belatedly that her choice to call him after the King had been peculiarly apt.

Lady Alice had recognised him as soon as she saw him, as did William, both having witnessed his triumphant arrival in Dorchester some three weeks previously. The ailing 'boy' was Prince Maurice of the Palatinate, commander of the Western Army and nephew to King Charles of England. Jayne would have preferred not to know this, since it merely added to her worries, but Alice had drawn her from the kitchen to warn her of the danger they faced if it became known that Prince Maurice was gravely sick inside her house. Parliamentarians would be angered that one of their own had given him a bed and found him a physician, while Royalists would question whether a physician secured by a Parliamentary sympathiser would exert himself to achieve a cure. It went without saying that a female physician would be rejected by both sides.

Jayne asked if the servants knew his identity and, upon being assured they did not, she begged Milady to keep it that way. For herself, Jayne would continue to call him 'Charles' and speak to him in the same casual manner she had used hitherto, and she urged Lady Alice to follow her lead. Sir Walter would have nothing to fear from any of them, now or in the future, as long as he believed them ignorant of their visitor's true identity.

William had assisted Jayne some five hours later by repeating what Sir Walter had told him about Charles. He was playing three-card brag with two of the dragoons in the salon, and shook his head when Jayne entered to ask if Sir Walter and Molly had returned with salt. 'Not yet, sister,' he said, raising his head and looking deep into her eyes. 'Does all go well with Charles?'

Unsure how to answer, she spoke the truth. 'There are signs of improvement. The wound is drying and the fever beginning to abate.'

William gave a nod of approval. 'I'm glad to hear it. I'm pledged to remain here until he's able to leave, and I fear these fine fellows will fleece me of all I have if the wait is a long one. It seems Charles left his barracks without permission and Sir Walter has requested my help in returning him because I have a good knowledge of the back roads and alleyways.'

Jayne guessed she should ask the obvious question. 'Will he be punished if he's seen?'

'Most certainly. He'll lose his commission if Prince Maurice learns of his absence.' William lifted the corner of one of his cards, lying face down on the table, to remind himself of what it was before matching the bid of the previous player. 'The prince has little time for hotheads, and Charles is certainly that.'

'What did he do?'

The dragoon to William's left wagged an admonishing finger. '*Es ist besser, dass sie das nicht weiss,*' he muttered.

'She's my sister—*meine Schwester*,' William answered. 'She'll get it out of me eventually.'

Perhaps the dragoon had sisters of his own, for he nodded and returned to the game.

'Charles was wounded in a duel with another officer,' William explained, 'and it will not go well for him if Prince Maurice learns that two of his subalterns wilfully excluded themselves from duty over a matter of honour. Such things are frowned upon when the greater enemy is Parliament. You'll do Charles a service if you can restore him to health before his absence is discovered.'

Jayne wondered if she was supposed to accept this story without challenge, and decided not. The dragoons would expect her to be curious. 'What of the other man? Can his discretion be relied upon?'

William smiled slightly. 'Charles was the victor, sister. His opponent is dead, and the body was found by soldiers shortly afterwards. Since his purse was missing, they reported him set upon by Dorchester thieves. The matter would have ended there had Charles's wound not begun to fester. He has no innocent reason for his injury, so could not consult the camp's physician for fear of questions being asked.'

Jayne shook her head. 'You're draining my sympathy for him,' she warned. 'Had he been bettered, my thoughts would be kinder.'

'Don't be too harsh on him, kitten. He's a lovestruck youth who fought in defence of a lady's honour.'

Kitten? She would have rapped his knuckles had he truly been her brother. 'Then I'm not surprised Prince Maurice seeks to outlaw such practices,' she said tartly. 'Enough blood has been shed already without besotted youths adding to it.' She moved towards the door, acknowledging to herself that she only felt safe in this house full of soldiers because it was William and not Andrew who was protecting her. Nevertheless . . . *kitten!* 'I can't promise Charles will be well enough to leave before dawn breaks, brother, so I suggest you limit your losses. Father will not be amused to hear you've wasted your allowance yet again.'

One of the dragoons laughed. 'Don't listen,' he told William, raising one hand and working the fingers and thumb in mimicry of a duck quacking. 'All sisters are the same.'

Every so often, Jayne broke off from her writing to check the colour of Charles's face and the regular rise and fall of his chest. Asleep, he looked even younger than when he was awake, and she struggled to believe he had any authority at all, let alone command of an army. She thought of the drunken troops at the King's Head and the loutish cavaliers on the streets of Dorchester, and wondered if they behaved as they did because Prince Maurice condoned their ill-discipline or lacked the ability to control it. Either way, it had been criminally irresponsible of the King to put him in charge of so many men.

At around three o'clock in the morning, she looked up to find him awake and watching her. 'Do you know who I am?' he asked.

'Not your name,' she said, 'but my brother told me how you were wounded, and that Prince Maurice will punish you if he learns of your foolishness.'

'What story did your brother give?'

'The one he heard from your friends. Being a man, he finds the idea of fighting over a lady's honour more admirable than I do. Women have better sense than to kill each other over words said in malice.'

His eyes, a deep brown, showed a glint of amusement, but whether at the tale or her chastisement of him, she couldn't tell. 'You might think differently if it was your honour that was questioned,' he said.

'How would I know? The falsehoods jealous officers tell each other inside their barracks are never heard by the lady.' She moved to kneel beside him again and take his wrist in her hand. 'You seem much better. Your heart is steady and your wound has dried enough to be stitched.'

'What does "stitched" mean?'

'Drawing the edges together with a needle and catgut. Hippocrates, the father of medicine, was using the method to heal wounds even before Christ was born. Does your head still pain you?'

'No, but I'm devilishly hungry. Will you summon a servant to prepare a meal for me?'

'I will not. The household worked tirelessly on your behalf yesterday and are now asleep. You must accept what I make for you or beg one of your friends to do it. Which do you choose?'

'Can you cook?'

'Not at all, but I believe there's some bread and cheese in the pantry.' She rose and walked to a door at the side of the hearth. 'Cold mutton, also,' she said, returning with two platters and placing them on the table. 'Are you strong enough to sit on a stool or would you rather rest against the pillows?'

'I need my clothes if I'm to sit on a stool.'

Jayne shook her head. 'You may wear your britches but not your shirt or jacket. Both are filthy from the blood and pus that leaked from your wound; they should be thoroughly cleaned before you use them again. If you're willing to wear a servant's garments, the scullery is near and I've seen laundered shirts and tunics inside it.'

'Bring whatever you like. I'm too hungry to care.' But he seemed to change his mind, for he held up his hand to stop her leaving. 'Go quietly and return alone,' he instructed. 'I want only your company while I eat.'

Before she allowed him to pull on the tunic, she told him she must suture the wound. As she threaded a needle with catgut, she warned him the procedure would hurt, but perhaps he wanted to prove his courage, for he made no sound, staring past her with eyes wide open and jaw firmly closed.

'You have three separate stitches,' she told him, 'each tied with a knot. In a week from now, you must ask your friend Sir Walter to snip through them and draw them out by their knots. To leave them in will cause a different sort of infection because the catgut will turn sour. Do you understand?'

'I will summon you to do it,' he said.

'You may try, Charles, but I have other patients to tend. Sir Walter will perform the task as ably as I, once I've shown him what to do.'

He asked to read her notes and she watched him scan through her ledger as he chewed on mutton and cheese. She knew his mother to be the King's sister, so she didn't doubt he was as well versed in English as German and understood each word she'd written. He seemed most interested in the billing amounts she'd put beside certain entries and the lengths of time in hours that she'd recorded.

He placed his finger on a wheelwright's notes. 'The hours represent how long you were with this person, and the pounds, shillings and pence are what you charged him?' he asked.

'Yes.'

He turned to the notes she'd made on George Lansdowne, a neighbour of her father's. 'The same here?'

'Yes.'

'Both men paid the same for each hour of your time, yet you describe Peter as a wheelwright and George as a landowner. Why did you not request more from the rich man?'

'It wouldn't be fair. My service to George was no greater than to Peter.'

'Some you don't charge at all.' He turned the pages. 'There's a woman here called Marianne whom you treated for seven days without payment. Why is that?'

Jayne took the register from him and read the notes. 'She had six living children, another four who had died at birth, and a drunkard for a husband. The family survived through the money she earned as a seamstress. Had I demanded a fee, the children would have starved.'

'You write that she had dropsy in her legs and you made her lie for several days with her feet raised above her hips to reduce the swelling. Who cared for her children then?'

'The oldest.'

Charles shook his head. 'It was you, for you record the time you stayed with her as seven days. Did you chastise her husband as cruelly as you've chastised me?'

'A hundred times worse. He was a lazy good-for-nothing who stole her earnings for ale and forced himself upon her whenever the mood took him.'

'Did your lecturing cure him of his drinking?'

'No,' said Jayne with a laugh, 'but it persuaded him to leave a house where he wasn't appreciated. That was three years ago, and Marianne has blessed me for it ever since. She's no longer required to make babies every year, saves her money for food, and has increased her earnings by teaching her two daughters to be as competent in dressmaking as she is. The dropsy returns from time to time, but never so badly as when she carried the burden of a thieving drunkard for a husband.'

He closed the register and rested his chin on his hands to stare at her. 'You seem to find more to criticise in men than in women.'

The stare was intimidating, and, had the question come from Prince Maurice, she might have dissembled. Was that where his authority lay? she wondered. In the recognition that a king's nephew had the power to destroy the hopes and ambitions of anyone who angered him?

'Only men who are irresponsible,' she answered lightly. 'There's nothing to admire in a grunting hog who brings hardship on his family through his own selfish greed.'

'Or in one who fights for the honour of a lady?'

Jayne nodded. 'No slight, however bad, is worth the death of a brother officer when the country's at war. Your friends say Prince Maurice thinks the same, which is why they brought you here instead of seeking help from an army physician. For the same reason, they hope to return you to your barracks without the guards seeing you. They fear questions being asked about how you were wounded and why you absented yourself without permission.'

'Do you believe them?'

'If you mean, do I believe Prince Maurice will punish you for your disobedience, then yes, I do,' she said. 'And your friends will be punished equally, since he'll know they assisted you. You should fear him as they do, Charles. He'll treat you as badly as he's treating the people of Dorset if he thinks you're his enemy.'

A flicker of anger flashed in his eyes. 'I was told you were a Royalist. I wouldn't have trusted you had I known you were a Parliamentarian.'

'Then be glad I'm neither,' said Jayne, reaching for the register and placing it in her satchel. 'The best physicians care nothing for their patients' beliefs, only their recovery—and judging by your appetite and new-found irritability, I've completed my task.' She rose from her chair. 'Being a woman, I'm forbidden to use the title of "doctor", but you can trust my discretion as surely as any male physician's. Nothing that has passed between us will be repeated.'

'Where are you going?'

'To fetch Sir Walter. Dawn is still a good two hours away, so he has time to return you to your quarters before it gets light.'

'I forbid you to leave,' he said with sudden petulance. 'You've yet to dress the wound and name your fee.'

Jayne took a candle from the table and headed for the door. 'The fee you can work out for yourself because it will be the same per hour as George and Peter. As for the dressing, I shall do that in front of Sir Walter once I've explained how to remove the sutures. The bindings will need to be replaced each day to ensure the wound remains clean and dry, and he should learn how it's done in order to replicate it.'

'Do you forsake every patient as easily?'

She held his gaze for a moment. 'Be grateful I came at all, Charles,' she said, lifting the latch and leaving the room.

Sir Walter could hardly hide his pleasure at Charles's peevish rebukes to Jayne as she bound his wound with clean linen strips in the tight shape of a figure of eight about his shoulder, with a holding strap around his back and chest to keep it in place. He was less pleased to be told the job would be his for the next few days, and that in one week he must snip the catgut and remove the stitches. Jayne instructed him on the necessity of using only clean linen at the site of the cut, and warned Charles to keep his left arm immobile for at least two weeks, since movement would tear the scab and delay the process of healing.

Charles showed more appreciation of William than Jayne, accepting Captain Swift's advice that he was less likely to be noticed on the streets of Dorchester if he wore the clothes Jayne had given him. Dressed in tunic, shirt and britches, he would be taken for the captain's servant as long as they walked a few paces ahead of Sir Walter and his dragoons. The idea seemed to appeal to Charles, and without a thank you for Jayne or any mention of payment, he opened the rear door and gestured to William to lead the way. It was left to Sir Walter to make the farewells, and he did so grudgingly.

'You proved a better physician than I expected, Mistress Swift.'

'Should I take that as compliment?'

'As you please.' He gave a small duck of his head. 'My regards to Lady Alice.'

Jayne arched an amused eyebrow. 'You waste your breath, sir. Lady Alice has given orders that your name is never to be mentioned in her presence again. She has a great dislike of bullies and thieves, whichever army they serve.'

He stepped into the street. 'It's of no matter,' he said with an indifferent shrug. 'If I'm in need of your services again, I'll send a messenger to Swyre. Your brother tells me I can always find you there.'

Jayne moved forward to close the door behind him. 'Do so, sir, but you won't be happy with my reply. I offer my services for free to deserving patients, not sullen hotheads who bring trouble upon themselves.'

'Blame yourself for your lack of reward, Mistress Swift. Charles favours those he admires, not those who toady to him.'

Jayne laughed. 'I also, Sir Walter.' She placed her hand on the door. 'Your friend dislikes rejection, so I suggest you consult a different physician if the wound fails to heal. Good day to you.'

NINE

THE SUN HAD BEEN UP three hours by the time William returned, dressed once again in the buff coat, knee-length britches, white stockings and black shoes that he'd worn the previous morning. He was surprised to find both the front and back doors bolted on the inside, and had to knock several times before Molly spoke from the other side of the kitchen panels. She remained suspicious even after he'd given his name, demanding to know if he was alone and only opening the door once he'd sworn an oath that he was.

'Lady Alice was certain Sir Walter would use you to gain entry,' she told him, pushing the heavy iron bolts back into place.

'Why?'

'Because you told him you were Mistress Swift's brother, and he will think that gives you some influence over her.' She knew all his secrets and was well used to his changes of clothes and appearance, but she scolded him nonetheless. 'You've been absent too long. Sir Walter and two dragoons came pounding on the door an hour and a half ago, demanding that Mistress Swift accompany them. She refused and bolted the doors to prevent their entry.'

'What did they want with her?'

Molly rolled her eyes to heaven. 'If Sir Walter was telling the truth, Prince Maurice has learnt of her service to Charles and is offering her the post of private physician to himself and his entourage. As a reward for acceptance, he's willing to use his royal prerogative to grant her the status of doctor.'

'And she refused?'

'Most strongly. She told Sir Walter only a university can make her doctor, and she didn't choose to favour princes over paupers in order to acquire an illegitimate title.'

William gave a grunt of amusement. 'What was his answer?'

'He said she was foolish to make an enemy of a man as powerful as Prince Maurice—which is probably true, but it made no difference to Mistress Swift. She sent Sir Walter away with a flea in his ear, reminding him to dress Charles's wound as she'd instructed.'

William looked for Jayne's satchel on the table, but it had been removed along with the mattress in front of the hearth and the many candles that had lit the room through the night. Only the bathtub remained. 'Is she with Lady Alice?'

Molly shook her head. 'She left as soon as Sir Walter had gone. Milady begged her to wait for you to escort her, but she said she'd attract less notice on her own. If Sir Walter has given orders to prevent her leaving the town, the guards will be looking for a well-dressed woman in the company of her brother, not a poor farmer's wife carrying a sack.'

'She's right,' said William.

Molly studied him with disfavour. 'Maybe so, but it's a churlish way to treat a lady who hastened to our rescue and hasn't slept all night. If you weren't so heartless, you'd have come back sooner and offered her assistance. Who's to say Sir Walter won't be waiting for her at Swyre? She says you were very free with the information that he could find her there.'

William ran a thoughtful hand around his jaw. 'That wouldn't be helpful,' he agreed. 'If her brother's in residence, she'll not explain his changed appearance easily.'

'She shouldn't have to, since I'm guessing it was your idea to masquerade as Captain Swift,' Molly said sourly. 'Do you have no concern for her safety? She could be seized from off the road if men are stationed at her father's gate to intercept her.'

'They'll not recognise her any better than the guards in Dorchester will,' he said reasonably. 'She'll ride on by and find a different way in.'

'You promised to protect her.'

William acknowledged the point with a nod. 'I'll talk to Milady. If she's confident these bolts will hold against unwanted visitors, I'll follow Mistress Swift.'

He kept his own horse, a nondescript eight-year-old brown mare, in a stable in Dorchester, and had her saddled and on the road within fifteen minutes of Lady Alice dismissing him. He made such regular journeys in and out of the town that his face was well known to the guards at the gates. Having searched his saddle packs several times in the early days of the occupation and finding them full of brightly coloured swatches of silk and satin, they believed him to be a cloth merchant trading in exotic fabrics from the east, and rarely bothered with him now. Today was no different. He brought the mare to a halt to give them a chance to search him, but they waved him through with nods and smiles.

Calculating that Jayne's walk across the fields, the saddling of her own horse and necessary conversation with the innkeeper would take above an hour, he rode the highway to the King's Head at a fast gallop, hoping to reach it before she left.

He was disappointed. Both she and her mare were gone and the innkeeper refused to say which route she'd taken or how long it had been since her departure.

'Had I not recognised you from yesterday, I would have denied she'd ever been here,' Timothy finished. 'The soldiers left at dawn this morning, their memory of her arrival purged by drink, and no one else was party to her coming or going. I'm pledged to keep it that way.'

'Did Mistress Swift give a reason for wanting such a pledge?'

'If she did, it's not your business to know.'

'Indeed.' William nudged his mare backwards. 'My respects to you, sir. Be sure I shall tell Mistress Swift that you honoured your word.'

Timothy smiled cynically, as if he doubted William would be given the chance. 'You do that,' he said, turning away. 'It'll please her to know there's one man she can trust.'

William pondered these words as he took the highway to Bridport, recalling Jayne's fear of him inside the bakery. Their paths had come close to crossing only once in the year since they had first met in Dorchester. With Dorset under Parliamentary control, Royalist sympathisers had had the choice of leaving the county or accepting Parliamentary governance. Most, being landowners, had chosen to stay.

Two such were Jayne's father, Sir Henry Swift of Swyre, and her uncle, Joseph Swift of Littlemoor, both of whom were prodigious letter writers. Neither stinted in the grievances they expressed, nor the detailed information they shared with their Royalist friends and relations outside Dorset, and their careless confiding of their thoughts to paper made for interesting reading. Sir Henry invariably added postscripts about his daughter's continued refusal to accept any of the suitors he found for her, but he wrote the words without rancour, as if he'd long since accepted that she had the right to reject them. It was rare for a father to be so tolerant, and William liked him for it.

The system of public delivery of mail had been set up by King Charles during the early years of his reign. Through a series of 'posts' some twenty miles apart—often located in taverns, with the innkeeper acting as the postmaster—salaried riders carried the mail along designated roads. The process was slower than paying a messenger to deliver a single letter, because each postmaster was charged with sorting the letters to ensure they travelled in the right direction, but the cheapness of the system made it attractive. Nonetheless, it was notoriously open to theft, error and mistake, and a wiser monarch would have cancelled it on the day he raised his standard at Nottingham.

Perhaps he'd hoped the leakage of information would work in the Royalists' favour. If so, he was wrong. In Dorset, where most of the postmasters were for Parliament and knew William as a high-ranking Parliamentary officer, they readily gave him access to letters from known Royalists. Seals were prone to cracking or tearing away from the paper when they rubbed against others in a mailbag, but William preferred to use silversmiths, who had the sharp blades and steady hands needed to cut the seals from the paper and restore them afterwards with fresh molten wax to hide the cuts. He had five he trusted in different parts of the county, none more than two hours ride from a post, and it was a rare letter that was delayed by longer than eight hours.

There was as much to read in the letters Sir Henry and Joseph received as in those they sent. They had sisters living in Oxford, where the Royalist headquarters were located, and the women were freer than they should have been with news of their husbands' and sons' regimental locations and movements. The desire to commit compromising information to paper seemed to be a family failing, for Sir Henry's two younger sons, Philip and Benjamin, were equally profligate in their reports of Royalist movements in the West Country and the north.

Sir Henry's letters were usually brought to the post by a servant, but on a day in November the previous autumn, it was Jayne who made the delivery. The nearest post to Swyre was the Saddlers' Inn on the Bridport to Dorchester highway, and William was in the back chamber when she entered through the front. The innkeeper, hearing her call, whispered a warning before hurrying to prevent her crossing the beer-stained floor of the bar to look for him. This gave William time to retreat to the kitchen quarters, where he viewed her departure through an unglazed window. He wouldn't have recognised her had the innkeeper not said who she was. Dressed as a poor farmer's wife, she bore no resemblance to the handsome woman he'd met in Dorchester, and he was curious to know why she'd chosen to disguise herself.

The innkeeper couldn't say, though he imagined her father had something to do with it. She'd caused Sir Henry enough despair by riding alone before the war, when she was seen only by local people, and the innkeeper doubted he'd tolerate her doing the same before strangers. There were too many Parliamentary troops from other counties on the highways, and tongues far and wide would wag if Sir Henry's daughter was known to wear britches beneath her gown in order to ride astride. Such conduct was shameful in a lady, but of no account in a peasant woman.

At the time, William had been more amused than persuaded by this explanation, for he questioned how soldiers from outside Dorset would know the 'shameful lady' was Mistress Swift. However, her remark the previous morning about the poor travelling more safely than the rich suggested a different reason for dressing as she did, and William wondered what had happened to make her afraid. He would have guessed at robbery had she put less effort into making herself plain and unattractive. Instead, he suspected her terrors had a darker origin.

~

At Winterborne Abbas, he spotted a matron standing at her open door, and stopped to ask if she'd seen a farmer's wife pass by.

'Maybe I have, and maybe I haven't,' she answered. 'Who's asking?'

Who indeed? William gave a respectful duck of his head. 'Sir Francis Stickland, ma'am. My mother, Lady Alice, is acquainted with the goodwife and begs me to borrow a few moments of her time. I'm told she rode this way.'

'By what name does Lady Alice know her?'

William chose honesty. 'Mistress Jayne Swift.'

'Is your mother in need of a physician?'

'She is.'

'She'll not do better than Mistress Swift.'

'So I'm told.' He looked along the highway. 'Did you see her? Time presses, and I'd like to speak with her before she reaches Swyre.'

The matron shook her head. 'She never rides the roads. If you're right to say she's ahead of you, she'll be on the bridleway that skirts Abbotsbury Common. There's a track to the south a mile farther which will take you there.'

William thanked her and spurred his mare to a gallop again. The matron's warm praise of Mistress Swift set him questioning why Prince Maurice had been so discourteous to her when she pronounced him well enough to leave Milady's house. What had passed between them, he wondered, that made him hostile one moment and a supplicant for her services the next? Had he realised belatedly that she might have saved his life?

His own conversation with the prince had been limited to idle chitchat and urgings for him to slow his pace each time they approached the end of a darkened street. Their goal had been a sprawling house to the north-west of the town, vacated by Denzil Holles on news of Bristol falling, and William's task had been to lead the party there by the least frequented routes. He was fully aware that Sir Walter's only concern was to keep the prince from being recognised by the people of Dorchester, but there were so few abroad that the journey had proved uneventful, and he enjoyed the irony of delivering the King's nephew to the home of a Member of Parliament. He was ignorant of whether Prince Maurice knew who the previous tenant was, but was amused to hear him express dislike of the place, saying he preferred the elegance and comfort of Lady Alice's house.

'Thank her for me, Captain Swift,' he instructed, as William prepared to make his farewell.

He spoke as a prince, but William answered him as Charles. 'I will if she's an early riser,' he said, stifling a yawn, 'otherwise

I shall ask a servant to give her the message. Knowing my sister, we'll be on the road long before Lady Alice leaves her bed.'

'Do you always do what your sister wants?'

William produced an engaging grin. '*You* did, Charles, so why should I be any different?' He tipped his hat. 'Farewell, my friend, and steer clear of trouble in future. You won't always have the good fortune of being treated by Jayne.' He turned before the prince could respond. 'Your servant, sir,' he said to Sir Walter. 'God willing, we'll meet again.'

As he walked away, he heard Prince Maurice mutter in German that the Swifts had an ill-mannered habit of turning their backs on him, and Sir Walter reply in the same language that they wouldn't if they knew his status. He wondered now if that was Prince Maurice's reason for wanting Jayne as his personal physician—a childish desire to have her acknowledge him as her superior—for William's assessment of him was the same as Jayne's: the commander of the King's Western Army was more boy than man.

The track south took him to Broom's Barrow, which was elevated enough to give him a view of the rolling farmland stretching towards Dorchester to the east and Abbotsbury Common to the west. He narrowed his eyes to search in both directions, but all he saw were sheep and cattle on the common land and two or three travellers making their way by foot along the paths that crossed it. He was on the point of leaving, thinking the matron had led him false, when he took a last look to the east and picked out the slowly moving shape of a horse some quarter-mile distant. The animal was making its way around stooks of straw in a harvested cornfield, and its rider was sprawled forward across its mane. From so far away, he couldn't tell if it was Mistress Swift, but the giving way to sleep suggested it might be.

He rode to meet her rather than wait on the track, slowing to a halt when her mare pricked up her ears and whinnied at his approach. The sound caused Jayne to wake and she jerked upright, pulling on her reins and looking in alarm at the mounted figure some thirty yards ahead of her. William raised his hand in greeting. 'It's William, Mistress Swift,' he called. 'Lady Alice sent me to escort you safely home.' He thought he heard a small sigh of relief and hoped that meant she felt able to trust him.

Her words were hardly welcoming, however. 'I've reached this far without you. Why should I need you now?'

William nudged his horse forward. 'Milady worries that Sir Walter may have sent men to wait for you at Swyre.'

She answered irritably. 'And what help will you be to me if she's right? You can hardly pretend to be my brother, since Sir Walter's men will have met him already. And why do you think escorting me *once* will suffice? If Sir Walter's intent on delivering what his master wants, his men will keep returning—or, worse, will set up camp in Swyre. I shall become a prisoner in my father's house.'

William made a gesture of apology. 'I'm sorry, ma'am. I should never have put you in this position.'

She studied him for a moment. 'It's not your fault. The decision was as much mine as yours, and neither of us knew I'd be ministering to a petulant child who thinks he can take whatever he wants.'

'He was most churlish towards you before he left.'

'All men are when they don't get their own way.' She signalled her intention of bringing the conversation to an end by tightening her reins and adjusting her feet in the stirrups. 'I thank you for coming, William, but I have no need of you. It's a long time since I entered my father's house through the front door.

Sir Henry doesn't like visitors to see his daughter dressed as a peasant, and I doubt Sir Walter's men will think to guard the kitchen quarters.'

He made a small bow. 'As you wish, ma'am, but may I offer a word of advice before we part? Assuming Sir Walter's men are indeed at your father's house, ask one to take a letter to Prince Maurice explaining why you're refusing his request. He'll call the dragoons away if your excuse is a good one.'

'How do I address him?' she asked cynically. 'As Charles or His Royal Highness?'

'His Royal Highness, ma'am, since as far as you're concerned they're two different people.'

'And what explanation can I give other than that I don't wish to humour him?' She shook her head in annoyance. 'I didn't spend five years learning to be a physician in order to waste my time amusing a prince. I have other patients more in need of me than he is, as he discovered for himself when he looked through my ledger. He's acting out of spite because he would have preferred to continue our conversation in the kitchen rather than return to his barracks.'

William nodded gravely. 'That should serve the purpose if you couch it in less condemnatory terms, ma'am. A man has less reason to feel foolish about a woman's refusal when she appeals to his better nature, and a reminder that there are many who depend on your skills will allow him to feel magnanimous.'

She smiled grudgingly. 'He wouldn't want me anyway. My only appeal was that I spoke to him as an equal. He'll grow bored very quickly when I'm obliged to curtsey each time I enter his presence.' She clicked her tongue to set her mare moving. 'Farewell,

William. If we meet again, I trust it will be under less trying circumstances.'

'I also, ma'am.'

She cast him a mischievous glance as she passed. 'Perhaps you should revert to calling me kitten,' she said. 'You're a shockingly bad footman, William, but you made a most convincing brother.'

He watched her set off at a trot, and then steered his mount in the direction she'd come, spurring it to a gallop to persuade her he was returning to Dorchester. Jayne would have good reason to distrust him if he appeared to ignore her wishes, but he was curious to know how events would unfold. Moreover, he found he was developing a grave exception to Prince Maurice's hubris in thinking he could own such a woman.

Once she was out of sight, he circled around to bring himself back to Broom's Barrow, from where a footpath travelled west in parallel with the bridleway beside Abbotsbury Common. Set higher than the common and lined by trees, the path was wide enough to be taken at a canter, allowing him to move ahead of her without being seen. Every so often he paused to watch her slower progress through gaps between the trees, but, as before, she was the only rider visible in any direction.

He lost sight of her when he dismounted to make his way through dense woodland to the north of Swyre, which brought him to the edge of Sir Henry's estate, but glimpsed her briefly before she disappeared behind the magnificent house that sat in open parkland ahead of him. Beyond, the sea formed a sparkling expanse of blue some quarter-mile distant, and he found himself wondering why a woman born to such beauty and wealth had chosen to work as a jobbing physician rather than exploit the opportunities her family's status gave her to rise higher in life.

Even Lady Alice, made of similarly rebellious stuff, had accepted a husband in order to acquire a title and position.

William searched for the start of the driveway, and found it some four hundred yards to his right. He hobbled his mount in a grassy clearing inside the woodland and made his way quietly through the trees, shadowing a dirt road that skirted the estate. As he neared the pillared entrance, he retreated deeper into the woodland and then took up a position behind the wide trunk of an oak tree.

Molly's instincts had been correct. Four dragoons, one of whom he recognised from Lady Alice's house, leant lethargically against the stone pillars. For the most part, they searched the road to the north, but every so often they turned to stare towards the house, as if hoping to be relieved of a tedious duty.

William had some sympathy for them as he lowered himself to the ground and prepared for a long wait. He had no particular plan in mind, other than to observe events as they occurred and, if necessary, intercede on Jayne's behalf if her father was careless enough to make her leave with Sir Walter.

TEN

Jayne led her horse to the stables and left it with a groom before entering through the servants' quarters. The kitchen was alive with industry, and her arrival brought the customary curtseys and bows from maids and footmen. She learnt from Sir Henry's valet that visitors from Prince Maurice's staff had arrived some half-hour previously. The master and Andrew were entertaining them in the salon, although Steven felt 'entertaining' was hardly the right word, since the visitors were largely silent and had refused to state their business. Jayne asked for their names, and her heart sank to hear that one of them was Sir Walter Hoare.

She took the servants' stairs to her chamber and flung off her peasant clothes, instructing her maid to make haste to transform her into a lady. All the while she set her mind to constructing a plausible reason why a stranger had accompanied her to Lady Alice's house and given his name as Captain Andrew Swift. Her maid, seeing that she was troubled, asked if she could help.

Jayne sighed. 'Only if you can think of a way to divert my father's anger, Kitty. He'll have learnt by now that I allowed a man to escort me to Lady Stickland's house and then introduced him as my brother.'

Kitty clicked her tongue as she drew the bodice of a blue silk gown together at Jayne's waist. 'You take too many risks, ma'am,' she scolded. 'Is this man someone you know?'

'I'm acquainted with him, but as to *knowing* . . .' She shook her head. 'Lady Stickland claims him as her footman but I doubt that's his real position.'

Kitty began fastening the hooks. 'A male servant would be an acceptable chaperone, ma'am, particularly one in the employ of Sir John Bankes's sister. I've heard Sir Henry boast several times that his daughter is physician to the Lord Chief Justice.'

'I can't embroil Lady Alice in this masquerade, Kitty. Sir Walter Hoare is unaware that she had any previous knowledge of William, and it would be wrong to paint her as a liar now.' She lowered herself to a stool to allow Kitty to remove the braids Molly had refashioned that morning. 'In any case, he didn't behave like a servant while in Sir Walter's company. I'd have taken him for a Royalist captain myself if I hadn't known better. He has the handsome looks of a cavalier.'

'Then make him so,' said Kitty simply. 'The countryside is awash with Royalists, and surely one is gentleman enough to escort a lady. Could it be you met him when you were tending Sir John?'

Sir Walter rose to his feet when Jayne entered the salon. 'Mistress Swift,' he said, ducking his head. 'I'm surprised to see you.'

Jayne assumed her most composed expression, giving no indication of the dreadful churning in her stomach. 'I can't think why, since this is my home, Sir Walter.'

'Your father and brother believed you absent from it.'

Jayne smiled at Andrew, who was lounging in a chair, and gave Sir Henry's hand an affectionate squeeze. 'Only yesterday and last night, sir. May I ask why you're here? I can't believe Charles's condition has relapsed in so short a time.'

Sir Walter frowned at her. 'How did you reach this house before we did? And why was your father unaware of your presence?'

Jayne answered only the last question. 'I've no idea, Sir Walter. Perhaps you should ask him.'

Sir Henry stirred. 'You're mighty impertinent, sir. You enter my house uninvited, announce your intention of waiting for my daughter without any explanation as to why, and then quiz her as though she were a servant because I refused to allow you access to her. Explain yourself—and, in future, address her with proper deference, since her rank is the equal of yours.'

'Forgive me, Sir Henry, but my curiosity overrode my manners. The last time I saw Mistress Swift was at nine o'clock in Lady Stickland's house in Dorchester, and not even a racing carriage could have brought her here ahead of me.'

Jayne shook her head. 'You're mistaken, sir. The last time you saw me was an hour before dawn when you left Milady's house to return Charles to his barracks. We've had no communication since.'

'You spoke to me through the front door three hours after sunrise.'

'Not I, sir, for I left as soon as it was light. It must have been Lady Alice who answered you. She assured me she would keep her doors bolted in order to prevent you imposing yourself on her again.'

'It was your voice, Mistress Swift.'

'It can't have been,' she said bluntly, studying him with feigned surprise. 'What do you claim to have said to me, and how do you claim I answered? If it pertains to my fee, I'm more than happy to submit my account now.'

He stared at her. 'Where is the man who accompanied you? And why did he call himself Captain Swift, when I discover now that he was an imposter?' He gestured to Andrew. 'This gentleman tells me *he's* your brother.'

Andrew smiled sourly. 'I don't take kindly to ne'er-do-wells using my name, sister.'

'He's hardly a ne'er-do-well, brother. He shares the same rank as you and forms part of Sir John Bankes's garrison at Corfe Castle.' Jayne turned to her father. 'My escort's name is Captain Harrier, Papa. I've been acquainted with him as long as I've been physician to Sir John. We met by chance on the outskirts of Dorchester and, since the town is full of drunken infantrymen, he offered to accompany me to Lady Stickland's house.' She produced a tremulous smile. 'I confess to finding groups of undisciplined soldiers alarming, so I was most grateful for his kindness.'

Sir Henry studied her for a moment. 'Why did he adopt the name of your brother?'

'Because I asked him to, Papa. It was meant as the smallest of falsehoods because I worried that Lady Alice would disapprove of my being chaperoned by a man unrelated to me. Our expectation was that he would deliver me safely to her door and then leave, since neither of us anticipated that soldiers were billeted in her house. Captain Harrier was forced to defend me from Sir Walter's dragoons when they drew their swords on me, and he chose to remain in order to protect both Milady and myself.'

It was hard to know what Sir Henry made of this, since it was the flimsiest of explanations, but his impassive expression led Sir Walter to assume he wasn't troubled by the news. He was taken by surprise, therefore, when Sir Henry rose to his feet and advanced upon him. 'Is this true, sir?' he demanded, thrusting his chest against Sir Walter's. 'You ordered armed men to threaten my daughter?'

Sir Walter retreated a step. 'Mistress Swift's description is exaggerated, sir. She was never in danger. Her protector drew his own sword as readily.'

'Then I owe him a debt of gratitude. The same cannot be said of you, however. You seem to take delight in imposing yourself on people who would rather be spared your company, Sir Walter. Oblige me by leaving before the two of us come to blows.'

This time Sir Walter stood his ground. 'I am here by command of Prince Maurice, sir. I have private business to discuss with your daughter, relating to her skills as a physician, which must be concluded before I depart.'

'Nothing is private where my daughter is concerned. Speak.'

Briefly, Sir Walter closed his eyes, clearly all too aware of how his proposal might sound to a father. 'His Highness Prince Maurice of the Palatinate requests that Mistress Swift attend upon him as his personal physician. As reward for her services, he will use his royal prerogative to grant her the title of doctor. He has tasked me with returning her to Dorchester as soon as possible.'

Sir Henry frowned at Jayne. 'Do you understand this request? If the prince is sick, why does he ask for you? Are there no competent physicians attached to his regiment?'

She shook her head. 'I don't know, Papa, for I've had no dealings with Prince Maurice.' She turned to Sir Walter. 'Is it you who gave the prince my name, sir? If so, I can't think why, for you were most grudging about my skills before you left Milady's house with Charles.' She searched his face. 'What ails the prince? If it's something mild, I beg you to seek out another physician; I've had no rest for a day and a night, and my maid tells me a messenger came at dawn to tell me that Marianne Prewitt has the dropsy again.'

'His Highness sees advantage in retaining a private physician in the event he or his staff are wounded in battle, ma'am. Your name was suggested.'

Jayne gave a surprised laugh. 'Advantage to whom? Certainly not to me or my many patients. Would the prince have them die so that I can sit around idly waiting for something to happen to him?'

'Most men would view the offer as an honour, ma'am.'

'I'm sure they would, sir, but a man's reputation wouldn't be tarnished by becoming a camp follower to provide such a service. In any case, it's not worth discussing, since my father will refuse on my behalf. He tolerates my helping the poor and destitute of Dorset, but would never countenance my debasing the family name by seeming to play courtesan to a prince. Am I not right, Papa?'

'You are, daughter. The prince has strange ideas if he thinks the ladies of Dorset can be sequestered as easily as cattle.' He glared at Sir Walter. 'Oblige me by telling His Royal Highness that Mistress Swift is not for barter, sir. *More*, that her father is offended by his effrontery in making such a proposal.'

'No effrontery was intended, sir. He sought to elevate your daughter by giving her the title of doctor.' Sir Walter turned again to Jayne. 'Does that not tempt you, Mistress Swift?'

'Not at all, if it means abandoning the impoverished women who rely on my skills, Sir Walter.' She held out her hands in supplication. 'Will you explain that to Prince Maurice and beg him most earnestly to allow me to continue my work with the likes of Marianne, whose six children depend upon her ability to work? I'm sure if he knew of her, he would agree that I should put her interests before his. I spoke to Charles about her at length and he was most sympathetic to her plight.'

Sir Walter exchanged a glance with his companion, a fellow aide to Prince Maurice, and upon receiving a nod, removed a purse from inside his jacket. 'You may wish you'd decided otherwise when the war is over and the King restored, Mistress Swift. Friends in high places will be of value then.' He offered the purse. 'Charles asked me to give you this in remittance of your fee, should you refuse Prince Maurice's invitation. He has worked it out according to the hourly amounts you charge your other patients and trusts it's acceptable to you.'

Jayne took it with a smile. 'It is, sir. Please thank Charles for me, and be sure to bind his wound as I instructed. If it knits together cleanly, he should have no more trouble from it.'

She held out her other hand and he raised it to his lips. 'Farewell, Mistress Swift. If I happen to travel to Corfe Castle to see my cousins Sir John and Lady Bankes, should I seek out Captain Harrier and give him your respects?'

'Certainly, sir,' she answered lightly. 'He will not have forgotten you.'

William had moved closer to the pillared entrance, curious to learn what was causing the dragoons to keep breaking out in ribald laughter. Thoroughly bored by their guard duties, and with their attention now directed entirely at the house, they didn't notice his quiet progress through the woodland behind them. The conversation involved a stream of questions from the three who hadn't been in Lady Alice's house to the one who had, and his answers about Prince Maurice were enlightening.

Some of the German dialect was unintelligible, but William had no trouble understanding the man with whom he'd played brag for several hours. Inspired by his friends' interest, he gave bawdy descriptions of what he said he and his fellows had done with Lady Alice's maids, though he reserved his lewdest claims for Mistress Swift. It was no wonder Prince Maurice had fallen under her spell, for she had kept him naked for fifteen hours and used come-hither eyes and witchery to seduce him.

This led to questions about what had ailed the prince, and the brag player repeated the duel story. But it seemed German dragoons found it easier to believe that a female physician was a witch than that Prince Maurice had been wounded by a fellow officer. Who would dare challenge him? Under pressure, the brag player relented. A blockhead of an English colonel by the name of Burleigh, he said. With only a dagger to defend himself, he had berated the prince for abandoning Carnarvon's pledges to abstain from plunder, and the prince, off his head with drink, ran him through.

Shortly afterwards, William heard the voice of Sir Walter ordering his men to collect their horses from the grazing land inside the pillars before speaking with another man. 'Did you believe her story about Captain Harrier serving with the Corfe garrison? She seemed unconcerned when I said I might seek him out.'

'Will you?'

'Not unless I must. Lady Bankes delivers more lectures on how this war should be fought than the King.'

This answer was greeted with a laugh. 'The story was credible enough, though I'll wager it was meant for her father. I can't see Sir Henry forgiving a secret lover, though he might excuse a member of Sir John's staff. I suggest you worry more about Lady Alice. If she sees advantage to Parliament in speaking out, Burleigh's death is sure to be questioned.'

'She'll regret it if she does,' came the grim reply, before hooves sounded on the dirt road and the column departed.

William made his way back to his mare and led her through the woodland to where he'd seen Jayne take a pathway across a field to the rear of the house. She'd told him it was a long time since she'd entered by the front, and hoping the same applied to her departures, he prepared himself for another long wait.

His mind was taken up with the story of Burleigh, whose body had been dispatched to his family two days previously. William knew little about him except that he'd been a colonel in Prince Maurice's regiment and was liked and admired by his men, all of whom had stood with heads bowed as the wagon carrying his coffin had left through Dorchester's eastern gate. William had had no reason to question the reason given for his death—'sudden collapse'—for Burleigh was said to be in his middle years and greatly fatigued by the effort needed to take Bristol. William had recorded the death as 'natural', but there was still time to amend it to 'murder at the hand of Prince Maurice of the Palatinate'.

With the war going badly for Parliament, he knew the importance of unearthing information detrimental to the Royalist cause. In normal circumstances, he would have had few reservations about using what he'd learnt, but this time he had many: principally, the debt of gratitude he owed Lady Alice. He knew for a certainty that Sir Walter would hold her to blame if the King's nephew was exposed as a murderer, and for the first time in the war, he was forced to confront the quandary many others had faced—to betray the cause or to betray a friend?

From where he was positioned, on an incline to the east of Swyre House, he could see the port of Lyme Regis on the other side of Lyme bay. Unlike Weymouth and Dorchester, Lyme had refused to surrender to Carnarvon, scorning his promises of peaceful conquest. Poole to the east had been similarly defiant and, along with Lyme, was all that was left to Parliament in Dorset. If ever there was a time to strike a blow against the King, it was now.

His attention was caught by the sight of two mounted figures emerging from behind the house and ambling towards him. One was unmistakeably Mistress Swift, riding side-saddle, the other was a handsomely dressed man of some fifty years who William guessed was her father. Realising his opportunity to speak with Jayne was gone, William took hold of his mare's noseband and retreated deep into the woodland. He couldn't blame Sir Henry for wanting to protect his daughter after Sir Walter's visit, but he cursed him nonetheless.

The only letters William had ever intercepted from Jayne were those she wrote to her tutor, Doctor Richard Theale of Bridport.

Her missives invariably involved medical matters, being either a sharing of successful treatments or a request for advice, while his were largely advisory, although he complimented her frequently on the clarity of her notes. From the firmness of his handwriting, William had expected a man of similar age to Sir Henry Swift, and was surprised to be shown into the presence of one who looked nearer to eighty years old.

It hadn't been hard to find Doctor Theale, who was well known in Bridport, and in return for a penny an urchin had led William directly to his door and promised to hold William's mare while he was inside. A maid had answered his knock and led him to Theale's office, announcing him as Captain Harrier of Corfe Castle.

The elderly man studied William with curiosity and then gestured to a chair at the side of his desk. 'You're far from home, sir. How may I help you?'

William lowered himself to the seat. He hadn't seriously considered trying to manufacture a fabrication but, if he had, he would have abandoned it in face of the intelligent gaze that was fixed on him. 'By allowing me to write a letter to your pupil Mistress Jayne Swift of Swyre and enclosing it in one from yourself, sir. It's a matter of urgency, and I'm willing to pay a messenger to carry it. However, it will be less troublesome for Mistress Swift if her father believes the letter has come from you.'

'I don't doubt it,' said Theale in amusement, 'but why should I lend myself to such a deceit? If you desire her services as a physician, Sir Henry will allow you to present yourself in person. If it's an affair of the heart, you must find a way to manage that yourself. I'll not permit my name to be used for the purpose of enabling secret trysts behind her father's back.'

William shook his head. 'It's neither, sir, and to prove it you may read the letter when I've finished. If you gift me some paper and the loan of a pen, I shall do it now.'

'Not until I've had a spoken explanation first, Captain Harrier.'

'It's not in my power to give you one, sir, because the matter concerns Mistress Swift and one of her patients. She may choose to offer an explanation later, but I cannot break faith with her by doing so now. Allow me to write, and you will see that what I say is intended only to benefit her.'

William was subjected to a searching stare before, with a shrug, Theale took a piece of paper from a drawer in his desk and placed it together with a quill and inkwell in front of his visitor. He nodded when William asked if he might draw his chair closer, and then resumed his study of a book which lay open before him, leaving William to work in silence. He wasn't prepared for the speed with which William composed his letter, for he frowned in astonishment to have the page returned to him in under five minutes.

'Do you always write so fast, Captain?'

'When the matter is urgent, sir.'

The old man read what he'd written.

Dear Mistress Swift,

Be assured that I would not have involved Doctor Theale in this subterfuge unless I believed it necessary. Through means too long to explain here, I have learnt that you named your escort of yesterday as Captain Harrier of the Corfe Castle garrison. Since this story will not stand scrutiny if your father or brother decides to satisfy himself

*on the matter, may I pay you a visit to give Captain
Harrier some substance?*

*I have no right to ask for your trust, Mistress Swift,
but I beg you to believe that I seek only to safeguard you
and Milady from further unwelcome intrusions into your
lives. At present, Milady's cousin Sir Walter shows no
inclination to call upon his relatives at Corfe Castle in
order to verify your story; however, that may change if
your father decides to search me out. Sir Henry is bound
to mention the circumstances under which he learnt my
name, and Lady Bankes will demand explanations from
Sir Walter and Milady.*

*The fault is mine for not supplying you with a less
troublesome reason to explain our acquaintanceship, and
I beg your pardon for imposing this further worry on you.
Nevertheless, I believe I can rectify my fault if you allow
your father to meet me.*

*To ensure that Sir Henry does not suspect collusion,
it is imperative that you greet your visitor with surprise.*

I shall await your reply at Doctor Theale's house.

*Your obedient servant,
William Harrier*

Theale looked up. 'You and my pupil seem to have spun quite
a web of deceit, Captain. Is the cause a worthy one?'

'It depends how you value worth, sir. A man was restored to
health through Mistress Swift's skills, but her life has become
complicated as a result.'

'And you seek to uncomplicate it?'

'If I can. The falsehood was a small one and never intended for her father's ears.'

'Why was it used at all?'

William answered honestly. 'For the protection of a houseful of women, sir. By accepting the falsehood, Mistress Swift assisted them as much as she did her patient.'

It was three hours before the messenger returned with a carefully sealed, one-line note for Doctor Theale, giving William permission to visit. In the intervening period, the urchin had earned two more pennies by feeding and watering William's mare in the doctor's stable, and the old man had shared a meal with his visitor, regaling him with stories from a life spent working in the fields of science, philosophy and medicine. William found him an entertaining companion, despite the many subtle prompts that were designed to trick him into revealing truths about himself and his relationship to the people mentioned in his letter to Mistress Swift.

Once the messenger had left, William stood to take his leave. 'I thank you most sincerely for your hospitality and your kindness, sir. It has been a pleasure to make your acquaintance.'

Theale chuckled. 'It is I who should thank you, Captain Harrier. It's a rare day when something out of the ordinary happens. May I give you a word of advice before you meet Sir Henry?'

William smiled. 'I would welcome it, sir.'

'Sir Henry presents himself as a bluff and jovial man, but that doesn't mean you should underrate his intelligence. His wife and daughter have quicker minds, but Sir Henry's no fool. Corfe Castle is not as valuable to the Royalist cause as Sir John and Lady Mary like to pretend. Historically, its purpose has been to prevent invasion from the sea, but now it stands only as a symbol of power. This is not to say the King would be happy to lose it; rather that he's unlikely to send his best officers to defend it. To this end, it is guarded by local men, none of whom has your confidence or ability. Sir Henry will suspect you of fraud unless you give him good reason for why you were posted there.'

'What would you suggest, sir?'

'Something debilitating that required a period of recovery and brought you to the attention of Mistress Swift. The ague, contracted abroad, perhaps . . . or an injury to the leg that prevented you joining a cavalry regiment.'

'Would a limp serve the purpose?'

Theale gave another throaty chuckle. 'As long as you can maintain it. Malingerers place a pebble in their boot to remind them which leg to favour. You might be wise to do the same.'

Close to Swyre, William discarded his merchant's attire in favour of the doublet, hose and wig he'd worn for Sir Walter, since a purveyor of fabric would seem even more out of place in the Corfe garrison than a confident cavalier. His saddle packs might hold exotic silk at a cursory glance, but buried beneath were the disguises he used most frequently, and it was a simple matter to re-enter the woodland where he'd hidden that morning and change his appearance to something more befitting the role of a captain. Lady Alice loved to refer to him as a chameleon, and he always said in response that he'd learnt the art of transforming himself from her and Gilbert Jackson.

A groom advanced to meet him as he reached the forecourt of the house, and he bent forward in his saddle to ask if Sir Henry was at home. Being told that he was, he gave his name and instructed the groom to discover if Sir Henry was willing to receive him. While he waited, he circled his mare on the wide expanse of gravel, leading her first on one rein and then the other.

'Is your mount ill-trained?' asked a voice from the entranceway.

William looked towards the sound and guessed from the man's age and extravagant attire that he was the older brother. He approached on horseback, thinking Jayne had been right to laugh at the idea of William impersonating him, since William was decidedly taller and leaner than the man whose name he'd appropriated. 'Not so much ill-trained as having a preference for pulling to the left,' he answered amiably, dismounting and handing the reins to the groom who hurried outside to take them. 'I live in hope of curing her of it. May I know to whom I'm speaking?'

'Captain Andrew Swift,' came the curt response. 'You're well acquainted with the name because you used it yesterday at my sister's request.'

William crossed the ground between them, walking with an uneven tread. 'It's a fine name, sir,' he said, offering his hand. 'I trust I did nothing to dishonour it.' He smiled slightly when his gesture of friendship was rebuffed. 'You have my sincere apologies if my borrowing of it offends you, Captain Swift.'

Andrew scowled at him with dislike. '*Stolen*, more like. Do you plan to use it again?'

'Not now that I've met you, sir. I doubt I could pass for you, even in the dark.'

A hearty laugh sounded in the hall, and William saw the figure of Sir Henry coming towards him. 'Your servant, sir,' he said, bending his knee. 'I'm Captain William Harrier, most recently of the Corfe Castle garrison but now with orders to join the King's Regiment of Horse at Oxford. Do I have your permission to enter?'

'You do,' said Sir Henry, walking forward. 'Stand aside, Andrew. The captain deserves our thanks, not our censure.' He extended his own hand. 'My daughter tells me you defended her from armed men inside Lady Stickland's house, Captain.'

William gripped the hand warmly. 'I did only what her brother would have done, sir. It was a most unexpected welcome, and deeply shocking for Mistress Swift.'

Sir Henry ushered him into the salon and presented him to a pretty woman who sat at an embroidery frame. 'My wife, Lady Margaret. This is Jayne's rescuer, my dear. Captain Harrier.'

Lady Margaret offered her hand, and as William bent over it, he saw that her eyes had the same intelligence as her daughter's. 'Have you come to see Jayne?' she asked.

'Only to assure myself that she's safe, ma'am. My intention was to escort her home, but I had business with the commander of the garrison and she was gone by the time I returned to Lady Stickland's house.' He turned to Sir Henry. 'Milady, who tells me she has a deep affection for your daughter and a strong distrust of Sir Walter, begged me to follow. I pray her concerns for Mistress Swift's safety were misplaced and that she arrived home without trouble.'

Sir Henry assured him she had, but went on to describe the events of the morning in loud and colourful terms. Sir Walter was impudent offal for daring to invite Jayne to play bauble to a prince in front of her father, and he was in full spate about the 'shameless effrontery' of Prince Maurice's proposal when Jayne entered the room and begged him to stop.

'You're making Captain Harrier uncomfortable, Papa. He owes the same allegiance to Prince Maurice as he does to the King, and to decry one is to decry the other.' She smiled apologetically at William. 'You were kind to come, sir, but I fear your journey was wasted. I heard you say that Lady Stickland was worried for me, but my ride home was uneventful, and once here I had my father's protection. I do thank you most heartily for the care you showed me in Dorchester.'

William bowed. 'It was small repayment for the care you've shown me, ma'am. I'd not have ridden again so soon had you not helped me rebuild the strength in my shattered leg.'

A gleam of humour flashed in her eyes at the falsehood. 'Thank Sir John for allowing me to treat all the garrison's ills, sir. Do you still practise the exercises I taught you?'

'I do, ma'am. They are most beneficial.'

Andrew, who had sprawled himself ill-manneredly along a sofa, eyed William with a frown. 'We weren't at war when my sister treated Sir John. How did you receive your injury?'

William turned towards him, wondering if he resented all visitors or just those who had a connection with his sister. By way of explanation, he told a half-truth. 'I fought for eight years in Europe, sir. My last attachment was with the Comte de Guiche's army in the winter of '41 and spring of '42, when he was tasked with halting the Spanish advance into northern France at Honnecourt. My horse was hit by artillery, and I broke my thigh as I fell.'

'Was the battle won?'

William shook his head. 'Sadly not. We took such heavy casualties I was lucky to survive. I received word later that some seven thousand of the Comte's army were killed, wounded or captured.'

'An inglorious defeat then.'

William smiled slightly. 'The dead died gloriously enough. It takes courage to ride at full gallop against superior artillery . . . as you'll know from your own experiences of war, Captain Swift.'

The taunt was intentional, for he'd read in Sir Henry's letters that only the younger sons had left Swyre to fight for the King. The eldest had remained at home, taking the title of captain and assuming command of the footmen and farm labourers who made up the estate's irregular militia. Sir Henry referred to him as 'the heir', but it was hard to tell whether the phrase was intended as mockery or respect.

Andrew dismissed the comment with a flick of his hand. 'You and my sister seem overly keen to promote your bravery, sir. But tell me this: why did Sir Walter's men draw their swords on her? I find that part of her story hard to believe if they were merely billeted in Lady Stickland's house. Do you care to explain why it was necessary to defend her?'

Richard Theale had advised William not to underestimate Sir Henry's intelligence but hadn't warned him of Andrew's. He'd expected suspicion from the father but not from the brother, and he was unsure how to respond since he didn't know if the question had been put to Jayne. 'With respect, sir, I don't care to explain anything without your sister's permission.' He looked at Jayne. 'Do I have it, Mistress Swift?'

She held his gaze for the briefest of moments. 'By all means, Captain Harrier. My parents will be as interested as Andrew to hear the reason, since fatigue has left me disappointingly silent on the matter.'

William acknowledged her answer with a nod and turned back to Andrew. 'Your sister's manner of dress did not suggest a lady of learning, sir, and Sir Walter assumed Lady Stickland had played him false when she assured him she'd summoned her brother's physician. He reacted angrily out of fear for the wounded soldier he'd brought to Milady's house, who needed a doctor and not a laundress.'

Andrew gave an abrupt laugh. 'Who can blame him? Jayne shames us all by her choice of dress.' He studied William closely. 'Why was Sir Walter so keen to have this soldier mended?'

'For the same reason you show keenness to follow a superior's orders, Captain Swift. Sir Walter didn't want to disappoint Prince Maurice. I understand His Royal Highness has a particular fondness for the young subaltern, having known him since childhood. I was told they practised their swordsmanship together.'

Sir Henry leapt to the conclusion William wanted him to draw. 'And still do, presumably? Am I right to think it was the prince who wounded him?'

'I assumed from Sir Walter's desire for discretion that this was the case, sir. The Dorchester Puritans would seize on any accident if they thought it would harm the King's cause.'

'Indeed, indeed! They're a scurvy lot.'

Andrew, less easily persuaded, glanced at Jayne. 'Is that your view, sister?'

'You know better than to ask,' she answered, marvelling at how easily William had manipulated the truth. 'I've never yet broken a pledge of silence to a patient.'

'You should teach Captain Harrier to do the same. He has a loose mouth.'

William eyed him for a long moment, then turned to make a bow to Sir Henry. 'Your servant, sir. It has been my pleasure to make your acquaintance.'

'Are you departing so soon, Captain Harrier? Will you not accept some refreshment before you go?'

'I'm afraid I can't, Sir Henry. I still have much to do before I leave for Oxford at dawn tomorrow.' He bowed to Jayne's mother and then to Andrew. 'Milady, Captain Swift.' And, finally, to Jayne. 'May God go with you, Mistress Swift.'

'You also, Captain Harrier.' She offered her hand and he bent to kiss it. 'And never forget to do your exercises,' she said as he turned strongly on his left leg to leave. 'Your continued good progress depends on them.'

She thought she caught the whisper of a laugh as he limped his way across the hall, but it might have been the brush of the front door across the stone flags of the floor as the footman opened it. Whichever, she was the only one who heard it, for her father and brother were at each other's throats again, the one praising their visitor, the other sneering at him. If there was an ounce of amusement to be found in their constant bickering, Jayne would have smiled to hear them both accept Captain Harrier for what he said he was, but, as ever, she preferred to distance herself. With a curtsey for her father, she prepared to leave the room.

'You'd better not be running after him,' Andrew warned. 'You'll make a fool of yourself if you do. He's only interested in your dowry.'

Jayne wouldn't have answered had weariness not robbed her of patience. Following Sir Walter's departure, to satisfy her father she had been obliged to pretend that Marianne Prewitt was indeed in need of her services, only to return to find William's messenger awaiting a reply. Her one ambition had been to sink onto her bed and fall asleep, but, recognising that it was her error and not William's to name Corfe as his garrison, she had stayed awake, watching for his arrival. And now she had Andrew's jealousy to contend with.

She'd never seen this side to his character before the war, and she regretted deeply that the easy affection they'd always had for each other had soured. He upset the whole household with his bad-tempered barbs, and Jayne's only explanation for his changed behaviour was the one she delivered now.

'Isn't it time you brought some sense to bear on your feelings of inferiority, brother?' she asked coldly. 'You achieve nothing by dressing like a popinjay and pouring scorn on everything others do and say except to expose your own failings. The choice to stay here was yours, though I deeply regret that Sir Henry gave you the option, for your behaviour grows worse each time a letter comes from our brothers, showing how far they now outstrip you in skills and maturity. We've been sadly deprived of Philip and Benjamin's company since the war began, but must tolerate yours whether we wish it or not.'

Andrew shrugged his indifference. 'Cease your preaching, sister. Your views carry no weight with me.'

Sir Henry tut-tutted his annoyance at both of them, but Jayne ignored him. 'I'm well aware of that,' she said. 'The only voice you listen to is the angry little simpleton inside your head who blames his unhappiness on everyone but himself. Your single reason for trying to denigrate Captain Harrier was to make yourself seem better by contrast, but all you succeeded in doing was to paint yourself as an ill-mannered fool.'

'I care nothing for the opinion of a fortune-hunter.'

Lady Margaret intervened. 'I doubt he's that,' she said, raising her head from her embroidery. 'He would have stayed longer and sought to ingratiate himself with Sir Henry if it was Jayne's wealth he was after. The objective of every fortune-hunter is to gain access to the father, and Captain Harrier wouldn't have wasted the opportunity had that been his purpose.'

Andrew scowled. 'Perhaps I saw him off. Perhaps you should be thanking me rather than criticising me.'

Lady Margaret shook her head. 'Nothing here impressed him, Andrew, least of all you. If you saw him off, it was to your sister's detriment.' She turned to Jayne. 'I fear Captain Harrier's standing may be above ours, my dear, so I hope your feelings for him are indeed just those of physician for patient.'

Jayne reached for her hand. 'They are, Mama. Our conversations have been very few.' She studied her mother curiously. 'But why do you think his unwillingness to linger speaks to high status rather than an urgency to return to Dorchester?'

'Only a man rich enough to purchase, equip and maintain chargers on foreign soil would have been attached to Comte de Guiche's cavalry. A commoner would have fought on foot.'

1644

*With Parliament achieving successes in the north
of England, the Royalists attempt to consolidate
their control of the south-west by laying siege
to Lyme Regis.*

ELEVEN

Lyme Regis, 20 April 1644

THE NEWS THAT PRINCE MAURICE was parading his army outside Lyme's Town Line reached Jayne as she was lancing yet another carbuncle on the neck of yet another of the Parliamentary garrison's soldiers. She believed the cause of the outbreak to be a poor diet and general lack of cleanliness, but there was little she could do except lance the painful boils, clean the wounds with brine and urge the men to bathe themselves regularly in the sea.

This advice was greeted with hollow laughter, since none had time for bathing. When the men weren't manning the Town Line—a six-foot-high earth bank behind a deep trench that had been constructed by the people of Lyme during the preceding twelve months—they were sunk in sleep or searching for food. The Parliamentary town, with its strong Puritan leanings, had been under threat of siege since refusing to surrender to Lord Carnarvon the previous year and, as the ramparts were more than a mile in length, it required a thousand men to defend them, with most sleeping at their replacements' feet and rarely changing their clothes or eating more than bread and thin soup. Before the war, the population of Lyme had been under a thousand, but now, swollen by Puritans seeking refuge from towns under Royalist control, the number exceeded three thousand, and all were crammed into the confined space between the earth-bank ramparts and the sea.

The trench and ramparts had been constructed under the guidance of Colonel Robert Blake, the commander of the garrison, and Jayne had come to his attention when one of his aides, John Metcalfe, had begged permission to bring Mistress Swift to the town for the purpose of treating his ailing wife. The woman suffered from recurring ague, and Mistress Swift was the only physician who had ever been able to give her relief. Colonel Blake had granted Metcalfe leave to escort Jayne from her home, warning that she would have to depart again before nightfall, but on learning of her skills he decided to keep her another two days. There were too few town physicians to cope with the outbreak of boils amongst the men of the garrison, and he promised Jayne fair remuneration if she would lance the worst of them.

Jayne had been allocated a room in a house overlooking the harbour and began work on the Friday morning, after asking John Metcalfe to send word to Sir Henry that her return would be delayed. She was assisted in her work by two doughty matrons who told her the house had once been a hospital, though it hadn't been used for more than a year. The women's nursing skills were limited but Jayne was grateful for their presence when she saw how many men needed treatment; she doubted her nerve would have held had she been obliged to face such a crowd alone. The first day she treated in excess of one hundred men, and began again at dawn on the next when a long queue formed in the street outside.

In the preceding weeks, the news reaching Swyre had concerned only the north and east of Dorset, with skirmishes between Royalists and Parliamentarians being rumoured from Shaftesbury to Poole. Since Lyme was situated in the far west of the county, Sir Henry had been unconcerned about her travelling there, but he'd sent word back to Metcalfe that he must return her to Swyre no later than four hours after noon on the third day of her visit.

The poor man was trembling now as he informed Jayne that Prince Maurice and six thousand Royalist soldiers were gathered outside the town. 'Your father will never forgive me, ma'am. He'll have my head for endangering you.'

'He's not so savage,' said Jayne calmly, squeezing pus from the putrid carbuncle into a rag. She nodded to a pile of cloths on a table beside her and gave instructions to one of the matrons. 'Wet a fresh one in the bowl and then hand it to me, please,' she said, wondering why neither seemed able to learn that she was following the same routine each time. She discarded the pus-filled rag in a wooden chest for burning and then pressed the brine-sodden cloth against the wound in the sufferer's neck. 'Take a stool outside the door and hold the cloth in place until I call you back to put a dressing on the cut,' she told him before asking how many others were waiting.

'Only five, ma'am. You've treated more than one hundred and twenty already, for I've counted them as they came out.'

She smiled. 'Will you tell them I need just a few moments with Captain Metcalfe? I will not be long.' She asked the matrons to leave also and then turned to Metcalfe. 'Will the town surrender?'

'No. Colonel Blake is committed to the fight. It may be that I can persuade a fisherman to take you out by sea, but the price will be high.'

'I have but five shillings with me. Will a fisherman do the job on a promise that my father will pay?'

Metcalfe shook his head. 'Payment will have to be made in advance, ma'am, and I question whether any will agree to desert the town. Our fisherfolk are as dedicated to the defence of Lyme as every volunteer who guards the ramparts.'

Jayne recalled her conversation with William last September about why the unpaid defenders of Dorchester had surrendered. 'Are they all volunteers?'

'They are, ma'am. The town has been out of money since we made our stand against Carnarvon. Parliament sends supplies of food by ship, but when the weather's bad we can go days without eating. The women do their best to stretch the rations, but it's not easy.'

Jayne nodded. Her father had said several times that Lyme would have been starved into submission if the King hadn't lost control of the navy.

Metcalfe spoke again, worried that her silence indicated despair. 'Would you like me to ask my father to pay on your behalf, ma'am? I can't say for certain that he has the necessary coinage, for there's been no commerce here these last six months, but I'm sure he will help if he can.'

Jayne smiled. 'It's a kind thought, John, but I imagine he would rather keep what he has to ensure the safety of his family and household.' She pondered for a moment. 'Who has charge of this hospital?'

'No one, ma'am. The last incumbent was Doctor Chaffin, but his sympathies were with the King and he left in acrimony after we refused Carnarvon's terms. The other two physicians prefer to work out of their houses, and the barber surgeon performs his operations wherever his patients are located.'

Jayne was surprised. 'Did you not tell me there were upwards of a dozen physicians in Lyme the first time you summoned me to tend your wife?'

He nodded. 'Most have left—three or four out of sympathy for the King, the rest out of recognition that there's no money to be made from a town under siege. I doubt they're a great loss, since they only sought custom from the foreign ships that used to dock here. As long as they carried leeches and quicksilver, the credulous sailors believed they could cure anything.'

Jayne was sure he was right, but two physicians and a barber surgeon were hardly sufficient for a population of three thousand. It needed but an outbreak of the flux and all would be infected. With sudden decision, she rolled her sleeves higher up her arms, and leant forward to place her hands on the table at the centre of the room. 'Would you be willing to ask Colonel Blake if I might have charge of this hospital?' she asked. 'I would rather make myself useful than sit in idleness. If there are women with knowledge of nursing and disease, I would have them at my side, and because I have no wish to set myself up as competition to the male physicians and the barber surgeon, I would appreciate a meeting between the four of us. Do you think Colonel Blake will agree to these requests?'

Metcalfe bowed. 'For certain, ma'am. He has a good understanding of how desperate our situation is likely to become. I'll return when I've spoken with him.'

A half-hour later, when the last of the carbuncles had been lanced and Jayne had had time to compose herself, Captain Metcalfe escorted her to Gaitch's Fort, one of the middle forts in the Town Line, and led her up the five wooden steps inside. There were four such edifices built into the earth-bank ramparts, at a quarter-mile distance from each other, all housing cannons on their raised floors. From there, the view towards the hills that surrounded Lyme was clear, and Jayne glimpsed Prince Maurice's army through a slit in the wall as she reached the last step. The sight was intimidating—six thousand infantry and cavalrymen, gathered in serried rows on Uplyme Hill, a steep grass-covered scarp that towered above the town—and her mouth dried with fear. It was one thing to pretend courage in a house overlooking the harbour, quite another to pretend it here.

Fortunately, she wasn't required to speak for several minutes, giving her time to run her tongue about her mouth to produce some saliva, because Colonel Blake was being berated by two elderly men in Puritan dress. Metcalfe whispered that these were the physicians, while a younger man to the side, less obviously Puritan judging by his tunic and britches, was the barber surgeon. Unsurprisingly, the physicians were arguing that a woman should not be put in charge of the hospital, and their protests became shriller when they saw Jayne. If this was Mistress Swift, she was too young to be given such responsibility. Colonel Blake was misguided if he thought a woman could be a doctor, even more so to think one yet to reach thirty had any medical experience at all.

What was surprising, however, was that the barber surgeon spoke up for her. He looked to be in his mid-forties, some fifteen years younger than the two physicians, and it seemed he was well acquainted with Richard Theale. Many was the time he had ridden to Bridport at Doctor Theale's request to assist in the setting of bones, and he'd heard the doctor speak of Mistress Swift as the best and most diligent student he'd ever had. In his opinion, Lyme was lucky to have her, and Colonel Blake correct to give her management of the hospital.

He ducked his head to Jayne. 'I am Alexander Hulme, ma'am, and will assist you in any way I can.'

She smiled, recognising the name immediately as the master barber surgeon that Richard always employed. 'You're most kind, sir,' she said, 'and be sure Doctor Theale speaks as highly of you. I believe you relocated his shoulder after he fell from his horse three years back. He said your methods were painful but effective.'

Hulme's pleasant face split in a grin. 'There was a deal of wrenching involved to force the arm into its rightful place again, ma'am, but he'd have lost the use of it if I hadn't done what was necessary. Captain Metcalfe tells me you're looking for women with nursing skills. My wife, Susan, is more practised than most and knows others as able. Shall I ask her to call upon you?'

'Please do, sir.'

'And with haste,' murmured Colonel Blake, staring through another slit. 'The prince is bringing forward his artillery.' He turned to the physicians. 'Will you accept Master Hulme's recommendation of Mistress Swift, gentlemen, or do you wish to argue further? I hardly need remind you that the Western Army outnumbers the garrison by upwards of five thousand, and the burden of dressing wounds will fall on you if you refuse Mistress Swift's help. What is your choice?'

Prince Maurice's assault began the following morning. By then, Jayne and Susan Hulme, with the help of the two matrons, several women and three young maids, had swept the hospital clean of dust, washed and scrubbed the floors, stools and tables, and begged and borrowed fifteen mattresses to lay in the upper and rear chambers. Jayne reserved the downstairs front room for treatment, placing stools around the walls and a solid oak table at its centre. One of the maids asked if the table was to hold medicines, and Jayne shook her head, saying its purpose was to allow a wounded patient to lie on his back.

To this end, she urged Susan to persuade her husband to join them and spread the word that wounded men should be brought to the hospital. 'We'll have more success working together than apart,' she said. 'I can assist him in the setting of bones, and he can assist me in the cleansing and sewing of wounds. I have catgut and needles in my satchel, but if he has supplies of his own, he should bring them here. Will he agree, do you think?'

Susan chuckled. 'I doubt I'll be able to keep him away, ma'am. He's been saying for months that it's a crying shame to leave the hospital locked up.'

'Who locked it?'

'Doctor Chaffin, who owns it. He swore he'd return once the war was won and sue the town for compensation if he found it had been used. He's mighty hopeful of a Royalist victory.' She broke off to listen to the sound of musket fire in the distance. 'Which might come sooner than he thinks,' she said wryly, making for the door.

The first day of the assault brought only minor injuries, often self-inflicted through carelessness—such as two broken toes from a keg of gunpowder being dropped—and Jayne began to wonder if she'd imagined war to be worse than it was. They learnt from the injured that the Royalists had tried to take some empty houses outside the Town Line, but the Lyme defenders had retaliated by setting the buildings alight with fire arrows. The resulting smoke had been so dense that it had allowed a band of Royalist infantrymen to crawl into the trench below the earth bank and dig away at a section of the base in order to cause a collapse. Their efforts proved fruitless not only because the bank was too well constructed but also because the Royalist musketeers on the raised slopes of Uplyme Hill—firing indiscriminately—wounded more of their own men in the ditch than the garrison's defenders.

The next few days followed a similar pattern, enlivened occasionally by the discharge of cannons from both sides of the Line. Injuries remained minor on Lyme's side despite a bold sortie by two hundred Parliamentarians into enemy territory to seize a battery and some thirty-five prisoners. Colonel Blake's interrogation of these men suggested Prince Maurice's troops were suffering worse than his, because a large number had been conscripted against their will and showed little appetite for fighting. To correct their cowardice, mounted dragoons rode behind them, slashing wildly with their swords to keep them moving forward. Out of sympathy, perhaps, Blake allowed the prisoners to desert by creeping along the shoreline at night and vanishing towards Devon.

The assault proper began on the following Sunday, and Jayne realised that the first week had been a mere testing of Lyme's defences by the Royalists. For the next ten days, the town came under constant bombardment from Prince Maurice's batteries, with one thousand heavy shot fired upon the town on the first day, and countless more in the days that followed. The noise was continuous, for the cannons in the forts were fired as relentlessly, and Jayne wondered if she would ever get used to the shock of the explosions or the crack of splintering timbers as heavy iron balls carved through roofs and walls.

Throughout, she and Alexander Hulme dealt with a constant stream of wounded. Those who defended the ramparts had bullet injuries to the head, arms and shoulders, since musket fire from the Royalist ranks was as unremitting as battery fire. The lucky were grazed by the lead shot, leaving bloodied burn tracks on their skin; the unlucky required the half-inch balls to be dug from their flesh. In every instance, unless a bone was broken and needed splinting, the men returned to their posts as soon as the wounds were cleansed and bandaged; as indeed did the women, children and elderly who came with injuries caused by falling cannonballs.

Many of the women dressed as men and stood with their husbands and brothers on the steps behind the earth bank to persuade Prince Maurice that the garrison was better supplied with troops than it was, and Jayne wished her father was there to see them. Nothing could be more different from Sir Henry's descriptions of Puritans as intolerant religious bigots than these open-minded men and women who worked together in defence of their homes.

Jayne found their courage inspiring, and envied the women their tunics and britches. For herself, as everyone else was obliged to do, she spent the eight weeks of the siege in the same plain dark woollen gown in which she'd arrived, since water was precious and the laundering of clothes impossible. Susan Hulme found her a spare apron which she was able to interchange with her own, achieving a semblance of cleanliness by washing each in the sea by turn at the end of the day.

The evening of 6 May saw the fiercest fighting. The town had been shrouded in thick fog all day, and Colonel Blake, fearing the Royalists would use it to advance upon the Town Line, had warned his men to expect an attack. But the attack never came and, as the light began to dim, he allowed one half of his troops to go in search of food. By so doing, he played into the Royalists' hands, for Prince Maurice had done precisely what Colonel Blake had predicted—sent his infantrymen under cover of the fog to hide in the hedgerows beyond the trench and wait for the command to storm the ramparts. The order was given at seven o'clock, and such was the fury of the assault that savage hand-to-hand fighting ensued, and in places the earth bank was overrun, allowing some one hundred Royalist soldiers to advance into the town.

Jayne would remember that night for the caterwauling of women who used their voices to intimidate the intruders. Her own nerves were quite frayed by the hideous sound, and she would have sworn on oath that the engagement lasted until dawn had she not been told afterwards that it endured a bare two hours once the troops at their supper learnt of the affray. Food was abandoned in their haste to return to their posts, and with double the numbers behind the earth bank, the Royalist attack was repelled. Nevertheless, the injuries were many, and the hospital quickly filled with slashing and stabbing wounds, all needing tourniquets and sutures to stem the flow of blood.

At some stage during the night, Susan Hulme drew Jayne's attention to the two elderly physicians who stood in the doorway, watching the industry inside. They appeared astonished to see so many working so hard to manage the queue of wounded. In the previous week, Susan had recruited ten mature women willing to learn how to cleanse wounds with brine and then apply dressings. Another ten worked inside the kitchen to create bandages from donated garments, first scrubbing them clean and then immersing them in cauldrons of boiling sea water to purify them. All this was visible to the physicians, as was Jayne and Alexander's stitching of the worst of the slashes while greybeards held the patients still on the table and children whispered words of comfort in their ears.

'You're welcome to join us, sirs,' said Jayne as she tied the last of the sutures on a five-inch gash in a man's leg and carefully released the tourniquet. 'Your help will be much appreciated if you can bring us more catgut and have the knowledge and skill to use it.' She moved away from the table, leaving Susan to bind the wound with clean strapping. 'But perhaps you had a different reason for coming?' she suggested when they didn't answer.

One, whom Jayne knew to be Doctor Fisher, stepped into the room. 'Are you charging for your services, Mistress Swift?'

Jayne shook her head. 'None of us is, sir. We work as volunteers just as every man and woman of Lyme. Are you not doing the same?'

'We've had no patients for a week.'

'Then join us,' she urged. 'Some of these brave men have been waiting a long time to have their wounds cleaned and dressed. We took the most serious first, but even those with lesser wounds are in need of care.'

Doctor Fisher addressed the men sitting on stools. 'Will any of you accept my treatment over Mistress Swift's?'

There was an uncomfortable silence.

'What is it she does differently?'

Alexander Hulme spoke when this question also went unanswered. 'She works quickly and efficiently, sir, and uses brine and boiled dressings to prevent wounds becoming infected. If you need proof of her methods, look to the men whose carbuncles she treated, few of whom have had a recurrence.'

'I'm one such,' said a grizzled soldier, nursing his injured left hand in his lap and gesturing to a healed patch of skin on his neck with the other. 'I've had boils before but none went away as quickly as this, and so I've told anyone who asks.'

The other physician, Doctor Whiteway, addressed Jayne. 'What of the four humours, Mistress Swift? If you work quickly, how can you assess which is out of balance?'

Jayne heaved an inward sigh, unwilling to be drawn into an argument about a practice that Richard Theale had taught her was outdated. The theory of humours was that four liquids—blood, phlegm, yellow bile and black bile—held equal importance in the body, and that an imbalance between them caused disease; yet it was twenty years since William Harvey had demonstrated that blood was pre-eminent because it circulated around the body through the pumping action of the heart. She answered tactfully. 'The humours relate only to disease, sir, not to wounds caused in battle.'

'But carbuncles and boils represent disease, do they not? I'm told you were as quick in your lancing as you appear to be in your stitching, which tells me you gave no thought to choler being the cause of the eruptions.'

'And what would you advise for an imbalance of yellow bile, which is the cause of choler, sir?'

'To reduce the heat and dryness of the body through regular immersions in cool water.'

Jayne beckoned the soldier forward and asked him to rest his hand on the table. 'Will you tell this doctor what advice I gave you once I'd lanced your boil, sir?'

'To bathe daily in the sea for the purpose of cleanliness, ma'am.' He cast a thoughtful eye towards the physician. 'And for the cooling of yellow bile, of course.'

Jayne hid a smile as she stooped to examine the man's palm, which had a gash from side to side where he'd warded off a sword before plunging his own into the enemy's belly. By keeping his hand half closed, the edges of the wound had begun to knit together beneath a scab, and she was reluctant to break it open again. She asked him if he thought the cut was a deep one and he told her he doubted it, for the scurvy Royalist clearly didn't believe in sharpening his blade.

'Then I'd rather leave this as it is, my friend, though you must keep your hand closed until the scab falls away.' She took some strips of dressing from a basket beneath the table and crumpled them into a ball. 'Grasp this,' she instructed him, pressing the ball into his curled palm and then using another strip to bind a figure of eight about his wrist and fingers. 'You may use your right hand as much as you like, but you're not to open your left until I give you permission to do so. Should you feel feverish, you must come here immediately, otherwise I shall expect to see you again in four days. Complete healing will take rather longer, but I need to be sure the scab is healthy. Do you understand?'

He nodded. 'Fever will mean the wound is infected, but a healthy, unbroken scab will mean it's healing of its own accord. Do you not have enough catgut to stitch it, ma'am?'

'We could certainly do with more,' Jayne said wryly, 'but even stitched you would still have to keep your hand closed for two weeks. To flex it would be to tear the skin around the sutures, and that would do even more damage.'

He nodded again. 'My brother's the quartermaster for the town, ma'am, and has responsibility for ordering the supplies that are brought in by ship. With your permission, I'll ask him to add catgut to the list. It'll likely be a week before it arrives, but it will free you and Master Hulme to use what you have in the meantime.'

Jayne smiled her thanks, adding that more barrels of salt would also be useful, since sea water wasn't as clean as brine, and then, as he departed, she turned her attention to the next man in the queue. 'If you wish to stay, sirs,' she told the physicians, 'you will help us greatly by examining the wounded and bringing the most severely injured to the front. If we have some order in the queue, our nurses can clean and dress the minor cuts while we manage those that need stitching.'

She hadn't expected them to accept the invitation, but perhaps they felt the need to restore their reputations in the eyes of the town. Whatever the reason, they removed their coats and worked as assiduously as everyone else for the next three hours, earning the gratitude and respect of those they helped. By the time the end of the queue was reached, every bed in the hospital was in use, being given to those whose injuries were so severe they were unable to stand or walk. Susan Hulme estimated that, in the five hours since the fighting had started, three physicians, a surgeon and a dozen nurses had treated in excess of one hundred and fifty men, and not one of the patients had died.

Jayne had barely rolled out her mattress in the kitchen and lain her weary body upon it when one of the night nurses ran in and shook her vigorously. 'Colonel Blake is at the door and requests that you accompany him, ma'am. I've said you're too tired but he won't take no for an answer.'

Jayne sat up and rubbed her eyes. 'Has he said what he wants?'

'No, ma'am, only that you must take medicines and dressings.'

Jayne stifled a groan. 'You'd better bring him to me, Bridey. I'm quite respectable, having nothing to wear but this gown.' She reached for the tankard of fresh water she'd placed beside her mattress, first taking a long drink and then wetting a cloth and holding it against her face. She heard boots tramping across the front room. 'Do you have more wounded for me, Colonel?' she asked, leaning forward to press the cool fabric against her eyes.

'I'm afraid so, Mistress Swift.'

'Then we must send for Master Hulme and the doctors Fisher and Whiteway. I'm too drained to manage on my own.' She gave her face a last wipe, then folded the cloth in her hands to study him. He was a man of middle age and pleasant features, but she was always surprised by his smallness of stature. He was shorter than she was, and yet the strength of his character made him a compelling leader. 'You look weary too, Colonel.'

'I am, ma'am.' He paused. 'John Metcalfe assures me you have no allegiance to either side in this war and seek only to bring succour to those who need it. Is that true?'

She nodded.

'The same cannot be said of the physicians and surgeon, all three of whom have sworn allegiance to Parliament.'

'Why does that matter when we're in a Parliamentary town?'

'The man I need you to treat is a young Royalist captain, Mistress Swift. His name is Francis Blewett and he's badly wounded. He led his troop into the town with great bravery in order to secure the port for Prince Maurice.'

'We heard they'd been captured.'

'Only twenty, ma'am. The rest are dead. Captain Blewett is being cared for by Ann Metcalfe in her husband's house. She begs your assistance for she is still weakened from the ague and cannot cope with his injuries.'

Jayne pushed herself to her feet and took a moment to steady herself. 'Am I right to think you know Francis Blewett, sir? Your concern for him seems stronger than mere admiration for a young man's courage.'

'I'm his godfather, ma'am. His mother is my cousin, and I stood sponsor for him on the day he was baptised. Both his life and his soul are my responsibility.'

﹏

Jayne knew as soon as she saw the pallor of Francis's face and felt the rapid pulse in his wrist that there was nothing she could do to save him. His eyes were wide open and showed fear and pain in equal measure. Ann Metcalfe had done her best to staunch the blood that seeped from the wound beneath his ribs, but Jayne believed that most of the bleeding was happening inside. She had seen the same symptoms—grey sweaty skin, racing heartbeat and crusted blood on the lips—in a patient of Richard's who had been stabbed in the chest during an angry fight in the lead-up to war, and the only comfort Richard had been able to offer was relief from pain.

Richard's patient had died in under an hour but Francis had lingered for upwards of four, and Jayne could only assume that whichever internal organ had been pierced was bleeding more slowly than in Richard's patient. Ann had propped pillows beneath his back, which she said had allowed him to breathe more easily, but the obvious swelling of his abdomen suggested to Jayne that this was where the blood was collecting. The whimper of pain that issued through his nose when she touched a light finger to the skin beneath his ribs seemed to prove it, though she didn't think altering his position would make him any more comfortable. In the end, she knew she could do only what Richard had done and ease the poor man's passing, since the greatest sadness for any physician was to acknowledge how limited his ability really was.

She asked Ann to bring her a small glass of water, heavily sweetened with sugar, and then leant forward to smile into Francis's eyes. 'I have some medicine which will free you of pain and allow you to sleep, Francis. It needs to be swallowed, so will you show me that you can open your mouth?'

He tried to do so but his lips were sealed with encrusted blood.

Jayne took a salve from her satchel and smoothed it gently around his mouth to loosen the crusts before dipping a small silver spatula into a bowl of water at his side and inserting it carefully between his lips. Next, she saturated the corner of a cloth and squeezed droplets down the spatula to moisten his tongue. 'Is that better?'

He nodded. 'Who are you?' he managed.

'I'm Jayne Swift,' she said, discarding the cloth and filling a silver teaspoon with water. 'Your godfather asked me to help you, Francis.' She removed the spatula and dribbled water from the spoon into his mouth.

'Is he here?'

'He is, and I will call him to speak with you as soon as the medicine has taken away your pain.' She nodded to Ann to put the glass of sweetened water on the table. 'You will find it a little bitter, Francis, but its curative powers are truly marvellous. Its name is laudanum.'

She was speaking for the sake of speaking, but in truth the pain-killing properties of laudanum were astonishing. She had a single small bottle of the remedy and had seen the relief it had brought Richard's patient some two years previously. From pain, the dying man had moved to a state of euphoria, and when sleep came, it had been peaceful. She uncorked the bottle and poured a teaspoonful of the brown tincture into a larger spoon, adding another of sweetened water, before holding the spoon to Francis's lips and urging him to take it all. He did so, wincing at the bitter taste, but within minutes his eyes lost their fear and his taut body began to relax.

Jayne rose from her knees and moved to the door of the chamber where Colonel Blake was waiting. 'Stay at his side until he sleeps, and say all you wish to say,' she whispered. 'He will be greatly comforted by your presence.'

She could see from Blake's expression that he knew the poor boy was dying, for he'd been around battlefields too long to believe that one so pale could survive. Nevertheless, he gave no hint of it as he took Jayne's place at Francis's side and praised his godson for his courage and honour. The scene, lit by candlelight, was painfully intimate, and Jayne's eyes welled with tears to see the affection the two men had for each other. There was no greater tragedy in this hideous war than that differences of allegiance had set loving friends against each other.

She and Ann moved away from the door so as not to intrude on the men's final moments together. Ann's fever and shivers had calmed thanks to the infusions of cinnamon and chamomile Jayne had brought when she first came, but she was clearly exhausted by the day's events and Jayne ordered her to bed. For herself, she sat on a stool in a corner of the anteroom, listening to the murmur of voices from the neighbouring chamber and judging the passage of time by a marked hour-candle on a sideboard. Despite her sadness for Francis, she remained detached enough to record how effective laudanum was in achieving a peaceful death.

Richard Theale had learnt of the remedy through reading the works of Paracelsus, a Swiss physician from the previous century, and his attempts to replicate Paracelsus's recipe had put him in the way of a young student called Thomas Sydenham. Thomas lived at Wynford Eagle, some seven miles to the north-east of Bridport, and the pair had met by chance at the home of the only merchant in Bridport able to acquire a necessary ingredient of laudanum—opium poppy seed from Asia. A few minutes' conversation had revealed a shared interest in Paracelsus.

Richard had taken Jayne to meet Thomas some three months before the war started and she admired his practical approach to science and medicine. He accepted what his experiments told him, rejecting anything that couldn't be proven through results. Since Richard did the same, she was unsurprised that a strong friendship had developed between her elderly tutor and this ardent nineteen-year-old Parliamentarian. By working through different permutations of Paracelsus's ingredients, Thomas had isolated opium as the reliever of pain and, on Richard's advice, had ground the seeds to a fine powder and dissolved them in alcohol, thereby producing an infusion, albeit a bitter one, that could be fed by spoon.

The hour-candle showed that nigh on thirty minutes passed before Colonel Blake came to tell Jayne that Francis had died. 'We had a fine talk,' he said gruffly. 'Death held no terror for him. He was clear of mind and free of anxiety until the end.'

'May I check?' asked Jayne, rising from her stool. 'I expected him to sleep for a short while before he passed.'

But it seemed not. Francis had lived and confided his thoughts to his godfather until the moment his heart stopped beating, and the look of serenity on his face was beautiful to see. His eyes were closed and a small smile curved his mouth, and Jayne thought how greatly this contrasted with the fear she'd seen earlier.

'I'm so sorry,' she said.

'No need to be, ma'am. You gave him a sweeter death than most physicians could have done.' Colonel Blake nodded to the bottle of laudanum. 'What manner of medicine is that?'

'A reliever of pain,' she said, leaning down to draw a coverlet over Francis's body and face. 'I wish I had a hundred more bottles. There were many in the hospital today who would have benefited from it.'

'Place the order and the ships will bring it.'

'I wish I could,' she answered with a sigh, 'but I'm only one of three people who know how to make it and, in war, the necessary ingredient is unobtainable. Parliament would rather import weapons from Europe than poppy seeds from Asia.' She replaced the bottle and her silver spoons in her satchel. 'You said twenty of Francis's companions were taken prisoner, Colonel. Are any of them wounded?'

'They're not your business, Mistress Swift.'

She shook her head apologetically. 'They are because I choose to make them so, sir. They were your godson's men and, had he lived, I believe he would have asked me to help them. I regret his passing most deeply and would help his friends if I can.'

Blake smiled slightly. 'You're an annoying woman, ma'am. We'll neither of us be liked for mending Royalists.' He gestured towards the door. 'They're in the town gaol. I'll escort you there and then summon Master and Mistress Hulme to assist you.'

TWELVE

JAYNE DOUBTED SHE'D EVER SEEN such a sorry-looking group of men. The gaol was lit by a profusion of candles in sconces which gave off heat, smoke and light in equal measures, and she wasn't surprised that the prisoners were taking shallow breaths. Many bore similar laceration wounds to those she'd treated earlier in the hospital, and all were battered and bruised from being punched and kicked after their weapons had been removed. They were crowded into a cell barely large enough to hold seven or eight, which meant only the two most injured were able to sit.

Seeing how little space she would have, even using both chambers, Jayne was tempted to ask Colonel Blake to have the men marched to the hospital, where she could treat them more easily and in cleaner conditions. However, to do so would invite anger from the people of Lyme, and she doubted Blake or his prisoners would agree to it. It was evident to her that the gaoler, a giant in Puritan dress, had done his share of the kicking, for even when Colonel Blake ordered the cell door to be opened, none showed an inclination to walk out into the gaoler's anteroom.

She asked the colonel if the gaoler might be allowed to sit outside in the street, making more room for her to examine and treat the prisoners. 'I'm happy for him to leave the door open, so that he can see what is happening,' she said. 'Indeed, I would welcome it. Fresh air will help dispel the unhealthy odours in this building.'

'I can't afford to have you taken hostage, Mistress Swift.'

'Then ask these men to give their word that they will do no such thing, sir.' She addressed the prisoners. 'I am a physician, come to treat your wounds,' she told them. 'You are not obliged to accept my help, but I offer it in good faith, for I take neither side in this war. My pledge is to treat all who need me, regardless of their beliefs or allegiances.'

'Do you treat the men of the garrison?' asked one.

'I do. Today, I have stitched and dressed more wounded soldiers than I can count.' She smiled at his immediate look of distrust. 'Would you have had me refuse them when they bleed and feel pain the same as you, sir? My job as a physician is to heal my patient, not stand in judgement on his thoughts.' She gestured to the youngster at his side. 'Your friend is close to collapse. You will do him a kindness if you allow me to find out why.'

'He can't breathe.'

'All the more reason to send him out to me.'

With a shrug, the man prepared to thrust the other forward, but Colonel Blake held up his hand. 'First, give your parole,' he said. 'I will instruct the gaoler to move into the street if each of you makes the pledge.'

The paroles were given so readily that Jayne guessed it was clean, cold air they wanted as much as attention to their wounds.

The heat and stench coming from the cell was truly appalling, and she advised the prisoners to remove their jackets as they began to file into the anteroom.

'You must cool yourselves as best you can,' she told them before turning to Blake. 'They need water for drinking, and buckets in which to urinate, Colonel. My nose tells me the gaoler expects his prisoners to do their business where they stand, and there's no quicker way to spread disease than by leaving waste to fester. If you wish the people of Lyme to stay healthy, you must allow these Royalists some dignity.'

Blake closed his eyes briefly. 'Come dawn, you'll be begging me to release them back to Prince Maurice.'

'Not begging, sir,' she answered, 'merely pointing out that a town under siege can ill afford another twenty mouths to feed. Lyme will earn more admiration by showing mercy than by leaving these men to starve in squalor . . . or, worse, executing them for daring to breach your defences.'

He turned towards the door. 'You have strange ideas about war, ma'am. Respect is given to the winners, not to those who treat their enemies with kindness.'

~

The open doorway, and the gaoler's obvious displeasure at being forced to sit outside, had drawn neighbours and passers-by to stand and stare. The light from inside the building spilt onto the street, and the anger of the watchers was clear to see. The prisoners were made nervous by their presence, but Jayne took strength from the gathering crowd. For all her fine talk to Blake, she knew she could not have faced a group of twenty soldiers on her own.

With the help of the man whose friend had been close to collapse, she created a space in a corner of the antechamber and asked for the two who'd been seated inside the cell to be brought to her first. Both had deep cuts across their arms, which were bleeding freely despite the rags that had been bound about their injuries, and she was shocked by the dirt and faeces on both the rags and the men's skin. She applied tourniquets to stem the flow of blood and then appealed to the gaoler for a bucket of clean water from the well. He refused, saying he couldn't leave his post.

Jayne singled out an older woman in the crowd of watchers. 'Will you help me, ma'am?'

'I will not. I'd rather die than give succour to Royalists. You have no business treating them.'

There was a stir of movement as Alexander Hulme shouldered his way through the throng. 'You're a mean-hearted creature, Maggie,' he said to the woman. 'Where's your gratitude for the help Mistress Swift has given the garrison this night, or in the weeks that have gone before? She's not from Lyme, so it's no more her business to assist us than these Royalists, but she does so freely. Would others were as generous.'

The woman bridled. 'Do you say I'm *not* generous?'

He moved past her. 'You should know better than I. One of Mistress Swift's patients this evening was your husband, and a pail of water would have been small repayment for the kindness she showed him.' He placed a sack of salt at Jayne's feet. 'Susan is following with catgut and dressings, ma'am. If you hand me the buckets from inside, I'll fill them for you.'

'There are none,' she said, 'not even for waste. These men have had nothing to drink since they were brought here, and all are covered in their own filth. We must use flagons and buckets from the hospital unless you can find some closer, Alexander.'

Hulme turned to the crowd again. 'Well?' he demanded. 'Is there a Christian amongst you? It's written in Matthew that Jesus said: "Love your enemies, bless them that curse you, do good to them that hate you, and pray for those who despitefully use you."'

'Cease your preaching, Hulme,' growled the gaoler. 'Every person here is better versed in the Bible than you.'

'Nonetheless, he speaks the truth,' called a man's voice. 'We defend our city for God and Parliament, and both demand that we do it in obedience to the Word. There's no reason to hate these men for fighting bravely. We lost none in the battle they brought to our streets, but they lost eighty—and I, for one, have sympathy for them.'

And so it seemed did others, for within five minutes a large array of pitchers and pails, brimming with clean water, were brought to the gaol.

Jayne tasked the man who had helped her create space in the corner with ensuring that every prisoner had water to drink. He gave his name as Peter Tucker, his age as thirty-two and his county of birth as Cornwall. He had assumed leadership over the others, some of whom were as young as sixteen, by virtue of being the oldest, but he told Jayne he had no higher rank than they. They were all just common foot soldiers, pressed into service by Prince Maurice's German dragoons on the promise of plunder from each town that was subjugated.

She begged the gaoler's permission for the prisoners to stand in the street while she sluiced out the cell and anteroom. He gave the permission readily, amused by the idea of a woman of her status dealing with urine and faeces, but he hadn't bargained on Alexander and Susan helping her, insisting he move so that they could sweep and wash the waste into a communal cesspit some five yards from the gaol's doorway. As polluted water was added to the ordure inside, a stench drifted through the metal grating that covered the pit, and the watchers took hasty steps backwards to avoid it. By doing so, they created a spacious circle outside the gaol which allowed the prisoners to move a little away from each other and breathe the cool night air.

Since Jayne saw more sense in examining them there than in the cramped conditions of the gaol, she asked Alexander and Susan to clean and stitch the wounds of the two with tourniquets and then moved amongst the men to assess the severity of their injuries. In this, she was ably assisted by Peter Tucker, who had made his own appraisals during the hours they'd been confined in the cell. He'd used rags torn from shirts to bind the worst of the cuts and slashes, and called these men forward first. Most were bare-chested, because it was their own garments that had been used, and their bruised and bloodied state showed clearly in the flickering lamplight.

Jayne wondered whether it was their injuries, their soft West Country accents or their youth that most affected the onlookers, because the crowd thinned each time she removed a soiled rag to inspect the lacerations beneath. She sent a silent thank you to God that none of Prince Maurice's German mercenaries were in the mix, for a guttural Teutonic voice would have shouted 'enemy' more surely than the lilting burrs of Cornwall and Devonshire. Peter asked her afterwards if the crowd had dispersed through shame to see their countrymen so ill-used.

'I don't know,' she answered honestly. 'How much shame do you feel when you rob a family of their hard-earned savings?'

'We call it "spoils", not robbery. Things are different in war.'

'By which you mean that as long as there's a word to make your thieving sound better, you're happy to do it?'

'We have to have some reward for fighting, ma'am. None of us would engage otherwise. This lad would go home tomorrow if he could.' He was holding a bowl of brine while Jayne cleansed a large area of raw skin on a youth's back where he'd been dragged by his feet across cobbles.

'The people of Lyme would celebrate if he did,' said Jayne. 'It's a foolish sort of war where men on both sides dream of living peacefully at home but are forced into battle because their leaders refuse to listen to each other.'

'Do you speak of Prince Maurice and Colonel Blake?'

'No,' she said with an amused smile, 'though nothing would please me more than if those two negotiated a truce, since I, too, would like to go home.' She smoothed a salve of comfrey oil over the graze and then took a long dressing which she bound several times around the youth's chest. 'This will protect the wound until it heals,' she explained, 'but be wary of bending or stretching. The process will take longer if you tear or crack the scabs.'

The youth eyed her bitterly. 'It hardly matters,' he said. 'You're just patching up dead men. We'll be hanged tomorrow.'

Jayne tied off the dressing. 'And who will you thank if you aren't?' she asked.

'God. We've prayed a thousand prayers since we were taken prisoner.'

'He must be busy then,' she responded lightly. 'I warrant every person in Lyme says as many prayers each time your artillery starts firing.' She looked at Peter. 'If I were to guess at why the crowd dispersed, I'd say it was out of reluctance to feel the same compassion for you as they do for their sons and neighbours. It's hard to fight men for whom you have sympathy.'

'Meaning they must keep hating Royalists if they're to defend their town?'

Jayne nodded.

'Why don't you hate us, Mistress Swift?'

'For the same reason I don't hate the people of Lyme. You're no more responsible for this war than they are.' She moved on to the next youth needing attention. 'The fault lies with the King and Parliament.'

~

At some point during the night, Peter whispered to Jayne that a man was watching her from the shadows beyond the pool of candlelight. He had stood a quarter-hour, listening to every word she said, and Peter feared he intended harm to Mistress Swift. He nodded in the direction she should look, but by the time she'd turned there was nothing to see except a shadowy figure disappearing into a side street. Absurdly, she thought it was William Harrier, and she would have called after him had common sense not prevailed. Wherever William was, he was not in Lyme or she would have seen him before.

~

Dawn was breaking when Jayne finally returned to her bed, and she slept the sleep of the dead for the next seven hours. Nothing disturbed her, not even the nurses who were tending the fifteen patients on the mattresses upstairs and in the room at the back.

'But what of cannonballs and artillery?' she asked. 'Why did *they* not wake me?' Because there were none, she was told. No gun had been fired in anger since the sun had risen.

These answers were given by Susan Hulme, who woke her shortly before noon. 'You need to rise, ma'am. The truce has ended and the fighting is about to resume.'

Jayne rolled onto her back. 'What truce?'

A strange one, it seemed. Envoys from Prince Maurice had ridden under a white flag to request the release of Captain Francis Blewett. When told he was dead, they'd asked for his body so that it might be buried with due reverence by his Royalist companions. All the while the guns had remained silent, and the voices of Colonel Blake and the envoys had sounded loudly in the still air.

Colonel Blake shouted that Parliamentarians were not wanting in reverence towards a corpse. Captain Blewett had been washed and shrouded and placed in a coffin, the cost of which had been borne by Colonel Blake himself. Was it Prince Maurice's intention to repay this money? When the answer came back in the negative, Blake said he wasn't surprised, since the commander of the Western Army was better known for taking than for giving. Nonetheless, Lyme was not so poor that they would hold a brave man's body hostage for want of compensation.

He went further and said that if Prince Maurice pledged to keep the peace until the coffin was returned, he would release the twenty Royalist prisoners who had fought alongside Captain Blewett. They would emerge through the gates at noon, bearing the coffin upon their shoulders, and nothing would be done on Lyme's side to impede or endanger their progress. Thereafter, the war could resume, though Blake's challenge to Prince Maurice was to engage with the garrison face to face. To this end, Blake was willing to create a breach in the earth bank, so that Prince Maurice might send in his army, ten abreast, in the hope that so mighty a force could prevail against the stout-hearted defenders of Lyme.

Jayne stared at Susan, aghast. 'Has he lost his wits? What if Prince Maurice accepts?'

'He has already, ma'am. His commanders have been forming their regiments into columns of ten for the last two hours. They wait only for the prisoners to emerge with the coffin.' She shook her head. 'I passed them being marched to the gate on my way here, and they didn't look happy. Given the choice, I suspect they'd rather desert than be forced to keep fighting.'

Jayne sat up and began running her fingers through her hair to bring some order to it. 'There'll be more wounded than we can cope with,' she said. 'What possessed the colonel to act so foolishly?'

Susan moved behind her to smooth the curls at the back. 'According to Alexander, it's not so foolish. Colonel Blake wants to show the impossibility of a frontal attack. He's confident our men can hold a breach if only ten come at them at a time and the musketeers will fire on those behind. Alexander believes the Royalists' wounded will far outnumber ours.'

Alexander's prediction was correct. The Royalists withdrew in under two hours, carrying their dead and wounded with them. Their casualties, mostly from musket shot, were said to number in the hundreds, while only three Parliamentary soldiers had died and the injuries brought to the hospital were minor ones. The episode gave new hope that Lyme could withstand the siege indefinitely as long as the navy kept supplying them, and this hope burnt even more brightly when an entire week passed without Prince Maurice launching an assault on the town.

A strange event happened towards the end of this uneasy peace. Jayne was summoned from the hospital to speak with Colonel Blake in Gaitch's Fort, and once again she was required to mount the wooden stairs and look upon the Royalist army through a slit in the wall. The sight was no less menacing this second time, because the artillery batteries were more noticeable, being concentrated to the west of Lyme. Blake drew her attention to three figures some fifty yards from the trench. Two were smartly dressed in the uniform of Prince Maurice's dragoons; the third wore the jacket and britches of a foot soldier. He stood slightly ahead of his companions, bearing a white flag, and Jayne recognised him immediately as Peter Tucker.

'Are you acquainted with this man?' Blake asked. 'He claims to know you.'

She nodded. 'He's the leader of the prisoners you returned with your godson's body, sir. What does he want?'

'We don't know. He says he has a message for Mistress Swift, which he insists on delivering in person. He's willing to approach closer and call it out to you if you show yourself on the earth bank. Are you prepared to do that?'

'If you say I should, Colonel, but it's an odd request, don't you think?'

'Very odd, since the message must come from Prince Maurice. Are you acquainted with him also, ma'am?'

'It would be unlikely if I were, sir.'

Blake's expression was unreadable, and Jayne couldn't tell what he made of her non-committal reply. 'I thought it might be a ploy to divert our attention from an attack elsewhere, but there's been no movement anywhere along the Line.' He seemed to reach a decision. 'I'm curious to know what he has to say, but I'm conscious his words will be heard by the men in this fort and for fifty yards on either side. I will therefore honour your choice to refuse if you have secrets you'd rather keep hidden.'

'There are none on my side, sir,' said Jayne honestly, thinking the only secrets she knew were Charles's. And if Prince Maurice wanted to reveal those, she was quite capable of expressing the same surprise as everyone else to learn she'd once treated the King's nephew.

With a small bow of appreciation, Blake opened a narrow door which led onto a wooden platform atop the earth bank and ushered her ahead of him. He ordered the nearest soldiers to mount their steps and stand ready in case of trouble, and then called to the messengers to approach. 'You can see that Mistress Swift has come,' he said. 'Now state your business.'

Peter was visibly shaking as he stopped at the edge of the deep trench, and Jayne wondered what was causing his terror: the dragoons who seemed to be guarding him or the muskets levelled at his heart? When he appeared unable to moisten his mouth enough to speak, she addressed him directly. 'There's nothing to fear, Peter,' she said. 'Colonel Blake is a man of honour and will not order his men to fire on you.'

He fixed her with a haggard gaze. 'There's everything to fear if you give the wrong answer, ma'am. I was sent to make this request because I said you were willing to treat all wounded men, whatever their allegiance, and I'll be flogged if I'm shown to be a liar.'

'But you haven't lied, Peter. Everything you've said is true. Do you wish me to shout that aloud? I can't promise my voice will carry as loudly as Colonel Blake's, but I'm willing to try.'

Peter shook his head. 'I need you to accompany me to our camp in order to treat the Royalist wounded, ma'am. My words were reported to Prince Maurice, and he summoned me to his tent to say what I knew about you. I spoke in praise of your kindness and now he wants to know if you were being truthful about your willingness to treat all who need you. We have many wounded, but none of our surgeons is as able as you.'

Jayne turned to Blake. 'How should I answer?'

'It's not my place to say, Mistress Swift. You're a visitor to Lyme and therefore not subject to my command, but in two years of war I've never heard of a physician crossing the lines to treat both sides.'

Jayne considered for a moment. She had no illusions about why Prince Maurice was making this request, for nothing would amuse him more than to use her own declared neutrality to steal her away from the garrison.

She addressed Peter again. 'Please give my respects to Prince Maurice and tell him that I'm more than willing to lend my services to the Royalist wounded. His concern for his troops is entirely to his credit, though I fear you've allowed him to think too highly of my abilities if he believes I can mend your many injured on my own. Colonel Blake tells me they run into the hundreds, but perhaps you have a more accurate figure?'

One of the dragoons stepped forward to prevent Peter answering. 'Colonel Blake exaggerates,' he said in strongly accented English. 'There is but a handful needing attention.'

Jayne smiled down at him. 'I'm glad to hear it, sir, for it would be a tragedy indeed if hundreds were being tended by inadequate barbers in the filthy squalor of an army camp. In such conditions, more die of poisoned blood and camp fever than from wounds.' She gestured behind her. 'Lyme hospital can easily take a handful, and I'm sure Colonel Blake will be generous enough to allow them through the gates under a flag of truce.'

The dragoon shook his head. 'Those are not His Highness's wishes, ma'am. He asks that you come to our camp.'

Jayne's eyes lit with humour. 'Then he must make the request himself, sir. I am superintendent of a hospital which overlooks the harbour. If His Highness has the courage to enter Lyme alone and on foot in order to find me, I will match his bravery by walking, unchaperoned and unprotected, amongst his men.'

'He cannot do that, ma'am.'

'And neither can the daughter of Sir Henry of Swyre flaunt herself before an army, sir. If you have the prince's ear, persuade him to send his most severely injured to the gate in the confident knowledge that I will do my best to save them. Peter Tucker spoke honestly when he said I take no account of allegiances when people need help.'

Colonel Blake was more surprised than Jayne when the dragoon returned some quarter-hour later to say her invitation had been declined. Had the roles been reversed, he told her, he would have sent as many wounded as he thought he could get away with into the Royalist camp. There was no better method of assessing an enemy's strength than placing spies in their midst, and her mention of the hospital being on the harbour would have allowed the prince's men to watch at close quarters as the ships were unloaded.

Jayne watched the dragoon retreat up the hill. 'Perhaps Prince Maurice fears losing them forever, sir. Peter and his companions couldn't have been clearer that they'd rather be in Cornwall than here. They fight because they must, not because they want to.' She clasped her hands in apology. 'Nevertheless, my offer was rash and extremely ill-considered . . . though in truth I couldn't think of anything better to say.'

'You could have refused.'

'I'd have made a liar out of Peter if I had.'

'Yourself also?'

She acknowledged the point with a nod. 'I've made a principle of being neutral. I'd hate to abandon it at the first sign of difficulty.'

Blake turned to look at the mass of tents assembled on Uplyme Hill. 'Perhaps the prince hoped you'd bring him information. He must be wondering how well or badly we're faring after weeks of bombardment. Do you agree, Mistress Swift?'

She laughed in genuine amusement. 'I've no idea, Colonel. You're asking me questions that only God can answer. May I return to the hospital? I believe my talents are better applied there than in trying to read your enemy's thoughts.'

As she made her way to the seafront, Jayne saw that a new ship was anchored outside the Cobb, a man-made boulder wall that curved out into the sea and protected the harbour from the vagaries of the wind and tide. Like everyone else, she watched eagerly for fresh arrivals, because the only source of food was the navy. As often as not, more barrels of gunpowder were unloaded than those containing salted meat, grains and beans, but the women of Lyme stretched every keg of food as far as they could. The cooking was done in large cauldrons in a warehouse near the docking area, and people gathered to eat in the vast hall that had once been stacked high with textiles. Rationing was taken seriously, and anyone who misappropriated another's share was condemned publicly as a thief, although the only people who tried were children. Adult Puritans viewed their limited diet as a test of dedication to their cause, and thanked God heartily for their daily wedge of bread and bowl of flavourless broth.

Made of weaker stuff, Jayne dreamt of being back in Swyre, smelling the sweet odour of roasting beef, mutton or pork in the kitchen. She had a strong longing to be home, for despite the ready acceptance she'd received from the people of Lyme, she was missing her family most dreadfully.

John Metcalfe came to the hospital to find her as night was falling. She and Susan were removing bandages from a patient whose leg had had to be amputated above the knee by Alexander the week before, and she asked John to wait while she examined the stump. By necessity, she'd had to cauterise the flesh to stop the bleeding, but through regular applications of calendula oil the blistering had calmed and the scabs looked healthy. Nevertheless, she worried for the man's state of mind. He rarely spoke, and when he did it was to say he'd be better off dead. Leaving Susan to apply fresh dressings, she rose from beside his mattress and accompanied John into the front room.

Assuming he'd come for help for his wife, Jayne lifted her satchel from beneath the table and began sorting through the contents. 'Ann works too hard,' she told him. 'I warned her yesterday she'd have a relapse if she overtired herself, but she wouldn't listen and just kept carrying logs to the fires in the warehouse.'

He smiled. 'She won't listen to me either, ma'am, but she's not the reason I'm here. I've brought you a visitor who came in on the ship this noon. He waits outside for permission to enter.'

Jayne frowned. 'Who is he?'

'Samuel Morecott, ma'am, Parliamentary surveyor of the western ports. He says he's husband to your cousin.'

THIRTEEN

THE SMARTNESS OF SAMUEL'S APPEARANCE put Jayne's bedraggled gown, unkempt hair and sea-washed apron to shame. He bowed gracefully and favoured her with a smile, though she didn't doubt both were for Metcalfe's benefit. He seemed to feel it was incumbent upon him to make a speech, naming the many dignitaries who had assisted him up the Parliamentary ladder, and Jayne guessed he was trying to impress Metcalfe, for few of the names he mentioned were known to her.

She spent the time studying his face, wondering how so contemptible a man could have become even more handsome since the last time she'd seen him. The sun had bronzed his skin and he looked as well as she'd ever seen him. It was a mercy Ruth wasn't there. In the nigh on two years since their separation, her cousin had come to see her escape as a blessing, but Samuel's beauty would have reignited all the feelings she'd once had for him. To receive a smile would have disarmed her completely, and his many cruelties would have been forgiven and forgotten.

Samuel concluded his pompous oration by telling Jayne he'd just spent two hours with Colonel Blake, receiving the colonel's report on Lyme's continued ability to defend herself. 'He mentioned your presence here, cousin, and I was surprised to learn of it. Your family's allegiance to the King is well known, so I question how committed you are to assisting the garrison.'

Jayne allowed a second or two to pass before she answered. 'As committed as I was to saving your son, Samuel. You wouldn't recognise him if you saw him now. He's grown a good three inches since he left your house and is as happy and healthy as a four-year-old should be.'

He ignored her jibe. 'Colonel Blake tells me you treated some Royalist prisoners, and as a result Prince Maurice was encouraged to request you attend the wounded in his camp. Do you care to explain yourself in this matter?'

She eyed him with amusement. 'Which matter? The dressing of wounds in the gaol or Prince Maurice's invitation?'

'Both.'

'Royalists bleed as freely as Parliamentarians, and Prince Maurice is impertinent. What other explanation is there?'

'That you're exploiting the trust Colonel Blake has placed in you to send information to the enemy.'

She stared at him open-mouthed. 'How?' she protested. 'I've had no communication with anyone outside Lyme since I came here.'

'You sought out the Royalist prisoners, spent half the night with them and then asked Colonel Blake to return them to Prince Maurice the following day. The colonel was foolish enough to do so without discovering what secrets you'd passed to them.'

Jayne turned anxiously to Metcalfe. 'There were no secrets, John. The gaoler was witness to every conversation I had, as were Alexander and Susan Hulme. If the colonel shares Mister Morecott's concerns, he should question them, for they will say I spoke only of my distaste for war and my wish that we could live in peace with each other.'

Metcalfe nodded. 'Don't fret yourself, ma'am. The colonel did precisely that before he returned the prisoners, and informed this gentleman of it a bare half-hour since.' He glanced at Samuel. 'However, Mister Morecott has warned him that he's concerned enough about your father's allegiance to the King to express doubts about you in his report.'

Jayne was so relieved not to have lost the colonel's confidence that she had little care for anything Samuel wrote. 'Does it matter? The worst that can happen is that Colonel Blake will be instructed to dispense with my services.'

'He wouldn't want to do that, ma'am. The men of the garrison value you too highly. They'd rather be treated by you than the other physicians.'

Jayne saw a look of displeasure cross Samuel's face. 'Then perhaps the colonel should write a report of his own,' she suggested. 'I'm more than happy to explain why Mister Morecott bears a grudge against me. The last time we met he threatened me with a horsewhipping for changing his son's medication in order to help the poor child live.'

She was pleased to see that Samuel's intelligence hadn't improved with his looks. Instead of laughing off the remark as a jest, he placed the fault on her. 'You behaved badly, cousin. I was within my rights to chastise you.' He jabbed a finger at Metcalfe's face. 'My son was cured by prayer and his previous physician's infusions, not by anything this woman did.'

Metcalfe took a step backwards. 'I'm in no position to judge, sir. I can speak only of my personal knowledge of Mistress Swift's ability, which has brought relief to my wife and all who have received care in this hospital.' He paused, clearly debating with himself how much to say. 'Your ship sails in an hour, sir, so I'm surprised you're wasting time on our medical arrangements. Previous port surveyors assessed our defences and took stock of our provisions, but you've done neither.'

'I believe I have a better understanding of my role than you do, Captain Metcalfe.'

'I hope so, sir, for Lyme's most pressing concern is that Prince Maurice has trained his artillery on the harbour. Colonel Blake drew your attention to it several times, but the reason for the prince's actions seems to have escaped you.'

Samuel's lips thinned in irritation. 'Do you lecture me?'

'Only to suggest that Parliament would prefer some warning of the imminent loss of one of its ports to learning of your dislike for Mistress Swift, sir. The prince's clear intention is to fire on incoming ships in order to prevent fresh supplies reaching the town, and should he succeed, Lyme will fall. We cannot hold the Town Line without ammunition and food, for starving men make poor soldiers.'

'I assumed Colonel Blake wrote of such matters in his own reports.'

'We're at war, Mister Morecott. The colonel rarely has time to dictate more than a few lines before he's called to one of the forts to repel an attack. He relies on the port surveyors to make detailed assessments of the dangers we face.'

Jayne blessed John for trying to deflect Samuel's attention away from her, but she worried that he was telling falsehoods to do it. The colonel sent a letter with every ship that departed, usually delivered on board by John, who had asked several times if Jayne would like to add a letter of her own. She always declined, for only Colonel Blake had the authority to apply a seal to what he wrote. All others must allow their words to be read as insurance against the passing of secrets, and Jayne had been unable even to start a letter to her father without foolish tears dripping onto the page. She hoped it was enough that Blake had requested a message be sent to Sir Henry, informing him that his daughter was safe, though she doubted either of her parents had taken comfort from hearing such news through Parliament.

As she listened to John flimflam Samuel with imaginary deficiencies in Lyme's stores, she found herself wanting to scream. John and Colonel Blake had no more in common with Samuel than her father had with Sir Walter Hoare or Prince Maurice, and yet stubborn belief forced them to align themselves with people they would ordinarily avoid.

With a sigh, she broke in on their conversation. 'You're a good friend, John, and I thank you most sincerely for your help, but it will pain me greatly if Mister Morecott includes your name with mine in his report. Two years ago, he hacked the head from a dying priest to use as a football, and he'll destroy your character with as little conscience if he sees advantage to himself in doing so.' She turned to Samuel. 'Write what you like about me, Samuel, for I couldn't care less about the opinion of self-serving men in London. If you choose to write lies about Colonel Blake or Captain Metcalfe, however, I shall beg Lady Stickland and every Parliamentarian I treat to say what they know about you. Be sure your cruelty to the priest, your abandonment of your wife and child, and your cowardly desertion of Dorchester in her time of need have not been forgotten.'

Samuel clenched his fists. 'Be silent, woman!' he snapped. 'Whatever your position here, you are as nothing compared with the surveyor of the western ports.'

'Indeed. Your purloining of your wife's allowance and your shameless fawning on Denzil Holles have served you well, Samuel.'

Metcalfe stepped between them before Samuel could strike her. 'Control yourself, sir,' he said sharply. 'I've no idea how you conduct yourself elsewhere, but while in Lyme you will behave like a gentleman.' He placed a hand beneath Jayne's elbow and turned her towards the back room. 'I suggest you join Susan and your patient, Mistress Swift. I'm sure they have more need of you than Mister Morecott does.'

She gave him a nod of gratitude and walked away, amused to hear Samuel's blasphemous swearing as Metcalfe manhandled him into the street. Nonetheless, she was conscious of an opportunity missed. Had her visitor been anyone else, she would have asked him to take word of her to her father.

Prince Maurice's bombardment of the harbour commenced three days later. Because the hospital overlooked the Cobb, it was within reach of the guns, although whether through luck or God's intervention, the building was never hit. Many houses on either side were less fortunate, and Jayne, Alexander and the nurses were kept busy with the stream of wounded who presented themselves at their door. There were more broken shinbones than before, with patients describing cannonballs thudding onto the cobbles and skittering in unpredictable directions. The elderly, being the least agile, were unable to skip aside, and accommodation had to be found for them in the centre of the town once their legs were set and splinted. Jayne would never forget the generosity shown by the women of Lyme during this period. The queues to offer rooms, board and care to people they hardly knew were as long as the queues of those needing treatment, and the favoured mode of transport for greybeards who couldn't walk was a wheelbarrow. She came to understand that when hardship and adversity were shared by all, kindness invariably triumphed over selfishness.

Evidence of this came in the persons of Doctor Fisher and Doctor Whiteway, who had chosen to transform their houses into hospitals, accepting trained nurses from Jayne and demanding no payment in return for their services. In consequence, she and Alexander were able to send patients into safer parts of the town and, on the occasions when the bombardment of the Cobb became unbearable, join and work with the other two physicians in their homes. She couldn't tell if they considered her an equal, for they never deferred to her, but she found it pleasing that both had adopted her habits of cleanliness in their surgeries and the use of brine in the treatment of wounds.

On 22 May a supply boat carrying a full load of malt and beans from a ship anchored outside the Cobb was sunk, and attempts to rescue the cargo brought yet more casualties to the hospital. Most of the men were suffering gunshot wounds, delivered by ranks of Royalist musketeers on the hill to the west of the town, and though none of them died, all questioned the sense of trying to save food that was destined to sink anyway.

Prince Maurice clearly took a different lesson from the incident. Seeing how much easier it was to attack the smaller boats inside the Cobb than the ships at anchor beyond the range of his artillery outside, he ordered his musketeers to rain fireballs and fire darts on the supply barges that were moored against the dock. Realising the danger this presented, Colonel Blake sent a hundred men from the garrison to drive the musketeers back, but though they had initial success in dispersing the ranks, they were forced back across the Town Line by Prince Maurice's cavalry. The musket fire resumed, and by nightfall every barge was ablaze. So intense were the flames that the entire town was lit by their glow.

Dawn the next day showed the true extent of the damage done by the fires. Only a handful of the supply barges had survived, and few believed they would still be intact by the evening, because Prince Maurice had no reason to cease his onslaught. For the first time, Jayne sensed that despair had entered Lyme, and like everyone else she found herself praying for a miracle.

It came in the late afternoon when shouts were heard from lookouts at the eastern end of the harbour that a fleet was approaching. The call was taken up around the town and people gathered along the shoreline to see the truth for themselves. Eight ships, including a ninety-gun warship which flew the colours of the Admiral of the Fleet, the Earl of Warwick, hove to in deep water some four hundred yards from the Cobb's boulder wall, and every watcher called their arrival a blessing from God, until the Royalist artillery unleashed the most ferocious bombardment to date.

The Earl of Warwick responded by firing his own guns, and the haze of smoke that drifted across the town, coupled with the deafening sound of exploding gunpowder, left most in Lyme confused and ignorant about what was happening. Nightfall brought merciful respite, but come dawn the hideous barrage began again. This time, Prince Maurice trained his guns on the town as well as the fleet, intent, it seemed, on trying to destroying both at the same time.

The casualties were so numerous that Jayne and Alexander turned away any whose cuts didn't require stitching or bones setting, but despite their taking only the most severely wounded, the floor of the hospital was still covered in patients unable to sit or stand. By mid-morning, more than thirty had died, most from calamitous blood loss. Their bodies were removed by teams of women, who took them to be buried in the graveyards of their churches, where Puritan preachers spoke movingly of the saintliness of their lives and their predestined places in heaven. Each time one was borne away, Jayne felt a little part of her go with them, for so many of the faces and names had become known to her over the past weeks.

She used the last of her laudanum on Maggie, the woman who had refused to bring a bucket of water to the Royalist prisoners in the gaol, and whose belly had been penetrated by a wide, foot-long shard of wood. Her pain was so grievous that her eyes were starting from her head, and she kept begging Jayne to forgive her, as if she felt she were being punished for the sin of denying her help. Jayne forgave her again and again, until the laudanum dulled her agony and allowed her to die in peace, but the poor woman's passing left its mark on her.

Whether it was sadness at Maggie's death, or a recognition that she now had nothing left to ease the pain of others, she felt suddenly drained of the strength and will to continue. She had promoted a lie when she persuaded the people of Lyme that the hospital was a place of healing, for her skills were too paltry to mend the damage that artillery did to the human body. Tears of despair gathered in her eyes and coursed down her face and, but for Susan seeing her distress and reaching down a hand to assist her to her feet, she would have remained kneeling beside

Maggie's body, incapable of moving of her own volition. Yet even as she rose, Susan was signalling for the corpse to be removed, seemingly unaffected by the tragedy it represented.

Alexander looked up from the table where he was splinting a child's arm. 'She needs food and rest,' he told his wife, nodding at Jayne's pale face.

'We all do,' said Susan bluntly, grasping Jayne by the shoulders and shaking her fiercely. 'Pull yourself together, ma'am, and recognise that every injured person in this room has a right to feel sorry for himself. There are many still in need of our help and we cannot manage without you.'

Jayne stared at the floor for a moment and then wiped her eyes with the hem of her apron. 'It's you we can't do without,' she said huskily. 'Your strength puts me to shame, Susan. Who would you like me to see next?'

'Colonel Blake, ma'am. John Metcalfe sent word that he's wounded and is refusing to leave Gaitch's Fort for fear our troops will lose heart if they see him go. John asks that you attend him as soon as you're able.' She pulled Jayne's satchel from under the table and placed it in her arms. 'Now would be a good time to do so, because the walk and fresh air will revive your spirits.' She lifted the flap of the satchel and added fresh dressings and a bottle of brine to the contents. 'Be sure to avoid the sides of the roads,' she instructed, leading Jayne to the door. 'There's more danger from collapsing walls and burning thatch than there is from cannonballs.'

Jayne discovered the truth of this for herself as she made her way towards the fort. Debris and smouldering straw lay everywhere, with houses showing gaping holes in their facades and roofs. She couldn't believe that so much damage had been wreaked in two days and wondered what the next two would bring, since Prince Maurice seemed determined to reduce Lyme to rubble and ash. Yet the threat of complete annihilation of their town was being worn lightly by her people, who seemed more intent than ever on holding together against adversity. Tables ran along the centre of every street, allowing the elderly, wounded and children to sit or lie beneath heavy oak planks, while women battled the inevitable fires from falling thatch, using blankets and boots to smother the flames. Yet more passed buckets of sea water from hand to hand in order for those at the front to enter a stricken building and quench the flames inside. By such means, they prevented fire spreading from house to house, thereby delaying Prince Maurice's hopes of a mass conflagration destroying their town.

How trivial Jayne's sudden despair in the hospital seemed by comparison, for it was not just Susan's strength that put her to shame but the strength of every woman in Lyme. While their men stood ready on the ramparts to repel each new attack, mothers, wives, sisters and daughters were fighting behind them to preserve the only homes they had, and Jayne guessed it was this that Susan had wanted her to see. If anything could revive her spirits, it was surely the sight of women proving themselves the equals of men.

*

The interior of Gaitch's Fort was filthy with the dust thrown into the air each time a cannon was fired on the upper storey. For the moment, the cannons were silent—due to a lack of gunpowder, Jayne learnt from the young soldier who escorted her inside. The ships outside the Cobb carried fresh supplies, but, with the harbour under constant assault from Prince Maurice's artillery and most of the barges destroyed, there was no way to bring the kegs ashore. The soldier seemed resigned to Colonel Blake's view that Prince Maurice would give the order to storm the length of the ramparts in a frontal assault once he realised the defenders had neither cannon nor musket fire. The day had seen several skirmishes as the prince tested the garrison's strength, but as yet there had been no unified push to put the entire Town Line under attack at the same time.

'It's why the colonel can't leave the fort,' the soldier explained, taking Jayne's satchel and gesturing towards the wooden steps. 'He needs to be seen if the troops are to fight well.'

Jayne questioned the sense of this when she found the colonel seated on the floor with his back propped against the wall. It was a fine ambition to stand with his men, but hardly practicable if his wound wouldn't allow him to do so. John Metcalfe knelt at the colonel's side, trying to replace his boot, and 'clumsy oaf' was the least of the imprecations being showered on the captain's head.

Metcalfe greeted Jayne with relief. 'I was afraid you wouldn't come, Mistress Swift. The colonel's foot's too swollen to take his boot.'

Blake glared at him. 'You should never have taken it off,' he snapped. 'I told you to leave it be.'

'What happened?' asked Jayne, taking her satchel from the soldier and kneeling beside Metcalfe.

'Fifty Royalists tried to scale the ramparts two hours ago and the colonel led men into the trench to prevent them.' Metcalfe pointed to a ragged hole in the upper leather of the boot. 'A dragoon fired on him from above and he took a ball in his foot for his bravery. I hoped it might have passed through and become lodged in the sole of the boot, but it hasn't.'

Jayne bent to look at the burnt and blackened entry wound. 'You're lucky it was only your foot, Colonel. How many were killed?'

'None. Three of our men attacked the dragoon before he could reload and the Royalist assault was repelled by the rest, but it'll not be long before they try again.'

Jayne turned to the young soldier and asked him to remove his jacket so that she could form it into a support for the colonel's foot. 'Are you sure you want me to treat you on this squalid floor?' she asked Blake. 'The hospital has the merit of cleanliness and several kind nurses to soothe your discomfort when I dig out the musket ball.'

Blake gave a grunt of a laugh. 'I'm already discomforted.'

'You may think so,' she said, folding the youngster's jacket and placing it beneath Blake's heel. 'If you're lucky, the ball is nestled between two of the twenty-six bones that make up your foot. If you're unlucky, it's lodged *inside* one and will need considerable cutting and wrenching to remove.'

'Then spare me some of your laudanum, Mistress Swift. My men need to see me upright at the ramparts, not cowering on the floor.'

Jayne shook her head. 'I can't, sir, for I used the last of it an hour ago.'

'I trust it went to good use.'

'It did. There are many in the hospital with wounds far worse than yours.'

Blake smiled. 'You're a cruel woman, Mistress Swift, but I don't doubt you speak the truth. Do your worst. I shall endeavour to endure your rummaging with fortitude.'

Jayne had learnt a great deal about removing unnatural items from swollen human flesh over the last few weeks, principally that blind 'rummaging'—even with the smallest pair of pincers—was a great deal more painful than a quick, sharp incision that allowed her to see what she was looking for. Nonetheless, she first needed to feel for the ball, since such objects often travelled away from the entry wound after encountering bone. With a warning to Blake that she was about to hurt him, she shifted her position so that she could grasp his foot between her hands and apply strong pressure around the wound with her thumbs.

She gave a murmur of satisfaction when she located the ball above the gap between the higher bones of his first and second toes. 'Your boot must have taken most of the force,' she said, releasing her grip. 'The penetration is neither as deep nor as erratic as I feared.' She took her sharpest knife and a pair of silver pincers from her satchel. 'John, oblige me by cupping the colonel's heel in your hands and holding his foot steady. And, Colonel, please take a deep breath and count off the seconds in your head while you hold it.'

'Why?'

She smiled. 'Because I believe I can conclude this procedure before you reach sixty. You can tell me afterwards if I've succeeded.'

It was a trick that rarely failed, particularly with male patients. A held breath kept them still, and most were so keen to prove her wrong that they put their efforts into counting rather than tensing against anticipated agony. Colonel Blake was no exception. Even if he felt the quick, clean nick Jayne made to extend his wound or the press of the pincers as she gripped and extracted the half-inch musket ball, he was so prepared for a minute of pain that anything shorter was a relief.

Thereafter, she cleansed the wound thoroughly with brine and bound a dressing tightly around it to contain both the bleeding and the swelling. She asked him to move his toes and, though the movements were small due to bruised and torn muscles, she was confident the bones hadn't fractured.

'I need to apply thicker and stronger dressings if you're to stand, sir,' she said. 'Your arch and ankle need supporting, and you'll not be able to walk unless we can find you a firm, supportive boot that's at least three sizes larger than the one you have.'

Blake snorted another laugh. 'You're asking the impossible, Mistress Swift. If we had spare boots, I'd have given them to the two hundred men of the garrison who've had nothing on their feet for weeks. Everything falls to pieces when you stand night after night and day after day on the steps of a damp earth bank.' He nodded to her satchel. 'Do the best you can with the bandages you have. If my troops can fight barefoot, then so can I.'

'But not yet,' said Jayne, pushing herself upright. 'I need to be sure the wound is binding before I add more dressings. Remain seated until I return.'

'Where are you going?' he demanded.

'To beg a boot off a patient whose leg had to be amputated,' she said. 'He keeps it beside his mattress in the hospital to remind him that he once had need of it.'

'Send this young soldier to fetch it.'

Jayne shook her head. 'It'll not be given to a stranger,' she said. 'I can't even promise it'll be given to me.'

She entered the hospital through the kitchen to avoid the press of people at the front, and raised a finger to her lips to prevent the women boiling dressings from drawing attention to her. 'It's better no one knows I'm here,' she whispered. 'I have to return to Gaitch's Fort within five minutes.'

'What do you need, ma'am?' asked a matron.

Jayne nodded towards the door of the back room. 'Something only Jack Young can give me, Faith, though I fear the request will upset him.'

The matron chuckled. 'Then you're in for a surprise, ma'am,' she said, 'for I've never seen him so chirpy. A gentleman came looking for you some half-hour since, and he waited with the bed patients rather than clutter up the front room. He left again five minutes ago, but not before winning Jack's heart.'

'What gentleman?'

The woman shrugged. 'You'll have to ask Jack, for we never heard his name nor recognised him either, but he claimed you as his friend, Mistress Swift.'

Lady Margaret always told her daughter that if wishes were horses, beggars would ride, but Jayne's heart fluttered a little, nonetheless, as she made her way into the back room. There were, after all, very few Parliamentary gentlemen who might claim her as a friend.

'Faith tells me you've had a visitor,' she said, squatting beside Jack's mattress.

For the first time, she saw him smile. 'I have, ma'am, and a fine person he is too. He raised all our spirits.'

His neighbour nodded. 'He praised us for our courage and said the whole country knows of the battle for Lyme. It seems no one can believe that such a small garrison has held off the Western Army for so long.'

The remark gave Jayne the opportunity to plead Robert Blake's case, so she put his needs before her curiosity. 'But not for much longer unless I can help the colonel to stand,' she said. 'He's been wounded in his left foot and needs a larger boot than his own to accommodate the dressings. I wondered if he might borrow yours, Jack.'

Jack shifted his gaze to the floor beside his mattress, where both his boots stood. They were lower cut and of sturdier construction than a gentleman's boot and had the added merit of laces to bring the uppers together about the arch and ankle. He hesitated for a moment. 'Is the captain a man of his word, Mistress Swift? I told him you'd tried to find a woodworker to turn a leg for me but that all the experienced men are on the ramparts. He said there are plenty of such people in London and promised to have a peg sent on the next ship that leaves for Lyme. Should I believe him?'

'I can't say unless you tell me his name, Jack.'

'Harrier, ma'am. He came in this morning off the Earl of Warwick's ship.'

'Oh my goodness!' She caught his hand and squeezed it joyfully. 'I hoped it was he, and can say nought else but that you should trust his word completely. If he says he will send you a new leg, be sure he will.'

Shyly, Jack returned the pressure of her fingers. 'In that case you may give my boot to Colonel Blake with my blessing, ma'am, and tell him my prayers go with him. Lyme would have folded a long time ago but for his leadership.'

FOURTEEN

JAYNE WAS ON HER KNEES, lacing Jack Young's boot onto Colonel Blake's foot, when steps sounded on the wooden stairs behind her.

'Warwick sends his respects, Robert,' said William's familiar voice. 'He hopes to share a brandy with you when this fight is over.'

Blake looked up with a surprised laugh. 'Is that you, William? By God, I'm glad to see you, sir. I was beginning to fear no one would make it ashore.'

William walked forward to clasp Blake's hand in both of his. 'The prince certainly isn't making it easy for us,' he agreed. 'I came in by skiff two hours before dawn and met with Jeremiah Fullerton to assess what's left of the supply barges. Was it his idea or yours to use women to pull those that weren't sunk into the lee of the eastern wall of the Cobb?'

'His. He's a fine harbourmaster and saw the sense of moving them out of range under cover of darkness, though he told me it was his wife who mustered the women. They'd have salvaged more if the bombardment hadn't begun again at dawn. Did you see that we've taken men off the ramparts to rebuild the five least-damaged boats?'

William nodded. 'They're not far off completion. All being well, we should be able to start unloading men and munitions this night.' Even as he spoke, he was reaching down to assist Jayne to her feet. 'Excuse me while I greet Mistress Swift, Robert. She and I have a long acquaintanceship.' He raised her fingers to his lips, his eyes creasing in an amiable smile. 'I trust I find you well, Jayne. Lord Warwick knows of your presence here and has asked me to thank you for your work on Lyme's behalf.'

He retained hold of her hand longer than he needed to, and Jayne felt an unwanted blush colour her cheeks. She had hoped they would meet in a more private place, for she had no idea how to address him in front of Colonel Blake. So many falsehoods peppered their history—particularly those involving Prince Maurice—that she feared misspeaking and arousing the colonel's curiosity. William's use of her Christian name suggested she could respond in kind, though she was hard pressed to understand why he was on such familiar terms with both the Admiral of the Fleet and the commander of the Lyme garrison.

She withdrew her fingers and took a moment to smooth her apron, which was stained with Maggie's dried blood. 'Thank you, William,' she said then. 'I'm both well and extremely flattered by Lord Warwick's interest, though I question why he's so knowledgeable about my movements.'

'He received conflicting reports about you—one from the surveyor of the western ports and the other from Colonel Blake. He asked my advice on the matter, and I was pleased to lend my weight to Robert's assessment.'

'Morecott's a damn fool,' said Blake contemptuously. 'He seems to think good physicians come two a penny in a town under siege.' He ducked his head to Jayne. 'You have my gratitude, ma'am. Had

I summoned Fisher or Whiteway in your stead, they would still be discussing whether it was black or yellow bile that had caused a musket ball to lodge in my foot. Allow John to escort you back to the hospital. I'd hate to be held to blame for keeping you from your work.'

The dismissal was clear and Jayne accepted it without demur, though it grieved her that her conversation with William had been so brief. She had hoped he might have news of her family or be willing to carry news of her to them, but it seemed this meeting must end, as all their meetings did, with more unsaid than said.

Over the next two nights, and without lanterns to betray their positions, the supply barges ferried in thirty-six barrels of gunpowder, munitions, food and, most welcome of all, thirty pairs of boots and one hundred pairs of shoes which had been donated by the sailors on the ships for the men on the ramparts. On the third night, following another day's relentless Royalist bombardment of the town and several frontal attacks along the Town Line which came close to succeeding, Lord Warwick reinforced the garrison with three hundred sailors from the fleet.

Jayne watched with Alexander and Susan as they came ashore, and despite the darkness she was certain she saw William marshalling the throng before marching them four abreast to the Town Line. The Hulmes were encouraged by the sight of so many coming to the garrison's aid, but Jayne was secretly dismayed at the thought of yet more patients to treat. The stream of those injured in the intense close-quarter battles on the ramparts was never-ending, while the shortage of everything necessary to treat them was nigh on disastrous. There was no catgut for stitching, precious little salt for the making of brine and such a dearth of old clothes to tear into dressings that Jayne had instructed her nurses to retrieve old dressings from patients who had healed. The washing and boiling of them was arduous, for she insisted that no blood traces should remain, but the matrons in charge of doing it never complained.

Even so, Jayne doubted Lyme or the hospital could sustain this level of effort for more than a couple of days. She was certain she could not. Her body and brain were so tired from lack of food and sleep that at times she could barely stand.

The following day, the artillery fell eerily silent and the anticipated assault against the Town Line began. Yet the strangest aspect of the morning was the scarcity of patients. Alexander drew a morose interpretation from this, suggesting the battle was so severe that men were fighting to the death and dropping where they died.

'Then we're in the wrong place,' said Jayne. 'We should position ourselves close to the Line.' She turned to Susan. 'Do you agree?'

Susan nodded. 'I do. We'll be a great deal more useful there than here.' She instructed the nurses to bag up every clean dressing they could find and bring as many flagons of water as they could carry. 'I suggest Alexander and I take half the nurses to Davy's Fort and you take the rest to Gaitch's, ma'am. Women will bring the wounded to us once word spreads of where we are.'

By choosing the two middle forts, each group was able to cover one half of the Town Line. Jayne chose to work outside where the air was cleaner and was greatly helped by the mothers, wives and sisters who were gathered outside the fort, ready and willing to assist in any way they could. She dispatched them first to find stools and tables, and then sent them along the Line to the west to support or carry men in need of treatment to the make-shift surgery. She discovered very quickly that the only workable treatment in most cases was the application of a tourniquet to stem the flow of blood down a man's arm and then a thick, tight dressing to absorb any new flows. There was no holding a sword or pike when the hands were slippery with gore, yet few thought their injuries so bad that they weren't prepared to return to their posts afterwards. The women worked unceasingly, collecting rope and strong wooden pegs for the fashioning of the tourniquets, supplying Jayne and her nurses with constant fresh water, and fashioning stretchers to carry the most severely wounded to Fisher and Whiteway.

Some two hours after noon, Jayne was summoned into the fort to tend the officer in command. He was blind in one eye from blood that was pouring from a diagonal slash across his forehead but, like his men, was refusing to leave his post. Jayne removed her apron and laid it over the filth on the floor, instructing him to lie down with his head upon it. She then turned his face to the side so that the blood dripped onto the fabric before using a full flagon of water to sluice the scabs and debris from his eye. Without catgut to close the wound, she could only place a thick pad across it to absorb the blood and use a crisscross pattern of dressings about his head to hold it in place. As she helped him to his feet, she told him his sight would be bleary for upwards of an hour and warned him he wouldn't be able to judge distance until it cleared.

He moved to look out along the earth bank. 'I've no trouble seeing the lines of Royalists waiting to storm the Line,' he said grimly.

'But you'll not see the sword tip that's within inches of your heart,' said Jayne, retying her saturated apron. 'Be wise and avoid hand-to-hand fighting until your vision is restored.'

'I doubt that's possible,' he murmured, beckoning her forward. 'We can't withstand another hour of this.'

Jayne wished afterwards that she'd made an excuse to leave, because she could never forget the brutality of what she witnessed or the dread she felt to see Royalists moving in waves towards the bank. Their numbers were vastly superior to the garrison's, and she understood suddenly how sheltered she'd been in the hospital, treating wounds when they arrived but never seeing how they were made.

In places, the bank was falling away under pressure from boots, hands and bodies, and to prevent the Royalists clambering through the gaps, Parliamentarians were dropping into the trench and fighting them there. As far as Jayne's eyes could see, soldiers were chopping and stabbing each other, quite careless of the tumbled corpses that lay sprawled at their feet. Every man was splattered with blood—whether his own or someone else's—and Jayne had no way of telling a Parliamentarian from a Royalist. If there had ever been emblems on their dress to distinguish one side from the other, months of rough living had torn them away.

Behind every Royalist was another to take his place, while the men of the garrison had only women to support them, and for the first time Jayne picked a side. There was no justice on earth or in heaven if the bravery of Lyme's people came to nought. She thought of how hard they had toiled to defend their homes, and her eyes filled with tears to think they might lose them now.

Perhaps the officer thought her concern was for herself, because he made a gesture of apology. 'Forgive me, ma'am. I was wrong to show you this.'

'No, sir, you were right,' she answered, wiping her eyes on the sleeve of her gown. 'It's past time I saw the true awfulness of war. The courage our people show in the hospital is nothing to the courage I see here.'

As if to prove her wrong, shouts arose some fifty yards from the fort as men on the Lyme side of the earth bank began to retreat and scatter. What began as a handful quickly became a stampede and, cursing profanely, the officer ordered one of his subalterns to alert Colonel Blake to a breach in the line.

'It's those lily-livered mariners,' he growled, drawing his sword and instructing the other subaltern to accompany him. 'I knew they'd run.' He nodded to Jayne before heading down the steps. 'Get yourself back to the hospital while you still can, Mistress Swift. There's no safety for you here.'

But Jayne remained where she was. She told herself she wanted to see what happened to the officer, but in truth her attention was entirely fixed on the mariners. She was searching for a figure she recognised, but it was impossible to make out individuals amongst the melee. The fleeing sailors appeared to be fighting their comrades in their eagerness to escape, and the confusion grew worse as Royalists streamed towards the breach and began to clamber over the bank. On either side of the rapidly crumbling structure, the weary soldiers of the garrison did their best to stem the flow, but their efforts were fruitless. The fear of the men at the centre of the breach was so infectious that those at the margins began to pull away too, creating an ever-widening gap for the Royalists to exploit.

Jayne learnt later that none of the mariners had been involved in such close-quarter fighting before, being more accustomed to firing cannons at a distance than looking into a man's eyes as he killed him, but, watching them scatter, she cursed their cowardice as roundly as the officer had done. Were they so lacking in spirit that they couldn't stand their ground for an hour, when the poorly fed, barefoot men of the garrison had stood theirs for nigh on two months? She knew she should warn her nurses and the women outside of the impending danger, but she couldn't bring herself to move. Yet it wasn't fear she felt so much as a deep despair at Lyme's imminent defeat, for she had little doubt that Prince Maurice would loot the town of everything of value before setting it ablaze. And what would become of her people then?

Her eyes welled with tears again at the utter hopelessness of it all when a single sailor advanced towards the place where the rout had begun. In his left hand he carried the Earl of Warwick's colours, in his right a sword, which he levelled at the Royalists forcing their way through the bank. His deep-throated roars of encouragement to his fellow mariners resounded loudly along the line, and within seconds flight transformed into unity. A tall figure, easily recognisable as William, thrust through the crush on the eastern side of the breach, bringing twenty uniformed sailors with him, while a dozen Lyme defenders, led by the half-blind officer, surged forward from the west.

Garrison gossip said afterwards that the Royalists never retreated faster than when the reinforcements joined shoulder to shoulder with the mariner, but Jayne couldn't attest to the truth of this because she left before the confrontation began. She was too afraid to see what happened next, for she doubted her heart could withstand the sight of William being killed.

Jayne took her nurses back to the hospital as soon as it became clear that the tide of the battle had turned in Lyme's favour. She left word at the fort that all men with still-bleeding wounds should present themselves urgently for treatment, but she hadn't anticipated that her first patient would be Edward Moizer, the courageous mariner who had raised Lord Warwick's colours and rallied his comrades. He was cradling his left hand inside his jacket front, and the two friends who accompanied him refused to let anyone but Mistress Swift examine him.

Edward was a sturdily built man of middle years with a weathered face and bright blue eyes, and he remained remarkably cheerful despite having lost two of his fingers. It seemed Royalist musketeers had begun firing from Uplyme Hill when Prince Maurice saw that his troops were being beaten back from the breach, and a chance shot had hit Edward's hand where it clasped the colours.

'Was the prince not worried about killing his own people?' Jayne asked as she cleaned the stumps to see how much damage had been done.

Edward grinned. 'Put it this way, ma'am: I'd not want to be fighting for him. He's more careless of his own troops' lives than he is of ours.'

One of his companions stirred. 'Sir William says it's because his need to win makes him reckless.'

Sir William? Jayne asked Edward to put his hand in a bowl of brine while she laid dressings on the table. 'You're fortunate it was your last two fingers that were taken and that both sheared at the bottom joint,' she told him. 'Your grip won't be as strong but you should still be able to raise Lord Warwick's colours when the need arises.' She smiled. 'Was it Sir William who sent you to me?'

'It was, ma'am. He said you're the best physician in Dorset.'

'I believe I saw him come to your aid at the breach. Is he well?'

'He'd be here himself if he wasn't, ma'am. He speaks most highly of your skills.'

Jayne pressed on his hand to keep it submerged. 'We've met once or twice in the past, but with all the excitement of the day I've quite forgotten his surname.'

'Harrier, ma'am.'

'And am I right that his family home is in Winterborne Stickland, to the north of Dorset?'

Edward Moizer shook his head to express ignorance. 'I heard tell his father encumbered the family estates with debt, which is why Sir William went to fight in the European wars, but I can't say if there's any truth to the story. He's a fine commander is all I know.'

'Indeed.' Jayne dried his hand and then applied a salve of calendula and St John's wort flowers to the stumps before dressing each individually and enclosing them in a secure diagonal bandage across his palm and around his wrist. 'To avoid infection, you must keep this in place for a week,' she told him, tying off the ends. 'Try to use your hand as little as possible and do not immerse it in water until the stumps are healed. Are your orders to return to your ship or to remain in Lyme? If the latter, you may come here in three days so that I can check your progress.'

Edward's companion spoke. 'Sir William says we'll stay till the siege is over if the Royalists keep attacking the Town Line.'

'Is that what will happen?'

The man shrugged. 'It depends on whether the King sends a relief force, ma'am. Prince Maurice lost vastly more men than we did this day. We counted upwards of a hundred corpses in the ditch beneath our short stretch.'

'Will they be removed?'

He nodded. 'Colonel Blake has offered an hour's truce this evening for that purpose. The wind is blowing off the sea, so Prince Maurice is sure to accept. It'll not help his troops' confidence if they start to smell the odour of death.'

The following days saw more taunting than attacking. The Parliamentarians favoured sexual expressions such as 'cowardly limp-cocks' for the Royalist foot soldiers, 'foppish coxcombs' for the cavaliers and 'German arse-worm' for Prince Maurice. In return, the Royalists' slurs related to the low class and noxious religion of their adversaries. When they weren't 'dung shovellers' or 'fish-gut pickers', the defenders of Lyme were 'miserable Puritans' or 'godless heathens'.

As a form of war, it was preferable to constant bombardment and frontal attack, but Jayne wearied of it after a while. 'Why do they bother?' she asked Alexander.

'A taunt is like a battle cry, ma'am. Each side is looking to intimidate the other.'

'But it's all so pointless.'

'Almost as pointless as this siege, wouldn't you say, ma'am?'

She smiled. 'Have I converted you to neutrality, Alexander?'

'You're not far off, Mistress Swift. There's precious little merit in two months of fighting which results in a multitude of deaths but gains not a yard of ground for either side.'

On the third day of June, the Royalists made a fresh attempt to burn the town with fire darts and arrows. The weather had been unusually hot for more than a week and the dry thatch caught alight easily. As before, it was the women who fought the blazes, and though they succeeded in preventing the whole town going up in flames, upwards of thirty more houses were destroyed. The Earl of Warwick sent messages of hope to bolster the defenders' spirits, saying that a Parliamentary relief force was on its way, but such promises had been made from the outset of the siege without ever being realised.

There was more hope to be had from the confessions of two Royalist foot soldiers who deserted the prince's ranks on the night of 10 June. They approached the West Gate under a flag of surrender, expressing a desire to change sides, and upon being taken to Colonel Blake they revealed all they knew about Prince Maurice's army. It was in a state of disarray, with more dead from besieging Lyme than at Bristol, and rumour was rife that the prince's requests for reinforcements had been denied.

Jayne learnt all this from John Metcalfe when she paid one of her regular visits to his wife the following afternoon. Being of a similar age and background, the women had become close friends these last two months, and the Metcalfes' house was the only place where Jayne could kick off her boots, unhook her bodice and recline for an hour in contented peace. With John present, this wasn't possible, but Jayne found his words to be as good as a rest.

If the two deserters were to be believed, the Royalists were close to abandoning the siege. Not only had they sustained a huge number of casualties, but word had reached them that the Earl of Essex was leading a large Parliamentary force into Dorset from the north. If true, Prince Maurice would find himself trapped between Warwick's fleet and the garrison below, and a marauding army above.

Colonel Blake had been worried that the prince had sent the deserters to spread misinformation on the promise of payment, but Sir William Harrier had dispelled these fears by interrogating the two soldiers about their reasons for enlisting. They told him they'd had none, for they'd been quite ignorant about why war was necessary until they'd been press-ganged from their homes in Sidford in Devon as the Western Army marched towards Lyme. Neither was a willing recruit. They admitted to having been tempted by the assurance of plunder, but Lyme's resistance had shown them that their regular wages as farm labourers were more desirable than empty promises. Their ambition (said between sobs) was to make their way home to Sidford once the Royalists left, and never again allow themselves to be conscripted into the army of either side.

'None of us doubted they spoke the truth,' said John. 'Sir William's a clever man and he'd have tripped them up if they'd been spies. But you know this, of course, Mistress Swift. I understand you and he are well acquainted.'

'Well enough to know that he's clever,' Jayne agreed, 'but not so well that I can claim any great knowledge of him. We met two years ago at Lady Stickland's house in Dorchester, and our paths have crossed once or twice since, but I've never conversed with him long enough to discover anything about his family or where he comes from.'

'The family had estates outside Blandford until his father forfeited them through non-payment of mortgages. It was a messy business. He hanged himself shortly afterwards, leaving his son penniless. I believe Sir William was twelve at the time.'

'Does he have brothers or sisters?'

John shook his head. 'His mother died a day after birthing him and his father never remarried.'

Jayne wondered how much of this to believe. It was a convenient story to account for why William had a title but no property to support it. 'Poor man,' she murmured. 'He seems to have had his share of tragedy.'

'His situation would have been worse if Lady Stickland hadn't taken up his cause.'

'How so?'

'His father's estate neighboured her husband's, and when she learnt that Lady Harrier had died and Sir Ralph was absent from the house, she made herself responsible for the baby. I'm told it was three months before Sir Ralph came looking for him, and Lady Stickland only agreed to release him on condition that Sir Ralph appointed her as an equal guardian. Without her interest, Sir William would have been sadly neglected.'

Jayne eyed him thoughtfully. 'How do you know so much about him, John? Was it Sir William who told you?'

He shook his head. 'My father took the trouble to acquaint himself with the family's history. Sir Ralph swindled him out of two hundred pounds worth of goods, and he was never able to collect payment or even serve him with a writ. Sir Ralph lived most of the time in London, first squandering his family fortune and then using charm and trickery to relieve honest Dorset merchants of their earnings. He favoured those in the west of the county because he knew the local magistrates wouldn't pursue him once he was outside their jurisdictions.'

'What did he do with the goods?'

'Sold them to merchants in London and kept the money for himself.' John smiled wryly. 'It's twenty years since he killed himself but Father hasn't forgotten him. When he heard that Sir William was in Lyme, he told me the story and warned me not to trust him. He puts great store by the adage that the apple doesn't fall far from the tree.'

'And you think it applies to Sir William?'

John shook his head. 'Not from what I've seen of him, ma'am. He learnt his soldiering in the European wars and, other than Colonel Blake, there's not a man I'd rather have at my side. Were we on closer terms, I'd advise him to change his name. It can't be easy living with the sins of his father.'

Jayne was tempted to say that William took different identities whenever the situation demanded it, and, moreover, was as adept at deception as his father had been, but she had no wish to plant doubts in John's mind. Instead, she turned the conversation back to the Royalists and when they might leave, and took heart from John's optimism that they would be gone before the week was out.

~

They left during the night of 14 June, although no one believed it until the sun rose the following morning and all could see that Uplyme Hill was bare. The siege had been lifted without fanfare, and Prince Maurice's army had vanished. Nevertheless, there was little celebration in the town at this sudden change of fortune. Stories abounded that it was a ploy: Prince Maurice had simply moved his troops and artillery to the other side of the hill in order to persuade Lord Warwick and his fleet to leave, and Lyme would be subjected to an even fiercer attack once the mariners had been withdrawn from the garrison.

A young soldier presented himself at the hospital at around eleven o'clock, bearing a note from Colonel Blake to Mistress Swift. It was brief and to the point: *I'm reminded that you're not of Lyme, Mistress Swift. Please inform me when you wish to leave.*

The words were so peremptory that Jayne took them more as an order than an invitation. She smiled to hide her hurt and showed the note to Alexander, begging him to take her answer to the fort. 'Please tell the colonel that I'm happy to leave now, Alexander. I have a great longing to see my family again, and since my mare is lodged in John Metcalfe's stable, I can be with them by evening if I depart before noon.'

Alexander had come to know Jayne very well in the last eight weeks. 'Don't read more into this than is there, Mistress Swift,' he said gently. 'I'm guessing John Metcalfe reminded the colonel that you have no obligation to remain, and he's releasing you in the only way he knows how. Would you rather I ask that he sends word to your father to come for you?'

Jayne gave a small laugh. 'By no means. I'm hoping to persuade Papa I was never in danger, but he'll not believe me if he sees how much damage has been done to the town. It's better I reach home before he hears that the siege has been lifted. Do you think John Metcalfe will agree to escort me?'

Alexander reached for his jacket. 'I'm sure of it, ma'am.'

Jayne spent the time he was away sorting through the hospital's implements, liniments and medicines with Susan. Her personal remedies had been exhausted within the first two weeks of her arrival and, though fresh supplies had come in regularly by sea, nothing was in such surplus that she felt justified in taking what was there to replenish her own stocks. After a few moments of consideration, she also donated three of her finer blades and a small pair of pincers to the hospital—being the best for extracting bullets and slivers of wood from flesh—telling Susan she would order replacements for herself upon her return to Swyre.

'But only at a price, ma'am,' said Susan with a sigh. 'Your stay amongst us has cost you dear, I think. With the town so bankrupt, you'll not even receive the reward Colonel Blake promised you for treating the garrison's carbuncles.'

Jayne smiled. 'It's of no matter. I abandoned all thoughts of payment when I heard that Prince Maurice was at the gates. It's reward enough that we're alive and the hospital still stands. You and Alexander will make fine custodians of it, Susan.'

Susan lifted the hem of her apron to her eyes. 'I'm a rough sort of person, ma'am, and not given to fine speeches, but I do thank you most heartily for placing such trust in my husband. He's stood by me these last ten years despite my barrenness, and it gladdens my heart that your faith in his ability has given him new-found confidence.'

Jayne drew her into a close embrace. She had known from the beginning that the Hulmes were childless for, unlike the nurses, they never used the excuse of little ones to absent themselves from duty. 'It's having you at his side that gives him confidence,' she said. 'Myself also. We only managed as well as we did because you brought calm and order to the running of the hospital. I dread to think of the chaos we would have faced had anyone less accomplished been in charge.'

Susan returned the hug for the briefest moment and then stepped away. 'You'll have me weeping,' she said fiercely before continuing her sorting of the medicines.

Alexander came a few minutes later with instructions for Jayne to present herself at the West Gate within the half-hour. This meant there was no time for goodbyes if she was to retrieve her mare from John Metcalfe's stable, and her departure from the place she'd called home for eight weeks was quiet and unobtrusive. It was how she wanted it to be, for she was no better at farewells than Susan. Or Alexander either, it seemed. He accompanied her to the Metcalfes' house, where John was waiting with her mare and his horse, already saddled, and then took his leave with a simple bow and a heartfelt wish that God would go with her.

As he walked away, Jayne asked John to lead both horses to the gate while she made her way separately on foot. 'If I'm seen with my mare, people will be curious,' she said, 'and I truly can't bear to have any more partings.'

Metcalfe stood for a moment in indecision. 'There's many will want to thank you for what you've done for them, Mistress Swift. All Lyme understands the debt of gratitude we owe you.'

'But I do so hate fuss,' she said, heading purposefully towards a side street.

FIFTEEN

JOHN WAS ALREADY AT THE gate when Jayne arrived, and she was relieved to see that the only other people there were a handful of guards who stood in the opening, staring at the hill opposite. John took her satchel and hooked it onto the pommel of her mare's saddle before asking if she was wearing britches beneath her gown, as was her custom when she travelled. If not, he would send a soldier in search of a pair.

When Jayne said she was, he stooped and laced his fingers to form a platform for her foot. 'You'll need to ride astride from the outset so that we can outrun any cavalry that may still be in the area, ma'am. Scouts tell us Prince Maurice and his army are retreating west towards Exeter, but I'd rather be safe than sorry.' He waited while she folded her gown across her knees and settled her feet in the stirrups before hoisting himself atop his own mount. 'Our route to the east will take us along the Town Line, ma'am, and the men of the garrison wish to take their leave of you. They hold you in high regard, and it will please them if you acknowledge their salute.'

Jayne eyed him with alarm. 'I hoped to leave quietly, John.'

'I know, ma'am, but Colonel Blake felt you should be honoured in this way. If we move at a fast trot, we'll be clear of the Line in minutes, and a wave will suffice as acknowledgement.'

He cut off any chance of protest by ordering the guards to stand aside and allow them through, and Jayne was obliged to go with him because her mare began champing at her bit when the other horse moved. The guards raised their swords in salute as she passed between them, showing no surprise to see her legs encased in britches. And why would they when so many of their women had dressed as men to persuade Prince Maurice the garrison was larger than it was?

Jayne felt a sudden and huge regret to be leaving, for she'd enjoyed feelings of equality these last eight weeks that she doubted she would ever experience again. Once the hospital had been established, her competence as a physician hadn't been questioned and her methods had been valued and copied by the doctors Whiteway and Fisher. Yet, in view of her dislike of war, she found it ironic that it was conflict that had allowed her skills to be appreciated. In peace, women were considered inferior; under siege, they were granted the same status and authority as men.

John took the outside position as they left the gate, forcing Jayne to ride between him and the Town Line, and being slightly ahead of her, he was able to dictate their pace—a painfully slow trot—which meant she could make out every person on the bank. There was hardly a face she didn't recognise, and the cheering was so loud it bounced back and forth against the steep escarpment of Uplyme Hill. Jayne's initial feeling was terrible embarrassment to be singled out in this way, but it was impossible not to respond with smiles when so many smiles were being directed at her. She fought hard to hold back tears, for it wouldn't do at all for these gallant gentlemen to see her weeping, but the battle was lost completely when John slowed to a walk as they reached Gaitch's Fort. He gestured towards the platform at the side of it, where Colonel Blake was standing with doctors Fisher and Whiteway, and Alexander and Susan Hulme.

The colonel raised his sword in salute. 'Allow me to honour you, Mistress Swift,' he called. 'Lyme could not have asked for a finer or more courageous physician to run her hospital. We owe you a debt of gratitude that can never be repaid.'

Any hope she had of answering was extinguished by the flood of emotion that welled in her throat when Alexander and the elderly doctors removed their hats and bowed, and Susan dropped a curtsey. The best she could do was make a bow of her own and smile through the river of tears that ran down her cheeks. She would have liked to have expressed her respect and gratitude to all five, but perhaps her entirely feminine response pleased them more, for their own smiles were shy and understanding. She managed to mutter to John that they should travel faster, for she was quite overcome, and he obliged her by returning their pace to a trot.

Near the end of the Town Line, two dozen men were gathered in a group outside the eastern gate. All had been so badly injured that they'd stayed several weeks in the hospital, and Jayne had come to know them well. At their centre, supported by two comrades who had each lost an arm, was one-legged Jack Young, who had donated his boot to Robert Blake. Deeply moved by the efforts they'd made to see her, Jayne brought her mare to a halt and, without care for propriety, slid from her saddle and embraced them all.

Even as they surrounded her, she understood how much Lyme had taught her. Two months ago, she couldn't have done this. It would have mattered not that she knew these men and had John to protect her: irrational fear would have kept her mounted and at a distance from them. And once again, it seemed, she had conflict to thank for curing her of her terrors. Enduring constant bombardment, knowing that death could come at any moment, had shown her how insignificant the events on the highway had really been. All she'd suffered was a ripped bodice and a few bruises, yet she'd allowed fear of what *might* have happened to haunt her for the next two years. How pitiful that seemed when viewed beside the bravery of the women of Lyme.

When each man had thanked her and wished her godspeed, Jack Young proffered his hands to help her remount. 'With my friends holding me, I'll not drop you, ma'am. My one leg has the strength of two since you persuaded me to use it again, albeit with crutches.'

She placed her foot in his palms and smiled down at him after he'd lifted her easily into her saddle. 'Thank you, Jack. May God go with you.'

'And with you, ma'am. It's rare for humble men such as ourselves to be treated with kindness and courtesy by a lady of your standing and we shall never forget it. You gave us hope where there was none, and we hold you in our prayers every day. God bless you, Mistress Swift.'

Mercifully, John Metcalfe set off again before the men were made uncomfortable by a fresh flood of tears. Richard would say it was most improper for a physician to sob in front of her patients, but Jayne doubted even he could have remained dry-eyed in the face of Jack's simple confirmation that she'd honoured her pledge to treat the sick to the best of her ability wherever she might find them. In any case, her emotions were in turmoil, for she felt she was leaving the best part of her life behind her.

John slowed to a walk as they entered some woodland beyond the Town Line. 'Was that so bad, ma'am?'

Jayne drew to a halt and took a breath to compose herself. 'No, it was considerate and kind, though I fear I've disgraced myself. Physicians aren't allowed to show weakness.'

He smiled. 'You never have, ma'am, which is why Colonel Blake and the garrison wanted to honour you. I'm instructed to give you the numbers of dead on both sides so that you will better understand the high regard in which you're held.'

She set her mare walking again. 'Will I be shocked?'

He drew alongside her. 'Almost certainly, since the disparity between the figures is startling. Our tally is one hundred and twenty, while the Royalists' is well in excess of two thousand. We know this from our count of the bodies removed and the numbers the deserters gave us of those who died in the camp. By their descriptions, most perished of fever and infected wounds, and the colonel intends to cite your name in the reports he writes to Parliament, for devoting yourself to Lyme. Had you accepted the prince's invitation to abandon the garrison, the numbers of dead might have been reversed.'

Jayne stared at him in disbelief. 'Are you sure the deserters weren't exaggerating the Royalist figures?'

'We don't think so, ma'am. Scouts searched their camp earlier this morning and reported seeing more than a dozen large burial pits to the east of Uplyme Hill. They came back with stories of human filth everywhere and vermin feeding upon it. In such conditions, poisoned wounds and fever would have been rife.'

'Then nothing I could have done would have made a difference,' Jayne said bluntly. 'The colonel should put that in his report as well. It's utter foolishness to force men to live in squalor for the purpose of fighting battles.'

John grinned. 'And Colonel Blake assures me you'd have said the same to Prince Maurice, ma'am. He says you can be powerfully persuasive when you choose and, since he believes you're acquainted with the prince, he's quite sure the young man would have listened to you.'

Ahead, the trees were thinning and she made out a mounted figure on the grassland beyond. There was something very familiar about the way the man sat his horse, and Jayne considered the unlikely coincidence of John raising the subject of Prince Maurice when the one person who could expose her as a liar appeared to be waiting for them. From there, it was a short step to believing that William had told the story already and, far from guessing that she was acquainted with the prince, Blake knew it for a fact.

As she and John emerged from the woodland, William advanced to meet them. 'My respects, Jayne,' he said with a smile and a small bow. 'I trust you're well.'

She adopted the lightest tone she could manage. 'You can see I am not,' she answered, drawing her mare to a halt in front of him. 'In my whole life I've never been so dirty and unkempt, nor so thin that my gown cannot hold its shape. Could we not have made our farewells in the hospital?'

'I hoped you'd allow me to accompany you to Swyre. Captain Metcalfe is agreeable to my joining you if you have no objections.'

Jayne had many objections, not least a deep suspicion about why he and John had made this arrangement behind her back. 'Shouldn't you return to your ship?'

He shook his head. 'It will be a few days yet before we leave. Warwick plans to come ashore tomorrow to congratulate the garrison. As long as Metcalfe and I return by midnight, all will be well.'

'We should make haste then,' she said, driving her heels into her mare's flanks. So long unridden, the animal leapt to a canter in five strides and, thereafter, raced across the grassland in a gait that was more akin to a bolt than a gallop. Jayne steered her towards the Bridport highway and exhilarated in every thundering hoof-beat on the hard ground of the road. There was as much freedom to be had in speed as there was in being considered an equal.

She reined in the mare when the outskirts of Bridport came into view, anger and hurt feelings giving way to common sense. For all she knew, the scouts had been wrong to say the Royalists were retreating west towards Exeter and had billeted themselves on Bridport instead, for unlike Lyme the town had supported the King from the outset of the war.

'Perhaps we should ride cross-country from here,' she said to John as he drew level with her. 'There's a ford across the river some half-mile to the north which will take us onto a bridleway that heads south-east towards the coast. The journey won't be so fast but it might be safer. I fear Parliamentarians may not be received kindly in Bridport.'

John looked down at his torn jacket and threadbare britches. 'There's nothing to say that's what we are, ma'am. Indeed, we're more likely to be taken for horse thieves than soldiers.' He looked towards the town. 'We'll not encounter Prince Maurice's troops. Sir William was part of the scouting troop that followed them five miles along the highway towards Exeter, and he saw the debris they discarded along the way, including men too sick to continue. Isn't that so, Sir William?'

William nodded. 'It is, although I agree with Mistress Swift, if only for my own safety.' A teasing twinkle entered his eyes. 'A less ferocious rate of speed would be welcome, Jayne. This brute I've borrowed seems intent on throwing me, and I'd rather be tossed into a hedgerow than onto compacted ground.'

'You might change your mind when you see the bridleway,' she warned. 'By recollection, there are more brambles than shrubs growing beside it.'

'I'll take my chances if it means we can have a few minutes' conversation before we reach Swyre.'

Jayne was tempted to say he assumed too much if he thought the desire for conversation was mutual, but in truth her annoyance with him was passing. His apparel was as filthy and threadbare as hers and John's, his frame as lean, and his face and hands bore so many bruises and scabs that she didn't doubt he'd been at the heart of the fighting. Nevertheless . . .

'John tells me Colonel Blake believes I'm acquainted with Prince Maurice. Do you know why?'

The question clearly surprised William. 'Should I?' he asked carefully.

'You're the colonel's friend. I thought he might have confided in you the same way he confided in John.'

'Not in matters concerning you.' He turned to Metcalfe. 'How did Robert come by such an absurd idea?'

John squirmed in discomfort. 'The prince's request for Mistress Swift to treat the Royalist wounded was so unusual that the colonel believed he must have had some previous knowledge of her.'

'And you didn't argue with him?'

'It wasn't my place.'

'Of course it was your place,' came the withering retort. 'You know Mistress Swift's circumstances as well as I, and, without wishing to seem discourteous to her, her father's modest status as a country squire precludes any chance of meeting a prince.' He turned back to Jayne. 'Please believe that I have not broken faith with you, Jayne. Had Robert raised this foolish notion with me, I would have disputed it as strongly as when Samuel Morecott attempted to paint you as a Royalist sympathiser. Can you accept that?'

Jayne could and did easily, for the plea was heartfelt, but John intervened before she could speak. Unaware that her question had related to trust in William rather than Robert Blake, he gave an anguished defence of his commander.

'You are greatly mistaken if you think Colonel Blake spoke in criticism of Mistress Swift, Sir William. His words were intended as a compliment, which is why I repeated them. He has such high regard for her that he was sure Prince Maurice felt the same, and was deeply afeared she would accept his invitation, if only to prove her willingness to treat both sides. It was this that led him to conclude they had a personal connection, for he doubted the prince would have challenged an unknown woman on such a matter.' He made a gesture of apology to Jayne. 'I regret most deeply if my words suggested he thought you a Royalist sympathiser, ma'am, for he has never once questioned your neutrality and was most grateful for the care you gave his godson. Please forgive my clumsiness in trying to praise you, and be sure I shall correct the colonel's error when I return this evening.'

Foolish tears began pricking at Jayne's eyelids again. 'I don't wish you to correct anything, John. I would rather keep the colonel's high regard than have him hear from you that I gave way to pique over a silly misunderstanding. Shall we agree to forget this ever happened and continue as friends?'

John bowed in relief. 'Most willingly, ma'am.'

William did the same. 'There's nothing I would like more, Jayne.'

She studied their thin, drawn faces. 'This is madness,' she sighed. 'You're both too weary to ride to Swyre and back in one afternoon. I question the sense of it anyway, since William cannot show himself to my father, and John will be given a tongue-lashing for placing me in danger. I'd make the journey alone except that Sir Henry will doubt I was ever in Lyme unless I have an escort to vouch for it.'

If John found the reference to William puzzling, he didn't show it. 'Don't trouble yourself on my account, Mistress Swift. I have no intention of leaving you.'

She shook her head. 'You need rest, John. We all do.' She pondered for a moment. 'As long as you're sure we won't encounter trouble in Bridport, I suggest you take me to Richard Theale's house. His footman has accompanied me before, and my father will accept his word that you delivered me safely to Doctor Theale.' She turned to William. 'We should say our farewells here, because Richard will be as confused by your presence as my father would be, since both believe you to be a captain in the Corfe Castle garrison.'

William gave his jaw a thoughtful stroke. 'I don't think Richard ever accepted that story,' he said, 'and, as to being confused, he always impresses me with the sharpness of his mind.'

Jayne frowned. 'You had reason to visit him again?'

'We discovered we share a common interest.'

'Which is?'

'His favourite student,' he said with a smile. 'It seems Richard delights in talking about you even more than I do.'

Jayne absorbed this information on a deep, indrawn breath. 'You truly are the most irritating person,' she said, nudging her mare to a walk and setting off down the gentle incline of the hill.

Richard received them with an absence of fuss, as if filthy, dishevelled people appeared at his door every day. He greeted Jayne and William as old friends, and took John's hand warmly, expressing pleasure to meet him. Certain they were in need of food, he took them to his dining room and instructed his cook to bring whatever meats, cheeses, butters and breads she had in her pantry. The result was a veritable feast compared with the thin, tasteless broths that had been their diet for weeks, though Jayne enjoyed the beaker of cool, fresh milk the most. Cows were a luxury that a town under siege could not afford.

News of the Royalist retreat had reached Bridport ahead of them, but Richard was keen to hear every detail of what had caused Prince Maurice to break camp. Between them, John and William did their best to enlighten him, describing the Royalists' inability to breach Lyme's defences and the rumoured approach of Essex's Parliamentary army, but he found their explanations wanting and turned to Jayne instead. 'To what do you attribute the prince's departure, my dear?'

'The same as you, I imagine,' she answered thoughtfully. 'Sickness. Two deserters spoke of camp fever and infection, citing a figure in excess of two thousand deaths, and it's inconceivable that so many died in the fighting when John tells me Lyme lost only one hundred and twenty. I haven't forgotten your lessons on war, Richard. The greatest killer is not the sword or the cannon, but the squalid conditions in which men live.'

'And William tells me you introduced such a strong regime of cleanliness in the hospital that it was copied by other physicians in the town.'

Jayne eyed him suspiciously. 'I must be losing my hearing,' she murmured. 'I could have sworn he spoke only of the garrison's brave defence of the ramparts.'

Richard chuckled. 'He told me four weeks ago. He's been most assiduous in keeping me informed of your welfare and achievements, and I in turn have done the same for your parents. You've won a lot of praise for your efforts, Jayne, and while Sir Henry continues to maintain his support for the King, he's immensely proud of what you've accomplished.'

Perhaps unreasonably, Jayne felt a surge of impatience with Richard and William. She had wanted to tell her father the story in her own way, not have it controlled and translated by others. 'How could you know what I was doing four weeks ago?' she asked William.

'I visited Lyme three times before I came in on Lord Warwick's ship.'

'By what means?'

'At night in a rowboat from Charmouth. Lord Warwick employs me to give and acquire information and wouldn't tolerate me for long if I failed in my duty to him.'

'I never saw you there.'

Humour gleamed in his eyes. 'You did the night you treated the soldiers outside the gaol. I would have spoken to you if I hadn't feared the prisoners would report our meeting to Prince

Maurice. I made my visits in darkness and left before dawn to avoid my boat being spotted.'

Jayne propped her elbows on the table and rested her chin on her hands to stare at him. 'Did you not think to offer me the chance to go with you? I warrant my father would have been happier to see me than make do with second-hand reports on my welfare.'

John Metcalfe stirred. 'You must blame Colonel Blake for that, ma'am. Sir William offered to take you with him each time but the colonel wouldn't allow it. He said you were too necessary to Lyme.'

Richard spoke when she didn't. 'Would you have accepted the offer if you'd known about it, my dear?' he asked. 'For myself, I was sure you would not, since you may never have the opportunity to run a hospital again, and certainly not with the assistance of a surgeon as fine as Alexander Hulme . . . which is what I told William.'

Jayne bit back the sharp retort that sprang to her lips. She owed her training and profession to Richard and could never repay him for what he'd given her, but she resented his assumption that he could speak for her. Even so, she answered honestly.

'I would not,' she said, 'though I would have welcomed the chance to send a private letter to my mother and perhaps receive one in return.'

John intervened again. 'Colonel Blake would not have allowed that either, ma'am. No unread letters were permitted to leave Lyme.'

William took an apple from a bowl and began to peel it. 'What would you have written to her?' he asked.

'I would have described the bravery of the women of Lyme, for it would have pleased Mama to learn of their intelligence and spirit.' She lowered her hands to the table and turned her attention to Doctor Theale. 'You're correct to say that Alexander's a fine surgeon, Richard, but neither he nor I could have performed as well as we did if not for his wife Susan, who took responsibility for the organisation of the hospital. With her assistance, I kept a record of every patient Alexander and I treated and will send you a copy as soon as I have time to make one. You will find that women feature throughout the document. Not only did they suffer the same terrible wounds as the men—both in fire-fighting and repelling attacks on the Town Line—but they died as bravely, worked as hard and, through their many decisions, helped Lyme withstand the siege as long as it did. I would like them to be accorded the same respect as their husbands, fathers and sons, but sadly, due to their inferior sex, I doubt that will happen.'

Richard seemed puzzled by these remarks. 'What greater respect could I show you than saying you would seize whatever challenge was placed before you, my dear? As, indeed, you did.'

Jayne stifled a sigh, wondering if he'd misunderstood her or truly thought she'd only been seeking praise for herself. 'My life would be calmer if I hadn't,' she answered dryly. 'It'll be a while yet before the sound of artillery stops ringing in my ears.'

William offered her a slice of apple on the point of his knife, and she knew from the teasing look in his eyes that *he* had understood her perfectly well. 'Calm doesn't suit you,' he said. 'If it did, you would spend your days at a frame, stitching pretty tapestries.'

She took the slice. 'It's never too late to start.'

He laughed. 'You'll be wasting your time if you do. Your proficiency lies with catgut not silk.' He passed her another slice. 'As for Mistress Hulme and the women of Lyme, Colonel Blake has praised them in every report he's written. I'm told that a song is being sung about them in London with the refrain, "By all 'tis known, the weaker vessels are the stronger grown." Is that respect enough for you when we poor men, being simple cannon fodder, get no mention at all?'

She leant towards him. 'It is not,' she said, 'for I'll make a five-shilling wager with you now that when the history of Lyme's glorious defeat of Prince Maurice is written, the only names recorded in it will be male.'

~

Despite her longing to be home, Jayne felt a growing melancholy as she approached Swyre with Richard's footman by her side. She foresaw hours—even days—of questioning by her family, and seriously doubted if she wanted to describe her experiences to people who hadn't been in Lyme. There would be no touch-points at all in her communication or their understanding, and she came to the sad conclusion that Richard's accounts of her management of the hospital were preferable. Her father would believe she'd been confined inside four walls for two months because he lacked the imagination to think a woman might have seen the fighting at first hand.

Halfway up the driveway of Swyre House, she reined in her mare. Four horses she didn't recognise were hobbled on the grass beside the forecourt, and she baulked at meeting visitors in her filthy, bedraggled state. 'My father has guests,' she told Richard's footman. 'We must return to the road and make our way to the kitchen quarters.'

'I fear it's too late, ma'am,' he murmured, nodding towards the arched entranceway. 'Your arrival has already been noted.'

Jayne watched her mother's maid stare in her direction for several long moments before disappearing inside the hall. 'The only person she'll tell will be Mama,' she said, swinging her leg across her saddle and slipping to the ground. 'We should proceed on foot along the grass verge so as not to alert anyone else.'

They were almost at the forecourt when Lady Margaret appeared in the doorway, her face more worried than welcoming. She tipped her head backwards to indicate that someone was behind her, and then placed her right hand on her left hip, making the motion of drawing a sword. Jayne could guess she was telling her that soldiers were in the house, but not what she was supposed to do about it. Retreat? Stay where she was? Pretend to be a visitor herself?

The decision was taken away from her when a dragoon wearing Prince Maurice's colours appeared at her mother's side. She knew him immediately as one of the two who had accompanied Peter Tucker to the ramparts, and any idea she'd had of playing the role of a poor farmer's wife vanished when she saw his answering recognition. Her mother said afterwards that she appeared unsurprised by the man's presence, but in truth she could barely breathe for panicking. Her first thought was that she was about to be placed under arrest for aiding Parliamentarians, her second that Prince Maurice himself was in the house. Either way, her impulse was to turn and run.

She was prevented by Andrew, who pushed past the dragoon and strode towards her. 'Sir Walter Hoare awaits you inside, sister,' he said loudly, before dropping his voice to a whisper. 'He's been here three hours and refuses to depart until he's spoken with you. He was sure you'd leave Lyme as soon as the siege was lifted but grows impatient with the delay.'

Jayne's mouth was so dry she could only manage a croak. 'What does he want with me?'

'He has a message from Prince Maurice.' Andrew's eyes lit with unexpected humour. 'There's no need to be alarmed, sister. Sir Walter looks and smells worse than you do and is mighty crushed by the prince's defeat.'

'Are you and Father not also?'

He took the reins from her hand and offered her his arm. 'Not me,' he said cheerfully, 'though I can't speak for Sir Henry. He's damned cross, but I'm guessing that has more to do with his dislike of Sir Walter than Parliament's success.'

⁓

As Jayne entered the salon, she was still toying with the surprising idea that Andrew might be a secret Parliamentarian. It would explain a great deal, particularly his refusal to join his brothers in the King's army. She pushed the thoughts from her mind when she felt the tension in the room. Sir Henry and Sir Walter, both red-faced and angry, were squaring up to each other in the middle of the room, and two uneasy-looking dragoons were fingering their sword hilts beside the window.

'Gentlemen, gentlemen!' cried Lady Margaret sharply, entering behind Jayne and putting a protective arm about her daughter's waist. 'There are ladies present. If you cannot remember your manners, I will take Jayne away and you will not see either of us again until tomorrow.'

The threat was enough to persuade Sir Walter to step back. 'My apologies, Lady Margaret. I found myself unable to agree with your husband's assessment of our recent battle.' He ducked his head to Jayne. 'Ma'am.'

She had no time to respond before Sir Henry plucked her away from her mother and folded her in a warm embrace. 'The disagreement was mine,' he boomed against her ear. 'I questioned whether Sir Walter's account of the engagement was accurate, since there's no reason for the Royalists to have withdrawn if they fought as well as he claims.'

Jayne planted a kiss on his cheek and then pulled away to offer her hand to Sir Walter. 'You and your men look tired, sir,' she said. 'Have you eaten since you came to the house?'

He nodded, bending to kiss her fingers. 'Your mother was kind enough to offer refreshments.'

'I'm glad, sir, for I received the same kindness from Doctor Theale in Bridport. Had you known of my intention to stop there before travelling on to Swyre, you could have saved yourself a journey. My escort from Lyme left me in his care, and Doctor Theale's footman accompanied me the rest of the way.'

The words were for her father, but Sir Walter answered as she withdrew her hand. 'I was unaware there was another address where I might find you, ma'am—and why was your escort not afraid of the reception he might receive? Am I wrong to believe Bridport supports the King?'

'He looked as little like a Parliamentarian as you do a Royalist, sir. Two months of living in the same clothes has taken its toll on everyone's appearance. It was John Metcalfe, Papa. He sends his respects and begs pardon for not escorting me the whole way, but neither Richard nor I would allow it. He was so weary he could barely sit his horse by the time we reached Bridport.'

Sir Walter smiled sourly. 'You seem to have managed the journey well enough, Mistress Swift.'

'Stitching sword wounds isn't as arduous as making them, Sir Walter,' she said calmly. 'But you know this yourself. Hand-to-hand fighting is savage and hard, and every man I treated was debilitated by it.'

He stared at her for a moment and then beckoned to one of the dragoons, who approached with a small wooden box. 'Prince Maurice asks me to give you this, Mistress Swift. He doubts you've received a reward from Lyme for your services but he wishes to pay for the care you gave twenty of our foot soldiers. His Highness has calculated the amount as per your hourly charge, and requests that you count the coins aloud to be sure he hasn't short-changed you.'

Jayne raised the lid. 'It hardly seems necessary, Sir Walter, since he's written the amount on a slip of paper.' She read the words aloud. '*Thirty pieces of silver.*'

'Do you understand the reference, ma'am?'

She nodded. 'Rather better than Prince Maurice, I imagine. If he's looking for the Judas who condemned so many of his men to death, I suggest he holds a mirror up to himself. It wasn't I who forced them to live in squalor for two months, encouraging camp fever to rage and wounds to fester.'

'It's the nature of war, ma'am. Had you accepted either of Prince Maurice's invitations, you could have alleviated the suffering. He now believes your protestations of neutrality to be false.'

She closed the box and handed it back to him. 'Then please thank him for his offer but tell him I cannot accept. I only take payment from people who have faith in my honesty.'

'He will expect a fuller answer than that, ma'am.'

She retreated a couple of steps to put some space between them. 'If you have the courage to criticise him, you may tell him this, Sir Walter: the battle was lost when he first set up his encampment. Had he enforced rigorous cleanliness through the digging of latrines, a constant supply of water for washing and more space between tents, fewer men would have died. The best stratagem is to keep infection out, not try to deal with it once it has entered.'

'You have simple ideas of what is possible in war, Mistress Swift.'

'Perhaps so, but surely you and Charles persuaded Prince Maurice of the cleansing qualities of brine? He should have sent his wounded troops to bathe in the sea, which was only a few hundred yards from your camp.'

Sir Walter's eyes narrowed in annoyance, but whether because he believed she was mocking him or because neither he nor the prince had thought of such an obvious solution, Jayne couldn't tell. 'Only a fool would deplete his army's strength for the purposes of bathing, ma'am.'

Jayne resisted the temptation to say that to lose two thousand through sickness was a greater foolishness. 'We must agree to differ, sir.' She turned to her father. 'May I take my leave, Papa? I am beyond exhaustion.'

'Of course, daughter.'

She took his hand. 'And will you accept that the same is true of Sir Walter and his men? You don't need the eyes of a physician to see how drained of energy they are. Please offer them hospitality this night. You have my word they fought as hard for victory as the defenders of Lyme.'

~

A letter awaited her when she descended the stairs the next morning. She opened it under the amused eyes of Andrew, who told her it had been left by Sir Walter Hoare. 'He and his men departed some three hours since, looking a good deal better than they did yesterday. Mother sent servants to shave them and clean their uniforms. I told her she was spoiling them, but she said it was in a good cause if it meant they would leave.'

Jayne read what was written.

My dear Mistress Swift,

I thank you most sincerely for your generosity in asking your father to provide us with lodgings last night and your kind commendation on how hard we fought during the battle for Lyme. Today, I ride to Oxford to give His Majesty details of the siege, and I go with a lighter heart knowing that you, who shared our experience of the last two months, saw valour on both sides.

Honoured lady, I could wish we had met under different circumstances, for I deeply regret my uncivil behaviour towards you and Lady Stickland last September. It's a poor excuse to say that my churlishness came from being charged with an unwelcome responsibility, but, nonetheless, I hope you can believe it.

My delivery of silver yesterday was a similarly unwelcome charge, but please understand that my allegiance to my King requires me to obey orders, even those with which I disagree.

> *Your humble servant,*
> *Walter Hoare*

'What does he say?' asked Andrew.

Jayne handed him the letter. 'He's excusing his rudeness to me.'

Andrew grinned as he scanned the page. 'I don't think so, sister. This reads more like a love letter. The absurd little man has a yearning for you . . . worse, seems to believe his feelings are requited. You shouldn't have held his hand so long, and you *certainly* shouldn't have applauded his bravery to Father.'

She took back the letter and tore it into pieces, wondering if it was Lyme's victory that had restored Andrew's good humour. Whatever the truth, she welcomed a return of the teasing manner that had always characterised their relationship in the past.

'He speaks honestly,' she said. 'We did indeed share an experience, and my praise of Royalist courage was merited.' She pressed the torn scraps into his palm and folded his fingers over them before clasping his hand affectionately between hers. 'But only those who were there will ever understand how thin was the line between victory and defeat.'

1645

After three years of unremitting hardship, resistance to the war grows in Dorset. The war turns against the King in the north of England, and Sir Thomas Fairfax and Oliver Cromwell take leadership of the New Model Army for Parliament.

1948

SIXTEEN

Swyre, Dorset, 9 March 1645

THE BATTLE FOR WEYMOUTH LASTED eighteen days, and news that Parliament had triumphed once again reached Swyre in the first week of March. Few in Sir Henry's house believed it, however, since rumours of a Royalist victory had been rife from the start of the engagement. In a detached way, Jayne found her family's excited devouring of each new titbit amusing, because her experience in Lyme had taught her how unreliable perceptions and word-of-mouth stories could be. But she was careful to keep her smiles to herself now that different allegiances and emotions gripped the house.

At the end of January, her uncle had learnt of a conspiracy by Weymouth Royalists to betray the town to Sir Lewis Dyve, one of the King's generals. Fearful that the plot would be discovered, thereby placing all Royalist sympathisers in jeopardy, Joseph had sent Ruth and Isaac and all his female servants, including those Ruth had taken with her from Dorchester, to the safety of Swyre.

Only his wife had refused to leave, saying she was acquainted with but one Parliamentarian—her butcher—and he valued her custom too much to chase her from her home.

The conspiracy had succeeded, and Sir Lewis Dyve had taken Weymouth for the King. But the victory was a hollow one, for nine hundred Parliamentarians, led by Colonel William Sydenham of Wynford Eagle, retreated across the River Wey and set up a garrison of their own in Melcombe, on the eastern bank of the estuary. The intent of both commanders was to secure the harbour at the mouth of the river, and the eighteen-day battle that ensued was savage and bloody, made more desperate for the Parliamentarians when another of the King's generals, Lord Goring, came to reinforce Dyve's army with his own, creating a combined Royalist force of six and a half thousand men.

For Ruth, rumours of Royalist victories were reason to celebrate, because it meant her parents would be spared reprisals, but the smiles of her hosts hid more divided feelings. As Jayne had predicted, her father had bedevilled her with questions about Lyme, and she'd been unable to hide her admiration for the people of the town. Matters had come to a head when news reached them in early July 1644 that Colonel Blake and a brigade of men had left Lyme in order to reclaim Taunton, thirty miles to the north. Sir Henry said the venture was doomed because Taunton was too far inland for Lord Warwick and the navy to come to Blake's assistance, but Jayne had argued strongly in the colonel's favour. He was a clever commander, she told Sir Henry, and wouldn't engage in a battle he couldn't win. Not only would he succeed in taking Taunton for Parliament, but he would hold it for as long as he was instructed to do so.

Andrew had departed in secret that night, leaving only a few lines in a letter to explain his decision.

Dear Sir Henry,

Please understand that, for your sake, I have tried hard to see merit in the King's cause. Sadly, it has proved impossible, for my head and heart have always been for Parliament.

My intention is to offer my services to the garrison at Weymouth, where I shall join my friends William and Francis Sydenham of Wynford Eagle.

I realise this will cause division between us, and may set me in conflict with my brothers, but I can no longer live a lie. It was never out of laziness or cowardice that I refused to enlist in a King's regiment, but through deep conviction that power should be vested in Parliament and the people.

Your son,
Andrew

Sir Henry blamed Jayne for his son's 'stupidity', saying she'd filled his head with exaggerated tales of heroism, but Lady Margaret said it had been clear to her for some time that Andrew had been wrestling with his conscience.

'Look to yourself before you criticise Jayne, Henry. Had you tempered your language towards Andrew these last two years, he might not have felt the need to prove himself. Did you never consider that he might hold different views from yours?'

Jayne watched an angry flush rise in her father's cheeks and intervened on her mother's behalf. 'I do bear some fault, Mama,' she said. 'I believe it must have been through me that Andrew met the Sydenham family.'

She described a day in April 1642 when Andrew had accompanied her to Bridport. He had business with a merchant but, being in no hurry, had escorted her to Richard Theale's house. Richard had invited Andrew inside, where he met Thomas Sydenham, a young medical student.

'Thomas is brother to William and Francis,' she went on, 'and all three are as deeply committed to the Parliamentary cause as you are to the King's, Papa. I'm ignorant of how Andrew came to know them so well that he claims them as friends, but I imagine he used his introduction to Thomas as an excuse to visit Wynford Eagle.'

'They're Puritans,' Sir Henry snarled. 'They prey on gullible boys like Andrew.'

Jayne thought how bitter his prejudice against the sect had become, and for no better reason than that Puritans supported Parliament. 'Yet I'm sure you'd enjoy their company if you allowed yourself to know them, Papa. They may follow the Puritan path, but they have all the attributes you admire in men: intelligence, strength of character, steadfastness and honour. It's only your different allegiances that make you strangers to each other.'

'I question why *you're* so well acquainted with them, daughter,' Sir Henry snapped.

Jayne answered honestly. 'Most of what I know about them was told me by Richard when he escorted me to Wynford Eagle one day to watch Thomas prepare laudanum, but I spent a pleasant hour afterwards speaking with Mistress Sydenham and her sons.'

She paused, wondering how cruel she could be in challenging his prejudice. 'Their conversation was lively, wide-ranging and stimulating, and quite different from the monologues in this house. Andrew will have felt at home there if he was leaning towards Parliament before he met them.'

Her father's colour deepened to purple.

'Take a breath before you burst, Henry,' Lady Margaret advised calmly. 'Nothing Jayne has said is so outlandish that you need have an apoplectic seizure over it. You love to call Andrew a boy, but he's past thirty years of age. Do you seriously imagine that one so grown is unable to decide for himself how this country should be governed?'

'Not if he's listening to Puritans,' Sir Henry said mutinously. 'They're the vilest of abominations, as evidenced by that evil creature our niece married.'

Jayne leant towards him with a teasing look in her eyes. 'Samuel Morecott's a poor example, Papa. Consider, rather, how honourable and fine are Colonel Blake and Alexander and Susan Hulme.'

He wagged a finger at her. 'I begin to understand why Prince Maurice sent you thirty pieces of silver.'

She smiled. 'He'd have done the same whether I'd accepted his invitation or not. I'm sure he blames everyone for his defeat except himself.'

Sir Henry gave a grunt of amusement. His greatest sweetness was his ability to abandon an argument as easily as he embarked on it. 'He'll not be heard kindly by the King if he tries such a trick on him. It's beyond belief that an army of six thousand, camped on high ground and with all the vantage points, was unable to overwhelm a miserable little enclave like Lyme.'

His words had proved true when a letter came a few days later from his youngest son, Benjamin, speaking of Prince Maurice's fall from favour and his loss of command of the Western Army. The King couldn't hide his disappointment in his nephew, not only for the prince's poorly managed attempt to take Lyme but also for his hasty retreat into Devon, leaving Parliament in control of south Dorset. Shortly afterwards, Lady Margaret received a letter from Andrew, begging forgiveness for leaving without a parting word and assuring her he was content with his decision to join the newly formed Weymouth garrison.

Thereafter, the war had become distant once again. In September, news reached Swyre that one thousand unarmed and starving men from the Earl of Essex's Parliamentary army had arrived in Poole from Lostwithiel in Cornwall. It seemed Essex had pursued Prince Maurice into Cornwall, only to find himself caught between the prince's army to the south and the King's to the north. Essex had escaped capture, but his troops had not; upon surrendering, all, including their officers, had been stripped of their weapons and ordered to march to Poole before attempting to engage with Royalists again.

To survive, they had stolen food from farmers and landowners along the way, and stories of pillaging were rampant. Their route had taken them north of Swyre, but Sir Henry received letters from Royalist friends who spoke of the immoral nature of Essex's defeated Parliamentary troops, alleging they were as willing to steal a maid's virtue as take a cow or a sack of grain. For this reason, her father had ordered Jayne to remain in the house until they were sure the danger had passed, but she reminded him that he'd heard the men had reached Poole before he ever received word that they were thieves and rapists. Nevertheless, she was doubly watchful whenever she rode alone to see a patient, for whatever was rumoured about Parliamentarians paled to insignificance beside the tales of Lord Goring's Royalist soldiers.

Even Sir Henry's friends had nothing good to say about them or their commander. They reported that Goring had adopted the title of 'Lord' to enhance his ambitions and refused any order to lay siege to a town where he deemed the pickings too slim to make the effort worthwhile. Instead, his army prowled the border between Dorset and Somerset, killing and plundering at will, and no maid or matron escaped the soldiers' lust. Jayne would have given as little credence to these stories as every other, had not Sir Henry's sisters in Oxford added their own warnings. In separate letters, both had urged their brother to be wary of Goring, with one describing him as 'wicked' and the other as 'dissolute'.

Jayne had sensed a growing despair across the county each time she ventured out, for everyone she met, regardless of allegiance, spoke of his or her desire for the war to be over. People were tired of having soldiers billeted in their houses and their stocks of food requisitioned. They were hungry themselves, and it made no difference if reparation was offered, since money had no value when produce was scarce. Sir Henry heard a rumour that a handful of landowners in north Dorset had declared themselves neutral and armed their farmworkers with clubs in order to beat off thieving soldiers from either side. They called themselves 'Clubmen', and as word of their resistance spread, it was said that more and more were buying clubs and joining the movement.

In October 1644, Jayne's brother Benjamin had arrived without warning, saying he'd been given leave to spend one night with his family before returning to his regiment on the morrow. He was dishevelled, dusty and deeply weary, but his joy at seeing his family again was clear. He kissed and clasped them all and then consumed an entire rib of beef before declaring himself full. To Jayne's eyes, he looked considerably older than his twenty-four years, and she wondered what he had seen and done to age him so quickly.

He was more interested in hearing their news than telling them his, although much of it he knew from the letters his father had sent him. He pressed Jayne for information on Colonel Blake, who was causing problems for the King in Taunton. According to Benjamin, Blake had rallied his garrison to withstand a Royalist encirclement the month before and, despite lack of food and gunpowder, had held the town until a Parliamentary force relieved him. The thrust of all Benjamin's questions was the same as those Sir Henry had asked—What manner of man was Blake?—but, unlike Sir Henry, he had little difficulty accepting Jayne's complimentary appraisal. Perhaps defeat was easier to bear if the enemy was a person to admire.

The one piece of information Sir Henry had left out of his letters was Andrew's decision to join the Weymouth garrison, and it fell to Lady Margaret to make the explanation. Benjamin had told his mother all he could about Philip, her middle son, who was stationed in Oxford, then pressed her for news on Andrew, and she and Jayne were pleasantly surprised by his easy acceptance of the fact that his eldest brother had enlisted for Parliament. Almost every man he knew had friends or relatives fighting on the other side, he told them, and Andrew's reluctance to side with the King had been obvious from the start. The conversation would have ended there had Benjamin not goaded his father, quite unintentionally, by questioning why Andrew had taken so long to declare his colours.

Sir Henry gave a derisive snort. 'He feared being disowned.'

Lady Margaret shook her head. 'He wouldn't have declared at all if that were the case.'

Benjamin turned to Jayne. 'What do you say, sister?'

'As little as possible,' she answered with a laugh. 'The subject is bad for Father's health.'

Sir Henry's colour darkened immediately. 'Answer, girl! Your brother should know of your own Parliamentary sympathies.'

'Only if you allow him to listen to what I have to say, Papa. He'll be deafened by your roaring otherwise.' She waited a moment and then turned to Benjamin. 'I believe Andrew thought the war would end quickly and that the King would win,' she told him. 'You and Philip thought the same when you enlisted, because I remember you telling me it wouldn't be long before I saw you again.'

Benjamin nodded. 'It's what we hoped for.'

'And if your hopes had come to pass, Andrew would have held his tongue out of respect for Papa and satisfied his own Parliamentary conscience by accepting every insult that was hurled at him.' She glanced at Sir Henry. 'But the war drags on without an end in sight, and it needed no more than Lyme's victory to persuade Andrew to follow his heart. My tales about the siege added nothing to the choice he made except a better understanding of how people who truly believe in a cause can triumph.'

Sir Henry glowered at her. 'Are you suggesting that those on the King's side do *not* believe in their cause?' he barked.

'I'm sure the officers do,' she answered tactfully, 'but I doubt their commitment is shared by the foot soldiers. The men I treated were reluctant recruits and only stayed on the promise of plunder and through fear of being beaten if they tried to desert.'

'Does she speak the truth, boy?' Sir Henry demanded of Benjamin.

'I'm afraid so, sir. A few enlist willingly in return for daily food and the chance of plunder, but most have to be pressed into service. There's little appetite amongst ordinary folk for leaving their homes to kill their countrymen. Do you say it's different for Parliament, sister?'

'I can speak only for Lyme,' she told him, 'and the situation there was different. Every man, woman and child was a willing volunteer because they were fighting to safeguard their homes.' She paused. 'Do you not long for home yourself, Benjamin?'

'More than you know,' he muttered grimly, turning a bleak gaze on his father. 'I've watched the King at close quarters, sir— the princes also—and none commends himself to me as well as Colonel Blake commended himself to Jayne. I see more petulance and arrogance than honour or decency.'

Lady Margaret caught her husband's hand before he could form it into a fist. 'Come, sir!' she admonished sharply. 'You have no higher opinion of Prince Maurice than Benjamin does. Have you forgotten how you railed against him for his shameless effrontery in trying to appropriate Jayne as his personal physician?'

'The King is not responsible for his nephew's behaviour,' Sir Henry growled. 'What do you find to criticise in your sovereign, boy?'

'I have no wish to upset you, sir.'

'Speak!'

Benjamin shrugged. 'Very well. He does not inspire the same loyalty in his troops as Colonel Blake seems to do. The one sets himself apart from the common men; the other, by Jayne's description, walks amongst them. Since I doubt Colonel Blake loses any authority by greeting those of lower status with warmth and friendship, I could wish the King and his nephews would do the same.'

'There's no equivalence between a monarch and a colonel.'

'There is one, sir: both expect their soldiers to die for them should the need arise.' Benjamin fell silent for a moment. 'I've lost more friends than I can count these last two years. And for what? Because the King would rather govern alone than with the consent of his people.'

Sir Henry slammed his palm onto the table. 'The people were turned against him by the Puritan faction in Parliament. You know this, boy, for I showed you the speeches of their leader John Pym before you enlisted. What have you read since that makes you think fanatical Puritans would govern better than your sovereign?'

Benjamin turned a pleading gaze on Jayne, begging her to intercede on his behalf. It was a pattern he and Philip had followed since childhood, for her younger brothers had always looked to her to rescue them from their father's anger.

She rested her chin on her hands. 'Benjamin will have read the same pamphlet as you last December, declaring that John Pym was dead, Papa. I remember you twirling Mama in your arms on Christmas Day and shouting with joy that God had struck down the evil bigot whose hatred of the King had caused this terrible war. You went on to argue that the zealots would lose their influence now their leader was gone.'

'You think Presbyterians any better than Puritans?' Sir Henry demanded. 'They're no keener to have bishops and rectors in their churches than were Pym and his fanatics, and I'm told that's the faction that now holds sway in Parliament.'

'I can't believe the war is only about bishops and rectors, Papa. Surely Benjamin is correct? It was often said in Lyme that conflict would have been unnecessary had the King agreed to govern with the help and advice of Parliament. And what is that if not consent by the people?'

Benjamin stirred. 'There are many in my regiment who say the same, sir, and the mutterings have grown louder since Prince Rupert's defeat at Marston Moor in July. The whole of the north is lost to us now, and most believe the King should sue for peace on the terms Jayne mentioned.'

Sir Henry was shocked by such negative words. 'Have you not taken heart from your victory over Essex at Lostwithiel last month?'

'There's precious little glory in victory when you're met with dislike wherever you go,' Benjamin answered. 'The King's army numbers over ten thousand, and we cannot feed ourselves unless we steal what we need along the way. We've heard tell that Essex's defeated army did the same, and there's hatred building for both sides. Have you heard of the Clubmen? We encountered them first in Somerset but we're told they're even better organised in Dorset.'

Jayne spoke when Sir Henry remained silent. 'Are these the men who have chosen neutrality over conflict? We've heard rumours, but we didn't know if they were true.'

'Believe it, sister. Resistance is growing across the south-west, but the King refuses to take it seriously. The Clubmen of Somerset pleaded with him to negotiate a peace, and he said he would, and then gave orders for the seizure of livestock and the impressment of men.' He pulled a wry smile. 'I fear he's about to do the same in Dorset, though I doubt his lies will be as easily accepted.'

This time it was Jayne who was shocked. 'Is he here?' she asked.

Benjamin nodded. 'I wouldn't have been given leave for this visit otherwise. The King and Prince Rupert are staying the night at Maiden Newton. The two haven't met since Prince Rupert's defeat at Marston Moor, and I warrant the King will be as angry with him for the loss of the north as he was with Prince Maurice for the loss of Lyme.'

He regretted his words immediately, begging his family to swear they would keep His Majesty's presence at Maiden Newton a secret. Parliamentary spies were everywhere, and his head would be on the block if it became known that Captain Swift had betrayed the King's location. They did so gladly, if only to lessen his worry, but Jayne asked curiously where the army was quartered, since ten thousand men could hardly pass unnoticed. At Kingcombe, Benjamin told her, some five miles from Maiden Newton, leaving His Majesty and Prince Rupert with but a handful of aides for protection. Any Parliamentarian clever enough to gain entry to the house in which they were staying could end the war by killing them both. Sir Henry said no such Parliamentarian existed, but Jayne found herself wondering where William was.

Benjamin was given leave to visit them once more during the fortnight the King remained in Dorset. He used the occasion to urge his father to order Andrew to return home, because he believed it was the King's intention to lay siege to Weymouth. There was talk that His Majesty had signed a treaty of friendship with the French and that a foreign army was being amassed on the other side of the Channel. In order to land so large a number of men, he needed a secure harbour, and the best for that purpose would be Portland, which was currently guarded by the Parliamentary garrison of Weymouth.

Since it was obvious to Jayne that Benjamin's anxiety concerned the unwelcome prospect of having to fight his brother, she found her father's response surprising. Sir Henry refused his help, saying he would prefer Benjamin to desert his post than Andrew his, arguing that the King would not be forgiven if he won the war with French troops. He told Jayne afterwards that Benjamin had merely been repeating some ignorant barrack room gossip, for His Majesty knew better than to incite a foreign invasion of England, and this had seemed to be proven true as 1644 turned to 1645 without any reports of fighting in Weymouth.

Sir Henry was forced to eat his words, however, when Ruth arrived at the end of January with twenty female servants, and word came two weeks later that the battle for Portland harbour had begun. Thereafter, Swyre held its breath through the many fluctuating rumours about what was happening, torn between concern for Andrew and concern for Ruth's parents. The few glimmers of light in the hideous gloom came in letters from Philip and Benjamin, who had the sense to inform their father that neither of their regiments was involved at Weymouth, and Lady Margaret shed private tears of relief that her sons would not be required to kill each other.

Confirmation that victory had gone to Parliament came in a letter from Joseph on 9 March. He asked Sir Henry to tell Ruth that he and her mother were safe, adding in a postscript that Lord Goring's ill-disciplined army had suffered considerably more casualties than the Parliamentary garrison. Sir Henry read the words aloud in the salon and, while his own feelings about another Royalist defeat weren't entirely clear, Lady Margaret's happiness was obvious.

An hour later, Ruth asked Jayne why her aunt had smiled to have the garrison's success confirmed. 'Does she hold a different allegiance to your father, cousin? Will it please her if Parliament wins this war?'

They were sitting on a bench at the rear of the house, watching a groom use a long halter to teach Isaac to ride a pony in circles around him. Ahead of them, a swathe of grassland ran between shallow hills towards the sea. Had the rising land on either side not obscured their views, they would have been able to see the Isle of Portland to their left and Lyme Regis to their right. Sir Henry had confessed to Jayne that he'd climbed the western knoll many times while she was in Lyme, searching for any indication of how the siege was going, and she knew he'd done the same these last few weeks in order to look towards Portland and Weymouth.

With a sigh, she placed her arm about Ruth's waist and explained that a Parliamentary victory, coupled with Joseph's postscript, meant that Andrew, too, might be safe. 'He enlisted in the Weymouth garrison last July, but Papa thought it kinder to keep you in ignorance that our loyalties have been divided.'

'But I knew this already,' said Ruth. 'Andrew came to visit us when he first arrived in Weymouth. He felt he should inform Papa in person that he'd given his allegiance to Parliament.'

Jayne eyed her with surprise. 'Why did you not tell us?'

'Because Sir Henry made no mention of it in his letters. Papa assumed he must have disowned Andrew and advised me to stay quiet on the matter.' Ruth's gaze followed Isaac. 'Will it please Lady Margaret to hear that Andrew visited us every week with his friends William and Francis Sydenham, and that a firm respect has grown between them and Papa? I wonder sometimes if they haven't persuaded him of Parliament's cause, for he's not as favourable to the King as he used to be.'

Jayne thought of Sir Henry's mounting criticism of the way the war was being fought. 'What of you, cousin? Do you still have a hankering for Puritanism and Parliament?'

Ruth gave a low laugh. 'For the sake of peace, I play whatever role is expected of me.'

'But in your heart?'

'I would have what my sweet Mary wants—a world where every voice is heard. She was most flattered that you remembered her, Jayne. As, indeed, were Sarah and Rose. They speak of you often because your entry into their lives was so startling, but they never believed you would hold their names and images in your memory.'

Jayne would have answered that Ruth's servants had made as great an impression on her as she on them, had angry shouts not reached them from the grazing land to their left. Both women turned to see what the argument was about, and rose together at the sight of uniformed cavaliers laying into Sir Henry and his field workers with riding whips. Shocked, Jayne urged Ruth to take Isaac inside and then, without pausing to consider the wisdom of her actions, picked up her skirts and ran towards the melee, screeching at the top of her voice.

She told Sir Henry afterwards that she did only what the women of Lyme would have done in the same circumstances. Being female was no excuse to stand back when one's men and property came under attack, and she'd seen for herself how effective caterwauling could be. The disagreeable high-pitched howling broke a man's concentration, and it certainly worked on the cavalier who was lashing at her father's face. He turned to see where the sound was coming from, and Sir Henry, infuriated, grasped at the whip and wrested it from his hand.

'Thieving scoundrel!' he roared, swinging the crop in a backwards arc at the horse's muzzle. Frightened by the sudden sting of leather, the animal reared, throwing its rider to the ground, and then bolted towards the road. With a torrent of oaths, Sir Henry stamped on the cavalier's groin before turning to attack another horse with the crop.

Jayne's pounding feet and incessant caterwauling brought her mother to the kitchen window at the eastern end of the house. Pausing only to see if her daughter was running to or from a threat, Lady Margaret flung open the door, raised her own skirts and set off in pursuit with cooks, maids and footmen close behind. In short order, the thirteen Royalists who had entered Sir Henry's property with the intention of stealing his livestock found themselves assaulted by farmhands on one side and howling women and footmen on the other. Unable to control their mounts amidst so much confusion, some beat a hasty retreat towards the road while others were dragged from their saddles and dumped unceremoniously upon the ground. Lady Margaret instructed her household to sit on their chests and legs to prevent them rising, while Sir Henry and the labourers rounded up the horses. Meanwhile, the cavaliers' intended target, a herd of Devonshire Ruby Red cows, stood in docile indifference some twenty yards distant, chewing their cud.

Jayne saw the same exhilaration in her father's face as he disarmed and counted his prisoners—six—as she'd seen in the faces of Lyme's defenders each time they'd repulsed an assault. Nevertheless, she felt compelled to spoil his fun by pointing out that the men's comrades had retreated only as far as the road.

'We'll not fight them off if they come back with their swords drawn, Papa.'

Sir Henry followed her gaze. 'Damned heathens,' he muttered, before instructing the farmhands to take the horses and weapons to the stables. 'Stand guard at the doors and arm yourselves with pitchforks. No one's to enter without my permission. I'll send word if and when I decide to release their mounts and swords back to them.' He turned to Lady Margaret. 'Do we have rope in the house, madam? These men will cause us injury if we take them into the house unbound.'

Lady Margaret shook her head. 'We store such things in the stables, sir.' She looked at her maid, who was sitting across a fallen cavalier alongside another maid and a thirteen-year-old footman. 'Is there something else we can use, Agnes? Even with Sir Henry's help, a dozen women and two young lads cannot restrain six healthy men.'

'We have old bedsheets, milady, but they'll need fetching and tearing into strips.' Agnes turned to see if a servant was free, but all were sitting on the prisoners. 'Perhaps Miss Jayne can go.'

Jayne was watching the road. 'I doubt there's time,' she said. 'Wouldn't it be simpler to remove their boots and britches, and use their hose for bindings? I doubt Royalist soldiers hide anything inside their trousers that we ladies haven't seen before.'

Mary, erstwhile cook to Samuel Morecott, was straddling the thighs of the first man to be felled. 'I wouldn't be too sure about that, ma'am,' she said with a laugh. 'Whatever this one has between his legs has shrivelled away to nothing. If it wasn't for the hairs on his chin, I'd think he was a girl.'

'We'll soon find out,' said Jayne, stooping to grasp the heel of his left boot.

The man tried to kick her away, but Mary thumped the side of her fist onto his groin, while Lady Margaret's weightier cook, who was sitting astride his chest, pinned his arms beneath her knees.

'Enough!' he snapped. 'Will you accept our parole?' he demanded of Sir Henry. 'We'll not resist or attempt to escape if you allow us to stand. You have my word on it.'

'Do you command these men?'

'I do.'

'Your name and brigade.'

'Sir Edward Hamway of Lord Goring's Regiment of Horse.'

Sir Henry gave a grunt of disapproval. 'Lord Goring is a man without morals. I'm told he's already ravaged and plundered most of the West Country. Why should I have confidence that your parole is worth anything?'

'Because I swear it by God as a high-ranking gentleman, sir. We do what we must to support the King's cause, but dishonesty is as foreign to our natures as it is to yours. I beg you to believe that.'

Jayne saw her own scepticism of this honeyed plea mirrored in the face of every woman there, including her mother's, but Sir Henry seemed satisfied with it. He instructed the maids to rise and then gestured for Sir Edward and his companions to follow him into the house. Jayne's faith in her father's judgement had never been strong—he persisted in believing that a gentleman's word was his bond—but it weakened considerably as she watched Sir Edward signal to the men on the road. He spread his hands wide and then brought them together to form a circle with his arms. To Jayne, the message was clear: *Move apart and station yourselves about the house.*

Jayne and her mother were prevented from entering the salon by Sir Henry, who dispatched them to fetch refreshments for his guests. They heard him invite the men to seat themselves, followed by Sir Edward's warm praise for Swyre House and the magnificence of the furnishings.

Lady Margaret shook her head in irritation as they crossed the hall. '*High-ranking gentleman*, indeed! He's a practised trickster. He'll have your father eating out of his hand within two minutes, and he and his men will have vanished with our silver by the time we return.'

Jayne shook her head. 'I doubt it's silver that interests him, Mama. Lord Goring's troops need food, so I'll wager he's looking to charm Papa into gifting him the Ruby Reds.'

'Sir Henry's not so foolish. We'll have no means to feed ourselves if our stock is taken.'

'Then Sir Edward will break his parole and take what he wants by force. Never forget there are seven more of his men outside, still armed with swords. We'll not stand a chance if he summons them inside. They have but to hold a blade to Papa's throat and you'll give them whatever they want, Mama. We should have armed ourselves with clubs like the Clubmen.'

Lady Margaret paused before the kitchen door. 'What can we do to stop them?'

Jayne glanced towards her satchel, which sat on a table to the right of the front door. 'Use a different kind of club. Are you willing to return to the salon and ask Sir Edward if he and his men would like a tankard of ale while the cooks prepare food for them? They'll be thirsty after their ride, so I doubt they'll do anything rash until they've drunk it.'

Lady Margaret's gaze followed hers. 'And what will you be doing?'

Jayne's eyes filled with mischief. 'Preparing the tankards,' she said.

She chose half-pint earthenware vessels for the cavaliers and stood them around the edge of a large circular salver with an embossed silver tankard in the middle. Next, she instructed one of the cooks to fill a flagon from a keg of the frothiest ale and summoned her mother's maid Agnes to accompany her. 'You must carry the tray and offer a tankard to each man in the salon,' she said. 'I will walk beside you and fill them one at a time. The silver tankard is for Sir Henry and you should serve him last. Do you understand?'

Agnes peered at the half-inch of liquid at the bottom of each of the earthenware tankards. 'I believe so, Miss Jayne, but I hope you're not making me party to murder.'

'Nothing so dire,' said Jayne with a laugh. 'My intention is to send them to sleep.'

She apologised profusely when her clumsy handling of the flagon delivered more head in Sir Edward's tankard than liquid. He and his men appeared fully at ease in the salon, lounging on her mother's prized sofas and chairs in their dirty uniforms. 'Are you able to handle so much froth, sir?' she asked with nervous concern. 'Allow me to serve your men, and I will attempt to be more proficient in my pouring when I come back to you.'

He gave a gracious wave of his hand. 'A good head speaks to a good beer,' he said.

The other cavaliers were as gracious, happily lining their lips with foam as she and Agnes moved from one to the next. She took more trouble with her father's vessel, tilting it to minimise the head, and taking time to ask questions while she did so. Had Sir Edward satisfied Papa's curiosity about the battle for Weymouth? Did he understand now how one thousand men had defeated six thousand? It seemed so, for Sir Henry was less displeased with Sir Edward's excuses than he'd been with Sir Walter Hoare's after Lyme. Jayne stood politely in front of Sir Henry, listening to tales of bad weather and treachery, and when she judged that a good five minutes had passed, she made a second round to refill the cavaliers' empty tankards.

She had added five times the dose of valerian root tincture she'd normally use to help a patient sleep, because she was quite ignorant of whether diluting it with ale would render it ineffective. She hoped that by giving a small first dilution and waiting a few minutes the tincture would begin to work, for she was even more ignorant about what a second, larger dilution would do. Sir Edward remarked that the ale seemed less bitter on a second tasting.

Sir Henry blamed it on the froth. 'Your mother should have sent servants who know how to pour correctly,' he told Jayne.

'She was worried for their safety, Papa,' Jayne answered. 'We've heard so many stories of rape and assault in connection with Lord Goring's troops that she didn't want to place them in danger.'

Sir Edward gave a grunt of amusement. 'Are you not worried for yourself, Mistress Swift?'

Jayne glanced at one of his companions, who was yawning. 'Not any more, Sir Edward.'

'The stories you've heard are falsehoods, invented by Parliamentarians to blacken Lord Goring's name,' the cavalier said lazily. 'You shouldn't give them credence.'

'You assaulted my father, sir. Does that not prove the tales to be true? You must be accustomed to taking what you want without permission or you wouldn't have done it.'

Sir Edward stifled a yawn of his own. 'I'm a soldier, mistress. Do you question me for following orders?'

'I do, sir, for you're using the same excuse that every soldier gives for the crimes he commits.'

'There are no crimes in war, only casualties.'

Jayne smiled slightly. 'That must be Lord Goring's philosophy. I'm told he sees war as a means to enrich himself and cares nothing for the people he destroys in the process. Do you have no mind of your own, Sir Edward, but must always ape your superiors?'

Sir Edward scowled. 'You take too much licence, woman. Your father may tolerate your forwardness, but not I.' He made an effort to rise but slumped back when his legs refused to take his weight.

Jayne stooped to look into his eyes. 'You're weary, sir. Allow yourself to rest.'

He glanced in sudden alarm towards his men, two of whom were already asleep. 'Are we poisoned?'

'Deeply so,' she said, 'but not by me.'

SEVENTEEN

JAYNE HELD A FINGER TO her lips to urge her father to silence and then walked to the door to beckon her mother and two strapping footmen into the salon. Lady Margaret carried long strips of cloth torn from worn-out bedsheets, which she shared between herself, Jayne and Agnes, and each applied herself to removing the boots of the cavaliers before binding their feet in strong figure-of-eight hobbles. Jayne had urged them to be slow and gentle in their movements, for she couldn't be sure how deep the men's sleep would be. In the event, none of them stirred and, once they were bound, Lady Margaret whispered to the footmen to lift them from their chairs and lay them on their backs on the floor.

Agnes placed cushions beneath their heads to make them comfortable, and then assisted Jayne and Lady Margaret to hold their hands together across their groins in order to bind their wrists. Had Jayne had more confidence in the tincture, she would have preferred to lie them on their fronts and tie their hands behind their backs, but even if only one had woken, the struggle to contain him would have been hard. Instead, she twisted strips of bedsheet together to form strong ropes and then linked each man's wrists to his feet with tight knots. As a final touch, she asked the footmen to fetch blankets to cover them and keep them warm, for the longer they slept the less trouble they would be.

Throughout, she and her mother had ignored Sir Henry's rumblings, hushing him with fingers to lips, but now they escorted him into the hall and sat him in a carved oak chair. 'Speak low,' Lady Margaret whispered, gesturing towards the entranceway. 'Three of Sir Edward's men stand guard on the other side of that door, two are stationed outside the kitchen quarters and two more are at your office door. We believe they are awaiting his summons to force their way in.'

Sir Henry reacted more calmly than Jayne had thought he would. 'It was to be expected,' he said. 'They were bound to come looking eventually, but I'd hoped to persuade Sir Edward to accept a dozen older cows before they did.' He studied his wife and daughter curiously. 'Tell me why you thought putting him to sleep was a better solution? Our predicament remains the same. There are thirteen hardened fighters who want to relieve us of our stock, and we haven't the trained men or weapons to prevent them.'

Jayne dropped to her haunches in front of him. 'The number's now seven, Papa. Six of the thirteen are currently helpless and will remain so until you choose to release them. Mama and I believe we can render the others as helpless, but we'll need your assistance to do it.'

'To what purpose? We can't hold them indefinitely.'

'Pride?' Lady Margaret suggested. 'We're told the Clubmen fight hard to protect what is theirs. Will we not do the same?'

After all, it was ridiculously simple to tempt the men stationed around the house into drinking ale spiced with valerian root. Sir Henry began with the two outside the kitchen quarters, throwing the door wide and greeting them with bluff good humour while holding a tankard in each hand to show he was neither armed nor looking to fight. Sheltering beneath his right arm and clutching the flagon of ale to her chest was Lady Margaret's smallest maid, a girl of eighteen with a quick and clever mind but of such tiny stature she looked more like a ten-year-old. Together, their appearance was so unthreatening that, despite both soldiers holding unsheathed swords at their sides, neither raised them.

Beaming, Sir Henry informed them that he and Sir Edward had reached an accommodation about which cattle could be taken. The animals were being rounded up as he spoke, and Sir Edward and his companions were collecting their horses from the stables. 'He asks that you muster on the forecourt in twenty minutes, gentlemen, but urges you to refresh yourselves first. Will you accept some ale and a platter each of bread and mutton?'

The tantalising scent of roasting meat, and the indifference shown them by the dozen cooks working industriously in the kitchen behind Sir Henry, allayed whatever doubts they might have had. Thirst and hunger took precedence over caution—as, indeed, did sympathy, since both men begged Sir Henry not to chastise the maid for clumsiness. It was of no matter that she spilt more ale on the ground than in the tankards and had to run back inside to beg for the flagon to be filled again.

Sir Henry pointed to a bench against the wall. 'Seat yourselves, gentlemen,' he said. 'I can see you're weary.'

'We are, sir,' said one, as both lowered themselves gratefully. 'General Goring retreated to Dorchester, from where we've ridden this morning, but food is scarce for miles around. We haven't eaten well in days.'

'You'll feel better when your stomachs are full of bread and mutton.'

'We will, sir,' they agreed in heavy-lidded unison.

Sir Henry turned towards the sea, murmuring inanities about the blueness of the water, and when he looked back both men were asleep. He beckoned forward the footmen, who stood in the shadows at the back of the kitchen, to bind the Royalists' hands and feet, then took Mary and the maid to his office, where they performed a similar charade for the pair outside that room. Meanwhile, Lady Margaret had lured the three on the forecourt into the hall.

'Sir Edward asks that you join him, sirs,' she said, gesturing towards the open front door. 'We've prepared refreshments to celebrate an agreeable conclusion to his talks with my husband, and all are invited to partake.'

They peered suspiciously inside, but saw only Jayne with a salver of sweetmeats in her hands. 'Where is Sir Edward?' one asked.

Jayne placed the salver on a table beside another piled with breads and cold meat, and a third holding tankards and a flagon. She gestured towards the salon. 'Still with my father, sir. We expect them in a moment. Your fellow soldiers also.' She counted the tankards. 'Thirteen, and one for Papa,' she said with satisfaction, pouring ale into the nearest three. 'Sir Edward said you'd be thirsty, so Sir Henry instructed me to give each man a drink as he arrives.' She lifted the tankards by their handles and carried them to the men. 'Please,' she urged with a smile when they hesitated. 'They're only half filled because I must keep enough in the flagon for Papa and your fellows, but when all of you are here, I shall fetch more from the kitchen.'

They needed no further invitation and took the vessels gladly, making no demur when Lady Margaret ushered them inside and gave them hunks of bread. 'Seat yourselves while you can,' she urged, 'for you'll be required to stand when Sir Henry and Sir Edward emerge.' She moved across the hall to press her ear to the salon door. 'They're laughing,' she said, 'but I'll give you good warning when I hear the sound of their chairs being scraped back.'

When all thirteen soldiers were bound and laid on their backs on the salon floor, Jayne began to worry that a quintuple dose of tincture, coupled with ale, might indeed be poisonous. She knelt by each to feel the strength and steadiness of the pulse in their wrists, but found nothing untoward. Sir Henry, by contrast, began to see problems everywhere. This was no surprise to his wife and daughter, because he was acting according to his nature, which was to embrace an idea with enthusiasm and only look for the pitfalls afterwards.

He raged around the hall once the door of the salon was closed. 'I should never have agreed to this. What will we do when they wake? Keep them prisoner? Set them free so they can incite Goring to send his whole army to put us to the siege? *Kill* them?'

Lady Margaret clapped her hands to her ears. 'For goodness' sake, stop *shouting*, Henry! You'll give us all headaches. As to what we should do with them, I suggest we treat them as we would any violent thieves: escort them to the Bridport magistrate and have them tried for assault and attempted robbery. We, at least, should be on the side of justice, even if they are not.'

Such a straightforward solution hadn't occurred to Sir Henry, and he eyed her thoughtfully. 'We have enough men to do it,' he agreed, 'providing we rope the prisoners together and force them to walk. I doubt Justice Meredith will bring them to trial, however. The man's a Royalist through and through.'

'As are you, Henry, or so you've always told us. But perhaps that's another decision you've come to regret?'

To take the sting from her mother's words, Jayne offered her father the salver of sweetmeats. 'You'll be celebrated across Dorset if you succeed in holding thieving soldiers to account, Papa. People are being robbed of their food by both sides, leaving families to starve, yet the magistrates do nothing. Will you not make the attempt, at least?'

Sir Henry gave an abrupt laugh. 'I don't seem to have much choice,' he said, selecting a sweetmeat and popping it into his mouth.

His resolve was strengthened by Sir Edward's threats once he and his men were awake. Some came to their senses sooner than others, but all were restored within four hours. As each stirred, Sir Henry ordered him pulled to his feet so that his hands could be retied with rope behind his back, leaving three yards of tether to loop about the neck of the man who would walk behind him. Only when all were upright did he instruct his twenty farm labourers to cut the hobbles from around their ankles and assist them into their boots, warning that any who attempted to kick their captors would make the journey to Bridport unshod.

He informed them that he planned to lay charges against them before Justice Meredith, and Sir Edward cursed him for being a treacherous knave. Sir Henry should know that treason was punishable by death, and that every member of his household would be deemed complicit in what he was doing.

Sir Henry was unmoved. 'How is it treasonable to seek justice against thieves?'

'We fight for the King.'

'You may think you do, sir, but I doubt the King would agree with you. For myself, I would hang my head in shame to be defeated so easily by a handful of women.' He turned to his labourers, instructing them to form the prisoners into a line and attach them together by their tethers. 'Make the nooses loose enough for them to breathe,' he said, 'but not so loose that they can slip out of them.'

Sir Edward tried to resist being taken to the front. 'I'm the same status as you,' he appealed to Sir Henry. 'Allow me to ride.'

Sir Henry glanced towards the door where his wife and daughter were standing. 'What do you say, ladies?'

Lady Margaret answered first. 'He has no honour, husband. He'll spur his horse to a gallop the first chance he gets and leave his men to face the magistrate alone.'

'Jayne?'

'Mama speaks the truth, Papa. An honourable leader chooses to stand with his men, not look for ways to set himself apart.'

Sir Edward eyed her with dislike. 'What does a woman know about leadership?'

'Enough to suggest that you ask the magistrate to try only you for this crime, sir. Your troops have no culpability in the matter if the excuse you gave me earlier has any validity.'

'How so?'

She looked at his fellow prisoners and saw that all were listening. 'You're their superior officer, sir. They were obliged to follow your orders whether they wanted to or not.'

~

It was close to midnight by the time Sir Henry and the farmhands returned. Lady Margaret and Jayne, who had decided against going to bed, heard their voices raised in song as they made their way down the driveway, and hurried to the door to greet them. The men moved as a throng, picking their way by the light of two or three lanterns on poles, and the tune they were singing was 'The Wild Rover'. At their heart was Sir Henry, his arms draped across the shoulders of two of his labourers, his voice bellowing out the chorus.

'And it's no, nay, never . . . No, nay, never, no more . . . And I'll play the wild rover . . . No, never, no more . . .'

'They've been at the ale,' said Lady Margaret. 'Your father never sings unless he's drunk. It's a mercy they've made it home at all.'

In truth, neither woman had thought Sir Henry would triumph, for he was vacillating even before he left. Wouldn't it be simpler to give Sir Edward a dozen head of cattle for a promise not to come back?

Surprisingly, it had been Ruth who firmed his mind. Her own father would applaud him for seeking justice, she said. Prince Maurice's troops had plundered their home of silver when Weymouth surrendered to Lord Carnarvon, and Joseph had been suing for reparation ever since. His greatest grudge was to have been robbed by Royalists when he had given his allegiance to the King.

Now, woken from sleep by the increasingly raucous rendering of 'The Wild Rover', she slipped down the stairs to join Lady Margaret and Jayne at the door. 'They must have won the case,' she said. 'They'd not be in such good spirits otherwise.'

Lady Margaret took a candle-tree from the table and held it high so that the men would see them in the doorway. Cries of salutation came back to them over the strains of the chorus, with Sir Henry's voice the loudest.

'Ladies!' he roared. 'We come to celebrate victory! Bring ale for my worthy friends!'

'We'll do no such thing,' Lady Margaret muttered to Jayne and Ruth. 'God willing, he'll fall asleep the minute he sits down. I've never seen him so inebriated.'

She drew the girls aside to allow the farmhands to walk Sir Henry through the doorway, telling them to lay him on the floor when their struggles to prop him in the carved oak chair proved fruitless. The oldest of the men, who held his drink better than his companions, explained Sir Henry's condition. It seemed they had paused at every tavern along the route home to toast the magnificence of the law, and by the time they reached the Saddlers' Inn, Sir Henry was incapable of sitting his horse.

'We thought it safer to leave the animal there and take it in turns to carry the master, milady. I shall retrieve the horse as soon as it is light tomorrow.'

'Thank you, Arthur, and what of the case? How was it won?'

Arthur pulled a wry smile. 'Through Sir Edward ignoring Miss Jayne's advice, milady. He insisted on being treated differently from conscripted troops, and his men took against him as a result.'

'They said it was he who ordered them to steal?'

'Even more, milady. They told the magistrate he had money in his saddle pack to be used as reparation, and had promised them a half-crown each if they succeeded in taking the cattle without payment. Justice Meredith ordered the pack to be brought to the court and discovered they were telling the truth. The bag of coins contained a chitty, signed by a quartermaster, setting a limit on how much Sir Edward could spend per head of cattle. I believe the amount was two pounds, so it would still have amounted to theft, since a single Ruby Red is worth at least ten, but Sir Edward's intent to commit felony was proved.' He chuckled. 'It was a mercy you persuaded Sir Henry to deliver their horses along with them so as not to be accused of thievery himself.'

Lady Margaret smiled. 'What punishment did the magistrate give?'

'Two nights in the town gaol for Sir Edward and the forfeiture of his and his troop's property, including the horses and the bag of coins. His men were released but none wanted to return to their regiment. They preferred desertion to explaining how they came to lose their captain, their mounts and their weapons.'

'Did Sir Edward argue against the sentence?' Jayne asked.

'Only if the same threats he made against Sir Henry can be considered argument, Miss Jayne. He cursed the magistrate for a traitor and said he'd lay charges against him for treason.'

Jayne laughed. 'How did Justice Meredith answer?'

'He declared himself a loyal Royalist and said he wouldn't tolerate anyone making false accusations against him,' said Arthur with another chuckle. 'Then added three hours in the stocks to be served on Sir Edward's release from the gaol in two days' time. He'll be a sorry man by the time he leaves Bridport, I think.'

Word came shortly afterwards that Lord Goring had marched his army into Somerset. Sir Henry was relieved to hear they'd left Dorchester but warned Jayne that this decision meant the King had given up on Weymouth in order to retake Taunton. The town stood on the only major route out of the south-west, and whoever controlled it also controlled the movement of people and supplies in every direction. Colonel Blake had resisted the first siege some six months previously, but Sir Henry doubted he could withstand another if the King's armies came together to surround him.

Over dinner one evening at the beginning of April, he asked Jayne if she still favoured neutrality. 'I sense your admiration for Colonel Blake may have persuaded you to Parliament's side,' he said. 'Am I right?'

Jayne took a moment to answer. 'I've always supported the people's right to have their voices heard, Papa. It's using war to achieve such ends that offends me. Therefore, in answer to your question, yes, I still favour neutrality and will continue to do so even after the conflict ends. I have no wish to judge anyone for their beliefs, now or in the future.'

'You were not so generous to Sir Edward Hamway.'

She smiled. 'You know very well I judged Sir Edward for his thievery, not his beliefs, Papa. Do you think I'd have acted differently if he'd been a Parliamentarian?'

He searched her face. 'I don't know,' he said. 'Let me ask a different question. Why do you never say anything to the detriment of the Parliamentarians in Lyme? Is it because you see them as models of virtue or because you don't want me to think badly of them?'

The point was well made. 'I wasn't aware I was doing that, Papa, but if I am, it's because you find so much to criticise in them. You assume that all Parliamentarians are Puritans, and your intolerance of that sect leads to intolerance of anyone who supports Parliament.'

'Name me a Parliamentarian who isn't a Puritan.'

Jayne sought for a name other than William Harrier. 'Your son Andrew,' she said, 'and several of your farmhands and maids who keep their views to themselves for fear of being dismissed.'

'Which ones?'

When Jayne shook her head to indicate that she wasn't prepared to say, Lady Margaret answered. 'More than you realise, Henry. Their families are as involved in this wretched war as ours and they blame the King for refusing Parliament's peace terms. You say his reasons are good, because Parliament's intention is to tie his hands, but not all agree with you. Most think a small loss of authority a paltry price to pay for the lives of husbands, brothers, fathers and sons.'

'The King fights for a principle: that his authority is absolute and bestowed on him by God. To give up *any* power would be to admit he's wrong to claim a divine right to rule.'

Ruth, who was sitting next to him, laid her hand over his. 'But is that not the issue in question, Uncle?' she asked. 'I can find only a few verses in scripture that support what the King claims, and they are in Proverbs Sixteen. Verse ten says, "A divine sentence is in the lips of the king; his mouth transgresses not in judgement," and verse twelve, "It is an abomination to kings to commit wickedness, for the throne is established by righteousness."'

'Do those words not convince you, niece?'

Ruth gave his fingers an apologetic squeeze before releasing them. 'Sadly not, for they seem to be contradicted by verse twenty-one of Daniel Two, which says, "God changes the times and the seasons. He removes kings and establishes kings," and also by verse twenty-four of Job Thirty-four, "He breaks in pieces mighty men and sets others in their place." Do you wish me to continue? I have found many more that speak to God's readiness to depose kings than those which grant them authority.'

Sir Henry groaned. In contests of biblical knowledge with Ruth, he lost every time. 'Are you arguing that God is using Parliament to rid us of this one?'

'I argue nothing, sir, but I believe that's how Puritans see this conflict. As long as they remain on the side of righteousness, they will defeat those who do not.'

Sir Henry turned to Jayne. 'Is she right? Is that how the Puritans of Lyme viewed their battles with Prince Maurice?'

Jayne nodded. 'You asked me why I never say anything to their detriment, and that is the reason. Even though food was in such short supply that theft should have been common, I never saw an adult in Lyme break a commandment as easily as Sir Edward Hamway.' She paused. 'It's a subject that interests Richard Theale. He wonders why Royalist soldiers seem more corrupted by this war than Parliamentarians and gave me the reason in his last letter.'

She kept to herself that the reason had been supplied by William, who had visited Bridport some two weeks previously on his way to speak with Blake in Taunton. It seemed he had fought alongside Andrew at Weymouth and had asked Richard to send word to Jayne that her brother was alive and well. She counted herself fortunate that Andrew wrote to Lady Margaret the same day, for she was unable to think of a single good excuse for why her tutor might know of Andrew's welfare before his mother.

'Did he cite differences of religion as the cause?'

'No, Papa. Lack of payment. If a man is rewarded for fighting, he behaves better than one who fights only for plunder. According to Richard, Parliament has been more consistent in paying their troops because they can still raise taxes, while the King is so pressed for funds he allows his armies to run rampant. And man's nature being what it is, Royalist soldiers have embraced dishonesty with enthusiasm. I'm sure Ruth can give you a biblical text to support that supposition.'

'Matthew Fifteen, verse nineteen. "For out of the heart proceed evil thoughts, murders, adulteries, fornications, thefts, false witness and blasphemies." Jesus was teaching his followers to worry more about their inner selves than the polished outer selves they present to others. Jayne may be right to say that payment is enough to curb a man's sinful nature, but most Puritans would argue that the struggle for goodness is the same for the rich as for the poor.'

Jayne eyed her cousin fondly. 'Yet Parliament seems to be taking more practical steps to keep their soldiers in check. Richard says their armies are to be joined together under the command of a single leader, Sir Thomas Fairfax, with every man paid a weekly wage. This force is to be called the New Model Army.'

Sir Henry frowned. 'Is this rumour or fact?'

'Richard believes it to be fact, Papa. He's heard that the second-in-command to Fairfax will be Colonel Oliver Cromwell, who is as respected and successful as Robert Blake. It's said Colonel Cromwell won't tolerate ill-discipline amongst his troops and insists they pay for everything they use, which is why he and they are liked by the people.'

'He sounds too good to be true,' said Sir Henry acidly. 'Why have I never heard of him?'

Jayne laughed. 'You have now, Papa.'

EIGHTEEN

A LOUD HOLLER RANG THROUGH the hall of Swyre House, alerting the household to an approaching army. A footman shouted that it numbered one hundred; a maid cried that it was twice that size. Sir Henry, roused from a doze, scrambled to his feet, swearing perdition on all who invaded his property. Lady Margaret ran to the kitchen, calling to her servants to gather around her and make ready to defend themselves. Jayne, recently returned from a tiring night-time delivery, sank onto a chair in the salon and closed her eyes. Someone could wake her when the house began to burn, she called, but until then she intended to remain where she was.

Dorset had seen so much tumult since Parliament regained Weymouth that she couldn't begin to guess which army to expect. The siege of Taunton occupied most of the conversation, for no one understood how Robert Blake and his tiny garrison had held out for so long. Lord Goring had joined with the general in command of the Cornish regiments to encircle the town, but their inability to agree had led them to withdraw their armies and leave the siege to different leaders. The general had retreated west to Cornwall while Goring headed east towards Shaftesbury. Such division in the Royalist camp should have benefited Blake, but Goring's choice to once again patrol the border between Somerset and Dorset prevented Parliamentary relief forces reaching him.

Formal notification of the creation of a new Parliamentary army of twenty-two thousand men had arrived in the second week of April, and in the days that followed rumours circulated that Sir Thomas Fairfax was bringing this huge force to Dorset in order to confront Lord Goring. There was no evidence to support these rumours, however. The only verifiable stories were those that said the behaviour of Goring's troops had become so appalling that ever more men were taking up clubs in defence of their homes.

In Dorset alone, the Clubmen's numbers were said to be in the thousands, and Sir Henry attested to this after joining a gathering of some three hundred on open land to the west of Swyre. He reported back to Jayne and Lady Margaret that what had begun as single individuals attempting to protect their property had grown into full-scale rebellion against the war. Petitions begging for peace were being prepared and, once signed, would be sent to the King and Parliament. Every man in Dorset would be asked to add his name, and Sir Henry said he was minded to do so. He found he had more in common with the gentleman farmers, vicars and merchants who had been at the gathering—many of whom he knew—than he did with the likes of Sir Edward Hamway or Samuel Morecott.

Jayne counted it a small victory that Sir Henry was finally seeing merit in neutrality, but Lady Margaret warned her against saying anything. In two or three weeks, he would claim the idea as his own, she said, and their lives would become easier when he did. Jayne's brothers would be treated with equal warmth when they returned, and the servants would not have to guard their words in front of him.

Now, Sir Henry was making so much noise ordering his footmen to follow him out of the back of the house in order to round up the farmhands that Jayne abandoned her chair to move to the window. She was joined by Ruth and Isaac, who had been reading quietly together beside the fireplace.

'What do you see?' asked Isaac.

'Men on horseback,' said Jayne, stooping to lift him in her arms. 'Can you tell if they're for the King? You say you know the colours of his different armies.'

Isaac gave an embarrassed wriggle. 'Not *all* of them,' he answered. 'I know Prince Maurice's wear red sashes.'

The leading horses were still some two hundred yards distant, and the wide red bands worn diagonally across their riders' chests were clearly visible. Nevertheless, Jayne doubted these were Prince Maurice's troops, because every man in the long line of horse that stretched back towards the gates was dressed in a buff jacket, a dark leather breastplate, thigh-length boots, and a peaked iron helmet with face and neck guards. Together, they represented a unified whole, looking quite unlike Prince Maurice's ragtag soldiers, who had dressed in any manner they chose.

Ruth laughed suddenly. 'I may be mistaken,' she said, 'for it's hard to see faces behind the bars on the helmets, but isn't that Andrew leading them? Do you see how he rides one-handed with his right arm hanging at his side? Andrew rode in such a way every time he visited us. Papa thought it absurdly affected and challenged him to do the same at a gallop.'

Jayne studied the horse as much as the man. Andrew's was a rich red bay with a single white sock. 'And did he?' she asked.

'Most impressively so. He instructed a groom to set an apple on a post and plucked it off with his free hand as he passed. What do you think?'

'It's certainly his horse,' said Jayne, setting Isaac on the floor and leading him by the hand into the hall. She pointed to the door on the other side. 'You must run to the kitchen and fetch Lady Margaret,' she urged him. 'Tell her Andrew has come and that your mother and I have gone outside to greet him.'

The boy took to his heels, and Jayne put her arm about Ruth's waist to hasten her out of the entrance. To her left, she saw Sir Henry and his farmhands rounding the corner of the house. Sir Henry carried a club which he'd purchased in Bridport, and the labourers held their pitchforks like spears. The distance between them and the column was a bare fifty yards, and she watched in alarm as every rider, including Andrew, reached for his sword.

'Oh, my goodness!' she said, picking up her skirts. 'We must run, cousin. There'll be regret on both sides if they come to blows.'

A woman could get used to caterwauling, she thought. The screams were hard on the throat but their effect on men was unvarying. Both Sir Henry and Andrew turned to discover what the disturbance was, and Jayne was given a few extra seconds to reach the space between them. Red-faced and breathless, she bent forward to place her hands on her knees, as Ruth, unused to strenuous exercise, sank to the ground beside her.

'Remove yourselves, women,' roared Sir Henry. 'This is a Clubman's house and we prohibit intrusion by either side in this wretched conflict.'

Jayne raised a hand. 'Allow me to breathe, Papa. All will be explained in a moment.' She took two deep breaths, then straightened and turned towards the column. 'You must remove your helmet, Andrew,' she called. 'You're dressed so similarly to your companions that you're quite unrecognisable.'

Andrew's abrupt reining in of his horse to avoid riding into her had brought the men behind him to a stop, and he gave an instruction to the rider beside him to order them to dismount. Then he removed his helmet, hooked it on the pommel of his saddle and nudged his mount towards his father. 'My respects, Sir Henry,' he said, dropping to the ground and making a deep bow. 'Be assured we come with no ill-intent and will leave again within the hour. I found I could not pass so close to my home without reminding myself of faces I have missed. Are you well, sir?'

There was no hesitation in Sir Henry's response. He gripped Andrew's arms and pulled him into a tight embrace. 'Who would have thought it?' he said. 'Who would have thought it?'

They were words Jayne might have used herself, because Andrew looked very different from the stout, gaudily dressed young man of a year ago. Lean and with short, cropped hair, he appeared taller and older—and to Jayne's eyes a good deal more confident. The simple buff uniform flattered him where fancy doublet and hose had not, and the creases about his eyes, scored into his skin by the elements, suggested he had learnt to smile more often than frown. She certainly had the sense that war had helped him, though whether because he'd found freedom away from his father or because he truly believed in what he was fighting for, she didn't know. Perhaps both.

Released from Sir Henry's hug, he was promptly embraced by Lady Margaret, who arrived in a flurry of skirts to cover his face with kisses. For her part, Jayne contented herself with relieving him of his horse, so that he could clasp the hands of the farm workers, all of whom he knew well. As she watched them greet Andrew, a soldier approached and asked if she would like him to lead the horse back to the column. His face was hidden behind the bars of his helmet but his voice and stature were unmistakeable.

'It would please me even more if you led him yourself, Jayne. I have as much desire for a few minutes' conversation with the good doctor of Swyre as your brother does.'

How absurd that her first thought was what a wreck she must look, since she still wore her workman's boots and the dress of a poor countrywoman from riding to the delivery last night.

'I doubt Papa would approve of my walking and speaking with a common soldier, William. It's a bare ten minutes since he was planning to poke you all with pitchforks.' She offered him the reins. 'You have my permission to take the horse yourself, however.'

She heard the ghost of a laugh as he took the strap in his hand. 'Some other time, then.' He stooped to assist Ruth to her feet before leading the animal away.

Ruth wore a puzzled frown as she watched him return to the column. 'Is that Lady Stickland's footman? I remember his name was William.'

Jayne couldn't deny it, since Ruth seemed to have a clear recollection of him. 'Yes.'

'You were right to rebuff him. He must feel your previous acquaintanceship gives him licence to be overly familiar.'

'Indeed,' said Jayne, taking Ruth's hand and guiding her towards Andrew. 'But let's enjoy the moment and worry about impertinent footmen later.'

Later came sooner than she'd wanted. When pressed by Lady Margaret to enter the house and partake of refreshment, Andrew declined, saying he couldn't expect to be treated differently from his men or the other officers travelling with him. But Sir Henry baulked at such nonsense, instructing Lady Margaret to have sweetmeats and cordial brought out to the troops and giving Andrew leave to invite his brother officers inside.

'Royalists feel free to come and go as they please,' he said gruffly, 'and I'll not have you thinking we're open to one side but not the other.'

Andrew glanced at the club in his hand. 'In truth, I was thinking the opposite, sir: that neither side is welcome. We find the same resistance everywhere, for both armies have imposed too heavily on the people they claim to represent.' He gestured towards the column. 'We hope to regain trust by behaving differently, so you have my personal surety that these men will do nothing to offend against your hospitality.'

'Are you part of this new army under Sir Thomas Fairfax?'

'We are, sir. Every man has undergone two months' training in Lyme and we now have orders to join the rest of the cavalry in Hampshire under the command of Colonel Cromwell.' He turned to Jayne. 'John Metcalfe sends his respects, sister, and asks to be remembered to you, as indeed did others when they learnt I was your brother.' A smile lit his eyes. 'Your name is held in high regard and I was proud to share it.'

Jayne was more embarrassed than thrilled by the compliment. 'Are you sure you're not someone masquerading as Andrew?' she asked. 'We're more used to insulting each other than exchanging pleasantries.'

He grinned. 'I'm not so proud of you today, sister. Those garments get worse every time I see them. My men will think I'm related to a vagrant.'

She smiled back before turning to Lady Margaret. 'Allow Ruth and me to oversee the refreshments, Mama. You've been yearning to see all your sons, and you shouldn't waste your hour with Andrew by spending it in the kitchen.'

She waited for her mother's nod and then hastened towards the front door with Ruth scurrying beside her, asking plaintively why they were in such a hurry. Jayne said they had many mouths to feed, but the truth was she didn't want to be in the salon when Andrew brought the officers inside. She knew for a certainty that William would be one of them, and while Andrew may have been easily convinced that a Royalist captain in the Corfe garrison had had a change of heart, she doubted the same would be true of Sir Henry and Lady Margaret. The kitchen held many more attractions than feigning surprise that her erstwhile saviour had switched colours or dealing with Ruth's bewilderment over how a footman had mysteriously become a knight.

When there was no more to be done in the matter of refreshments, Jayne retreated to her bedchamber and instructed her maid, Kitty, to loosen her braids and help her into a gown. Her intention was to absent herself until Andrew and his colleagues were ready to leave, but this idea was thwarted by Agnes, who entered the room and stood arms akimbo in front of her. 'Your father and mother are most insistent that you present yourself in the salon, Miss Jayne. If I return without you, Sir Henry says he will come himself.'

'Beg another few minutes for me, Agnes. Kitty has barely fastened me into this gown and has yet to finish my hair. I promise to be downstairs before Andrew leaves.'

Agnes stamped her foot. 'It won't do, Miss Jayne. I'll lose my post if I return without you.'

'You'll never lose your post, Agnes. My mother has too much regard for you. Tell me what's being said in the salon.'

'I'm sure you can guess that for yourself, Miss Jayne, since Miss Ruth tells me Captain Harrier spoke to you on the forecourt. Your mother recognised him immediately as your escort of two years ago, and now your father bedevils him with questions.'

So, Captain Harrier and not Sir William . . . 'Have you heard his answers?'

'By no means,' snapped Agnes, shooing Kitty away and settling Jayne's bodice neatly above her hips. 'There's nothing more Kitty can do for you. You look as fine as I've ever seen you. Now, come.'

With a sigh, Jayne followed her from the chamber. 'You're no help at all,' she chided. 'What am I to say that won't make matters worse?'

'Nothing,' advised Agnes. 'Do as your mother and Miss Ruth do. Work at a tapestry and leave the men to sort their differences between themselves.'

Jayne recalled her last conversation with William in Richard Theale's house. Nothing would annoy him more than for her to sit daintily before a frame, making tiny silk stitches, she thought. The only pity was she had no aptitude for the task, as he had rightly guessed. For preference, she would have slipped through the door of the salon in the hopes of going unnoticed for a minute or two, but Agnes whispered to a footman to announce her, and the chance to learn what was being said was lost. All talk ceased as every gaze turned to watch her entrance.

'There you are!' Sir Henry boomed angrily. 'We thought you were hiding from us.'

Jayne dropped him a curtsey, trying to read the different expressions of those in the room. Lady Margaret and Ruth sat with heads bowed on a sofa, William and Andrew stood impassively beside Sir Henry, Sir Henry looked heated and two younger officers lingered uneasily in front of the window. 'I took Andrew's words to heart, Papa,' she said lightly, 'and decided it would be discourteous to him and his guests to appear again as a vagrant.' She flicked Andrew a smile as she rose. 'Do you approve, brother?'

'You're a sight for sore eyes,' he said, walking forward to fold her in his arms. 'Be cruel to William,' he breathed in her ear before drawing away and raising his voice again. 'Allow me to introduce my fellow officers.' He gestured to the men by the window. 'Lieutenant George Greenwood, my second-in-command; Captain Abel Poulter, who rides with us to Hampshire to take charge of his own troop; and your one-time escort'—he nodded to William—'Captain William Harrier, who will leave us at Dorchester.'

Be cruel . . . Jayne couldn't count the number of times she and Andrew had begged each other to do the same whenever they needed rescuing from their father's anger. The trick never worked on Lady Margaret, for her anger wasn't so easily diverted, but it never failed with Sir Henry, who invariably took the side of the child being savaged. Whether he would do so on behalf of a stranger, however, was anyone's guess.

She moved to the younger officers. 'I'm pleased to meet you, sirs,' she said, offering her hand. 'I trust you enjoyed the refreshments.'

'We did, ma'am,' they said in unison, taking turns to stoop over her fingers.

'You also, Captain Harrier?' she asked, turning to extend her hand to him.

He lifted it to his lips. 'Indeed, ma'am. Thank you for the trouble you've taken on our behalf. Your transformed appearance is as splendid as your food.'

Jayne responded coolly. 'You're rather more transformed than I am, sir. Last time we met you were a dashing King's man, now you're a sober-looking Parliamentarian. How so? Do your opinions change with the wind?'

Andrew answered for him. 'Captain Harrier was forced to serve under Lord Goring and he grew to detest the man. He deserted at Weymouth in order to help the garrison defend the town against rape and pillage by the most immoral troops in the King's army. We were pleased to have him, for he brought details of Goring's plans and placements.'

Jayne wondered if Andrew believed this, or if it was a story he and William had concocted. From their ease of manner, they seemed to have become friends despite the animosity of their first meeting in Swyre. 'You'll disappoint Sir Henry, Captain Harrier,' she said, withdrawing her hand. 'He thought you a man of honour when he spoke with you before.'

'How is my honour marred by turning my back on rapists and thieves, ma'am?'

'You pretended sympathy with their cause and then betrayed them. I'd not think well of Andrew if he'd sold the garrison's plans as easily. Whatever your views of Lord Goring, you surely had some feeling for his men. How many of them died as a result of your treachery?'

Sir Henry admonished her sharply. 'Mind your tongue, girl. Captain Harrier is our guest and should be treated with courtesy. We make it a point in this house to be civil to all, irrespective of belief.'

Jayne was tempted to say that, since Sir Henry had never knowingly entertained a Parliamentarian, the claim was exaggerated. Instead: 'You weren't so forgiving of Sir Edward Hamway, Papa,' she countered mildly. 'You called him a scoundrel and delivered him to the Bridport magistrate, yet I can't believe you think attempted theft worse than betraying the King to his enemies.'

Sir Henry scowled at her. 'Why this sudden love for your sovereign? You've never shown such attachment to him before.'

'I question the honour of any man who betrays his companions to the enemy, Papa. A soldier, be he Royalist or Parliamentarian, should lay down his sword before he turns spy for the other side.'

The word 'spy' was derogatory enough to attract a sterner admonishment. 'Cease immediately! I grow tired of your sanctimony.' He addressed William. 'Excuse my daughter, Captain Harrier. Her self-righteousness about her own neutrality leaves her ignorant of the struggle others have with their consciences. I confess I've had many myself since I learnt that the King was intending to employ a French army to subdue his people. Victory will have no meaning if the spoils go to France.'

William ducked his head in acknowledgement. 'There are many in the Royalist ranks who agree with you, sir, myself included when I was amongst them. Nonetheless, apologies are unnecessary. I'm aware from my previous brief acquaintanceship with Mistress Swift that she has strong views about the foolishness of war. Each of us wrestles with the rights and wrongs of it, but the Clubmen more than most, I think.'

It was a clever prompt to turn the conversation towards safer territory. The Clubmen represented a neutrality they could all embrace, since people from each side of the political divide were drawn to the movement. Sir Henry spoke of Dorset's despair at the behaviour of both armies, while Andrew explained that Parliament's recognition of this despair had given rise to the New Model Army. He listed the rules the men were required to follow, adding that strict adherence to them entitled each man to a salary and the right to name his profession as soldier.

He turned to Jayne, who had quietly withdrawn to sit on a footstool beside Lady Margaret. 'Do you approve, sister?' he asked, using the same phrase she'd used earlier.

She was tempted to tell him not to test his luck. 'How can I not?' she murmured. 'Only the most uncaring would argue that war isn't immeasurably improved by the imposition of rules.'

The irony escaped her father and brother, but a smile twitched at the corner of William's mouth. 'The hope is that the conflict will end sooner if people understand that Parliament fights *for* them and not *against* them, Mistress Swift.'

'I don't doubt it, Captain Harrier, but it's a fool's errand. Too many of my patients go hungry these days, and the only people who understand or care about their situation are the Clubmen. The New Model Army will not supplant them easily in the affections of Dorset folk.'

'And nor should we, unless we can bring an end to the conflict, ma'am. I have no quarrel with the Clubmen's desire for peace—there's not a person in the country who doesn't feel the same—but declarations of neutrality do not win wars. Only battles can do that.'

'And how many more must there be before Parliament or the King surrenders?'

William shook his head. 'I don't know, ma'am. All I can say with certainty is that Parliament's army, under the command of General Sir Thomas Fairfax and Colonel Oliver Cromwell, will conduct itself well both off the field and on it. And if that leads to ultimate victory, the peace that follows will be fair and just.'

⁓

Lady Margaret waited until she heard the crunch of boots on gravel as Sir Henry accompanied Andrew and his fellow officers to the column. 'Would you care to explain that little charade to me, daughter?'

Jayne moved from the footstool to a chair. 'Which part needs explaining, Mama?'

'Who is that man?'

Who indeed? 'If you mean Captain Harrier, you should ask Ruth, Mama. You'll have more faith in her honesty than mine.'

Lady Margaret looked at her niece in surprise. 'Are you also acquainted with Captain Harrier?'

'Hardly acquainted, Lady Margaret. I met him once at the time of Isaac's illness. He was kind enough to protect me from Samuel's anger and then convey my household and me to Weymouth.'

'*Convey?* How?'

'Lady Stickland lent us her carriage, and Captain Harrier drove it. He was most considerate, but I was so taken up with concern for Isaac that we had little conversation.'

'Why did Lady Stickland's coachman not drive the carriage?'

Ruth studied her hands.

'You can tell the truth,' Jayne said. 'Mama won't rest until you do.'

Ruth raised her head with a sigh. 'I knew him only as William,' she told Lady Margaret. 'He served Lady Stickland as both footman and coachman, though his relationship with her was unusual. She took his advice more often than is normal between mistress and servant. Today is the first time I've seen him since and, had Jayne not called him William, I would not have recognised him. He speaks and behaves quite differently from the footman I met three years ago.'

Lady Margaret turned to Jayne. 'Was he a footman when he pretended to be your brother and then presented himself here as Captain Harrier of the Corfe Castle garrison?'

'I'm doubtful he was ever a footman, Mama. Ruth spoke truthfully when she said his relationship with Lady Stickland was unusual, and you yourself thought him a person of consequence.'

'Then why did he claim to be a servant in Lady Stickland's house?'

Jayne thought back, picturing her first meeting with the indomitable matriarch. *Allow me and my footman to accompany you*, Lady Alice had said when Jayne had declared her intention of going to Samuel's house. 'The claim wasn't his, Mama. It was Lady Stickland who described him as such, and Ruth and I accepted that that was what he was.'

Lady Margaret studied her for several long moments. 'You'll need a better story than that if your father decides to question you,' she said. 'Captain Harrier had no choice but to come inside after one of the younger officers spoke his name in front of Sir Henry. His clear intention was to remain with the column, just as yours was to remain in your chamber until the visitors had departed, but Sir Henry wouldn't allow it. He was curious to know why Captain Harrier had changed sides.'

'Weren't we all, Mama?'

'Not you, daughter, and not your brother either. I believe you both know he's always been a Parliamentarian. Ruth, too, in all likelihood.'

Ruth looked alarmed. 'Not I, Lady Margaret. My knowledge of Captain Harrier is even more limited than yours.'

Lady Margaret ignored her. 'You showed too much reluctance to meet him, Jayne, and when you did you were overly harsh in your criticism. If you're lucky, your father will think you don't like Captain Harrier. If you're unlucky, he'll be wondering whether it was yourself or Captain Harrier you were trying to protect.'

'From what, Mama?'

'Questions about the propriety of your behaviour.' Lady Margaret wagged a finger at her. 'The pair of you seem to take rather more interest in each other's welfare than is usual amongst chance acquaintances, and that suggests a closer relationship than you've been describing.'

'But not as close as you fear, Mama,' Jayne said mischievously. 'Whoever and whatever Captain Harrier is, he is first and foremost a gentleman.'

'He'd better be,' said Lady Margaret tartly. 'Sir Henry will run him through, otherwise.'

In the event, the single reprimand Jayne received from her father was that she'd taken too long to change into her gown. Had she appeared sooner, he'd have learnt more about the King's most recent rejection of Parliament's peace terms. As it was, he'd had two or three minutes only to read a report which Captain Harrier carried in his saddle pack, stating that negotiations had taken place in Uxbridge during the month of February. The terms were fair to both sides. In return for keeping his throne, the King would grant certain powers to his people through their elected representatives in Parliament. The talks had been conducted over three weeks, but once again the King had refused to compromise, preferring conflict over resolution. The New Model Army had therefore been tasked with ending the war as quickly and decisively as possible.

NINETEEN

THE NEWS THAT LORD GORING had been given command of
the King's Western Army spread through Dorset and Somerset
in early May. It was greeted with alarm by Clubmen because it
confirmed their belief that the King was deaf to their pleas for
peace. There would be nothing left to the south-west if Taunton
fell and his most ruthless leader gained control of the region.

Certain that Parliament would attempt to relieve the garrison
at Taunton, Goring ordered General Berkeley and General Hopton
to subject the town and its people to constant bombardment while
he and his army continued to blockade the border between Dorset
and Somerset. By 10 May, a third of Taunton's houses had been
reduced to rubble, and the garrison retained hold only of the
castle, the church, a blockhouse called Maiden's Fort and a deep
entrenchment across the marketplace. Without food and low on
ammunition, any other commander would have surrendered, but
Robert Blake's refusal to lay down arms acted as a clarion call
of defiance to his troops. All vowed to fight and die rather than
gift hated Goring an easy victory.

Nevertheless, since there was no escape for the Parliamentarians, Goring showed no inclination to press an attack, preferring continued bombardment to assault. Known for his laziness as much as his prodigious appetites, he claimed it was only a matter of time before a mediocre upstart like Blake conceded defeat.

During the night of 11 May, Goring's most trusted informant, a man who had succeeded in infiltrating Parliament's armies, made his way to the general's headquarters—a house on the border between Dorset and Somerset. Dressed in black, and with a scarf masking his face, he went unnoticed by the guards at the front and slipped quietly down the side of the building to let himself in through the door to the kitchen quarters. More accustomed than most to moving in darkness, he trod softly around the soldiers asleep on the floor and followed the noise of drunken laughter.

Goring shook his head in disbelief at the sight of William Harrier in the doorway. They had fought together in Europe and their friendship was of long duration. 'I swear to God I'll never understand how you make your way past my guards,' he muttered, his words slurred by cognac. 'Do you come to congratulate me on my new command or chastise me for not pressing the assault?'

William removed his scarf with a grin, acknowledging the salutes of the aides who lounged along the table at Goring's side, all of whom knew him well. 'Both, but allow me to congratulate you first. Even Robert Blake is saying the war is all but over with you in control of the south-west.' He walked forward to grasp Goring's hand warmly across the tumbled bottles that littered the oak surface. 'It's good to see you, George. Have you drunk the cellar dry or is there some brandy left for me?'

Goring nudged a half-filled bottle towards him. 'How fares my dwarfish enemy?'

William raised the bottle to his lips. 'Reduced to skin and bone and filled with melancholy since I told him Fairfax is still five days away.'

Goring laughed. 'Rather longer if he's forced to confront me first. There are no easy ways around my blockade.'

'Indeed,' said William, replacing the bottle on the table and reaching inside his coat for a letter. 'But Berkeley and Hopton would rather not rely on that. I spoke with them both and they're keen to press the attack at noon tomorrow or the day after.' He handed the letter to Goring. 'Berkeley's put the request in writing, and I said I'd ride back with your answer.'

Goring dropped the letter to the table. 'What would you advise?'

William shrugged. 'It depends how eager you are to meet Fairfax. He'll keep advancing as long as there's a chance of retaining Taunton but will likely retreat if Berkeley and Hopton succeed in taking it first. His New Model Army is very green and I can't see him testing it against yours without good cause.'

'All the more reason to confront him, then. If we put the New Model Army to flight, the war is won.'

Word of Parliament's triumph at Taunton spread through Dorchester on the morning of 15 May as Jayne made her way past boisterous crowds to Lady Alice's house. She was reminded of the first time she and the matriarch had met. The crowds thronging the streets on that occasion had come to see the executions of priests, but today they were celebrating Robert Blake's victory.

Jayne had learnt the details from Timothy Ellis at the King's Head, who in turn had received them from a messenger the previous evening. The rider had paused at the tavern for a pint of ale, and his dramatic account of how the New Model Army had come to Blake's rescue gladdened the hearts of all who heard it. Yet it seemed the victory owed more to trickery than conflict. Despite Sir Thomas Fairfax marching his men seventy-eight miles in nine days in order to relieve the beleaguered town, they were still some fifty miles distant when they heard it was close to falling. Gambling that Goring would choose to track him and his army, Fairfax dispatched two thousand mounted dragoons to cover the remaining miles to Taunton at a gallop while he feinted north-west to entice Goring into pursuit.

The stratagem had worked. For reasons unknown, the besieging Royalists at Taunton had assumed the two thousand dragoons had been sent by Lord Goring to reinforce them in their attempt to storm the castle, and had then fled the field in panic when they realised their mistake. The following day, Goring, said to be ablaze with anger at Berkeley's and Hopton's incompetence, had abandoned his pursuit of Fairfax and joined his army with theirs in the hope of reinstating the cordon. But he was too late. With the garrison strengthened and Fairfax moving up on his rear, he chose sense over valour and abandoned the siege on 14 May.

Timothy had allowed Jayne the use of a chamber so that she might change from her countrywoman's garb into the same attire she'd worn on the day of Hugh Green's execution. Dorchester's Puritan leanings had returned in strength since Parliament had regained control of the town, and dark-coloured gowns with white aprons and bonnets were again the garments of choice for women. It was truly said that nothing changes, Jayne thought, as she stepped from the crowd into Lady Alice's doorway, though the only real difference between now and that morning three years ago was that today she was here by request.

Molly answered her knock and smiled to see her look warily about the hall. 'You're safe to enter, Mistress Swift. There are no soldiers this time.'

Jayne moved inside. 'You disappoint me, Molly,' she teased. 'I've yet to experience an uneventful visit to Lady Alice's house.' She allowed the maid to remove her cloak. 'Does she know you wrote to me?'

Molly shook her head. 'And I beg you to keep it a secret between us, ma'am, or she'll never trust me again. Had she allowed it, I would have summoned you sooner, but she refuses to acknowledge there's anything wrong with her.'

'She may guess why I'm here,' Jayne warned. 'It's not as if I make a habit of calling upon her without invitation.'

'I hoped my letter would prompt you to think of a reason why you might, ma'am. Another patient in Dorchester, perhaps? Milady will accept that someone called upon your services and you chose to drop in because you were passing.'

'You know full well that won't satisfy her unless I give her a name, a diagnosis and a treatment,' said Jayne, lowering her satchel to the floor. 'Bring this when I call for it,' she instructed, 'and, meanwhile, I shall attempt to convince her that I'm not a meddling physician.'

～

Jayne didn't need Molly's written description of 'tremors in the hand' and 'rigidity of face' to recognise that Lady Alice had shaking palsy. It was an incurable disease, more often found in men than women, and usually associated with advancing years. Alice did her best to hide the symptoms by clasping her hands in her lap and using her voice and eyes to express emotion, but

Jayne didn't doubt she knew what ailed her and had chosen denial over fluster and pother from well-meaning friends and servants.

She was seated near the window of her front parlour, watching the crowds outside, but though she must have seen Jayne's approach, she made no mention of it. Instead, she invited Jayne to draw up a chair beside her and asked her to relate everything she knew about the battle for Taunton. Jayne repeated what Timothy had told her, adding her own description of Robert Blake from her time in Lyme.

'I never doubted he'd hold out until a relief force came,' she finished. 'The word "surrender" doesn't seem to feature in his vocabulary. Papa heard from a Royalist friend who resides near Taunton that Blake's response to a demand during the earlier siege that he and his men lay down their arms was'—she deepened her voice—'"I have four pairs of boots and will eat three of them before we yield."'

Lady Alice's ability to laugh was not diminished and nor was her competence with speech, although the stiffness around her mouth meant her delivery wasn't as crisp as previously. 'William considers him as fine a commander as Fairfax and Cromwell,' she said, 'and that's praise indeed. He spoke unstintingly in support of both Blake and you after Lyme, Jayne. I understand you took on the management of the hospital after becoming trapped inside the town.'

'With the help of a surgeon and some fine nurses, milady. I couldn't have done it on my own.'

'I'd rather you called me Alice, my dear. Deference doesn't suit you any more than it suited William when he posed as my footman. Poor Molly had the Devil's own job teaching him to play the role of a servant.'

Jayne had had every intention of raising the subject of William herself, since curiosity about him was the only plausible excuse she could think of for her visit, and she was amused that Lady Alice had pre-empted her, if only to deflect attention from her palsy symptoms.

'He's a most mysterious person,' she said. 'One minute he's a footman, the next my brother, then a Royalist, then an aide to the Earl of Warwick and now a captain in the New Model Army. Or, at least, that was his guise three weeks ago when he accompanied my brother and his cavalry troop to my father's house.'

'He bears a rather higher rank than that, my dear, but I'm sure he had good reason to demote himself. He feared he caused problems for you during that visit. Was he right?'

In the circumstances, Jayne decided lies were justified. 'I'm afraid so, and it's why I've come to see you, Alice. Mama believes I know more about William than I do, and my inability to answer questions about him makes her suspicious. When he presented himself as a captain in the Corfe Castle garrison, she thought him a person of consequence, but since Ruth told her he was your footman, she fears he's a Puritan fortune-hunter in the same mould as Samuel Morecott.' She pulled a rueful smile. 'She takes pride in her judgement of people, and it annoys her to be wrong.'

Alice laughed again. 'Well, you can certainly quell her fears about his being a Puritan. William lost his faith in God a long time ago and regards all religion as chicanery. As to being a fortune-hunter, he'll not marry at all unless he can pay off his father's debts through his own efforts.' She studied Jayne curiously. 'Are you truly ignorant of his history?'

Jayne nodded and gave the most honest answer she could. 'All he's ever told me is that he comes from a long line of Harriers.'

Alice considered for a moment. 'The name's notorious in certain parts of Dorset, but I can't see that I'll be betraying William's trust by explaining why. He never hides who his father was.'

She went on to relate a tale similar to the one John Metcalfe had recounted to Jayne, though rather more detailed. William's father, Sir Ralph Harrier, was the only son of the Duke of Granville, but Ralph's dissolute ways had led to an estrangement between them. Alice described Ralph as both the most charming and the most disagreeable man she had ever met. It was hard to believe that two such opposite characters could exist in a single person, but she had witnessed both sides of Ralph at close quarters. He was consumed by an addiction to gambling and had sacrificed every relationship in pursuit of winning at dice and cards.

'His wife adored him, but even she couldn't persuade him to stop. It was very sad. The need to gamble was a recurring hunger that kept drawing him deeper and deeper into debt. I hoped he might try to repair his life after Estelle died and left him with William, but he didn't.'

'What caused her death?'

'The midwife cited childbed fever, but I think melancholy the more likely reason. Estelle couldn't see a future for herself or the baby after Ralph absented himself towards the end of the pregnancy. He left without explanation or farewell, and she had no confidence he would return or feel affection for the baby if he did.'

Lady Alice had begged Estelle several times to stay at Winterborne Stickland, but every invitation was met with refusal. The fragile young woman preferred to remain where her husband could find her than chance his coming and going again without her knowledge.

'I wanted to shake some sense into her,' Alice finished. 'It was a mystery to me that any woman could love a man who behaved as badly as Ralph did, but she was barely twenty years old and her tears were so heartfelt I couldn't bring myself to do it.'

Jayne watched a man turn cartwheels on the cobbles outside. 'Ruth was the same with Samuel,' she murmured. 'She would have taken him back in the blink of an eye if he'd ridden to Weymouth to apologise ... still might, if she ever sees him again. He was more handsome than ever when he came to Lyme. Was that where Ralph's charm lay? In his looks?'

Alice nodded to a bureau in the corner. 'See for yourself. There are some charcoal sketches of him in the bottom drawer which I made the summer before William was born. I intended to turn them into a portrait for Estelle, but there seemed little point after she died.'

Jayne left her chair to kneel beside the bureau. In the bottom drawer was a single scroll which, unfurled, stretched to two feet in length and showed the same face from different angles. The likeness to William was clear, though Ralph was considerably prettier than his son. 'What became of him?'

Lady Alice clutched her hands more firmly together, as if memories induced stronger tremors. 'Nothing good. When he learnt he was about to be imprisoned for insolvency, he hanged himself from a beam in his hall. He was alone in the house by then and wasn't found until a bailiff came a week later to arrest him. His estate, Winterborne Houghton, was confiscated by the court as punishment for murdering himself, and his body was buried face down in an unmarked grave somewhere along the Blandford highway.'

Jayne rerolled the page and placed it back in the drawer. 'Where was William?'

'In Oxford. I had part-guardianship of him and paid for his education away from his father. Had I not, he would have been shockingly neglected.'

'Who lives in Ralph's house now?'

'No one. It's been empty for twenty years.'

'Why?'

'Ralph's father begged the King to let it go to rack and ruin so that no memorial to his son remained. Some of the pastures have been designated common land for the local farmers but the rest is wilderness.' Alice forestalled Jayne's next question with a shake of her head. 'I've never been privy to the Duke of Granville's thoughts, but I can offer guesses. Ralph was his only son and he was greatly disappointed in him. He gave Winterborne Houghton to Ralph as a marriage gift in the hope he would mend his ways, then cut all ties with him when he learnt Ralph had raised mortgages against it within a month of receiving the deeds. I have some sympathy with the duke's disappointment, because I felt it myself, but I can't condone his bitter destruction of a fine house or the cruel rejection of a grandson he's never met.'

'Is he still alive?'

'He is.'

Jayne did some addition in her head. John Metcalfe had said William was twelve when his father died, and Alice said the house had been empty for twenty years. 'The duke must be as old as Methuselah to have a grandson past thirty.'

Alice gave a snort of amusement. 'He's two decades older than I am, which would put him in his early eighties, and I'm told he's determined to live out the war. He's a committed Royalist and expects to be rewarded when the King triumphs.'

'How?'

'With his daughter's son being granted the right to inherit his title. He's been petitioning the King since Ralph's death to allow the dukedom to pass through the good seed rather than the bad.'

Jayne eyed her curiously. 'That must upset William.'

Alice shook her head. 'Quite the opposite. He's always said he hopes the petition succeeds. He has no ambition to be saddled with a title he doesn't want.'

'Is that why he sided with Parliament—to separate himself from his family?'

'I doubt he ever thinks about them, Jayne. He has more knowledge of yours and mine than he has of his own.' Alice paused to order her thoughts. 'His views were formed by his education at Oxford and his time fighting as a mercenary in Europe. You were right about that. His fluency in French, German and Spanish comes from eight years of brutal soldiering, and the lesson he took from the experience was that a commoner's life is worth nothing to men who have power. Hence his decision to support Parliament.'

Jayne leant forward to watch a young lad swing a maid in his arms. 'He uses his father's title when it suits him. Everyone in Lyme called him Sir William.'

'Only because Warwick's fleet is full of men who fought with him in Europe. He served the Protestant Union as Sir William Harrier in order to make his fortune, and the heir to a dukedom can earn considerably more than a humble farmhand. Has he ever introduced himself to you as Sir William Harrier?'

Jayne smiled. 'Never, but it might have helped me with my mother if he had. Sir William Harrier has a better ring to it than footman to Lady Stickland, particularly as I'm still quite ignorant as to why that impersonation was necessary.'

A twitch lifted the edge of Alice's mouth. 'In William's life, every impersonation is necessary, Jayne. He said you guessed he was a spy the first time you met him. Was he wrong?'

'I certainly guessed he wasn't what he said he was, but as to being a spy'—she shrugged—'I only came to that conclusion when he played the role of my brother for Sir Walter Hoare.' She paused for a moment. 'To be a spy is an unusual position for a man to hold. How did he come by it?'

'The Comte de Guiche recognised his skill for crossing lines in Europe and recommended him to Lord Warwick. In advance of the war, he was tasked with estimating Royalist strength across the south-west; now he works to assist towns under siege through the passing of information.'

'Both ways?' Jayne asked, recalling Timothy Ellis's account of how the Royalists at Taunton had mistaken the garrison's reinforcements for their own.

Alice nodded. 'There were as many Royalists fighting for the Protestant Union as there were Parliamentarians, and most regard William as a friend. The life of a spy isn't easy, Jayne. They know more of betrayal than loyalty.'

Jayne was tempted to repeat John Metcalfe's phrase that the apple hadn't fallen far from the tree, since betrayal seemed to have been Ralph's weakness also. 'That still doesn't explain why he posed as your footman, Alice.'

'I'm the only family he has, my dear. When he's not on his travels, he prefers my company to being alone. As a footman, he's of no interest to anyone, but we'd have drawn unwelcome attention to ourselves if he'd tried to pass himself off as an intermittent guest. Good Puritan widows don't entertain young male strangers who prefer to arrive in darkness.'

Jayne gave an involuntary laugh. 'Do you even have Puritan views, Alice?'

'When it suits me. I'm not so principled that I can't pretend to share the belief of others if the cause merits it.'

'The cause being William?'

Alice nodded. 'He's my son in all but name, and he's very necessary to Parliament's cause. Without his work, the likes of Warwick, Blake, Fairfax and Cromwell wouldn't be so well informed about their enemies' movements.' She paused. 'William senses you're moving towards support for Parliament. Is he right?'

'Not at all, since that would suggest I had Royalist leanings previously. I am where I was three years ago, wishing a plague on all warmongers and longing for the war to end.'

'I shall be sure to tell him that the next time I see him.'

Jayne reached out to place her palm on Alice's trembling hands. 'Will you also tell him that I'm upset he didn't ask me to offer you my services? He could have whispered concern for you three weeks ago in my father's house, but said nothing. Must I find out by accident that you have shaking palsy?'

Alice sighed. 'I can't abide fuss and swore him to secrecy on the matter. My father suffered the same, and the disease is as incurable now as it was then.'

'Indeed,' Jayne agreed, 'but there are ways to mitigate the effects and slow its progression. Will you allow me to try at least?'

She remained three days with Alice, administering infusions of henbane and St John's wort, and teaching Molly to knead and smooth an ointment of lavender oil into the muscles of her mistress's face, neck, shoulders and limbs. These were methods that Richard had used successfully to relieve the sudden strange tension that came upon a patient, causing both tremors and rigidity, and she saw the beginnings of the same benefit in Alice by the end of the second day. The matriarch had yet to reach the stage where walking became a slow shuffle, but Jayne hoped the early and continued application of remedies would delay its onset.

By the third afternoon, Alice was delighted to find that the tremors in her hands had reduced enough for her to hold a piece of charcoal, and she begged Jayne to sit for her. 'It's three months since I drew or painted anyone and it would please me to capture your likeness,' she said.

She asked Molly to fetch her easel and paper and then positioned Jayne in such a way that the light from the window fell across her face. Once started, she spoke hardly at all, and Jayne was given a sense of how such sittings must have worked when Gilbert Jackson was alive. It was easy to imagine how a handsome, garrulous actor might hold a subject's attention while Alice worked unnoticed behind him, for it was intolerably tedious to remain immobile without even the distraction of conversation.

Her position, facing the window, allowed her to watch the comings and goings in the street outside. The revelry over Blake's victory had passed, but there were enough people going about their daily business to keep her reasonably entertained. At one point, she caught a glimpse of a familiar figure walking along the pavement on the other side, and she gave a start of surprise when she recognised Samuel Morecott. Ignoring Alice's sharp reprimand, she surged to her feet to watch his tall figure disappear down a side street.

'You're a shocking fidget,' said Alice crossly. 'Do you ever sit still?'

'Not often,' said Jayne, returning to her seat. 'Why is Samuel in Dorchester? This time last year, he was Parliamentary surveyor for the south-west. Has he a different appointment now?'

'I prefer not to speak when I'm sketching.'

'I'll fidget less if you do.'

'Tiresome girl! Your mother should have taught you patience.'

'She did try.' Jayne smoothed her skirt. 'Now tell me about Samuel.'

'Only if you promise not to ask questions until I've finished. There's no capturing a mouth if it's in constant motion.'

'I promise.'

The story took time to tell because Alice kept breaking off to stare at Jayne before leaning forward to make strokes on the paper. Samuel had returned a month previously, having forfeited Denzil Holles's patronage, and was now trying to restore himself in the eyes of his former friends—without success. News of his indiscretions had reached Dorchester long before he arrived, and he found himself turned away from every door.

'Our Member of Parliament is a prolific letter writer,' Alice murmured, using the point of her finger to smudge a soft shadow. 'I doubt there's a leading Puritan who hasn't been informed of Samuel's wrongdoing. I'm told his first approach was to the commander of the Dorchester garrison in the hope of enlisting in the New Model Army, but he was summarily refused because of his bad character.'

She went on to express some sympathy for the foolish creature. London was a dangerous place for inexperienced young men from the country who thought they knew a card sharp from a gentleman and a woman of easy virtue from a lady. For all the surface prudery in the city, the corrupt underbelly was as vibrant as ever. Ralph had been similarly seduced by it the first time he ventured up to the capital, preferring the taverns and bawdy houses of the back alleyways to the straitlaced salons of the worthy.

'If Samuel's beliefs had been formed through conviction rather than to serve his ambition, he might have shown more strength. As it was, he squandered money on women and gambling and then used his patron's name to raise more. Holles tells me he's run up debts of close to a hundred pounds with no expectation of paying them off.'

She went on to say that Samuel would have been wiser to take himself to a town where he wasn't known. Denzil Holles might spend his time in London, but he was still the Member for Dorchester and knew the value of keeping his electors close. His strongest warning had been against lending money to the now disgraced recipient of his patronage.

She canted her head to one side to stare again at Jayne's face. 'Whatever Holles's other faults, he's not an adulterer. He married a new wife barely three years ago and took grave exception to hearing that his name was being cited in brothels.'

An involuntary smile played across Jayne's mouth.

'No smiling! Think of what your poor cousin must have had to put up with. If Samuel's appetites are as uncontrollable as they appear, she will have been forced to submit a great deal more often than she would have liked. Puritanism is a perfect excuse for men like Samuel to demand obedience of their wives in matters of the bed.' She straightened. 'I believe I've finished.'

'May I see?'

Alice turned the easel to face Jayne. There was only one image, and Jayne was startled by it. She had expected a demure and pretty face to look back at her, as in the portraits that had been painted of her mother, but instead she was gazing at something far less flattering. Indeed, but for the fact that Alice had sketched in the top of her sleeves and bodice, she would have thought the strong jaw and searching eyes were those of a man.

Alice chuckled. 'You don't look pleased.'

'I hoped I'd be prettier than Ralph, at least.'

'Thankfully not. I despise prettiness. You have strength, character and honesty in your face, my dear, which are far more attractive. When I look at you, I see a person I want to know. When I looked at Ralph, I saw a carefully constructed mask. Had I sketched him truthfully, I would have drawn him with the horns of the Devil, but Estelle wanted only the likeness she saw—a man of beauty. Your cousin Ruth is the same: Samuel's looks blind her to the reality of his nature.'

Jayne glanced towards the window. 'She's not alone in that, Alice. For all the judgements I've made of him, I never took him for a libertine. If anything, I would have said the opposite, that the fact he's sired only one child with Ruth meant he had little interest in lying with his wife. Are you sure the tales about him are true?'

'Very sure. I wrote to Denzil Holles for verification and the details he supplied conformed with the assessment William made of Samuel at the time of the priest's execution. Power excites him, particularly over those too weak to offer a challenge. According to Holles, he treated the women he bought in London extremely roughly, and I'll warrant he was as brutal with your cousin.'

Jayne had little difficulty believing this side of his character. All weak-minded bullies used cruelty to impose their will. 'Where's he living?' she asked.

'At the same address as before. The house has been vacant since the Royalists left. Your uncle should have found new tenants, Jayne. Samuel has nowhere else to go and will not be removed easily.'

Jayne took leave of Alice the following morning, but rather than return immediately to the King's Head she made her way to High East Street. She told herself she intended merely to look at the outside of her uncle's house and assess its condition, but the temptation to knock on the door grew greater the closer she came. Nothing would please her more than to find Samuel living in poverty; his pride could never survive the knowledge that every Swift would learn of his fall.

She came close to feeling some of the sympathy Alice had expressed when he opened the door and she saw hope in his eyes. Visitors must be rare, she thought, if a simple knock allowed him to dream that his fortunes were about to change. His sallow skin and hollow cheeks suggested he hadn't eaten for several days, and he'd lost all the prettiness he'd had in Lyme, with even his hair beginning to recede.

'What do you want?' he demanded.

'Confirmation that you're living here, Samuel. I was surprised to hear of it and am certain my uncle will be also.'

'You're meddling in matters that don't concern you,' he muttered.

'As you did in Lyme, Samuel. I've neither forgotten nor forgiven how you tried to destroy my character with Colonel

Blake. Consider my meddling a small return for the spite you showed me.'

He looked up and down the street, as if to reassure himself she was alone, and then, without warning, grasped her wrist and spun her past him into the shadows of the hall. For all his appearance of weakness, he was stronger than she was and had no conscience about slamming her against the wall and pressing his forearm to her throat. And as his hot, vile-smelling breath swamped her nostrils, Jayne thought of Alice's words. *Power excites him.*

TWENTY

STANDING IN THE DARKENED HALL with Samuel Morecott's arm against her throat, memories of the clutching hands and leering faces on the Bridport road came flooding back. But this time, far from disabling her, the memories served only to spur Jayne to action, for she'd rehearsed what she should have done that day so often in her mind that her response came as naturally as breathing. If Samuel had expected resistance, it certainly wasn't in the form of caterwauling, globules of spit and two sets of nails raking the sides of his face. He made an attempt to grab her wrists but, in doing so, released the pressure on her throat, and with nothing to hold her against the wall, she thrust against him, using all her pent-up rage to propel him backwards.

Her screaming was incessant, as were her kicks, slaps and spittle, and he was so shocked by her behaviour that he retreated of his own accord. Seeing the fear in his eyes, she knew that was why she'd come. To take revenge for being made to feel afraid on the highway. He lifted his hand in protest, as if to say he didn't deserve such treatment, but Jayne had already drawn the razor-sharp blade that she kept sheathed in a discreet leather pouch on the side of her satchel. She raised it to the level of his neck.

'You'll bleed to death in five minutes if I cut you here,' she said, pointing the tip at the artery that carried blood to his head. 'It was the wound the soldiers of Lyme favoured, for it never failed to kill.'

Her voice was husky from caterwauling, and Samuel clearly took it as a sign of tiredness, because he made another attempt to catch her wrists. But he signalled his intention too obviously, and his clumsy attempt to grasp the hand that held the knife resulted in a slice across his palm and then another across the knuckles of his right hand as he reached instinctively to clasp his left in pain.

Jayne angled the tip towards the centre of his neck. 'Or perhaps I'll sever your windpipe and deprive you of air. I can't think of a better revenge for your son than to leave his father to die slowly in darkness, gasping for breath.'

He ran his tongue across dry lips. 'If I thought you had a heart for murder, I'd invite you to do it.'

'You shouldn't test me, Samuel.'

Even as she spoke, she heard the sound of footsteps behind her in the corridor, and saw Samuel's eyes widen in relief.

'Will you help me, sir?' he cried. 'I see you wear the emblem of a colonel, so you have the authority to arrest this woman. She has no cause to threaten me in this manner.'

'I doubt that, Mister Morecott,' said William's voice. 'In my experience, Mistress Swift always has good reason for what she does.' He drew alongside Jayne. 'Are you well, ma'am?'

She cast him an ungracious glance. He was wearing the uniform of the New Model Army, with a soft felt hat in place of a helmet. The crown boasted a badge which she assumed was the emblem that Samuel had recognised. 'Quite well, thank you, and in no need of assistance.'

'I can see that,' he agreed.

'Then what are you doing here?'

'Alice was so convinced you'd come that she sent Molly to ask me to follow you. I caught a glimpse of you being whisked inside and then heard your screams. I felt obliged to respond, if only for Alice's sake.'

'Were you in her house all the time I was there?'

He shook his head. 'I had some unfinished business in Taunton and only returned to Dorchester last night.' He nodded to her knife. 'Do you intend to pin Mister Morecott against the front door indefinitely, or will you allow me to escort you out through the kitchen? I tend to agree with him that you don't have the heart for murder.'

'I'm sorely tempted,' she said, 'but he's so lacking in friends his body won't be found for days and the stink will upset the neighbours.' She stared hard at Samuel's face but, with his back against the door, he was too much in shadow for her to see it clearly. With a shrug, she replaced the bloodied blade in its pouch and elevated William from colonel to knight in order to further intimidate Samuel. Fortunately, despite William's face showing beneath his hat, Samuel didn't seem to recognise him as the footman of three years ago. 'Allow me five minutes to inspect the house, Sir William. My uncle will want to know what state it is in.'

'By all means. You have my guarantee that Mister Morecott will not move from this spot until you're ready to leave.'

She began with the kitchen. The outer door stood open, which must have been how William had entered, but there was no inner door from the corridor, and the mangled state of the hinges suggested considerable force had been used to rip it free. This was the room where Samuel was living, for a niggardly fire smouldered in the hearth and a mattress lay on the floor beside it. Some stale crusts of bread sat on the windowsill, but the pantry was as empty as it had been three years ago when Mary told her she had no money to purchase food. Did Samuel regret his meanness now? she wondered. There was surely no truer saying than 'as you sow, so shall you reap'.

The sound of a scuffle broke out behind her, quickly followed by a thud and a whimper of pain. Jayne looked along the corridor, and saw Samuel lying on his back with William's boot pressed across his throat.

'Mister Morecott forgot his manners,' William informed her. 'He seems to think all women are as free with their consent as the harlots of London.'

'It's his preferred slur,' Jayne said, recalling the terms Samuel had used against her and Ruth the last time she'd been in this house. She returned to the hallway and stared down at Samuel's face. From above, the ulcers about his nose and mouth were more obvious, and that annoyed her, for she had no wish to feel sympathy for him. 'It might be better to let him breathe unless you plan to murder him yourself.'

William raised his foot a half-inch. 'Are you ready to leave?'

'Not yet.' Jayne walked into the doorless front room and took in the absence of furniture and the remains of ripped wooden panelling on the walls. Through an open archway which led to a smaller chamber, she saw the same destruction of the panelling there and what looked like the splintered leg of a stool on the floor. She sighed as she returned to the hall. 'Everything made of wood has gone, presumably because it's cheaper to burn someone else's doors and furniture than purchase logs. Is this your doing, Samuel?'

'Answer,' William instructed when Samuel remained silent.

'No,' he rasped. 'It was the work of the Royalists who were quartered here.'

Jayne hardened her heart against his symptoms of thinning hair, ulceration of the skin and fevered eyes. All men knew the danger of lying with prostitutes. 'My uncle will still hold you responsible, Samuel. One of the conditions for your continued receipt of Ruth's allowance was that you maintain his house. He will want to know what plans you have to repair and refurnish it.'

'None. I'm without funds, having forfeited the allowance when I moved to London.'

'It was paid for several months afterwards,' she reminded him. 'Joseph wasn't aware you'd left until I informed him his house was full of soldiers. But for that, you'd be stealing his money still. It was never your intention to tell him how complete was your abandonment of his daughter and grandson.'

'It was they who abandoned me, and if I use the law to reassert my rights as a husband, they'll be forcibly returned to me.' With a sudden effort, Samuel made an attempt to thrust William's boot aside, but the raising of his hands served only to draw Jayne's attention to the red rash on his right palm. William's boot didn't move.

'You may hope for such an outcome, Samuel, but it won't happen. Ruth's single reward for being an obedient wife was the birth of her son, and nothing will persuade her to imperil his life again. She'll go into hiding before she submits to your tyranny a second time.'

'I doubt you know her as well as you think you do.'

Jayne lifted her satchel from her shoulder and lowered it to the floor. 'It matters not. My uncle has lodged a case for legal separation before the ecclesiastical court. On Ruth's behalf, he's arguing that three years of abandonment, following months of abuse and cruelty, merit a writ of "divorce from bed and board", and once the ruling is given, you'll never see her or Isaac again.'

She made no mention that the case was in writing only and had never reached the court. Joseph and his lawyer pursued the matter from time to time, but, since a wife was expected to accept her lot, requests on behalf of women rarely received attention. She dropped to a squat, the better to see the ulcers at the corner of Samuel's mouth, and then pulled her satchel onto her lap.

'I confess I came here to gloat at your fall from grace, Samuel, but despite your assault on me, I find myself moved to charity from what I've seen of your circumstances.' She removed her purse. 'Allow me to give you five shillings to mitigate your poverty. It's the same amount I gave your cook to feed your household and should keep you alive a few days more.'

She expected a response, but received only indifference.

'I'm ready to leave now,' she told William, placing the crown on the floor and rising to her feet. 'If Mister Morecott's wise, he'll use a portion of my money to purchase mercury pills from the barber surgeon. They cannot cure his disease, but they may slow the ulceration of the skin, particularly about the nose and mouth. There's no surer way for a man to display his immorality than to be seen to have chancres eating at his face. It's been known for a century that the infection can only be caught through sexual congress with a sufferer.'

For once, William's composure was shaken. 'Are you saying he has the great pox?'

Jayne nodded. 'Richard calls it by its Latin name, "syphilis". It's common in soldiers coming back from the European wars.'

William seemed undecided about whether to release Samuel or crush the life out of him. 'He would have passed it to you if you hadn't defended yourself.'

'Most certainly.'

'And now seeks to infect his wife.'

'He'll not be allowed near her,' Jayne said firmly. 'Once my uncle learns of his condition, he'll demand the court has him examined by a physician. Ruth, too, if necessary. I can guarantee she's free of syphilis, so, since Samuel is showing clear evidence of the malady, it will prove both his adultery *and* unsuitability as a husband.' She saw a strange little smile play across Samuel's mouth. 'What have I said that's so comical?' she asked.

'God must love me more than I thought to send you as my advocate, cousin. You've always despised me, so I don't say it wouldn't have amused me to give you the pox, but my only intention in bringing you inside was to urge you to silence without passers-by hearing what I said.' He shifted his attention to William. 'Allow me to stand. This woman will do more damage than she knows if she speaks out of turn. You have my word I'll not cause trouble for either of you.'

William exchanged a glance with Jayne then, upon receiving a nod, lifted his boot and stepped back. Even so, it was several seconds before Samuel was able to summon the energy to pull himself into a sitting position, and from there to a kneel and finally to his feet. He used the wall of the corridor to support himself and addressed his speech to Jayne.

'Let's be done with pretence. I'm told this period of the disease will soon be over and that I might live a few years more before blindness and madness take hold. Is that correct?'

Jayne nodded.

'And your preferred choice is that my father-in-law uses my disease in order to dissolve the marriage and keep his daughter safe?'

She nodded again.

'It'll not work. Nothing will bring Ruth back to me faster than to learn of my illness. Whatever unhappiness I've caused her will count for nothing beside her marital vows to cherish me in sickness and in health. She may even believe that by making me dependent upon her, we can rekindle some affection for each other. Would you agree that this is an accurate reading of her character?'

Frighteningly accurate, Jayne thought. Ruth's heart was never softer nor more generous than when she felt needed. 'It depends whether she's willing to forgive the manner in which you contracted the disease, Samuel. You can be sure I shall tell her.'

'You'd be wrong to do so. She forgives everything, and learning of my infidelities won't cure her.' He steadied himself against the wall and searched Jayne's face with fevered eyes. 'If you truly want to protect her and the child, you must stay silent about finding me here. I have an offer for her father . . . but that, too, you must keep from Ruth, for it will come to nought if she learns of it.'

The intensity of his gaze suggested sincerity, but Jayne recalled how easily he'd used a show of honesty to impress Ruth's parents. 'Why should I make myself party to your deceits, Samuel? You were right when you said I have only contempt for you.'

A tremor of emotion ran through him. 'For Ruth's sake.' He cupped his hands in entreaty. 'My only wish is to let her and the child live in peace.'

Jayne felt William stir in irritation at what he took to be a blatant untruth, but, for herself, she wasn't so sure. There was something very compelling about Samuel's insistence that Ruth remain ignorant of both his presence and his disease. 'If those are your feelings, why did you come back to Dorchester? News of you was bound to reach her eventually.'

'I had nowhere else to go when I lost—' He broke off abruptly as William stirred again. 'It's of no importance. I knew this could only end one way.' He searched Jayne's face again. 'Will you take my offer to Joseph?'

'I can't say until you tell me what it is.'

'Inform him that he can purchase my death for one hundred pounds. I know of a corrupt minister in Southwark who will record it in his parish register for a small fee and then notify my wife of my passing. I will ask that he names the cause as consumption. This will allow Ruth to marry again and leave me free to act as I choose under a different name. Make Joseph understand that this will be the best solution for everyone.'

One hundred pounds—the amount of his debt. 'What guarantee can I give him that you won't turn up like a bad penny when you've spent the money?'

'The evidence of your eyes. Do I look as if I'll be strong enough to do this again in even a year's time?'

He did not, but Jayne knew from reading Richard's records that sufferers could live for more than a decade after showing the sort of symptoms Samuel had. Nevertheless . . . 'I will do as you ask,' she said. 'If Joseph agrees, I shall request Sir William to deliver the money tomorrow and then escort you to the London road. Should you fail to honour your side of the bargain—namely, a letter to Ruth within the next month, announcing your death—I shall send bailiffs to find you. Are we agreed?'

'We are.'

William, clearly questioning Jayne's naivety in accepting Samuel's word, intervened. 'I stand witness to this agreement, Mister Morecott.' He punched one gauntleted fist into the other. 'And I advise you to honour your pledge, for it will be I who comes after you if you fail Mistress Swift, not timid Dorsetshire bailiffs who don't know one end of London from the other.'

Perhaps it was the smack of leather against leather that jogged Samuel's memory, because his eyes widened with sudden recognition. 'I know this man,' he told Jayne, levelling a trembling finger at William's face. 'He misleads you if you think him a gentleman. He was a mere footman when he threatened me before.'

Jayne passed the strap of her satchel over her head and settled the bag against her hip. 'You're mistaken, Samuel—but then you've always been a poor judge of character. I suggest you remember that when you feel tempted to break our agreement, because I have absolute faith in Sir William. If he says he will find you, he will.'

She moved aside to allow William to open the front door and stepped out onto the street. When the door had closed behind them, she placed her hand on William's arm and set out to forestall a lecture on misplaced trust.

'I'm *most* impressed to learn you're a colonel,' she said playfully. 'The last time I saw you, you were a mere captain.'

He eyed her with amusement. 'Your brother didn't think your father would accept that a Royalist traitor could hold a higher rank. But was it necessary to be quite so cruel to me? Had Sir Henry not taken me to his bosom, I would have felt entirely bereft of Swift friendship.'

'Consider it retribution for all the lies you've imposed on me,' she said severely. 'After Ruth informed my mother that, far from being a Royalist captain from Corfe, you were merely a servant in Alice's house, Mama has decided you're the worst kind of fortune-hunter.'

'How mortifying,' he murmured. 'Are you saying my efforts to appear uninterested in the value of your father's furnishings have been wasted? He has a particularly fine Correggio above his mantel, but I've made a point of averting my gaze from it each time I've visited.'

She pinched his arm. 'If I repeat that to my mother, you will be barred from our house forevermore.'

'You're not so unkind, Jayne.'

'Don't wager on it. I'm not happy with you for staying quiet about Alice's condition.'

He answered seriously. 'She fears becoming an object of pity. I gave my word I wouldn't speak of it with anyone.'

'As did Molly, but she thought better of it.' Jayne slowed as they turned off High East Street and would have released his arm had he not trapped her hand beneath his. 'We should go our separate ways from here,' she said. 'I need to make haste if I'm to speak with Joseph.'

'Will he agree to the proposal?'

She avoided a direct answer. 'Assuming he does, it will be in the form of gold sovereigns. May I meet you at Lady Alice's house tomorrow to give them to you?'

William urged her to keep walking. 'Walls have ears,' he said, 'and you're speaking too freely. Have you considered the weight of such a sum in coins? My estimate would be close to ten pounds, and you'll have to carry it the two miles from the King's Head.'

'I manage my satchel well enough.'

'Which has leather pockets to separate the bottles. A heavy sack that rattles with each step you take will tell every passing thief you have something worth stealing.'

'Would you be happier meeting me at the King's Head?'

'I'd be happier escorting you to Weymouth and taking charge of the money myself.'

'Joseph won't trust you if I'm the only person vouching for you.'

'Colonel Sydenham will stand pledge for my honesty. He's governor of Weymouth in all but name, and your uncle knows him well.'

'I'd rather not involve anyone else.'

They had reached a crossroad, and this time it was William who drew to a halt. 'Including your uncle, perhaps? Do you even intend to go to Weymouth, Jayne?' When she made no answer, he nodded to a house on the far side of the street leading to the right. 'We can talk freely in there, if you're willing to enter through the kitchen quarters and without a chaperone.'

She followed his gaze. The property was neatly proportioned and stood alone between two rows of terraced houses. 'Who owns it?'

'I do, but in the guise of a fabric merchant who's away more often than he's at home. Trade gives me a reason to travel far and wide without questions being asked. My neighbours are used to my comings and goings through the front door, but the kitchen quarters are my preferred route of entry when I'm in uniform and want to pass unnoticed.'

Jayne thought her description of William to Lady Alice as 'a most mysterious person' could not have been more accurate. Whenever she thought she was familiar with every compartment of his life, he provided a new one to confuse her.

Receiving a nod of agreement, he escorted her across the road and into a narrow alleyway bordered by walled gardens on either side. After passing upwards of ten properties, he lifted the latch on a wooden gate and ushered her into a small yard, shaded by a wide-spreading apple tree laden with blossoms. Such gardens rarely held more than a well and a herb bed, and she wondered who had planted the tree, and whether the privacy it offered was the reason William had purchased the house. It certainly lent weight to his assertion that entry through the rear would escape notice.

Perhaps recalling her fear in the bakery, he motioned her to stand aside as he pulled a leather thong from around his neck and bent to insert the key that hung from it into the padlock on the door. Once opened, he pushed the panelling wide and entered ahead of her, leaving her to decide for herself if she wanted to follow. She was too curious not to. The idea that William had a home of his own in Dorchester had never occurred to her, but it explained how he had transformed himself so quickly from merchant to cavalier in order to confront Sir Walter Hoare inside Alice's house.

The interior was what one might expect of a fabric merchant. In the room beyond the kitchen, bolts of wool and silk stood on their ends about the walls while two or three lay across a table in the middle. Beside them were a pair of shears and a measuring stick, and even though the only light in the chamber came from a shuttered window, Jayne could see that the tools were as dusty as the fabric they purported to measure and cut.

She followed William along the corridor to the parlour and found it to be as functional as the fabrics room. Shelves piled with what looked like scrolled receipts and a desk covered with ledgers, quills and ink gave all the appearance of an office, although the fine layer of dust over everything would have told anyone suspicious of William's activities that no trade had been done here for a long time.

'You must have very dull neighbours,' she said. 'Aren't they puzzled about why you never sell anything?'

He shook his head. 'They know me to be an importer rather than a shopkeeper. As far as they're aware, I do my business at the ports, receiving cargo off arriving ships and then arranging delivery to the customer.'

Jayne gestured to the scrolls. 'And these are the orders and receipts to prove it?'

'Indeed.'

'Are they genuine?'

He smiled. 'In so far as they were written by me and are good enough to stand scrutiny.'

'Has that ever happened?'

He pulled forward a chair for her. 'Only when the Royalists took Dorchester. Carnarvon demanded proof of my merchant status before granting me continued and unfettered passage through the town gates, and his aides were so impressed by what they found here, he placed an order with me.'

Jayne seated herself. 'For what?'

A laugh escaped his mouth. 'Cloth for Royalist uniforms. I was able to acquire twenty bolts from a company of weavers in France who supply the Comte de Guiche. A ship brought the cargo to

London, and from there it was transported by wagon to the tailors of Oxford. It's the only order I've ever fulfilled.'

Jayne found the irony as amusing as he did. 'Were you paid for the service?'

He lowered himself to the chair behind the desk. 'In a manner of speaking. The King's treasurer sent me a bill of exchange in the amount I requested; however, I've yet to find a banker willing to accept it. The King's credit isn't trusted even in Royalist strongholds such as Oxford and Cornwall.'

With the light from the window falling on his face, he bore a strong resemblance to his father, though his square jaw lacked the softness of Ralph's. 'Did you pay the French weavers?' she asked.

The question bordered on rudeness, but William, perhaps guessing the reason for it, opened a drawer in the desk and removed a piece of paper. 'I did, and this is their receipt.' He pushed it towards her. 'I believe in honouring my debts, Jayne.'

She read what was written but, since the amount was recorded in French louis d'ors, she had no idea what the sum represented. 'Can you afford to lose so much?'

'I don't propose to make a habit of it. My ambition has never been to earn my living through trade. The fruits of my soldiering are spread across the floors upstairs, and are worth considerably more than a handful of louis d'ors.'

Jayne would have loved to ask what those 'fruits' were, but she felt she'd been rude enough already. 'Perhaps Parliament will honour the King's bill of exchange once the war is won?' she suggested, pushing the receipt back across the desk.

William replaced the paper in the drawer. 'It warms my heart to hear you say the victory will be Parliament's, Jayne. I'd hate to think I'd wasted the last three years on a doomed cause.'

He rested his arms on the desk and leant forward to study her closely. 'Now be kind enough to answer my questions as honestly as I've answered yours. How do you propose to conjure up one hundred pounds for Samuel Morecott?'

'I can't. The most I can give him is ninety.'

'*You* can give him?'

'It's of no matter who provides the money, William, only that he's made to understand there can be no more. You're better equipped to persuade him than I, which is why I sought his agreement that you deliver it.' She shrugged at his immediate shake of his head. 'Then I'll deliver it myself. I've earned it fairly and may spend it as I choose.'

'It's a bare hour since you clawed his face and pointed a knife at his throat.'

'He shouldn't have put his hands on me.'

'Quite so, but that doesn't explain why you want to reward him for it.'

Jayne studied him for a moment. 'Think of it more as an incentive to honour his promise to make Ruth a widow within the month.'

William shook his head again, but this time in irritation. 'You're being remarkably naive, Jayne. He's been extorting money from Joseph since he married her, and leopards don't change their spots. He's playing you for a fool. Can't you see that?'

She smiled. 'Not as clearly as you do, seemingly.' She pulled her chair forward to rest her own arms on the desk. 'According to Alice he's been in Dorchester for a month, but as far as I'm aware none of my family knows he's here . . . and I doubt we'd ever have known if I hadn't seen him in Church Street.'

'Meaning?'

'If his intention was to take money from Joseph, why didn't he visit him as soon as he arrived, instead of presenting himself at the garrison with a request to enlist in the New Model Army?'

'I wasn't aware he had.'

'Alice said it was the first approach he made, and when the commander refused him he went to High East Street, where he appears to be living on stale bread crusts. But why starve himself, when he could have contacted Joseph at any time these last four weeks? He had no expectation that I would turn up and, even if he did, why ask only for the amount that will settle his debts?'

'How do you know what he owes?'

'Alice told me.' Jayne took a moment to recall her thoughts when Samuel, who knew Joseph could afford more, had stipulated a mere one hundred pounds. 'Richard says there are three ways to cope with the knowledge that you have a killing disease. The first is to close your mind to it and continue to live your life as normal, which is Alice's choice; the second is to give way to melancholy, which is the choice of those, usually the poor, who've never had reason to hope; and the third is to use your remaining time to make amends for past mistakes and offences. I believe the last is Samuel's choice.'

A twitch of cynicism lifted the corner of William's mouth. 'On what evidence?'

'The reason he gave. He wants his wife and son to live in peace.' Jayne shook her head at his expression. 'Your father's situation was similar, William, and Alice tells me you've been living with the consequences of his insolvency ever since. I'd hate the same to happen to Isaac when there's something I can do to prevent it.'

He studied her thoughtfully. 'Go on.'

'I'll count my money well spent if it means Samuel can expunge his debts and buy an untarnished death from a corrupt priest. As long as the Morecott name remains unsullied, Ruth can grieve as a widow should, and Isaac will be free to fashion whatever memories he likes about the father he barely knew. Is that not a goal worth pursuing?'

William folded his hands beneath his chin. 'Only if your wild assumption that Samuel intends to pay his creditors is correct. He said nothing to suggest it, so I don't share your faith that it will happen. And if you're right to draw a comparison between him and my father, he'll squander your ninety pounds at the gambling tables within an hour of returning to London. Is that how you want your hard-earned savings to be spent?'

Jayne gave a rueful smile. 'I may be wrong about that, but do you see no merit in my other arguments?'

Briefly, William returned the smile. 'Not enough to let you do this,' he said, pushing back his chair and rising to his feet. 'If you'll permit me to sort the matter for you, you'll return to Swyre, say nothing about seeing Samuel, and I'll endeavour to achieve the outcome you want without the forfeiture of your savings.' He moved around the desk and offered his hand to assist her from her chair. 'Will you trust me on this, Jayne?'

She rested her fingers on his in the full—and somewhat surprising—knowledge that not only did she trust him completely, but she was grateful to have the responsibility of Samuel's future removed from her. 'You know I do,' she said.

⌐⌐

A few days later, Jayne received a letter from William, enclosed in one from Richard Theale, dated 22 May.

Dear Mistress Swift,

I write in haste from Bridport before continuing on to Taunton. You were entirely correct in your belief that Samuel wishes to redeem himself. His preferred choice is to fight for what he believes in and, to that end, I have recommended him for enlistment in an infantry regiment currently stationed near Leicester. Mercury pills are diminishing his chancres, and be assured he is as intent as you said he would be on honouring his debts.

> *Your servant,*
> *William Harrier*

TWENTY-ONE

Swyre, Dorset, 2 July 1645

JAYNE THOUGHT SHE WOULD ALWAYS remember this war for
the shouts of warning that echoed around the house each time
soldiers approached along the driveway. It was a circumstance
that had become increasingly frequent since the Royalists' defeat
at Taunton. Deserting infantrymen had rampaged across the
countryside in search of food, only to be met with short shrift
by Dorsetshire Clubmen, who were now so well organised they
acted more like an army than a rebellious uprising.

Jayne's normal response to the alarums was to watch from
a window as Sir Henry and his field hands dispatched the
encroaching thieves with pitchforks and clubs, but today she was
occupied with a gangrenous wound on her brother Philip's thigh.

Philip had arrived two weeks previously, barely conscious, and
was carried into the house by a tearful Benjamin, who had laid
him on a sofa in the salon and begged Jayne to save him.

Jayne's immediate response had been to shoo her mother, Ruth and Isaac from the room before taking Philip's wrist in her hand and asking Benjamin what ailed him. She learnt that Philip had received a pike thrust to his upper leg four days earlier at Naseby. The battle had been lost but Philip and Benjamin had avoided capture by retreating with the King's cavalry to Leicester. Once there, Benjamin had bound the wound himself, having sought in vain for a surgeon to stitch it, then, fearing infection, had made the decision to bring Philip home. The two-hundred-mile journey had taken three days, with Benjamin supporting Philip in front of him on the final day and leading the spare horse on a rein. He'd wanted to look for a competent doctor in a town along the way, but Philip had refused, saying his sister was the only physician he trusted.

It was a misplaced trust, Jayne thought, as she removed his britches and cut away the filthy dressing. The tip of the pike had ripped a ragged six-inch gash up the side of his right thigh, and the effort of riding had caused it to gape and putrefy. The lightest touch on the swollen livid skin around the injury caused shudders of pain to run through Philip's body, and Jayne would have diagnosed gangrene even without the foul odour that permeated the air.

The single ray of hope was that he wasn't blue-lipped and shivering, which he would have been if poison was flooding his system. Richard had taught her that blighted flesh was preferable to blighted blood, being curable by amputation, but she had little confidence that Philip could survive the necessary severing and sawing of flesh and bone so close to his hip.

She ushered Benjamin into the hall and asked Ruth to find food for him, then instructed her father to send one rider to Lyme to seek out Alexander and Susan Hulme at the hospital on the Cobb and beg them to attend with haste upon Mistress Swift at Swyre, and a second to Bridport with the same request of Doctor Theale. In both cases, the messengers should ride at speed and state that Mistress Swift needed urgent help in treating a patient with gangrene of the thigh. She tasked Agnes with overseeing the moving of Philip's bed and her father's bathtub downstairs to the salon, her own maid with bringing her satchel, and her mother with the boiling of kettles and the preparing of clean dressings. Finally, she commanded them all to mend their anxious expressions so that Philip would feel pleased about coming home.

'He'll wish he'd stayed away otherwise,' she said. 'He expects cheerful sounds in this house, not the gloomy reticence of church.'

In the time it took Richard and the Hulmes to receive her summons and make their journeys, Agnes and Kitty stripped Philip of his stained and soiled garments, moved him to his bed and transformed the salon into a hospital by pushing the furniture against the walls and swabbing the floor of every last speck of dirt and dust. Jayne ordered footmen to carry the table in from the hall and bring a keg of salt from the kitchen, then instructed six of the maids to fill her father's bathtub with one-third boiling water and two-thirds cold.

Philip's whole body needed cleansing—she questioned if he'd bathed once in the last three years—but she doubted he was strong enough to take the shock of cold water. He was thinner than she'd ever known him, as indeed was Benjamin, so, while she and Agnes assisted him into the bath, she sent Kitty to ask the cooks to make some nourishing broth. She expected Philip to cry out when the salt stung his ulcerated flesh but, whether through bravery or because he'd lost feeling in the wound, he merely closed his eyes and released a small sigh of pleasure to be in warm water.

Jayne replicated the treatment she'd given Prince Maurice—fifteen minutes of immersion followed by three-quarters of an hour of natural drying—and Philip was close to his fourth period in the bath when she heard the sound of hooves through the window. She hastened outside to speak privately with whoever had come. It was one thing to tell others to hide their anxiety, quite another to maintain a smile on her own face for three hours.

Finding the newcomer was Richard, she clutched his hands with relief and poured out her concerns in a whisper. She hadn't told Philip what ailed him, but she believed he'd guessed from the smell that it was gangrene. His melancholy demeanour certainly suggested this. She had summoned Alexander to perform an amputation if Richard advised that this was the only course, but she begged Richard to try a different cure if he knew of one, for she was certain Philip would choose death over life if he was unable to walk or ride again.

Richard assured her he'd come prepared for such an eventuality, gesturing to a bulky sack that his mounted escort was lowering carefully into the hands of a footman. Richard wore his own satchel across his shoulder and, after instructing the footman to follow with the sack, he urged Jayne to lead him to the patient.

It is truly said that a trouble shared is a trouble halved. Jayne felt the weight of the world fall from her shoulders as Richard conducted his own tests on Philip. He agreed with Jayne that the blood seemed healthy, and his examination of the wound confirmed her diagnosis of gangrene. He explained this to Philip in a matter-of-fact way, adding that he didn't think the putrefaction was so advanced it couldn't be stopped.

'Which isn't to say you'll like the cure, young man,' he finished cheerfully. 'I know of only one way to cleanse a gangrenous wound like yours and that's to infest it with maggots. They have a taste for rotten flesh but none at all for the healthy. You'll also be at your sister's mercy for the next several weeks, since she'll be under instruction to keep you immobile in this bed until the danger of reopening the scab has passed.'

'Will I be able to walk at the end of it?'

Richard nodded. 'With a limp. The wound will widen and become impossible to suture, and whatever skin you manage to grow across it will be too thin and brittle to flex, leaving you with permanent stiffness in your leg. As for riding, I suggest you ask your father to have his groom school your mount to take instruction from your left knee and foot, since you'll have little or no control through the right.'

A tired smile lifted Philip's mouth. 'Then you may set as many maggots on me as you like, Doctor. I'll consider myself blessed to have a stiff leg rather than a dismembered one.'

The sack contained a glass bell jar with a writhing mass of maggots in its base. Richard told Jayne he began experimenting with the creatures after reading a report from a French surgeon in the previous century who noticed that wounded soldiers infested with maggots seemed able to recover from gangrene of their own accord. There appeared to be no logic to it, and yet Richard's first experiment, on a man with a gangrenous foot, proved it true. Always alert to the need to amputate should the attempt fail, he was astonished by the man's recovery. Since then, he had used the method successfully three times.

He acquired the maggots from a farmer's wife who cultivated them to provide nourishment for her hens. Reluctant to feed the birds corn which could be sold at a profit, she placed rotten meat in pails and harvested the myriad maggots that emerged from it. It was her belief that flies created the maggots, since bluebottles were always the first to visit the pails, and Richard concurred, for he had seen for himself that a maggot became a fly when it was left undisturbed inside a bell jar, though he had yet to discover how or why.

Had Jayne not trusted Richard, she could never have brought herself to touch the disgusting creatures, let alone insert them into Philip's wound. Her mind was in complete revolt against the idea that anything so repulsive could have a beneficial effect, and Alexander and Susan Hulme expressed the same disbelief when they arrived an hour later, though they consented to watch and wait until all were agreed that amputation was the only way to save Philip's life.

When Jayne couldn't hide her pleasure at seeing the Hulmes again, Richard had urged her to take them outside in order to catch up on news from Lyme. Philip needed only one medical practitioner in attendance at a time and Richard was happy to be that person for the next few hours. They found Sir Henry and Lady Margaret standing anxiously in the hall, and Jayne took the opportunity to introduce them to Alexander and Susan. In normal circumstances, a barber surgeon and his wife, being of the tradesmen class, would not have received such a formal presentation, but Jayne had spoken of them so frequently that both her parents greeted them warmly.

The Hulmes were touched to be treated with such courtesy and gave a good account of themselves in face of the many questions Sir Henry and Lady Margaret asked. So much so, that Sir Henry never expressed doubt again when Jayne spoke of the commitment of Lyme's men to holding the town for Parliament or the bravery of her women. He took more convincing that maggots might be an effective cure for gangrene, but accepted Alexander's assurance that an amputation would be performed the following morning if no improvement was seen overnight.

Nonetheless, he expressed unhappiness when the couple declined Lady Margaret's offer of a bed for the night, saying they had patients in Lyme hospital requiring attention. They pledged to return posthaste on the morrow if word came from Mistress Swift that an operation was needed.

Seeing that Sir Henry would prefer them to remain, Alexander gestured to Jayne. 'Your son is enjoying the services of the two best physicians in west Dorset, Sir Henry. My skill is to reduce men to half what they were before gangrene attacked them, and I beg you not to wish that wretchedness on Philip. The pain and shock of amputation are so severe that half don't survive the operation, and those who do become crippled in both body and mind. There's little enjoyment in life when an entire leg is removed, and if your daughter is willing to support a treatment which might prevent that, then so should you.'

Sir Henry fixed him with a piercing gaze. 'I'm not used to being lectured so forcefully, Mister Hulme. However, I shall do as you suggest and pray that you will not be called upon to make this journey again.'

Alexander bowed. 'I meant no offence, sir.'

Sir Henry answered with a bow of his own. 'None taken. It's rare for a father to learn from a stranger that his pride in his daughter is justified.'

358

Jayne had been touched by Alexander's praise, but she worried he'd given her parents false expectations of the maggot remedy. For herself, she had little confidence it would work and had been ever ready to call Alexander back for the tried and trusted method of amputation. Yet in the two weeks since the disgusting creatures had first been inserted into the wound, the gangrene had slowly diminished, and Jayne's anxiety for Philip had lessened by the day. Now, she was so sure the infection was in full retreat that there was room in her mind to be curious about why shouts were sounding in the house.

She urged Benjamin, who was lounging in a chair at the side of Philip's bed, to move to a window and tell them what he saw. She expected him to report ragged infantrymen in search of food, and was surprised when he described five cavalry officers dressed in the uniform of the New Model Army; but rather more surprised to see an expression of relief cross Philip's face.

'What haven't you told me?' she asked, picking maggots from his wound with a pair of tweezers and placing them on a plate.

'Nothing.'

She held a maggot close to his mouth. 'Tell the truth or you'll eat this for breakfast.'

Benjamin spoke from the window. 'We're deserters,' he said. 'I didn't ask leave to bring Philip home because I knew it wouldn't be granted, and our names will have been posted by now. If we're found, the best we'll get is a whipping and a reduction to the ranks; at worst we'll be hanged as an example to other officers. We've seen several such executions already.'

'Does Papa know?'

Philip shook his head. 'We're too afraid to tell him. He calls us his courageous sons and won't understand that neither of us wants to go back. We were weary of this war even before Naseby . . . wearier now that we've had two weeks of peace. This leg gives me an excuse not to fight, but Benjamin has none and I'll not let him return alone.'

Jayne placed the plate on the table and picked up a magnifying glass. 'You needn't fear Papa's response,' she said, stooping over the wound. 'He struggles with his own conscience over his support for this war, and he'll struggle even harder if he has to take responsibility for yours as well. He knows you only enlisted to please him.'

Benjamin watched the approaching horsemen halt before Sir Henry and his labourers. 'We should have done what Andrew did and waited,' he said morosely. 'He chose the better cause in Parliament. Naseby became a rout once Cromwell brought his cavalry onto the field. We call them Ironsides, because they're impossible to defeat, and Papa is about to find that out for himself. If these five demand entry, there'll be nothing he can do to prevent it.'

Jayne plucked a maggot from the deepest part of the gash. Like the rest, it had grown fat on its diet of necrotic flesh and she marvelled anew at how quickly the gangrene was being consumed. Richard had instructed her to replace the maggots with fresh ones every four days, as the creatures ceased eating on the fifth and grew a brown casing. To that end, he sent a carrier with a new colony each time they were needed, requesting that Jayne return the dormant maggots so that he might study and dissect them in order to discover how they became flies.

That morning's delivery had been accompanied by a note. *These I have cultivated myself from bluebottles which hatched from the first batch I brought you. A most interesting experiment! Would you believe that flies lay little white eggs on rotten meat?*

Jayne had scribbled in reply: *Philip makes such good progress, I'm willing to believe anything.*

She began seeding the new maggots around the edge of the wound where shreds of necrotic flesh remained. 'You'd not have lasted a week if you'd chosen Andrew's course,' she said mildly. 'The first time Papa called either of you a coward, you'd have rushed to enlist to prove him wrong. Andrew withstood two years of insults before he made the decision to leave.'

'Father has great admiration for him now,' said Philip. 'He praises Andrew's courage more than he praises ours.'

Jayne shook her head. 'You hear what you want to hear because you believe you've failed him, but you have my word that Papa makes no distinction between his sons.'

Benjamin gave a gasp of surprise and stepped hurriedly away from the window. 'We'll soon find out,' he said with a tremor in his voice. 'Father's bringing these men inside and one of them is Andrew.'

'Why should that trouble you?' asked Jayne.

'The man beside him is Oliver Cromwell. I know his face, for he took the field at Naseby without his helmet to show how little he feared us.'

*

When Jayne was summoned from the salon to meet her father's visitors, she was careful to close the door before bobbing a curtsey to each in turn. She was interested to see Cromwell in person, for he looked nothing like the picture her imagination had painted. She had expected him to be handsome and imposing, but, though six feet tall, he had limp sandy hair, unsightly warts on his forehead and an overly large nose. His most remarkable feature was his intelligent grey-green eyes, which assessed her as quickly as he was said to assess the enemy's disposition on a battlefield.

She dropped a curtsey. 'General Cromwell,' she murmured, having learnt his new title from Andrew's introduction. 'You do us a great honour.' She turned to those she recognised without need of introduction and offered each her hand. 'Colonel Harrier . . . Captain Metcalfe . . . Colonel Blake.' She smiled as Blake kissed her fingers. 'It's a joy to see you, sir. Are you well?'

'Never better, Mistress Swift.'

'And quite recovered from having to eat your boots in Taunton?'

He released her hand with a laugh. 'Thankfully, the New Model Army came to our rescue before that disagreeable meal was forced on me. Sir William rode through the night to tell me that relief was coming, and your brother and Captain Metcalfe arrived a few hours later at the head of two thousand mounted dragoons. I've never been so pleased to see friendly faces. We were near done by the time they arrived.'

Jayne saw the look of surprise in her mother's eyes to hear William given a title. 'You couldn't have asked for more accomplished reinforcements,' she said warmly. 'We hear nothing but good about the New Model Army. Isn't that so, Papa?'

'Indeed! Indeed!' boomed Sir Henry. 'Rumour has it the war's almost won since your Ironsides routed the King's cavalry at Naseby, General Cromwell. Can we expect peace before the summer's out?'

'With God on our side, anything is achievable, Sir Henry.'

'I pray you're right, sir.'

'I'd rather you prayed for Parliament's victory, sir. The war cannot end unless one side triumphs over the other.'

'Quite so,' said Sir Henry, looking to his wife to save him from having to drop to his knees and make the prayer there and then. Cromwell's reputation for godliness was second only to his reputation as a commander.

Lady Margaret stepped forward. 'Will you partake of refreshments in the parlour, General Cromwell? We have some fine ale, cheese and bread, and even as I speak, a haunch of beef is being turned on the spit.'

Andrew stirred. 'The salon is more befitting a man of General Cromwell's standing, Mama. He will think you inhospitable if you relegate him to a smaller room.'

Cromwell corrected him. 'I have simple needs and will be quite content with bread and cheese in the parlour, Lady Margaret.'

Jayne, seeing the mortification in her mother's face, spoke for her. 'You wouldn't wish to be in the salon, sir,' she told him. 'I've converted it into a hospital in order to treat a young man with a gangrenous wound on his thigh, and both the cure and the smell are unpleasant. It's for this reason alone that Lady Margaret offered the parlour.'

'The only treatment I know for gangrene is amputation. Are we keeping you from performing such an operation?'

'No, sir. I'm applying maggots to the necrotic flesh. My patient has no choice but to consume food in their presence, but all others prefer to eat elsewhere, myself included.'

Cromwell was taken aback. '*Maggots?*' he echoed. 'These gentlemen led me to believe you were an accomplished physician, Mistress Swift, not a dabbler in witchcraft.'

Jayne smiled. 'It's hardly witchcraft, sir. My tutor, Doctor Richard Theale of Bridport, has used the method successfully four times, and since writing of it to fellow physicians—both here and on the Continent—has learnt that it was known in Italy three centuries ago. The mystery is why the idea was abandoned, because the results I'm seeing are extraordinary. My patient has been undergoing the treatment for two weeks and the threat of amputation has now passed.'

'Do you believe this?' Cromwell demanded of William.

'I'm sure Mistress Swift will allow you to see for yourself if you're interested, sir. I confess I'm intrigued to see a cure that does not involve amputation.'

Believing Cromwell would be more suspicious if she refused him entry than if she allowed it, Jayne ignored her father's warning frown. She also saw merit in being honest about who was in the salon, since Andrew's surprise to see Philip and Benjamin would be obvious. 'May I alert the patient first, Sir William? He and his brother tell me they saw General Cromwell on the field at Naseby, and they'll be nervous about receiving him here, particularly in the company of four Parliamentary officers'—she glanced at Andrew—'one of whom is as closely related to them as I am.'

Andrew's eyes widened. 'Our *brothers*?'

Jayne nodded.

'Which is wounded?'

'Philip. Benjamin tried to find treatment for him in Leicester, but the conditions were so squalid he decided to bring him home. They're no danger to General Cromwell, for neither is armed, but I will ask them to give their parole if he requires it.'

Cromwell placed his hand on his sword-belt. 'Do I gather your family's loyalties are divided, Mistress Swift?'

'Only in respect of which side we chose at the outset of war, sir. In all others, our loyalty to each other is unwavering and we look forward to burying our differences once peace comes.'

His pale eyes studied her closely. 'Which side did you choose?'

'Neither, sir. My job is to save life, not encourage those who seek to destroy it.'

He seemed to approve of her answer, for he unbuckled his sword-belt and instructed his companions to do the same. 'Paroles are unnecessary,' he said, laying the weapon on a chair. 'Please assure your brothers we come in friendship, Mistress Swift, and ask permission for us to enter. I'm as curious as Sir William to see this maggot remedy of yours.'

There followed a strangely convivial two hours spent entirely in the salon, during which General Cromwell spoke as freely to Philip and Benjamin as he did to his own officers. To such an extent, indeed, that Benjamin's fear to see him arrive gave way to pleasure at being in his company, since Cromwell was clearly more at ease with military men than their civilian counterparts.

Jayne withdrew after she'd described the improvement the maggots had effected and the necessity of keeping the wound clean, leaving Philip to explain that weakened muscles and thin inflexible skin were preferable to the loss of his leg. She joined her mother and Ruth in the kitchen to assist in the preparation of refreshments, grateful that the presence of the cooks and maids meant Lady Margaret couldn't quiz her about William's apparent elevation to knighthood. The servants' chatter was entirely about Oliver Cromwell. They'd all heard rumours that Sir Thomas Fairfax and the New Model Army had been quartered in Dorchester for the last two days, but who would have thought that General Cromwell would want to visit Swyre?

'It's a mystery indeed,' declared Lady Margaret, dispatching Agnes and Kitty with tankards of ale and instructions to ask Sir Henry if he thought the general happy to remain in the salon. 'I wonder if we have you to thank for it, daughter, since you're acquainted with all four of his aides.'

Jayne looked at her in surprise. 'That's no reason for him to visit us, Mama. It's more likely they're on their way to Lyme, and Andrew begged the opportunity to pause in Swyre. Three of the four fought in defence of the town and will have told General Cromwell of the people's heroism.'

She realised she'd said too much when her mother favoured her with an ironic smile. '*Three* of the four?' Lady Margaret murmured. 'Remind me to listen more closely when you speak, daughter. I could swear the only names you've mentioned in connection with the garrison are Colonel Blake and Captain Metcalfe.'

Ruth, busy arranging cheese on a plate, came to Jayne's aid. 'Surely not, Aunt Margaret,' she teased. 'I've lost count of the people Jayne has talked about. Tell us again of the women who dressed as men to scare Prince Maurice into thinking the town was packed with soldiers, cousin. The maids and I love that story so much we could listen to it every day.'

~

Jayne never admired her mother so much as when Sir Henry required her to be gracious to his drunken friends. She had watched Lady Margaret repulse advances from men so addled with ale and brandy they didn't know if they were coming or going, but she rarely embarrassed them so badly that they dared not visit again. She seemed to take a harsher view of what she perceived as William's advances to Jayne, however, frustrating every attempt he made to speak with her.

On the third such occasion, he begged Lady Margaret's permission to walk with her and Jayne outside. 'I have a message from Lady Stickland which I promised to give your daughter, ma'am. The matter is delicate, for it concerns her illness, but not so delicate that another lady cannot hear it.'

He truly was a master of guile, Jayne thought, as Lady Margaret gave grudging assent. Only the most hard-hearted woman would refuse such a request, though she wondered if William was ready to be quizzed about it.

'How did Lady Stickland know you were coming to Swyre?' Lady Margaret asked as they emerged onto the forecourt, shaking her head when he offered her his arm.

'It was her idea, ma'am. I took General Cromwell, Colonel Blake, Captain Metcalfe and your son to meet her yesterday, and she thought it beyond chance that five of the six people in the room had reason to be grateful to your daughter. She urged us to break our journey at Swyre when Colonel Blake persuaded the general that a visit to Lyme would be worth his while.'

Lady Margaret eyed him sternly. 'What reason do you have to be grateful to Jayne, sir? Did you use her services in Lyme?'

He was relieved she'd added a second question because he had no acceptable answer to the first. 'I did not, ma'am, but many others did, including Colonel Blake. They all speak very highly of her'—he smiled at Jayne—'but none so much as Jack Young, whose knee was shattered by a cannonball. Your daughter took such care to minimise the scarring on his cauterised stump that his skin is smooth and he feels no pain when he walks with a peg. He asked me to thank her for it the next time I saw her.'

Jayne clapped her hands with pleasure. 'Did you take the peg to him yourself?'

He shook his head. 'I had it shipped. He wrote to me after he'd given it a month's trial and included his gratitude to you. I expect to see him this evening and will tell him how pleased you are at his progress.'

Lady Margaret intervened before Jayne could answer. 'I seem to recall Andrew telling us you were with Lord Goring's army before defecting to Parliament at Weymouth, sir, so which side were you fighting for nine months earlier at Lyme?'

'Parliament, Lady Margaret. The same I've supported since the war began.'

His honesty surprised her. 'Then you were lying when you presented yourself as a Royalist the first time you came to this house?'

'Not entirely, ma'am. My allegiance to Parliament has required me to masquerade as a Royalist several times over the last three years. Lord Goring considers me to be one of his closest friends, which allowed me to confuse him about Parliamentary strategy before Weymouth and Taunton. But I apologise most sincerely if my different guises have caused you or your husband offence.'

'Your offence is against my daughter, sir,' Lady Margaret said sharply. 'How long have you been asking her to lie for you?'

A smile twitched at the corner of William's mouth. 'I don't believe I ever have, ma'am, but I'm sure she'll correct me if I'm wrong.'

Lady Margaret rounded on Jayne. 'Well?'

Jayne knew her mother's memory to be razor-sharp and doubted that William's answer would suffice. 'The only occasion I can recall is when you posed as my brother, sir,' she reminded him. 'We both lied to Sir Walter about that, as indeed did Lady Stickland when I introduced you as Captain Swift. Thankfully, she gave no hint of recognition when she saw you, but it was a dangerous moment, nonetheless, since she was more in need of your protection than I was.'

William nodded. 'I'd forgotten.'

Lady Margaret clearly expected him to say more, and when he didn't, she addressed Jayne again. 'I need a fuller explanation than that, miss. The story you spun your father at the time bore no relation to the one you've just given.'

'I'm aware of that, Mama, but you'd have had no story at all if Sir Walter hadn't pursued me to Swyre and seen the real Captain Swift.' She took her mother's hand. 'I would have told you I'd treated a patient in Lady Stickland's house and that would have been the end of it, because you and Papa are always so good about honouring my promises of discretion to the people I tend.'

Lady Margaret squeezed her fingers. 'You're a tiresome child. At least tell me why Lady Stickland needed protection from Sir Walter.'

Jayne considered for a moment. 'I don't see any harm in doing so,' she said. She looked enquiringly at William. 'Do you, sir?' Receiving a shake of the head, she offered a story nearer to the truth. 'He brought armed dragoons to her house, took her and her servants prisoner and then struck her when she tried to explain that the Doctor Swift he'd ordered her to summon for a patient who needed treating was a woman. To protect herself and her household from worse beatings, she wrote the summons and then begged her maid to get word of their plight to Sir William. He waylaid me before I reached the house and, together, we devised a plan that would keep everyone safe, myself included.'

Lady Margaret glared at William. 'You and Lady Stickland had no business endangering my daughter, sir.'

'The choice was mine, Mama,' Jayne said mildly. 'Would you have had me turn my back on Lady Alice and her maids out of fear for myself? I don't recall you running and hiding when Sir Edward Hamway was threatening Papa.'

'But it makes no sense,' Lady Margaret protested. 'How did Sir Walter know your name?'

'He learnt it from Sir John and Lady Bankes and then pressed Sir John's sister to summon me.'

'But why *you* rather than a Dorchester physician?'

'He thought I was a Royalist.'

A long silence followed, ended finally by William.

'I believe enough time has passed for you to give the patient's name, Mistress Swift. Your mother will understand Sir Walter's threats better if you do.'

'I cannot, sir, for I gave my word never to speak of the matter.'

'But I did not,' he said gently, before turning to Lady Margaret. 'The patient was Prince Maurice, ma'am, and his aides were so desperate to keep the reason for his wound secret they sought for a discreet physician to treat him. It was their good fortune that the physician Lady Alice provided was your daughter, because there's not a doctor in Dorchester who could have drawn the poison from the wound as effectively as she did. However, it was Mistress Swift's *ill* fortune that the care she gave a spoilt prince encouraged him to become enamoured of her. Out of fear that Sir Walter had followed her to Swyre, Lady Alice begged me to do the same in order to thwart any designs Prince Maurice had upon her.'

Lady Margaret took several long moments to digest this wealth of information and then asked the same question that was in Jayne's mind. 'Why would his aides want to keep the reason for his wound secret? Was it shameful?'

'It was, ma'am, and of value to Parliament if the story became known, though I believe Sir Walter was equally keen to keep it from the King. His Majesty wouldn't have approved of his nephew being so drunk that he killed one of his own colonels for daring to question the wisdom of allowing his troops to steal from the people of Dorset.'

Jayne's surprise was obvious to her mother. 'Is that the truth?' she asked.

'It is, ma'am. The colonel had only a dagger with which to defend himself, and the wound he inflicted on the prince was small compensation for being run through by a sword.'

Lady Margaret was shocked. 'It sounds like murder.'

'Indeed, milady, for that is what it was. Colonel Burleigh was a decent man who didn't deserve to die in such a fashion.'

'Then why have we never heard about it? Was Parliament informed?'

'Not that I'm aware of.'

She seemed even more shocked. 'Why not, if you knew it? Does your support for the cause fluctuate as easily as your rank and title, sir?'

William bore her hectoring with patience. 'Only where your daughter and Lady Alice are concerned, ma'am. They decided the best way to protect themselves from Sir Walter and his dragoons was to pretend they didn't know who the patient was. The ploy served them well. They were released without harm and have been left in peace ever since, though I doubt that would have happened if the story had become common knowledge. The prince is known to bear grudges.'

Lady Margaret eyed him thoughtfully. 'On that we can agree. I haven't forgiven him for sending Sir Walter to blame Jayne for his defeat at Lyme.' She seemed to reach a sudden decision. 'You had a message from Lady Stickland, Sir William. Do you wish to deliver it in private?'

'That won't be necessary, Lady Margaret. I have the same confidence in your discretion as I have in your daughter's.' He ducked his head to Jayne. 'Lady Alice sends her regards, Mistress Swift, and asks me to tell you that the infusions of henbane and St John's wort, coupled with Molly's unremitting kneading of her muscles, now allow her to hold a paintbrush without trembling. She has no illusions that her shaking palsy is cured, but the symptoms are currently so mild she has embarked on two new portraits: one of Sir Ralph and one of you. She says yours will be the prettier and hopes that comforts you.'

Jayne smiled. 'Please tell her it does, Sir William.'

'She further asked me to express her condolences to your family on the death of Mister Samuel Morecott at Naseby. I trust his wife received notification of his death from the army chaplain?'

'She did, sir, and it warmed her heart to know he died bravely.'

'Be sure of it, ma'am. He was part of an infantry brigade which resisted Prince Rupert's initial charge, and such was his courage in stepping into a breach and rallying his comrades that his name was mentioned to Sir Thomas Fairfax. He sacrificed his life with honour, and his wife and son may rightly remember him with pride.'

Jayne held out her hand. 'Thank you, Sir William. For Ruth and Isaac's sakes, I bless the man who gave Samuel a chance to prove himself. I truly believe a glorious death is the one he would have chosen had he known he was destined to die young.'

He touched his lips to her fingers. 'It's what all soldiers wish, Mistress Swift,' he murmured, before bowing to her mother and taking his leave.

TWENTY-TWO

SIR HENRY REGALED HIS FAMILY with his views on General Cromwell after their visitors had left. He thought Cromwell overly dour, and questioned why he was so adored by his men. Philip and Benjamin said it was because he knew how to win. Soldiers couldn't care less how their leaders carried themselves as long as they secured victory. Predictably, this prompted Sir Henry to ask how they felt about their own leaders, and both admitted they had a low opinion of them.

Benjamin went further and said he wasn't surprised that Colonel Blake had beaten Prince Maurice at Lyme and Lord Goring at Taunton. Jayne was right to admire him, for he was older, wiser and more experienced than either of those commanders. In the next sentence he confessed to bringing his brother home without permission, stating apologetically that he and Philip felt they had enlisted on the wrong side.

Philip intervened immediately. 'The fault was mine more than Benjamin's, Father,' he insisted. 'It was I who persuaded him to enlist and I who first spoke of desertion. He bears no blame unless it's a sin to want to help his brother.'

Sir Henry moved to the window and stared across the forecourt. 'Let him who is without sin cast the first stone,' he murmured. 'I imagine we've all made choices we now regret.'

'Not Andrew,' said Benjamin. 'I've never seen him look so well nor so sure of himself.'

'His brother officers were the same,' agreed Philip. 'General Cromwell may be as dour as you describe, Father, but I can say, hand on heart, that none of the King's generals would have spoken with two Model Army soldiers in the open, decent way that General Cromwell did with Benjamin and myself.'

'He could hardly be rude to you in front of your brother's family.'

Lady Margaret raised her head. 'Cease cavilling, Henry. Once you conquered your fear of being infected with Puritanism, you were as impressed by him and his companions as your sons were. We all noticed the pleasure you took in Colonel Blake's company.'

When he didn't reply, Benjamin spoke again. 'I thought Colonel Harrier the most interesting. Andrew said he's been at every major siege in the south-west of England. Did you know him in Lyme, Jayne?'

Such an innocent question but with so many pitfalls! A simple shake of the head would have sufficed were Lady Margaret not already aware of William's presence in the town. 'I believe I came to know everyone in Lyme eventually,' she answered carefully.

'Was he part of the garrison?'

'Not at the beginning. He was an aide to Lord Warwick and arrived with the fleet towards the end of May. He was tasked with bringing three hundred seamen ashore to join the soldiers on the Town Line when Colonel Blake feared the garrison wouldn't be able to hold it.'

Lady Margaret saw a frown of puzzlement gather on Sir Henry's forehead and stood up, beckoning to Ruth and Jayne to come with her. 'I need your help in the kitchen or we'll have nothing to eat this evening,' she told them. 'Visitors are all very well but they make a shocking mess of my arrangements.'

She ushered them through the door and closed it firmly behind them.

'Upstairs to my chamber,' she ordered Jayne before turning to Ruth and asking her to oversee the preparation of food. 'I need an undisturbed hour with your cousin, my dear. Are you willing to say we're outside if Sir Henry comes looking for us?'

Ruth exchanged a glance with Jayne. 'Should I?' she asked.

'It might be best,' Jayne answered wryly. 'It won't take long for Papa to remember that Lyme came before Weymouth, and I doubt I'll survive a quizzing from both my parents at the same time.'

Once the door of Lady Margaret's chamber had closed, Jayne was obliged to report the details of every meeting she'd had with William, including the last with Samuel. In addition, she gave a full account of what Alice had told her in May—William's father's name and disreputable character, William's service abroad, his work for Parliament, and his disinheritance by the Duke of Granville—though Lady Margaret was more interested in Samuel. The whole family had been curious about him since Ruth had received notification of his brave death.

'From the way you thanked Sir William, I gather it was he who gave Samuel a chance to prove himself. But why? Did you ask him to?' She wagged a finger when Jayne didn't answer. 'Sir Henry will put the same questions to you, miss, and he'll bar Sir William from the house if you allow him to believe that your friendship with this man runs so deep he's willing to do secret favours for you.'

Jayne attempted a diversion. 'I doubt he'll come back, Mama. My guess is he'll stay with Cromwell until the war ends and then pursue his ambitions in London.'

'Don't be absurd, child; he has too strong a liking for you. If you don't return his regard, then allow your father to savage him. If you do, tell me about Samuel.'

Jayne smiled at this blatant bid to elicit her feelings. 'Are you looking to matchmake, Mama?' she teased.

'You've done all the matchmaking that's necessary, daughter,' Lady Margaret responded dryly. 'The only question is to what end. Would you choose a pauper with a tarnished name for a husband?'

Jayne avoided a direct answer. 'I'd leave William to argue his case with Papa and see which of them won, but it wouldn't be fair on Andrew.'

'Why not?'

'I suspect he owes his position on Cromwell's staff to William. They seem to have become firm friends since Andrew declared for Parliament.'

'Your father won't like that either,' Lady Margaret warned. 'He'll see friendship with your brother as a deceitful way to gain access to you.'

Jayne knew her mother wouldn't stop until she received an explanation. 'Very well,' she said with a sigh, 'I'll tell you what you want to know, but you must promise not to repeat it to Papa. Neither he nor Uncle Joseph has ever been able to keep a secret, and it will upset Ruth greatly to learn the truth.' She took her mother's nod for agreement and went on to relate every detail of her meeting with Samuel and her conversation with William afterwards. 'We left it that William would speak with Samuel again, and he promised to let me know what was decided through Richard. I received a letter from him a few days later.'

'Why Richard?'

'Papa would have questioned anything addressed to me in a hand he didn't recognise.'

'Are Richard and Sir William acquainted?'

Jayne nodded. 'For some time.'

Lady Margaret shook her head. 'I can't believe there's so much we haven't known. What was in the letter?'

'Very little. You may read it if you like. William said merely that Samuel had enlisted in an infantry regiment and his debts would be honoured. It was a later letter from Richard that was more enlightening. He said the means to settle the debts was the bill of exchange that William received from the King's treasury. Richard managed to sell it for half its value to one of his Royalist patients in Bridport and then sent the money to Samuel's creditors in London.'

Lady Margaret was more shocked than grateful. 'And what does Sir William expect from you in return for this generosity?'

'Nothing, since Richard wasn't supposed to tell me about it, and only did so when I began to doubt the debts would ever be paid.' She smiled at her mother's disbelief. 'I don't know what else I can say to persuade you, except that William did it for Isaac and not for me. He knows better than anyone the difficulties of living with the memory of a worthless father.'

Lady Margaret studied her curiously. 'Aren't you worried about that? There's no truer saying than "the apple doesn't fall far from the tree".'

Jayne was tiring of that adage. 'I worry about it all the time, Mama. I dread the day when I wake to find I've become as prejudiced against Puritans as Papa, and so keen on tapestry that I'm happy to sit at your side, chatting nonsense with ladies for hours on end.'

Lady Margaret smacked her wrist. 'There's no need to be rude. It was a fair question and one your father will ask when I try to explain Sir William to him. What am I to say?'

'The truth,' Jayne suggested. 'That he tolerated your discourteous questions with gentlemanly patience. It's a pity you've never met Lady Stickland. You'd understand him better if you had.'

'How so?'

'She's been his parent and teacher since the day of his birth. If he takes after anyone, I would suggest it's Alice. They're very alike.'

'Sir Henry won't accept that as a recommendation. He's disliked her ever since you told us she was a Puritan.'

'But a very unorthodox one, Mama. She reads the plays of Shakespeare more often than she reads the Bible.'

⌒

Jayne wasn't party to her mother's 'explanation' of William to her father, but she guessed it ran along the lines of 'don't stir up a hornet's nest unnecessarily'. The country was at war, Colonel Harrier might never return, and Sir Henry surely had enough faith in his daughter to know she wouldn't behave foolishly with any man, let alone one she'd believed to be a servant until recently. If she were that way inclined—as Jayne had pointed out to Lady Margaret herself—she'd have caused them trouble from the moment Sir Henry allowed her to ride alone to visit patients.

Whatever the explanation, Jayne was grateful Sir Henry remained silent on the subject. His desire to see her wed to a suitable partner had been a bone of contention between them for years. Ever since Jayne had turned sixteen, he'd seen off anyone he considered beneath her while parading her like a prize cow before the sons of his friends. His disappointment when she or they expressed indifference had led to interminable lectures about her behaviour. She must refrain from conversation with the clever ones who shied away from intelligent women, and show kindness and tolerance to those who hadn't progressed beyond learning to read and write.

Mercifully, the war had brought an end to this nonsense, but she didn't doubt Sir Henry still harboured hopes that she would find a suitable husband eventually. As Andrew had said at the time Sir Walter Hoare left his letter for her, Jayne should sink to her knees and thank God that Sir Henry had taken such a dislike to him, since an aide to the King's nephew represented everything he wanted in a son-in-law—a title, wealth and, above all, royal connections.

Some two weeks later, Sir Henry received news that Fairfax and Cromwell had routed Lord Goring's army at Langport in Somerset. The message came in a letter from a Royalist friend who described the battle as 'the most supine and unsoldierly defeat ever seen'. Goring's cavalry had broken in the face of two relentless charges by Cromwell's Ironsides and, seeing this, his infantry had turned and run. In the hope of preventing pursuit, Goring had ordered the town of Langport to be burnt, but the attempt had proved fruitless. In excess of two thousand Royalists had been taken prisoner and the rest had chosen to desert rather than follow their disgraced leader into Cornwall.

Sir Henry laid the letter aside, saying he wasn't surprised. Goring's undisciplined troops were neither deserving nor capable of winning a victory against a well-trained army. He went on to beg Philip and Benjamin's pardon for ever encouraging them to give their allegiance to the King. If he'd learnt anything over the past three years, it was that a man should not cling to an old order out of fear of change.

His sons said he had nothing to apologise for. They were grown men and able to make their own decisions, but his favourable mention of a well-trained army emboldened them to bring up the subject of General Cromwell and his companions again. Other attempts had been met with silence or deflection to a different topic, all of which had heightened their interest, for they guessed that Sir Henry's unwillingness to speak on the matter concerned Jayne's acquaintanceship with those who had been in Lyme.

In private, Jayne had tried to dampen their curiosity by reminding them that Sir Henry had been a fervent Royalist at the time of the siege. 'He convinced himself I'd fallen under the sway of Puritans and had persuaded Andrew to follow suit, and he lost his temper each time Mama tried to correct him.'

'No wonder she keeps changing the subject,' said Benjamin pensively.

'Indeed,' said Jayne. 'Dare I suggest you follow her example?'

They agreed, and held to the bargain until Sir Henry condemned the ill-discipline of Lord Goring's troops. They took it as an invitation to further excuse their own desertion, and asked their father if he thought the rest of the King's army any different from Goring's.

'You speak as if his troops were unusual, Father,' said Philip, 'but our own brigades were as bad. If we didn't steal, we didn't eat, and as often as not our men thieved food from each other. They fought amongst themselves more often than they fought the enemy.'

Benjamin nodded. 'Even before the New Model Army, we had to force them with whips and the flats of our swords to stand firm, and it grew worse when they knew they were going to face Cromwell's Ironsides. I truly envied the Parliamentary officers at Naseby whose men obeyed orders without hesitation.'

'They believe in their cause,' Philip said. 'Colonel Harrier told us General Cromwell only accepts officers who are dedicated to the same Protestant ideals that he holds.'

Sir Henry cast a frowning glance at his wife. 'I knew he was a damned Puritan.'

'A person can be a Protestant without being a Puritan, Henry. You're one yourself.'

'There's a big difference between his version of Protestantism and mine. The one is arrogant, the other modest.'

Benjamin spoke into the silence that followed. 'I saw no arrogance in General Cromwell,' he said carefully. 'He conversed as easily with our servants as he did with us.'

'Papa's comments relate to Colonel Harrier,' murmured Jayne when neither of her parents answered. 'He believes he has reason to distrust him.'

'And why shouldn't I, when two of my children have fallen under his spell?' Sir Henry barked. 'You're fond of quoting the Sydenhams at me, but the real devils are Harrier and the woman who took the place of his mother. My father had some acquaintanceship with the Grainger family and they rued the day their daughter married the son of the Duke of Granville. If ever there was a monster, it was Ralph Harrier.'

Jayne looked him in the eye. 'If they were aware of that, why did they allow the marriage to proceed? Were they such upstarts that they put a dukedom before Estelle's happiness?'

'Mind your tongue, girl.'

'I will not, for you're being most unjust, Papa. It was hardly Sir William's fault to be born to such an ill-starred couple, nor Lady Stickland's that neither the Duke of Granville nor the Graingers were willing to take responsibility for their orphaned grandchild. If you want monsters, I suggest you look to them rather than the generous woman who gave Sir William a home and an Oxford education.'

Lady Margaret raised a warning hand, but Sir Henry ignored her. '*Generous!*' he roared. 'She wanted a son she could raise in her own image. Do you deny that her brother has refused to speak with her since she embraced Puritanism?'

'I do. He visited her in Dorchester after I treated him for gout and mentioned me to her. It was the reason she rescued me from the crowd on the day of the priest's execution. She recognised the Swift crest on my satchel and guessed I was her brother's physician.'

'That was before the war began. He'll not forgive her willingness to aid and abet his wife's enemies. Lady Bankes stands alone in defending Corfe Castle for the King without any succour or support from her sister-in-law.'

'On the contrary, Papa. Lady Stickland writes to Lady Bankes every week, expressing her pride in her sister-in-law's courage.'

'Humbug! She's as dedicated to Parliament's cause as Harrier is.'

Jayne acknowledged the point with a nod. 'Indeed so, but that doesn't mean she's lost her affection for Lady Bankes. They've held different views for years but have never come to blows over it. Lady Stickland was a supporter of Parliament long before she was widowed, and Sir William adopted the cause when he left Oxford to fight as a mercenary in Europe. As to their Puritan leanings, I believe they both see sense in blowing with the prevailing wind rather than against it.'

Lady Margaret, who had the advantage of knowing that Alice read Shakespeare more often than the Bible, understood Jayne's meaning rather quicker than her husband did. 'They assume the mantle of Puritanism but don't subscribe to the principles behind it?'

Jayne nodded. 'Lady Stickland feigned Puritanism in order to be accepted into Dorchester society, but, since she was the only non-Catholic brave enough to visit Hugh Green in prison before he was executed, I suspect her true leanings are different.'

Sir Henry bristled angrily. 'Should I understand she poses as one thing while believing another?'

'Only in the same way that you do, Papa. You presented yourself as a Royalist to Sir Edward Hamway, expressed sympathy for Parliament to General Cromwell and claim to be neutral whenever you meet the Clubmen of Dorset. For myself, I think you're eminently wise to choose courtesy over unnecessary conflict, but don't paint yourself as any less of a hypocrite than Lady Stickland.'

Once again, Benjamin broke the ensuing silence. 'What are Colonel Harrier's beliefs?'

Jayne decided on honesty because she guessed her father would keep probing if he suspected her of lying. 'None,' she said. 'The European wars taught him to view all religion as chicanery.

He grew cynical when God was invoked by both Catholics and Protestants in advance of slaughtering each other.'

Sir Henry was shocked. 'What manner of man rejects God?'

Jayne pressed her palms together in a gesture of apology, for she knew she was about to deliver an even greater shock. 'One such as Richard Theale, Papa. Science is about learning and proving truth through observation and experiment, and God is elusive on both counts. Richard has more faith in maggots than he does in an invisible entity who can't or won't reveal Himself.'

He stared at her. 'Are these your views also?'

'I'm afraid so, Papa. With each man able to interpret the Bible as he chooses, God comes in so many different guises that if I had as many gowns as there are gods, this house could not hold them.'

Sir Henry surged to his feet and shook his fist. 'I knew I should never have let you study under that man,' he bellowed. 'He's betrayed my trust in every way—turned you against God, enabled a fortune-hunter to seduce you and led my son and heir into the vipers' nest of Wynford Eagle.'

With a sigh, Lady Margaret rose to press him back into his chair. 'Calm yourself!' she ordered. 'Have you forgotten that, but for Richard, I would be dead and Benjamin would never have been born? What other physician would have had the sense to overrule the midwife and cut into a mother's womb to save the life of her and her child? And would you have wished death on your farmhands at the time of the red flux, or amputation of Philip's leg when it's been saved by maggots? Regain some sense, Henry, and recognise that Richard is one of the few people you *can* trust. He's always held himself to a higher moral standard than most others you know, as indeed has your daughter.'

Ruth straightened above her tapestry and turned her soft gaze on Sir Henry. 'Have you never questioned God's existence yourself, Uncle?' she asked curiously. 'I envy you your faith if you haven't.'

He eyed her with suspicion. 'What sort of question is that from one who knows her Bible by heart? Do you seek to divert attention from Jayne?'

'Just a little, for she's not the only member of your family who has doubts. Your brother, my father, struggles with belief each time he's asked to accept that the bread and wine of the Eucharist represent the body and blood of Christ.'

'Has he turned to Puritanism?'

Ruth shook her head. 'He calls himself a sceptic, like Sir William, and for the same reason. God cannot be on both sides of a civil war at the same time.' She pulled a contrite smile. 'Do you mind if I annoy you further, Uncle?'

'Will it make a difference if I say I do?'

'Only to you, for you'll have to live with your curiosity about what I might have said.'

Sir Henry groaned. 'Speak then!'

'You're wrong to think Sir William a fortune-hunter. I know the type better than anyone and he does not conform to it. His appearances are infrequent, he makes no attempt to flatter you or Lady Margaret and, while he's clearly at ease in Jayne's company, he doesn't exploit the friendship in order to gain advantage or promote his own importance. In addition, his rise through the Parliamentary ranks suggests he's hardworking and ambitious to succeed through his own efforts, and those are not qualities possessed by men who pursue wealth and position through marriage.'

Philip shook his head in puzzlement. 'Should I understand that Colonel Harrier and Sir William are one and the same?' He took the absence of an answer for confirmation. 'And this is the Colonel Harrier who came here with General Cromwell the other day?' More silence. 'Well, he seemed a fine sort of fellow to me and Benjamin, and clearly a good friend to Andrew. Does he have an interest in you, sister?'

Oh, dear Lord! 'Of course not,' Jayne answered with a laugh. 'The daughters of minor gentry have no appeal at all. When peace comes, he'll venture up to London and find an appropriate match there, and Papa will wonder why he ever thought my tiny dowry might be of interest to him.'

Sir Henry scowled. 'It's not so tiny,' he grumbled.

'And not so large that it makes up for my refusal to keep my opinions to myself, Papa. Can you accept that your thirty-year-old daughter is destined to be a spinster for the rest of her life? There'll be so few men left when this war is over that old maids such as myself will be at the back of every queue.'

He reached for her hand. 'You'll always have a home here,' he said gruffly.

~

In the days that followed, most of the news that reached the house concerned the Dorset Clubmen. There were reports of mass gatherings across the county, most involving skirmishes with the New Model Army. Rumour had it that Sir Thomas Fairfax gave no credence to the Clubmen's professed neutrality, and had ruled them Royalists because of their belligerence towards his troops.

On the evening of 3 August, a rider came to inform Sir Henry that fifty Clubmen were being held prisoner in Sherborne, and a great assembly was planned for the morrow on Hambledon Hill, some five miles to the north of Blandford. The intention was to gather four thousand men who would march on Sherborne in order to confront Sir Thomas Fairfax and demand their comrades' liberty, and Sir Henry and the Clubmen of west Dorset were invited to join them.

Sir Henry agreed to spread the word amongst his neighbours and then sent the rider on to Lyme to alert the Clubmen there. To Lady Margaret's relief, he showed little enthusiasm for making the thirty-mile journey himself, but when messages came back that others were going, and Benjamin—bored with doing nothing—began pestering to be allowed to join them, he changed his mind. When all was said and done, he told Lady Margaret, he was sworn to peace, and the imprisonment of similarly sworn fellows should not be tolerated.

They left at dawn the next morning, accompanied by the local rector and some twenty farmers from the surrounding area. Lady Margaret expressed misgivings as she and Jayne watched them leave. Nothing good would come of this, she said. Sir Henry might believe in the peaceable nature of the Clubmen, but she doubted Sir Thomas Fairfax would when faced with four thousand of them. It was one thing to pit yourself against handfuls of hungry soldiers in search of food, quite another to wave clubs at the New Model Army. She would spend the day praying that Andrew was as distant from Sherborne as he could possibly be, for it would be a disaster indeed if he was ordered to attack his father and brother.

The party returned late the following afternoon, having spent the night in woodland and being too weary or wounded to move at faster than a walk on the journey home. Benjamin rode ahead to warn Jayne that her services would be needed and, by the time the rest arrived, she was ready to receive them. As it turned out, there was more wounded pride than wounded flesh, for none of the injuries was so severe that it needed sutures. In most cases, the flats of swords had left weals across backs, though the rector, Mister Crewe, and two of the farmers had pricks in their buttocks from sharpened tips, and Sir Henry had a swollen knee from tumbling down the side of Hambledon Hill.

Jayne hid her smiles as she smoothed comfrey oil onto bruises, bound ice-cold bandages about Sir Henry's knee and begged the rector and the two farmers to allow Sir Henry's valet to examine their wounds in the parlour so that he could describe them to her. Only Benjamin, who'd been on worse battlefields, was uncomplaining about the treatment they'd received at the hands of Cromwell's Ironsides. Sir Henry and his friends described it as a vicious bloodbath with no quarter given to the unarmed Clubmen.

The story took so long to tell, with each man contradicting the other, that Jayne begged her father to let Benjamin recount the details. Given permission, Benjamin stood to attention and gave his report in the clipped manner of an officer; but his version was so humorous that Jayne had to clamp her teeth together to keep from laughing. Rather less successful at controlling herself, Lady Margaret left the salon two or three times to stuff the hem of her apron into her mouth.

Benjamin's account ran as follows: Sir Henry and his cohort made good speed to Hambledon Hill. With the help of a local, they followed a track to the summit. Because it was a hill fort, the top was flat and very large, being in excess of fifty acres, and gave good command of the surrounding area. Once there, Sir Henry's group joined some four thousand already gathered, and, since the surface was grassy, they were able to hobble their horses and allow them to graze. Individuals amongst the throng took it in turns to speak, but the wind blew their words away, and when nothing anyone said was heard, the crowd grew restless.

By ill-fortune, a lieutenant and fifty dragoons, an advance party from General Cromwell's regiment, appeared on the skyline at the moment the Clubmen were at their most belligerent, and the more excitable amongst the crowd fired upon them. Sir Henry, along with others, questioned why anyone was bearing muskets, but by then it was too late. General Cromwell and one thousand mounted troops were gathered at the bottom of the hill. In short order, the Ironsides charged the slope and set about punishing the Clubmen with fists and flat swords.

As battles went, it was a shameful rout, with four thousand Clubmen taking to their heels and slithering and sliding down the sides of Hambledon Hill. Sir Henry and his group took shelter in woodland but, with their horses still hobbled at the top, had no means of leaving. Benjamin, the least bruised and battered, skirted around the bottom of the hill to discover what was happening and learnt from other Clubmen that three hundred of their comrades had been taken prisoner. Word had it they were being marched to Shroton church, where they would be held for questioning by General Cromwell.

Ignorant of whether guards had been posted on the summit and the roads, Sir Henry and his companions made the decision to remain in the woodland overnight. When dawn broke, Benjamin made his way up a sheltered track to discover if their mounts were still where they'd left them, and also to scan the surrounding countryside for the New Model Army. Imagine his surprise to see his brother and Colonel Harrier standing guard over their hobbled horses when he emerged onto the level land at the top.

With nowhere to hide, he advanced to speak with them and was relieved when they greeted him with good humour rather than anger. Andrew had been tasked with taking the names of every man who came to retrieve his horse, and most had done so the previous evening. Amongst the two dozen animals left, he had recognised both Sir Henry's and Benjamin's mounts and the emblems on some of the other saddles as belonging to Sir Henry's neighbours. With the light fading, and concerned for his father's safety, he had sent his company of soldiers back to their camp and waited with the horses until someone came to retrieve them.

Colonel Harrier, having learnt from Andrew's men that he was still on Hambledon Hill, joined him shortly after sunset and remained with him through the night. Upon hearing from Benjamin that none of their group had slept and all had cuts and bruises, he suggested they lead the horses down on halters rather than require their owners to collect them.

'They made a fearsome sight,' said one of the farmers. 'The woodland was shrouded in mist, and it wasn't obvious that only three of the horses had riders. We quite expected to be placed in custody and marched to Shroton.'

'Instead, we were treated with courtesy,' said another. 'Colonel Harrier informed us that General Cromwell had no wish to make war on Clubmen and urged us to hasten back to Swyre.'

Sir Henry let loose a profanity. 'He gave us a damned lecture for daring to harass the New Model Army,' he growled.

The Reverend Crewe, back from the parlour after having his left buttock cleansed and dressed by the valet, raised a calming hand. 'Come, sir, it was hardly a lecture. He argued quite reasonably that peace will come quicker if the King is forced to surrender. Since only the New Model Army is equipped to do that, we Clubmen should stand aside and allow them to do their job.'

A noisy debate ensued, with each man stating his own interpretation of what Colonel Harrier had said. On the pretext of needing Jayne to examine a cut on his arm, Benjamin drew her into the hall. 'Colonel Harrier stayed for Andrew's sake,' he told her, rolling up his sleeve. 'Had he not, it would have fallen to Andrew to give the lecture, and you can imagine what Father's response would have been to that.'

'Not good,' Jayne agreed, looking at a small scabbed cut amidst a sea of bruises before giving him a playful tap on the chest. 'You'll survive,' she said. 'You had far worse scrapes when you were a child. What else do you want to tell me?'

'Father should be grateful to Colonel Harrier. According to Andrew, orders were given that the ringleaders of the insurrection should be singled out and taken to Shroton. General Cromwell wants their names listed and each to be interrogated for the purpose of learning who else is involved. Any other commander would have arrested Sir Henry and hauled him to Shroton on the end of a rope.'

'Have you told Papa?'

'Of course not,' Benjamin answered. 'He'd have bitten my head off. But I thought you'd like to know, since Colonel Harrier will have spared him as much for your sake as for Andrew's.'

Jayne gave a mock shudder. 'Well, *that* you must definitely keep to yourself,' she said dryly. 'I'm no keener than you to have my head removed.'

TWENTY-THREE

AT THE BEGINNING OF DECEMBER, with the New Model Army now so dominant across England that many believed the war was drawing to an end, Sir Henry announced his decision to invite his brother, his two sisters and their families to Swyre for Christmas. Lady Margaret encouraged him to do so, but in private she told Jayne and Ruth that his sisters would disappoint him. Neither had answered his letters since August, when he wrote that the King's cause had been lost at Naseby and urged them to build bridges with Parliamentarians. As both women lived in Oxford, with husbands and sons still firmly in the Royalist camp, such advice had clearly not been welcome, and Lady Margaret doubted they would come.

She was right. Only Ruth's parents accepted the invitation, and by 18 December, Sir Henry, frustrated that their party would be so small, suggested his wife invite her brother and his family.

'I will not,' Lady Margaret answered firmly. 'My brother's a bore, my sister-in-law a giggling imbecile, and none of us can bear to be in a room with them. I count it one of the few blessings of this war that their annual summer visit has been postponed for three years. If Malcolm didn't resemble my father so closely in looks, I would think we had different parents.' She poked her needle into her tapestry with unnecessary force. 'Have you heard from Andrew?'

'Not since Cromwell took Basing House, and that was nigh on two months ago.'

'Then let's invite friends and strangers who might otherwise be alone. I can name two, and I'm sure Jayne can name many. Her greatest sympathy is for patients who have no one at home to care for them.'

Sir Henry hunched his shoulders. 'Christmas should be for family and the household,' he declared mutinously.

Lady Margaret turned to Ruth. 'Is that in the Bible, niece?'

'I don't believe so, Aunt. I can't recall a single verse where Christ reminded his apostles of the day he was born, and the only party I remember was the wedding at Cana where he turned water to wine. If that was like weddings today, there would have been more friends than family on both sides and I imagine most of them would have been strangers to Jesus.'

Sir Henry groaned. 'Name your two,' he instructed his wife.

'Lady Stickland and Doctor Theale. I'm intrigued to meet the first and always glad to see the second, particularly now that Philip is walking again.'

'Name yours,' Sir Henry instructed his daughter.

'The list is a long one, Papa, and some will need assistance to get here. How bounteous are you prepared to be?'

⌒

Philip, who could hardly be kept from his horse since retraining himself to ride through his left leg, took charge of delivering the invitations, while Benjamin organised as many wagons as he could find to transport those who would otherwise be unable to make the journey. Sir Henry ordered the slaughter of turkey cocks and fattened weaners from his pig pens, also the broaching of beer and wine kegs; Lady Margaret set her cooks to baking bread, plum puddings and mince pies, the maids to churning butter and the footmen to bringing the best of the cheeses from the cold store; Ruth and Jayne oversaw the making of beds.

When Philip returned with the news that upwards of seventy would be arriving on Christmas Eve, with some forty being children, Jayne begged her father to allow her the use of the tithe barn as a dormitory and bundles of straw from the threshing barn to serve as mattresses. Sir Henry, clearly startled that such a large number was coming, gave his permission readily but then began to fret about how to entertain so many visitors. They would need more food, more spiced ale and wine. And what games could they play? And who would provide the music for dancing?

Naughtily, Benjamin suggested they pray that every guest was a Puritan, for they were known to frown on frivolity, but Lady Margaret scolded him and then reminded Sir Henry that most of his farmhands played instruments. Had he forgotten their Christmases before the war, when the house had rung to the sound of lutes, fiddles, pipes and the tapping of feet while the children played hoodman-blind, stool-ball, leap-frog and snap-apple? The conflict had put an end to such fun, but it beggared belief that their guests had lost all memory of how to enjoy themselves. As to food and drink, those were her responsibility and she was confident there would be enough.

Ruth's parents, Joseph and Elizabeth, arrived on the afternoon before Christmas Eve, bringing baskets of holly, rosemary and ivy to add to the decorations in the hall and salon. Ruth's joy on seeing them was matched by Sir Henry's, and Lady Margaret and Jayne breathed sighs of relief at his sudden upsurge of spirits. After all, it had needed but a reunion with his brother to conjure up the many happy Christmases they had spent together in this house as children. Joseph knew every game that could be played and had brought his hunting horn to summon the guests to eating and dancing.

Nevertheless, there was caution on both sides until the two men established that their views on the war were similar. Since neither thought the King could win, their shared hope was an honourable end to the conflict and, on that agreement, they shook hands. Watching them, Jayne wondered how many other families around the country were seizing on the longed-for peace as a means to heal division. What better expression of harmony could there be than a mutual desire to see both sides lay down their arms?

At one point over dinner, Joseph asked Sir Henry what he knew of Colonel William Harrier. 'Governor Sydenham tells me he has some acquaintanceship with you and your family. Is he correct?'

'Some,' said Sir Henry. 'Why do you ask?'

'It would please me to meet him. He took the trouble to inform us of Samuel's passing, and I found his words moving. It seems Samuel begged him to write to me in the event of his death, asking in all humility that we find it in our hearts to forgive him and commend his memory to his wife and son.' He glanced across the table at Ruth. 'We do both, daughter, for Colonel Harrier wrote two sentences that stick in my memory. "Samuel died in the knowledge that he had many flaws, but he embraced death with great courage. His single request was that his wife and son, whom he never stopped loving, be allowed to remember him for that and not for his previous failings." Did the colonel write to you also, my dear?'

Ruth shook her head. 'No, Papa, but he spoke similar words to Aunt Margaret and Jayne when he came here with General Cromwell.' She raised her napkin to her eyes. 'I believe Samuel must have unburdened himself in the days before he died, and it gladdens my heart that the man he chose for his confessions was as kind as Sir William.'

Philip took pity on his uncle's confusion. 'Colonel Harrier and Sir William are one and the same,' he explained.

'He's acquainted with Lady Stickland, whose son you've done business with, I believe,' murmured Sir Henry.

Joseph nodded. 'Once or twice. He's a timid lad, not at all like his mother. I understand she left him in charge of the estate in the hope he'd grow in confidence, but he shows no sign of doing so.'

'Why do you call him a lad?' Lady Margaret asked curiously. 'Is he young?'

'Barely twenty-five, I believe. Lady Alice despaired of ever having children until he arrived, but I can't help feeling he's a disappointment to her. Despite her absence, he still relies on her to make decisions for him, just as his father did.'

'How well do you know her?'

'Fairly well. I met her whenever I had dealings with her husband and always welcomed her interventions. She had a better grasp of business than he did.' He chuckled. 'It didn't surprise me at all when Jayne told me it was she who came to Ruth's aid when Isaac had the croup. A lesser woman would have washed her hands of the problem.'

'Did Jayne also tell you she was a Parliamentarian?' Sir Henry asked.

Joseph folded his hands on the table. 'She did not, but I could have guessed that was where her allegiances lay. I've never met a more independent-minded woman. The first time I saw her she was dressed as a man, and I would have taken her for one had her husband not introduced her as his wife.'

Jayne spoke when no one else did. 'You'll meet her again tomorrow, Uncle, for Papa has invited her to join our party.' She flicked Sir Henry a mischievous glance. 'But he may regret his generosity if she comes in britches.'

It was the wrong thing to say, for it persuaded Sir Henry that that was precisely what Alice would do, and Jayne's qualms about introducing them grew through the night. What had seemed like a good idea when her mother first suggested it assumed alarming proportions in the dark hours of Christmas Eve morning. Sir Henry was already so prejudiced against Alice that their meeting could never be cordial and, imagining terrible arguments, she entered Philip's room at dawn and begged him to ride to Dorchester in order to rescind the invitation. He refused with a laugh, telling her not to be such a ninny. He'd spent a bare half-hour in Lady Stickland's company, and she'd had him eating out of her hand within five minutes. She'd do the same with Sir Henry. 'Worry more about our mother,' he warned. 'She may not take kindly to another woman capturing her family's affections.'

To anticipate an event is worse than to experience it, and Jayne wondered afterwards why she had ever feared that Sir Henry would forget his manners. She could see he was shocked by Alice's frailty, because he assumed the part of protector, entreating Molly to stand aside and allow him to assist Lady Stickland from her carriage. She was dressed in a deep blue taffeta gown, which was both modest and elegant, and Molly had fashioned her hair into a graceful knot on the nape of her neck. She gripped Sir Henry's hand as she descended and begged him to allow her to steady herself for a few moments.

'Take as much time as you need,' he said, beckoning Lady Margaret forward. 'May I present my wife, Lady Margaret? She has long wanted to meet you.'

'And I her,' said Alice, reaching out her free hand to Lady Margaret. 'I'm in awe of a mother who supports her daughter's ambition to be a physician. Were there more like you, Lady Margaret, there would be more like Jayne. It must please you greatly that her name is celebrated in Dorset for her skill and dedication.'

A flush of pleasure rose in Lady Margaret's cheeks. 'Indeed, it does, but the credit belongs to Jayne. She has won her reputation through her own efforts and not through anything Sir Henry or I have done.'

Alice released her hand. 'You're too modest, my dear. She is what she is because of her parents.' She turned to Sir Henry. 'I believe I've found my balance now, sir, but may I continue to lean on you as we walk to the house?'

'Of course! Of course!' he assured her. 'You have but to ask whenever you need my arm.'

As they made their way slowly to the door with Molly following behind, Alice praised the gracious lines of the house and the beauty of its location, and Sir Henry's chest swelled with gratification. Jayne was standing with Ruth and Philip behind the servants gathered on the forecourt, but, if Alice saw her, she showed no sign of it.

Philip leant forward to whisper in his sister's ear. 'She didn't look that frail when I saw her in Dorchester. Is she feigning?'

Almost certainly, thought Jayne. 'I expect the journey tired her.'

He grinned. 'There's no better way to win Papa's sympathy.'

Jayne nodded agreement, while guessing that Alice's dislike of pity meant the reason for the pretence was probably different.

Shortly afterwards, Benjamin arrived with a wagon full of women and children from surrounding villages. Amongst them was Marianne Prewitt, whose dropsy and drunken husband had interested Prince Maurice. Her two bonny daughters and four boisterous sons ran to embrace Jayne, as did every other child from the wagon, and it was several minutes before she noticed Lady Margaret standing to the side.

She moved towards her, bouncing a two-year-old in her arms. 'This is Aaron, Mama,' she said with a smile. 'Six months ago, he was so sickly we feared he wouldn't live, and now look at him. Have you ever seen such a picture of health?'

Lady Margaret touched the back of her finger to the toddler's cheeks. 'The same can be said of every child here. Each one is a tribute to your care, daughter, and it's my joy and delight to welcome them all to Swyre.' She beckoned Agnes forward. 'I have need of Jayne inside,' she said, taking the little boy and handing him to the maid. 'Will you show these ladies and their children to their beds in the barn? I shall send word as soon as food is close to being served but, meanwhile, I'm told Arthur and two of the other farm workers have games planned for them.'

Jayne watched Agnes shepherd the women across the forecourt. 'Is something amiss, Mama?'

'Lady Alice is in need of your help,' Lady Margaret said in an undertone. 'Her maid tells me she's trapped in the corner of her chamber, quite unable to move. I understand it's happened before, and on each occasion the paralysis has lasted above two hours. Is there something you can do for her that won't draw attention to the problem? Lady Alice is most insistent that we keep the matter to ourselves, out of fear that undue fuss will spoil the party.'

Jayne adopted the most serious expression she could. 'Did Molly say Alice feels as if her feet are glued to the floor?'

'Exactly that.'

'Then she needs an inhalation of rosemary oil,' Jayne said, plucking a remedy from the air. 'Will you ask Kitty to bring a kettle of boiling water to her chamber while I fetch my satchel?' She urged her mother towards the house.

Lady Margaret paused inside the door. 'Should I warn Sir Henry that she might not appear for dinner?'

'There's no need. She'll be herself again once she's had thirty minutes of scented steam. I've not known it to fail yet.' She took her satchel from the side table in the hall. 'You mustn't worry, Mama. I'm sure it's just weariness from the journey that has caused this small setback.'

Lady Margaret gave a distracted nod and then hurried to the kitchen in search of Kitty.

Jayne chastised Alice as Molly let her into the chamber and closed the door behind her. 'Your penance for making me tell lies to my mother is to remain in that corner until my maid brings a kettle,' she said severely. 'It won't do at all for Kitty to say I cured you of temporary paralysis without steam, since that was the only remedy I could think of on the spur of the moment.'

Alice gave a quiet laugh. 'How did you know it wasn't real?'

'Because it's only two weeks since I last saw you and your palsy hasn't progressed far enough. I guessed you were merely aping your father's more advanced symptoms.' She held a finger to her lips as she heard Kitty's steps on the landing. 'Allow her in, Molly,' she murmured, lowering her satchel to the bed and removing a vial of rosemary oil. 'Thank you, Kitty,' she said when her maid entered. 'You've been quicker than I could have hoped for. Will you fill the basin on the ewer stand?'

Kitty did so. 'Is there something more I can do, Miss Jayne?' she asked, with a glance of concern at Lady Alice.

'No, thank you, Kitty, except to keep from speaking of what you've seen to anyone but Lady Margaret.'

The young woman dropped a curtsey. 'You can be sure I will, Miss Jayne.'

Jayne waited until her steps on the landing were no longer audible. 'Her silence is more than you deserve,' she admonished Alice. 'She and my mother are now consumed with anxiety for you, but why is that necessary?'

Alice lowered herself to a chair. 'I wanted half an hour alone with you without your mother thinking we were sharing secrets behind her back. Your brother said it was her idea to invite me, but I'm guessing her real intention was to discover how much influence I wield over you.'

Jayne nodded, since there was little point in denying it.

'It clearly grieves her that you're unmarried. I was watching from the window as she delivered Molly's message, and she came close to weeping to see you hugged and kissed by other women's children.'

Jayne poured some drops of rosemary oil into the basin and wafted her hand through the steam to disperse it about the room. 'Kitty will be suspicious if the water and room are unscented,' she explained before perching on the end of the bed and eyeing Alice with amusement. 'If you join with Mama and Papa in pressing me to take a husband, you'll have no trouble winning their trust and friendship.'

'While losing yours?'

'Very likely. The subject of marriage causes more arguments in this family than anything else. I wouldn't mind so much if my brothers came under similar pressure, but they never do. My father thinks a son should take his time to decide on a wife while a daughter must accept the first buffoon who offers.'

Alice laughed again. 'So, I'd be wasting my time if I proposed an introduction to my son Francis? He's much in need of an intelligent wife with the skill and sense to manage his estate.'

Jayne flicked a startled glance at Molly. Was this a serious suggestion?

'You're unkind to tease Miss Jayne, milady,' Molly scolded. 'You know full well Sir Francis has his heart set on young Emmeline Cooper.'

'That doesn't mean I'm obliged to approve her. She's even more tongue-tied than he is and never makes the effort to converse with me. I'd much prefer you for a daughter-in-law, Jayne.'

'I'll take that as a compliment, Alice, though I doubt your son would want a wife who finds more enjoyment in your company than his.' She pondered for a moment. 'Have you considered that Miss Cooper feels intimidated by you? I thought you quite terrifying the first time I met you.'

'What changed your mind?'

'William. He spoke of your visits to Hugh Green in prison while we watched the two priests being driven to Gallows Hill. I suggested you must have been criticised for showing kindness to Catholics, and William said it made no matter whether you were or not. You cared nothing for what others thought as long as you believed that what you were doing was right. I remember wishing I was half as brave.'

'Don't be modest, my dear. I've hidden behind men and costumes all my life while you face the world as you are. If I'd had even one ounce of your spirit, I'd never have allowed Gilbert Jackson to take credit for my portraits.'

'Will your son have told Miss Cooper about that?'

'Certainly not! She and her parents were shocked enough to learn I supported Parliament without having their sensibilities further brutalised by stories of male impersonation.' A tremor began in her left hand. 'We must talk about something less irritating or I'll be quivering all over.'

Jayne smiled. 'What subject pleases you?'

'William. Tell me what your parents know about him and how they view him. I'd hate to make a faux pas if I'm asked a direct question.'

Jayne maintained her carefree smile with difficulty. 'My mother thinks him a rogue, and my father believes him a godless fortune-hunter, so the only faux pas you can possibly make is to suggest he regards me as anything other than a physician. The best help you can give me is to name a young woman like Miss Cooper in whom he has an interest.'

Alice glanced at Molly. 'Does such a person exist?'

'I don't believe so, milady. The only woman he ever speaks of with fondness is you.'

'Well, that won't do! I can hardly nominate myself as William's love-token. I must either invent a fictitious beauty or attempt to persuade Sir Henry and Lady Margaret that William has a fortune. Which would you prefer, Jayne?'

Jayne delivered as heartfelt a groan as any her father produced when Ruth cited biblical texts. 'I would *prefer* you say nothing at all. Can you not feign deafness?'

Alice shook her head. 'It won't help. William sent word that Andrew has invited him to spend Christmas Day at Swyre. They're planning to arrive at noon tomorrow and, from what you've just told me, a little preparation in advance of their visit might be wise. Your poor mother will be mortified if her party's spoilt by arguments about whether your brother's guest is acceptable.'

Mercifully, Lady Margaret had already decided that Jayne owed a duty to her female patients and their children and had asked her to sit with them rather than at the top table. Because of Isaac's age, she had made the same request of Ruth, and the two cousins took their places at the women's table as Philip and Benjamin entered the darkened salon with a mighty yule log upon their shoulders. They were followed by a footman carrying a single candle, and the head cook bearing a roasted boar's head on a platter with an apple between its jaws, and fruits, bay leaves and rosemary sprigs about its neck.

A fiddler played the first haunting chords of 'The Boar's Head Carol', and the assembled diners raised their glasses and sang the words. When they reached the last line of the chorus—'*Reddens laudes Domino*'—Philip and Benjamin tossed the yule log onto the burning embers in the hearth, and cheers rang through the room as flames and sparks roared and crackled up the chimney. Around Jayne and Ruth, the children jumped with joy and clapped their hands, only to *ooh* and *aah* as servants lit candles, and the salon with all its pretty decorations sprang to life.

Traditionally, Christmas Eve was reserved for the farm workers and their families, with the servants sitting down to join them once the food was on the tables, and this made for a jollier party than the more formal occasion of Christmas Day. Sir Henry seemed to be in particularly good cheer, to judge by the way his booming laugh kept bursting upon the room. Jayne watched him surreptitiously out of the corner of her eye, but whether it was Alice to his right or Ruth's mother, Elizabeth, to his left who was amusing him, she couldn't tell. Perhaps both, since all three faces were wreathed in smiles. Lady Margaret sat between Alice and Joseph. Once in a while, Jayne caught her gaze, but there was nothing to read in it. If Alice was spinning fantastical stories about William, her mother was not reacting to them.

By nine o'clock the children were flagging, and Jayne and Ruth accompanied them and their mothers to the barn. The farmhands had strung a hessian curtain across the space to give the women privacy when families with fathers joined them on the morrow, and Jayne lowered it to show them how cosy they would be. She lit a taper from her own lantern and touched it to the wicks in those strung on ropes from the rafters, and the soft light created a mood of enchantment. One of the children asked for a story and, with a laugh, Jayne dropped cross-legged to his mattress of straw and invited them all to do the same.

'I will tell you the story my mother used to tell me when I was your age. It concerns a slave called Androcles and a ferocious lion with a thorn in his paw. It teaches us that kindness to others is always rewarded.'

She and Ruth knew more than a dozen of Aesop's fables and took it in turns to recite them. Ruth did it out of kindness while

Jayne's motives were entirely selfish. She would rather linger in the barn than be forced to answer questions from her mother, but the ploy came to nought when she felt a draught on her cheek and looked up to see Lady Margaret at the edge of the curtain. By then, two of the toddlers were asleep at her side, and Ruth and the mothers were singing quiet lullabies to the rest. With a sigh, Jayne whispered to Ruth that it was time to leave, and together they roused Isaac.

Jayne turned up the wick on her lantern as they left the barn. 'I'm sorry, Mama. Have we tarried longer than we should?'

'It makes no matter. Lady Alice has retired, but Joseph and Elizabeth are waiting in the hall to say goodnight to Ruth and Isaac.' She handed her own lantern to Ruth. 'Hasten ahead, my dear. Jayne and I will follow at our leisure.' She waited until Ruth had put some twenty yards between them and then, unexpectedly, stood on tiptoes to kiss Jayne's cheek. 'I don't tell you often enough how much I love you, daughter.'

Surprised, Jayne raised the lantern to look into her eyes. 'You don't need to, Mama. You show it in the support you give me.'

'I wish that were true. Tonight, I've had a lesson in how to do it properly. You have a far worthier champion in Lady Alice than you do in me, Jayne.'

Briefly, Jayne closed her eyes. What had Alice been saying? 'I doubt that, Mama. She knows me only as a physician.'

Lady Margaret smiled. 'But that's what you are, my dear, and I'm ashamed that I needed a stranger to explain it to me.'

TWENTY-FOUR

THE RECTOR—CURED ALONG WITH every other Clubman in Dorset of attending gatherings—had clearly mellowed since his brush with General Cromwell's Ironsides, for he was gracious in welcoming newcomers to his church on Christmas Day, trusting that whatever their beliefs, they would find comfort in the service. This was a marked difference from the beginning of the war, when his sermons had been aggressively opposed to Parliament and any form of religion that did not accept priests, bishops and the King as its head.

Today, he spoke of the peace, forgiveness and love that Christ's birth had foretold, and strayed towards politics only once, when he asked the congregation to pray for an end to division. He used similar words to those Hugh Green had spoken on the day of his execution. 'We must abandon enmity and learn to trust each other again. Let us pray for those with whom we have disagreed as earnestly as we pray for our friends, and keep faith that God will guide the minds of those who rule us.'

Such sentiments were easily embraced, and the 'amen' that followed the prayer was heartfelt. Even so, Sir Henry could not resist glancing towards Alice and Joseph to see if their responses were genuine. They were seated on stone pews at the side of the chancel, while Jayne stood with the women and children in the nave, and she couldn't miss her father's relief to see that his guests were acting appropriately. He believed things should be seen to be done correctly in public, and Jayne wondered, as she had many times before, how he had ever managed to tolerate his daughter's refusals to conform.

Perhaps he read her thoughts, because he turned to look at her, and her smile of pure affection reciprocated the same from him. In such moments, Jayne never doubted that he wanted the best for her. The only difficulty was that his idea of the best rarely accorded with hers.

Quiet reflection gave way to noisy exuberance as another forty guests arrived by horse and carriage to join the festivities. Richard Theale was amongst the first, and Jayne took pleasure in introducing him to Alice, certain they would have much to talk about. Since so many of the guests were Jayne's patients, her company was in great demand, and she lost track of time until Agnes came to tell her that Lady Margaret requested her urgent presence in the kitchen.

Jayne pulled a wry expression. 'Please don't tell me the cooks have burnt the food, Agnes. Mama will be beside herself!'

'Nothing so serious, Miss Jayne. Milady wishes your advice is all.'

Jayne excused herself from a farmer and his wife, whose twins she'd delivered. 'What about?'

'If I knew that, I might have been able to advise her myself,' said Agnes, leading her through the crowd in the hall. 'I can't accompany you further, Miss Jayne,' she said, nodding to the door to the kitchen. 'Sir Henry has tasked me with overseeing faster refills of the ale tankards, and the kegs are in the parlour.'

'His tankard or everyone else's?'

Agnes giggled. 'Let's just say Sir Henry will be singing more than carols by the time darkness descends, Miss Jayne.'

Jayne didn't doubt she was right, and the songs Sir Henry preferred would be considerably ruder than 'The Wild Rover'. His favourite was 'The Cuckoo's Nest', a bawdy tale of lost virginity, which invariably caused Lady Margaret to shoo every woman, child and servant from the room. Her efforts were fruitless, however, since Sir Henry's voice was so loud there wasn't a person in the house who didn't know the words. Even Isaac had learnt them, and Jayne was smiling to herself as she entered the kitchen and approached her mother, remembering Ruth's horror when her son had delivered in his sweet little treble: 'At the bottom of the belly lies the cuckoo's nest.'

'You seem happy,' said Lady Margaret.

'Wickedly so, Mama. I was recalling Isaac's rendition of Papa's favourite tune, the one he loves to tease you with when he finds you particularly appealing. Agnes tells me he's well on the way to singing it, so it might be wise to make him eat something.'

'Wretched man!' said Lady Margaret crossly, beckoning to a maid and instructing her to seek out Sir Henry's valet. 'Tell him to water his master's ale and give him some bread and cheese. Under no circumstances is Sir Henry to break into song, and *certainly* not "The Cuckoo's Nest".' She took Jayne's hand. 'Come outside with me. I need your advice and I'd rather have it away from prying ears.'

She hurried Jayne to the back door and then paused to inspect her. Her look was so strange that Jayne wondered if her gown was gaping. 'Have I come adrift, Mama?'

'No, my dear. I was just thinking how well that shade of blue suits you.' She lifted the latch and ushered Jayne through the doorway. 'Andrew and Sir William tell me they're happy to chew bones out here, but I think we should make room for them inside. I'm sure, with a little squeezing, we can lay two extra places at the top table. What do you say, Jayne?'

William and Andrew stood beside their horses, clearly having ridden the path Jayne always took to the back door, and her surprise to see them was obvious to her mother because she hadn't expected their arrival to be so discreet. Jayne guessed this had been on William's urging, for it would never occur to Andrew that they might not be welcome. She was more surprised at how different they both looked out of uniform. William, wearing a gold-embroidered black coat over dark britches and boots, appeared every inch a duke, while Andrew, in well-fitting russet jacket and britches, resembled no one so much as his father, who had chosen the same colour for himself.

With a spontaneous laugh, she stepped forward and held out a hand to each of them. 'Of course we must make room for them, Mama, though I fear their finery will put the rest of us to shame.'

William's eyes lit with a smile as he raised her fingers to his lips. 'You and Lady Margaret outshine us both, Mistress Swift.'

Andrew pulled her into his arms. 'He speaks the truth, sister. I've never seen you look so well.'

Had Jayne been inclined to simper, she would have said 'tush' and smacked their wrists. Instead, she asked a footman to take their horses while privately blessing Kitty for insisting she wear blue ribbons in her hair to match her gown.

~

She lingered behind as Lady Margaret led Andrew and William through the crowd and was grateful when Ruth moved quietly to her side to lend support. Together, they watched Lady Margaret pause in front of Lady Alice and Richard Theale to allow William to pay his respects to both. Next, she gestured towards the rector, who responded to William's bow with one of his own, and then beckoned to Philip and Benjamin, who greeted their brother with playful taps on his arms and William with firm handshakes.

'Lady Margaret will seek out my father next,' Ruth murmured. 'He'll be effusive in his thanks for Sir William's letter and insist on introducing Mama. I don't doubt he will also mention that they share a friend in Governor Sydenham. It's a marvellously circuitous path Aunt Margaret is taking in order to oblige Sir Henry to be courteous.'

'I fear he's had too much ale to allow reason to override emotion,' said Jayne, seeing a frown gather on her father's brow as he recognised William. He turned impatiently to his valet and delivered a sharp order.

Ruth laid a comforting hand on her arm. 'Have faith in Lady Alice,' she advised, watching Doctor Theale escort the elderly matriarch to Sir Henry's side. 'She'll find a way to manage any trouble.'

Jayne wished she shared Ruth's confidence as the valet hurried towards her. 'Your father asks that you join him with all speed, Miss Jayne.'

She stifled a sigh. 'Thank you, Steven. Is he cross?'

'He will be if you don't reach him before Colonel Harrier does, Miss Jayne. Allow me to forge a path.'

Jayne approached Sir Henry with a smile. 'You asked for me, Papa?'

'I did,' he said. 'I have a question for you and I expect an honest answer. Your mother tells me you spoke with Sir William only twice in Lyme, once when you were attending Colonel Blake and again when Sir William and Captain Metcalfe escorted you to Doctor Theale's house. Is this true?'

'It is, Papa, though there was very little talking either time. Richard was party to the longest conversation we had, and by recollection we spoke of the courage shown by the women of Lyme.'

Richard nodded. 'I can confirm that, Sir Henry.'

Sir Henry frowned. 'I'd assumed he'd used the opportunity of the siege to become better acquainted with you.'

Jayne shook her head. 'I spent more time with Colonel Blake, and our conversations were few and short. There was little opportunity for anything other than fighting and binding wounds.'

Sir Henry looked past her. 'He approaches now. Move aside, daughter.' He stepped forward with his hand outstretched. 'I believe I've misjudged you, Sir William. Please accept my apologies for my churlishness at our last meeting.'

William took the hand and ducked his head in a bow. 'There's no need, Sir Henry. Had our roles been reversed and it was I who'd had a sleepless night, I would not have taken a Cromwellian lecture from you as courteously as you took it from me.'

Sir Henry gave a bark of laughter. 'I wouldn't have minded so much if I hadn't been sitting in wet grass all night. Do you know how undignified it is to accept a reprimand in saturated britches?' He waved to his brother. 'Sound the horn, Joseph. It's time to eat.'

~

The party was judged by all to be a success. With the afternoon sunny and crisp, the children were able to go outside to play games once they'd eaten, while the adults conversed long over their food. Come twilight, the tables were removed and the adults joined together in lines and circles to perform traditional country dances. Lady Margaret had given stern instructions to the band that they were never to leave so long a pause between tunes that Sir Henry saw a chance to sing his own songs, but he was better behaved than his wife and daughter had feared, preferring to lead Lady Margaret and Lady Alice as often as they wished in a dance.

Since most involved figures of eight, poussettes and promenades, there was constant interchanging of couples, but all too frequently, Jayne found herself being led down the line by William. On one occasion, she accused him of cheating, since no other man was partnering her so regularly, and he laughed and said she had amenable brothers.

'Would you rather they didn't give way to me?' he asked, linking his arm with hers and swinging her around.

'No,' she said. 'You're the only man tall enough to allow me to dance without stooping.'

On another occasion, he asked if Alice had told her to expect him.

'I took it more as a threat,' she said lightly. 'It was a bare few minutes since she'd offered me her son.'

Humour lit William's eyes. 'For what purpose?'

'She said she'd rather have me as a daughter-in-law than the timid beauty Sir Francis favours.'

Come eight o'clock, she sought leave from her parents for Ruth and herself to accompany her patients and their children to the tithe barn. The room had thinned of guests since the departure of those not staying the night, and with a sigh, because he was so clearly enjoying being with his family, Andrew stepped forward and said he and William must leave likewise, for they were required to be back with their regiment by noon on the morrow.

Sir Henry frowned. 'Where's the sense in riding at night when you can make faster speed in daylight?'

'We've done it many times before, Father.'

'Can we not accommodate them here?' Sir Henry asked Lady Margaret. 'They'll have a good four hours to make the journey once dawn breaks.'

William interceded. 'It's not necessary, milady. I believe we have a greater distance to travel than Sir Henry realises. The army is wintering to the north of Exeter, and four hours will not be enough time to cover the sixty miles without a change of mount. We'll do better to make steady progress through the night, and only spur our horses when the sun comes up. We'll be in no danger. The skies are clear, the moon is bright and we're used to riding in such conditions.'

Lady Margaret's relief was obvious. 'If you're sure, Sir William, for I confess there isn't a spare bed anywhere. Nevertheless, I worry that you must be tired if you rode from Exeter to reach us this morning.'

'We did not, milady. We stayed last night in my house in Dorchester.' He bowed over her hand. 'May I thank you most sincerely for your generous hospitality and ask permission to escort your daughter, your niece and their many charges to the barn? The stables are adjacent, so, with your blessing, Andrew and I will depart directly after performing the service for the ladies.'

'Is this by way of asking me if you can have a few minutes alone with Jayne, Sir William?'

'It is, milady.'

'Then as long as Jayne is agreeable, I have no objections.' She turned to her daughter. 'Are you, my dear?'

What a question, Jayne thought. To say 'yes' would be to lay her heart on the floor so that others might trample upon it whenever they felt inclined; to say 'no' would be to close a door she would rather keep open. She did the only thing she could think of and laughed. 'As long as Sir William's willing to carry Aaron on his shoulders and trot while his ears are used as reins,' she said. 'Mine are thoroughly sore from being an obliging pony this morning.'

William responded with a genuine laugh of his own. 'Lead on, dear lady. I warrant a Harrier can give the young tyke a more exciting ride than a Swift.'

And so he did, prancing at a trot around the forecourt and then moving to a long-strided canter along the track to the barn. The two-year-old, whose father had fought for the Royalists and was reported to have died of camp fever a month before his son was born, seemed to relish the attention of a man. He laughed with glee to be raised so high and wept tears of grief when William lifted him from his shoulders and returned him to his mother.

'I fear I've done more harm than good,' William said wryly as the woman dropped a curtsey by way of thanks.

'Not at all, sir. He will remember this night for a long time.' She turned shyly to Jayne, who stood with the other women and children. 'Will you be coming in, Mistress Swift, or should we say goodnight to you here?'

Jayne smiled. 'We shall say goodnight inside, Meg. I need but a few moments to make my farewells to my brother and Sir William before I join you and my cousin for stories and lullabies.'

Ruth needed no stronger cue to shepherd the group through the door, and Jayne wondered—as she did almost every day—why such a sweet-natured, loyal and insightful woman had been unable to find a better husband than Samuel Morecott. From time to time during the evening, she had seen her speaking with Andrew, and the comfort each took from the other's company was obvious. They had come to know each other well during Andrew's visits to Joseph's house after he joined the Weymouth garrison and Jayne wondered if she was foolish to hope something might come of the friendship. There was no bar to first cousins marrying in the Anglican Church, so the only resistance would come from Sir Henry, who expected Andrew to marry a lady of status and make sons of his own, not tie himself to the widow and child of a low-ranking Puritan upstart.

Andrew waited until the barn door had closed behind the women and then gave his sister a hug and said he'd walk to the stables alone. She caught his sleeve to stop him. 'Would you not like to make your goodbyes to Ruth and Isaac?' she asked. 'I'm sure it will please them greatly to make theirs to you.'

'I'll scare the women and children if I follow them inside, Jayne.'

'No, you won't,' she said firmly, pushing him towards the door. 'Several of the families with fathers excused themselves a half-hour ago, and Arthur and two of the fiddle players accompanied them to light lanterns and make soft music for the children. Can you not hear it? Do this courtesy for Ruth and Isaac, if not for yourself, brother. They have a great fondness for you.'

William watched Andrew disappear inside. 'Are you right to raise Ruth's hopes?' he asked.

'She's too modest to hope for anything. If I'm raising anyone's hopes, it's my own.' She smiled. 'I'm becoming like Alice. I want to pick my in-laws myself rather than leave the choice to my father and brothers, who can't tell a diamond from a bauble.'

'Does your mother have no say in such matters?'

Jayne pretended to think about it. 'I'm sure she must, though she seems to reserve her influence for after an introduction has been made. She's always very supportive when her children express distaste for a possible match.'

'Then I can rely on her to see off Walter Hoare if he comes looking for you once the war is over? Andrew tells me he has a fancy for you.'

I can rely . . . ? 'Andrew has a colourful imagination,' she said, 'but I'll see off Sir Walter myself if he's foolish enough to return. I'm extremely adept at making myself unacceptable to suitors.'

A dry laugh whispered on the night air. 'So your brother tells me. By his count, you've wounded the feelings of upwards of twenty.'

Jayne raised her lantern to shine the light on his face. 'Andrew's been telling you far too much. Should you not be discussing the war instead of me?'

'You're a more agreeable subject than war, Jayne. I never tire of having my curiosity satisfied . . . particularly when your brother is so forthcoming with his answers. I trust Alice is as obliging when you question her about me.'

Jayne gave an involuntary laugh. 'Our situations are not the same. You relish gossip, while I have a constant need to explain you to my parents. They're quite unused to men who appear in different disguises each time they come to our door.'

He studied her for a moment. 'May I ask why you do that kindness for me? I'm more accustomed to defending myself than having someone do it for me.'

Jayne lowered the lantern abruptly, closing the shutter so that neither of their expressions was visible. 'Except for Alice, William. She's your true defender. I can't imagine what she's said to my father, but he seems better disposed to you today than he was yesterday.'

She felt the brush of his fingers against her cheek. 'She'll have told him the truth,' he said, 'which is that my intentions towards you have only ever been honourable. Does that please or irritate you?'

Jayne heard the creak of the barn door and turned to see Andrew limned against the light inside. 'It pleases me,' she said quietly, stepping away and reopening the shutter on her lantern. She raised the light to shine on her brother's face. 'You look happy,' she said.

'And I dare say you do, too,' he said with a laugh, advancing to pull her into a hug. 'You'll not find a finer man than William, sister.'

Sir Henry and Lady Margaret were waiting in the hall when Jayne, Ruth and Isaac tiptoed through the front door an hour later. Lady Margaret bestowed kisses on Ruth and Isaac and sent them to their beds before inviting Jayne to join her and Sir Henry in the parlour. Ruth turned at the foot of the stairs and asked Jayne if she would like her to join them, but Jayne shook her head.

'I thank you for the offer, cousin, but Isaac needs his sleep and so do you. I wish you both sweet dreams.'

Sir Henry tut-tutted as he ushered his wife and daughter into the parlour and shut the door behind them. 'Does she think you need protecting from your own parents?' he demanded.

'Perhaps she fears you're going to sing at me, Papa. She still trembles with horror each time she remembers Isaac's faultless rendition of "The Cuckoo's Nest".' She hummed a few bars. 'Remind me how it goes.'

Lady Margaret wagged a finger at her. 'You'll not divert your father that easily. He has something to say to you on the subject of Sir William and I suggest you listen.'

Briefly, Sir Henry stared at the floor and then removed a folded piece of paper from the pocket of his russet coat. 'I can't see the point of a speech when Jayne can read the words for herself,' he said. 'Here.' He passed her the page.

24th of December, 1645

Honoured Sir,

Since I have no wish to take you from your guests on Christmas Day, I will leave this letter for you to read after my departure. My request concerns your daughter and I am happy to give you as much time as you deem necessary to consider it.

The war is drawing to a close and the King's surrender is expected by summer. I am told he still has hopes of raising armies in Ireland and Scotland, but few believe he'll succeed now that England is all but won for Parliament. I pray the majority view is correct because I long for peace as much as you do, Sir Henry.

Soldiering has taken me far and wide across Europe, and latterly through England, but my ambition has always been to make a life for myself in Dorset, the county of my birth. To that end, I petitioned Sir John Bankes, the Lord Chief Justice, to grant me the right to reacquire my father's estate near Blandford, and he did so in return for my promise to repay the mortgages Sir Ralph raised against it. I have now honoured those debts, and Winterborne Houghton is once again in the ownership of the Harrier family.

The property is in disrepair, but peace will allow me to give my full attention to its restoration. I was rewarded well for my soldiering in Europe and, while I feel bound to make good on the amounts my father owed the merchants of Dorset, I am confident I can meet that obligation and also return Winterborne Houghton to its former splendour.

Thereafter, I hope to secure a living through farming and service to my country as an emissary, for which I have some talent, being fluent in several languages. I will never be as wealthy as your daughter deserves, sir, but from my few conversations with her, I question if wealth is all she is looking for in a husband. She is a rare and extraordinary woman, not least for her superior intelligence and desire to forge her own path in life; and,

while our encounters have been infrequent and brief, my
respect and regard for her increase each time we meet.
*   I am ignorant of whether she reciprocates my*
feelings and have no wish to annoy her if she does not.
Nevertheless, I beg you to plead my case with her. It
would be my greatest privilege to be allowed to offer for
her hand.

Your obedient servant,
William Harrier

'Well?' Sir Henry demanded. 'How do you wish me to answer? I presume this comes as no surprise to you?'

Jayne shook her head. 'I'm more surprised than you, Papa.' She thought of Andrew's parting words and wondered if he'd had a hand in encouraging William to write the letter and persuading him to leave it on his departure. She wondered, too, if Philip and Benjamin knew of the plan, since they'd been absurdly keen to give way to William in the dances. Alice also, who'd been determined to paint Andrew's guest in the best light. She folded the letter and returned it to Sir Henry. 'Tell me first which answer you would like me to give, Papa.'

'Your mother insists the decision must be yours.'

'I'd still like to hear your opinion.'

Sir Henry gave a grunt of amusement. 'You've never wanted it in the past. I've lost count of the wealthy young men I've placed in your way only to have them dismissed as unworthy of consideration. Would I have had better success if I'd found one such as Sir William who was obliged to earn his living?'

Jayne smiled. 'It's what I've been doing, Papa. Have you forgotten that you only allowed me to work as a physician if I forwent my allowance? I have close to a hundred pounds saved and was planning to use it to purchase a small house where I could set up a surgery of my own.'

Sir Henry was shocked. 'Why would you want to do such a thing? Are you not happy here?'

Jayne answered the first question. 'I would have done it to prove I can, Papa. It shames me how many of my female patients support their families through what they earn, either because they're married to wastrels or their husbands are dead. It would please me to show I'm as capable as they.'

Lady Margaret stirred. 'You do understand that Sir William's rewards can only have come from plunder, Jayne? The armies of Prince Rupert, Prince Maurice and Lord Goring have merely followed the customs that are practised in Europe for the payment of troops.'

'I do, Mama, but I find it hard to be overly critical when the Correggio above the mantelpiece in our salon was looted from a chateau in France. I recall you telling me that my eldest Oxford uncle returned home with several crates of treasure in the early days of the European wars, which he touted in front of my grandfather in order to court Aunt Arabella. The painting was his gift of thanks for Papa's assistance in the venture.'

Sir Henry, who was still aggrieved that his sisters had snubbed his invitation, snorted in derision. '"Tout" is right,' he said. 'The man was shameless in parading his new-found wealth in front of my father. If Arabella hadn't been so smitten, I'd not have gone along with it.'

'Well, you can't accuse Sir William of anything so vulgar,' Lady Margaret murmured. 'He couldn't be clearer that supporting a wife comes well behind restoring Winterborne Houghton and paying off his father's debts. Do you understand that also, daughter?'

'I do, Mama,' Jayne answered solemnly. 'It's a thorny problem, is it not? Should we admire him for seeking to repair the damage his father did to the family name, or condemn him for daring to hope he might find a wife who would support such an ambition?'

'Do I sense you've already made up your mind?' asked Sir Henry. Jayne smiled again. 'I have, Papa.'

1646

In the hope of avoiding English retribution, the King surrenders to a Scottish army at Southwell outside Newark in Nottinghamshire on 5 May.

One month later, his nephews Prince Rupert and Prince Maurice surrender in Oxford and are banished from England by order of Parliament.

TWENTY-FIVE

Dorchester, Dorset, 8 May 1646

BELLS HAD BEEN TOLLING IN joyous celebration of the King's surrender for three days, and the streets of Dorchester were once again filled with happy people, most of whom were inebriated. Brawls became frequent as the ale levels rose, and Jayne stood up to watch from Alice's bedroom window as men threw drunken punches at each other. More often than not, Molly joined her and, together, they pondered the mystery of why, when the war was over, men still took pleasure in conflict.

Jayne said it would make more sense if defeated Royalists were lashing out at triumphant Parliamentarians, but for Dorchester Puritans to fight each other seemed to her the height of absurdity. What did they have to argue about? Molly scolded her for being naive. Puritan or not, it was the nature of males to fight. She had nothing but contempt for the whole selfish sex.

In truth, her anger was directed mainly at Sir Francis, who had neither appeared nor sent an answer to her urgent request two days ago that he visit his mother. Jayne had left Swyre within half an hour of Molly's letter arriving and was shocked to find that Alice was close to death. She had last seen her in the third week of April and, while it had been clear that standing and walking would soon be beyond her through lack of balance, her mind had remained sharp and her speech, though slurred, still understandable.

Now, a catastrophic collapse had rendered her senseless. According to Molly, she'd retired to bed upon hearing of the King's surrender and hadn't woken since, as if her only reason for living had been to witness the end of the war. Jayne thought it more likely the news had brought on an apoplectic seizure, but the result was the same. She lay in a deep coma, unresponsive to the chiming bells, the shouts of merriment from outside or the gentle stroking of her hands by Molly and Jayne.

To be certain there was nothing she could do for her, Jayne had written to Richard the previous afternoon, describing Alice's symptoms. She had received his reply that morning.

What a terrible sadness, but I'm sure Lady Alice would prefer this end to lingering on with ever worsening palsy. I believe you're right to suspect a seizure, and if the coma's as deep as you describe, she's unlikely to live beyond a week. I have no better suggestion than what you're doing already: keeping her mouth moist and ensuring she can breathe freely. Such seizures cannot be reversed, and the physician's single task is to assist the patient to pass as easily and comfortably as possible.

I know her death will cause you great grief, my dear. She was an exceptional woman who brought many good things to your life, not least your future husband.

*Remember her for that and not for the sadness of
her departure.*

It was good advice but not needed at the moment, for Jayne
had yet to experience sadness. Whenever Molly left the room,
she took the opportunity to speak to Alice about everything that
was in her heart, and it thrilled her when her voice or words
caused the corners of Alice's mouth to lift in a smile. Molly
confessed that she did the same when Jayne was away from the
bedside, and they felt a shared joy in the idea that Alice was able
to hear and understand them.

Jayne's rational mind told her it wasn't true, but it didn't stop
her drawing solace from each facial twitch. If she learnt anything
from her long hours at the bedside, it was that vigils were more
beneficial to the carers than the sufferers, since there was true
freedom in being able to express love and admiration without
embarrassment. By the third day, she decided it was mention of
William that was bringing the smiles. She spoke of him often
because of her and Alice's mutual love for him, and whether her
remarks were teasing or sincere, they received a response.

Jayne had written to him after receiving Molly's summons,
explaining that Alice had suffered a collapse and urging him to
ride south-west with all haste, but there was no knowing if the
letter would reach him. The last she'd heard, he was camped
outside Oxford, but, as the King had surrendered to a Scottish
army near Nottingham, Jayne felt sure William would have been
sent north to discover the terms of the surrender; and the chances
of her letter finding him were slim.

Whatever the truth, she was saddened for Alice that neither the
son she'd birthed nor the son she'd fostered were at her bedside.

⌐

A maid came to the room two hours after noon to say a coachman was at the door asking for Lady Alice. She'd told him Milady wasn't receiving visitors but he refused to leave, demanding to speak with someone of higher authority. With an angry sigh, Molly accompanied her downstairs, only to return within five minutes, begging Jayne to deal with him. He wouldn't say who he was or what purpose had brought him to the house and, more mysteriously, although he wore the livery of a coachman, there was no sign of a carriage in the street outside.

'When he demanded proof that Milady was indisposed, I said her physician was with her and he asked to speak with you, Miss Jayne. I trust you'll have better luck than I in persuading him you're telling the truth.'

Jayne doubted it, since he wouldn't be expecting a female physician; nevertheless, she descended to the hall. He stood inside the open doorway, a handsome young man in a fine livery of maroon jacket and britches adorned with gold braid in the form of a crest. He scowled to see yet another woman approach.

'I was promised Lady Alice's physician,' he said.

'You have her,' Jayne answered. 'My name is Mistress Swift and I have practised medicine for several years. May I have your name and the name of your employer? It's not my habit to divulge information about my patients to strangers.'

He seemed nervous suddenly. 'I'm not at liberty to give you a name, ma'am. My employer was expecting to see Lady Stickland.'

Jayne moved past him to search up and down the street. People were still thronging the cobbles but, as Molly had said, there was no sign of a carriage. 'Where is he?'

'I was obliged to leave the carriage in High East Street because the crowds were too dense to make further progress, ma'am. A groom holds the horses and my employer sends Lady Stickland his respects and asks that she attends upon him there.'

Jayne smiled slightly. 'Has he lost the function of his legs?'

'He's elderly, ma'am, and too frail to make his way through a drunken mob.'

Jayne shrugged. 'Then there's nothing to be done. Lady Stickland is quite unable to leave her bed.' She placed her hand on the door and began to close it, gesturing for him to step outside. 'Farewell to you.'

He remained where he was, turning his coachman's cap in his hands. 'I believe the master might be willing to converse with you, ma'am.'

Jayne made her disinclination clear. 'You have peculiar ideas about how ladies behave. I'm no more in the habit of accompanying strangers who refuse to tell me anything about themselves than I am in divulging information about my patients.' She made a second attempt to close the door. 'I shall send for the bailiffs if you refuse to remove yourself.'

The coachman took a deep breath, clearly considering the wisdom of what he was about to say, and then blurted out his words in a hurry. 'I am in the employ of Lady Maria Marston of Thatcham in Berkshire, ma'am. Her father, who lives with her, is the Duke of Granville and he has come to discover from Lady Stickland what manner of man his grandson has become and whether Mistress Swift, the woman he plans to marry, is worthy of the Granville name. His Grace is past eighty-five years old, and the journey has taken its toll on him; I fear for his health if he's obliged to travel seven hours back to his home without time to recover. Since I believe you may be the Mistress Swift in question, you will do me a great kindness if you agree to accompany me to the carriage.'

Jayne was so wrong-footed she fixed on the obvious absurdity in the story. 'No man of such advanced age would travel a distance without knowing if he'll be received,' she protested.

'His Grace assured me that Lady Stickland was expecting him, ma'am. My Lord asked for a bed to be set up downstairs, for he cannot manage stairs, and was led to believe he would be allowed to stay the weekend in order to regain his strength before making the journey home again.'

Jayne stared at him, aghast. 'Even if that's true, it's quite impossible now,' she said. 'Lady Stickland is in no position to entertain anyone. You must find rooms for His Grace in one of Dorchester's inns.'

The coachman's face twisted in agony as he revealed something else he knew he shouldn't. 'But he needs the attention of a physician, ma'am. We left Thatcham before dawn this morning and he is desperately weakened by the journey. His daughter refused to supply him with food, water or even blankets when she learnt of his intention to speak with Lady Stickland.'

Jayne would have disbelieved him had his anxiety for his master's health been less apparent. With sudden decision, she pulled him inside and closed the door. 'Allow me five minutes to ready myself and then we will go to the carriage together, but be assured you will have reason to regret this summons if I find you've led me false.'

She hastened back up the stairs and explained the situation to Molly. Had Alice informed her she was expecting the Duke of Granville? Not a duke, Molly answered, only a visitor, but that had been a fortnight since and all thoughts of the matter had fled her head when Milady collapsed. What did Miss Jayne want her to do?

'Be ready to instruct the maids to set up a bed in the salon and ask Cook to prepare some nourishing broth and custard,' Jayne told her. She would send word within fifteen minutes, if the coachman's description of his master was accurate.

As they made their way to High East Street, the coachman begged her to pretend she was ignorant of his master's identity; His Grace would refuse to speak with her if he thought she knew his reasons for coming. The matter of his grandson had been consuming him since it became obvious the King could not win the war, but even more so since learning of his grandson's betrothal to Mistress Swift. Jayne was tempted to say that her own reluctance matched the duke's, but she was pleased she hadn't when she saw how frail the old man was.

She stood aside as the coachman opened the carriage door, then leant in to study the two occupants. One, a tiny person dressed in a servant's uniform, sat cross-legged in the corner of the seat; the other, much taller and clad in fine attire, sat upright, staring forward. The coachman had told her that His Grace's valet was travelling with him, and Jayne had no difficulty distinguishing between them, though she was shocked to see that each was as ancient as the other.

She bobbed a perfunctory curtsey and addressed the duke. 'Your driver tells me that Lady Stickland is expecting you, sir, but, with regret, I must tell you she was confined to her bed three days ago and is unable to greet you. I have come in her place to offer what assistance and explanations I can.'

The cross-legged valet eyed her with disfavour. 'Are you a maid?'

She shook her head. 'I am Jayne Swift, daughter to Sir Henry and Lady Margaret Swift of Swyre. I am also physician and friend to Lady Stickland and cannot be away from her side for longer than thirty minutes.' She looked again at the duke. 'May I enquire who you are, sir? Your coachman asked me to converse with his employer but would not give your name.'

He turned to look at her, a flicker of recognition in his eyes.

'He can't speak for cold,' whimpered the valet. 'What's to be done? What's to be done?'

The crest on the carriage door had attracted a group of wide-eyed children, and Jayne beckoned the tallest forward, taking a penny from her pocket-purse. 'Do you know Lady Stickland's house in Church Street?' When he nodded, she pressed the coin into his palm. 'Run there as fast as you can and tell the maid who answers the door that Milady's guests will be arriving before the hour is out.'

She instructed the coachman to drive to the White Horse Inn, which was two hundred yards ahead, and accepted the help of the groom to mount the step and settle herself on the seat opposite the duke. His lips were blue and the skin of his face so thin and pale that it was almost transparent, but his grey eyes were bright with curiosity. 'As a physician, I strongly advise that you remain in Dorchester for the night in order to restore your strength, sir. The inn has beds and good food, but you will also be welcome at Lady Stickland's house. I believe she would want her invitation honoured.'

It was evident the old man wanted to answer because his mouth writhed in an attempt to form words, but no sound came out.

'Would water help, sir?' she asked, lifting the flap on her satchel and removing a stoppered bottle and a silver cup. 'I carry it to quench my thirst when I travel to see patients.'

His hands were trembling so violently that she leant forward to hold the filled cup to his mouth, replenishing it twice before his tongue was loosened enough for speech. 'Thank you,' he managed. 'What ails Lady Stickland?'

Jayne saw little sense in withholding the truth. 'I believe it to be an apoplectic stroke, sir. She had a seizure three nights ago and hasn't woken from it. Had I known you were expected I would have sent word not to come.'

A glimmer of humour appeared in his eyes. 'Where would you have sent it, since you don't know who I am?'

'Alice is a prolific letter writer and keeps her correspondence in fine order, sir. I would have found your acceptance of her invitation.'

He looked out of the window as the coach turned onto the fore-court of the White Horse Inn and drew to a halt. The continued dryness of his mouth and throat meant his voice was croaky, but the words were fluent. 'You would have found a letter from the Duke of Granville, inviting himself, Mistress Swift. Lady Stickland had no choice in the matter once I named today for my arrival. Knowing this, do you still wish to offer me a bed for the night?'

Jayne poured a cup of water for the valet and watched him slide to the floor to snatch it from her hands. 'Learning your name and title doesn't alter my opinion that you're in need of rest, my lord. Your manservant also. He's as much in need of attention as you are.'

The duke addressed the groom who had leapt from the driving seat and presented himself at the window. 'I'm in this lady's hands,

Harold,' he said, motioning to Jayne. 'You must take your orders from her.'

—

Doubting the groom would succeed in acquiring what was needed as effectively as she could, Jayne descended from the coach to make the arrangements herself. Rather than give His Grace the impression that she was used to entering taverns alone, however, she asked Harold to accompany her. They had advanced barely three steps before she was stopped by a hand clutching at her skirts.

'Don't be alarmed, ma'am,' muttered Harold. 'It's only Mister Adams. His wits are scrambled but he means you no harm.'

She reached behind her to take the valet's hand. 'Do you wish to come with us, Mister Adams?' she asked with a smile. 'I'm sure the innkeeper's wife will have sweetmeats for you.'

He clutched her fingers as tightly as a child. 'Will Milady see me?'

Harold obliged with a whispered explanation. 'He means His Grace's daughter, ma'am. He has a powerful fear of her.'

Jayne assured Mister Adams he was safe and then led him and Harold down the side of the building to the kitchen quarters, where she was greeted warmly by the innkeeper's wife, whose children she had treated for measles fever. The room was full of servants busy preparing food, and Mister Adams pranced with joy at the heat that came from the fires and the fragrant scents that perfumed the air.

'I'm in need of your sedan chair, May,' Jayne told the innkeeper's wife. 'Also a plate of food and some ale for my friend Mister Adams.' She sat the little man on a stool at the kitchen table and knelt beside him. 'These kind people will look after you until I can send the sedan back to bring you to your master. You have nothing to fear from Lady Maria, for she is in Berkshire and you are in Dorset. Do you understand?'

He pulled open a drawer in the table. 'Where's the food?'

May plucked a sweetmeat from a bowl and popped it into his mouth, before raising her eyebrows in query. 'Mind gone?' she mouthed at Jayne.

Jayne nodded and took a half-crown from her pocket-purse. 'Will you watch him until the chair returns, May? They have but to take his master to Lady Stickland's house in Church Street, so the wait shouldn't be long.' She rose to her feet and placed the money on the table. 'May I borrow some blankets also? His master is of even greater age and so cold that he can barely speak. They've driven for more than seven hours, so the bearers may have to lift him from the coach, since I doubt he'll be able to descend unaided.'

Clicking her tongue in concern, May sent a servant to summon the two burly chair-bearers, another to fetch blankets and a third for a flagon of ale from the bar. Meanwhile, she spooned stew from a steaming cauldron into a bowl and placed it in front of Mister Adams.

'Sixpence will suffice for two chair rides and the food, Mistress Swift. If you don't have pennies in your purse, I'll send a maid to fetch change for your half-crown.'

'There's no need, May. I was hoping the rest would cover the cost of housing and stabling His Grace's carriage and horses, and a room for his coachman and groom.'

May noted the title with an ironic lift of an eyebrow. 'Can he not pay himself?' she asked, casting her gaze over Harold's smart livery.

Harold, clearly thinking the question was addressed to him, shuffled his feet in embarrassment. 'I fear not, ma'am, for his daughter refused him money for the journey. He wouldn't be in such a weakened state if we'd been able to purchase a room and provisions along the way, and nothing we said persuaded him to turn back.'

May's response to this statement was a choice word for the daughter, followed by instructions to Harold on where to house the horses and carriage once the duke had departed. By then, the chair and its bearers were waiting outside the kitchen door and, taking the blankets, she accompanied the party to the front of the inn. It was hard to say what she made of the stiff, upright figure staring straight ahead, nor indeed what Granville made of her, for he merely shook his head when she asked if he was able to step from the carriage himself.

'Then allow the bearers to lift you out, my lord. They carry ale casks for a living, so your weight will be small by comparison.'

In the event, it required only one to scoop him into his arms and transfer him to the sedan. Once he was safely seated, May wrapped two blankets about his shoulders, tucking them down his back, and then another two over his knees and around his feet. 'Do you feel secure?' she asked, closing and bolting the door. 'I'll ask the bearers to walk slowly so that you don't suffer nausea.'

He nodded. 'Thank you, mistress. You're most kind. May I ask where Mister Adams is?'

'Eating and drinking in my kitchen, my lord. He seems happy enough being spoilt by my maids, and Mistress Swift has promised him a ride in the chair when it returns from Lady Stickland's house.'

'I fear you're making a rod for your own back, mistress. He's unused to kindness and will likely refuse to leave your kitchen when the time comes.'

May chuckled. 'He'll not refuse me, sire. If needs be, I'll carry him to the chair myself and feed him sugar drops while the bearers bring him to you.'

The duke studied her with amusement. 'Could you not have made the same delightful offer to me?'

She wagged a playful finger at him. 'There's a difference between carrying a leprechaun and a man of your stature, sire. I warrant you were above six feet when you were younger . . . and handsome to boot, if your present good looks are anything to go by.'

May was a master at using flattery to tease money from reluctant payers, but this time she spoke only the truth. Despite his advanced years, the duke was as tall as his coachman, and in the shape of his eyes and mouth Jayne saw a resemblance to the sketches Alice had made of Ralph. Unexpectedly, she found herself warming to him. She had imagined Granville to be a bitter and vengeful man, not one who tolerated senile valets and overfamiliar innkeepers' wives with kindness and courtesy.

~

Molly, thoroughly strained to have guests added to her anxiety over Lady Alice, peppered Jayne with questions once another bed had been added to the salon and Mister Adams had joined his master for a sleep. Would they expect more food later, having already consumed several bowls of custard and broth? Should the cook prepare dinner? Who would host the occasion? Did

Miss Jayne plan to wear a more appropriate gown? And what of poor Milady? Must she be abandoned in order that a duke might be entertained?

Jayne squeezed her hand. 'Nothing needs changing, including my gown, Molly. His Grace must accept us as we are or seek a bed and entertainment at the White Horse. May told me she has three empty rooms, so he'll not go wanting.'

A twisted smile lifted the corner of Molly's mouth. 'You should have left him there.'

Jayne sighed. 'I didn't feel I could. You've seen for yourself how frail he is. We'll pretend His Grace is a man like any other, show him what hospitality we can and continue to give our full attention to Lady Alice. In truth, I suspect we'll have more trouble from his valet, whose mind is so muddled he's likely to start wandering the house.'

She was proved right some three hours later, when the little man began haunting the kitchen in search of ale. Jayne was summoned from Alice's bedside when the cook lost patience with his intemperate rummaging through her cupboards. To restore peace, she gave a maid a penny to purchase a flagon from the nearest hostelry, and once Mister Adams was assured he would have his drink in five minutes, he agreed to sit obediently at the kitchen table while Jayne went to check on his master.

She found him in the parlour, standing upright behind Alice's chair and watching the passage of people through the window. He was using the high back to support himself, and Jayne wondered how he had managed to walk from the salon unaided in view of his inability even to step down from his coach. He'd clearly had no help from Mister Adams, for he was dressed only in a long, loose shirt which was rumpled from being worn in bed.

She moved alongside him, ready to reach out if her sudden appearance caused him to lose balance. 'Would you not be happier sitting, my lord?'

'I would,' he murmured, 'but I'm not confident about making my way around this chair. I was doing quite well until I reached it.'

'Amazingly well,' she said, cupping her right hand inside his armpit and her left beneath his forearm. 'When you feel you can trust me to hold your weight, release your grip on the chair and I'll assist you to the front.'

'You're tall for a woman.'

'I am, sire. My father puts it down to good food and a healthy appetite in childhood.'

Without warning, he let go of the chair. 'This being Sir Henry Swift of Swyre?'

'Indeed.' She drew him gently towards her. 'There's no hurry. Be sure to find your balance before you take a new step.' It required only three before she was able to lower him onto the cushioned seat. 'Do you wish me to summon your coachman and groom to dress you?' she asked, kneeling to position his feet on a stool. 'Or would you prefer to remain as you are with blankets to keep you warm?'

'Blankets will suffice for the moment,' he said. 'I'm enjoying watching Dorchester celebrate her victory. I can't recall seeing so many inebriated Puritans before.'

Jayne smiled. 'You're not alone, my lord.'

'Do you share in their delight, Mistress Swift?'

'In so far as it means the war is over, I do, sire.'

'And you're not angry to be forced to entertain a Royalist? You should know that my daughter and son-in-law will not allow a Parliamentarian into their house.'

'Well, thankfully, Lady Alice holds different views, sire,' Jayne answered easily. 'She recognised very early that her life would become intolerably boring if she only conversed with those who agreed with her.' She rose and stepped away. 'If you'll excuse me, I'll fetch the blankets myself. Everything's been at sixes and sevens since Alice's collapse, and I'd rather be certain you were warm than leave the task to a maid.'

More truthfully, she was worried about the iciness of his skeletal feet and the lack of flesh on his arm and shoulder. Dressed in a simple shirt, he appeared even less substantial than he had when he was fully clothed at the inn. She returned to the kitchen and asked the cook if His Grace's coachman and groom were in the house. Directed to an anteroom, she found them eating plates of cold meat in their shirtsleeves. They rose hastily to their feet as she entered, pulling on their jackets and rebuttoning them.

'I need one of you to help me dress His Grace,' she said, closing the door, 'but first I want answers to some questions. How long has he been residing with Lady Maria?'

'Four years,' said Harold after a brief hesitation. 'His estate in Somerset was overrun by Parliamentarians in the first weeks of the war, and Lady Maria deemed it safer to bring him to live with her.'

'Does he spend time with her family or is he confined to his room?'

The coachman, who'd given his name as Peter, shook his head. 'We can't tell you, ma'am. Lady Maria threatened us with dismissal if we talked about the household.'

'How will she know?' Jayne asked reasonably.

'She won't,' said Harold. 'There's little communication between any of the family members, ma'am. Sir Anthony inhabits the east wing, Lady Maria the west, and His Grace stays in his rooms at the rear of the house with only Mister Adams for company.'

Which would explain why he was so curious about what was happening in the street outside, Jayne thought. His life must have been starved of interest if he'd been restricted to a back room with only a senile valet for company. 'Does the family eat together?'

Harold shrugged to express ignorance. 'We're outside workers so live and eat above the stables, ma'am, but I've heard tell His Grace can't manage the food Milady orders for him, it being too tough for the few teeth he has left.'

'And I've heard tell she does it deliberately,' said Peter, apparently feeling that discretion was no longer necessary. 'She's not a kind person, Mistress Swift. Every one of us would leave her service if we could find a place elsewhere.'

Jayne nodded thoughtfully. 'May I ask why she allowed you to bring him here today? She could have refused him the use of the carriage as easily as money and blankets.'

'The carriage belongs to His Grace, ma'am, as do the horses. He said he'd drive it himself if she refused to supply a coachman and groom. Our instructions were to turn around as soon as he fell asleep . . . but he never did.'

Jayne thanked them for their answers and then asked which of them was stronger. When both agreed that it was Peter, she led him to the salon and instructed him to take every spare item from the duke's bag, along with the boots, hose, britches, jacket and cloak he'd worn on the journey. For her part, she took the blankets from the bed before opening the connecting door to the parlour and ushering Peter ahead of her.

'We've come to dress you, my lord,' she said. 'Peter your driver will lift you while I clothe you in double layers to give you warmth.'

She had expected thinness but not a frame so skeletal that every bone could be felt beneath the skin. Nevertheless, she hid her concern behind light chatter, and, once he was clothed in two of everything with a blanket across his lap and another about his shoulders, she asked if he'd mind being left alone while she sought out a maid to light a fire in the hearth.

He looked at her for a moment and then nodded towards two framed pictures hanging to the left of the door to the hall. 'Which artist painted those?'

Jayne followed his gaze and saw with surprise that they were the promised portraits of herself and Ralph. Having not been to the parlour since her arrival, she'd had no idea Alice had finished them or displayed them so publicly. 'Lady Stickland, my lord.'

'She's captured your likeness very well—my son's also. Were they made for my grandson?'

Such an idea had never occurred to Jayne. 'I don't believe so, sire. I think Alice merely wanted to prove she could still hold a brush.'

He seemed to lose interest immediately and turned back to the window. 'I don't require company, Mistress Swift,' he said. 'The antics in the street are keeping me entertained.'

Peter moved ahead of Jayne as they walked down the corridor, and turned with a bow to persuade her to stop. 'My Lord is more in need of a physician's attention than I realised, ma'am. Please believe I had no knowledge of how truly frail he is.'

'You've no reason to chide yourself, Peter. It was you who found him a physician.'

'Even so, ma'am, no daughter should be so cruel to a father.'

Jayne agreed with him but didn't pursue the matter. She could think of only one reason for the woman to neglect her father so shamelessly, and it couldn't be said aloud. With Ralph's son disinherited, Lady Maria's family stood to inherit the entirety of the Granville wealth, and that placed a higher value on His Grace's death than on his life.

~

Unwilling to abandon Alice, she asked permission of Molly to have Granville brought to Milady's chamber, explaining that he, too, needed attention. Molly protested that it wasn't her place to make such a decision, but Jayne assured her it was. She was Alice's most loyal friend, and if she preferred to spend the last hours alone with her mistress then that was how it should be. Molly shook her head. It would amuse Milady to have a man in her bedroom, she said.

Peter carried the duke upstairs, still wrapped in blankets, and His Grace expressed himself satisfied to be sitting as comfortably at Milady's window as downstairs in the parlour. He studied Alice's face for several long moments. 'Her sleep seems peaceful. Do you think she hears you?'

Jayne glanced towards the bed. 'Molly and I believe so, my lord. Would you like us to absent ourselves for a quarter-hour so that you may speak with her in private? She'll not be able to answer you but her smiles suggest she understands some of the words being said.'

He shook his head. 'I wouldn't know what to say, Mistress Swift, except to express regret for my discourtesy in not replying to her letters. She wrote to me several times in the early years of my grandson's life, and I considered each communication to be a meddlesome intrusion into matters that didn't concern her. I took offence that a woman thought she had the right to tell me how to behave.'

Jayne smiled. 'Would you have found it less offensive if her husband had chided you, sire?'

He grunted a laugh. 'He wouldn't have dared. No man would. Only this lady felt able to lecture me on my shortcomings as a grandfather. Is my grandson everything she told me he was, Mistress Swift?'

'I don't know, my lord, for I'm ignorant of what she wrote. All I can say with certainty is that she's a true and honest friend.'

'Do you say the same about my grandson?'

'I do, my lord, but my word will have no more sway with you than Alice's did. You must form your own opinion of Ralph and Estelle's son.'

'And how am I to do that?'

Molly felt emboldened to speak. 'Pray that Miss Jayne's letter has found him, sire,' she said. 'I feel in my bones that Milady is waiting for his arrival.'

The prediction had hardly left her mouth when a knock came upon the chamber door. The sound heralded the entrance of two maids with a bowl of tender mutton stew, another of sweet frumenty, and a platter of bread, butter and soft cheese. Nevertheless, the coincidence caused the duke to start nervously and clap his hand to his heart in shock, and it was clear to Jayne that he was more fearful than desirous of meeting William. To settle his anxiety, she said she believed William would have come by now if her letter had reached him.

Molly excused herself to eat downstairs and Jayne encouraged His Grace to quiz her about her family, since talk of Swyre was unlikely to provoke disagreement. She kept her stories deliberately frivolous, but, even so, his curiosity about her father's and elder brother's different allegiances raised the issue of war. He found it difficult to believe that Sir Henry didn't harbour animosity towards Andrew, but Jayne assured him he did not.

'He has no wish to see the division in the country replicated inside his house, sire. Had Andrew chosen to support Parliament out of spite, Papa might have felt differently, but he knew the decision was made in good conscience and after long thought. The same was true of our servants and farmhands, a good half of whom preferred Parliament's cause to the King's. Had Sir Henry felt obliged to dismiss them because of it, he would have lost his best workers.'

Granville appeared shocked. 'I wouldn't countenance such a lack of respect in my household. How could he trust employees who held a different allegiance from his own?'

'Through knowing and valuing them for far longer than the war has lasted, sire. Do you think your daughter's servants share her views? They may not voice them aloud, but I'll warrant there are more than she realises who would rather the King ruled with their consent than without it.'

Granville laid down his spoon, having cleaned his plate of the easily chewed mutton. 'Is that what you think the war has been about?'

Jayne rose from her seat to wring out a napkin in a bowl of cool water and lay it across Alice's brow. 'It is, my lord,' she said, dipping her finger into the bowl and running a trickle of liquid across Alice's lips. 'The gift of peace has always been in the King's hands. He had but to accept Parliament's terms.'

Food and warmth had revived both his colour and spirit. 'He'll never do it,' he said firmly. 'He's God's anointed and believes in the righteousness of his actions.'

Jayne placed her finger on Alice's wrist and marvelled again at the steadiness of her pulse. 'As do Sir Thomas Fairfax and General Cromwell believe in theirs,' she answered. 'The country's awash with virtuous men in search of authority. How can we find a peaceful resolution if both sides persist in the belief that God favours them?'

'The King will never bow to Parliament's will. He may have abandoned the war, but he'll not vacate his throne. Will that annoy my grandson, Mistress Swift?'

Jayne resumed her seat. 'I wouldn't think so, my lord. Like most Parliamentarians, his aim has always been to replace absolute power with shared power.'

He eyed her for a long moment. 'He comes from a noble line and you're a squire's daughter. What interests can you and he possibly have in common?'

The abruptness of the question and the derogatory stresses that Granville put on the words suggested a move away from friendliness, and Jayne found it ironic that food, kindness and companionship were allowing his authentic voice to emerge. 'Nothing that would excite you, my lord. We talk more about our work than anything else.'

'And that contents you?'

'A great deal more than being handed a trinket and told I have pretty eyes, sire. I appreciate your grandson's curiosity. Every other suitor I've had shied away from discussions about the effectiveness of maggots on gangrene.'

He closed his eyes briefly. 'You're not what I was expecting, Mistress Swift.'

'May I ask who told you about me, sire?'

'My daughter learnt of your betrothal from Lady Cooper, whose own daughter, Emmeline, is acquainted with Sir Francis Stickland.' He nodded towards Alice. 'This lady's son. Between them, they've been most forthcoming on my grandson's intentions towards you and his plan to make you mistress of Winterborne Houghton. Are they as correct on the second count as on the first?'

Jayne nodded.

'Then you've been deceived, Mistress Swift. You can never live in Winterborne Houghton. The property belongs to me, and only I may decide its future.' He gave a dismissive flick of his hand. 'My grandson knows this perfectly well.'

Jayne wondered briefly if she should let the issue go, but decided for William's sake that she couldn't. 'With respect, my lord, the property has never belonged to you. You gave it to your son at the time of his marriage, and in law a gift cannot be taken back. William won his case fairly in court, establishing his right to inherit the estate as Sir Ralph's heir on the condition that he redeem the outstanding mortgages. This has now been done, and the deeds of entitlement granting him sole ownership have been authorised by the court.'

'My rights granted me by the King take precedence.'

'Not in law, sire. Only the court that confiscated the estate at the time of your son's suicide had jurisdiction. The King moved outside his authority when he approved your petition, as Lady Alice and her husband argued in the legal objection they lodged on William's behalf. Being a minor, he couldn't lodge it himself, but he was able to refresh it on his return from Europe.'

Anger sparked in his eyes, but whether at the mention of 'suicide' or Alice and her husband's advocacy for William, Jayne couldn't tell. 'My daughter believes Lady Stickland is to blame for your family's future connection with mine. Is she right?'

Jayne stared at her hands so that he wouldn't see her own anger. 'If you explain why it's a cause for blame, I'll endeavour to answer, sire.'

'Lady Maria is closely acquainted with Lord and Lady Hamway, whose son Edward had reason to visit Swyre on official business. The portrait he paints of you and your parents is most unflattering, and my daughter is persuaded that you and they have used your influence with Lady Stickland to entrap my grandson into an inappropriate marriage.' He paused. 'What do you say to that?'

Jayne raised her head. 'Nothing, sire, for I don't choose to waste my breath.'

He gave another dismissive flick of his hand. 'That's a foolish response. In the absence of denial, you will force me to accept that what Lady Maria says is true.'

Jayne considered for a moment. 'Then allow me to defend Alice, since she can't speak for herself.' She leant forward to stare into the duke's eyes. 'The idea that she might be susceptible to another's influence is both laughable and insulting. Her intelligence is superior to that of most men and greatly in excess of anything enjoyed by small-minded, malicious gossips like your daughter and Lady Hamway. Far from my parents influencing her, she interceded on your grandson's behalf to influence them. Had she not, my father would have rejected William's offer out of hand, since he assumed a man who had been disowned and disinherited by his family must be the worst kind of fortune-hunter.'

Granville was unimpressed. 'And what argument did she use to persuade your father to the contrary? The promise of ennoblement through marriage?'

Jayne gave an abrupt laugh. 'She's not so dishonest, my lord. It's only you who sees merit in your title. William has no interest in it, and Alice would never betray his trust by using it as a lure to win over a reluctant parent. You make a grave mistake judging women by your daughter and families by your own.'

He made a perfunctory gesture of apology. 'I didn't mean to offend you, Mistress Swift. My single aim in coming here was to discover the truth.'

'But you have offended me,' she said, rising from her chair. 'It's of no interest to me if you choose to believe Lady Maria and Sir Edward Hamway, but I will not allow you to slander Alice. It remains a source of inspiration to me that William's decency and honesty were forged by a powerfully free-thinking woman—and not the weak, degenerate line from which he springs.'

TWENTY-SIX

SIR FRANCIS CAME EARLY THE next morning. He was as timid and hesitant as Joseph had described, but his anguish for his mother was very clear. He excused his tardy arrival, explaining that he'd been absent from home for three days, staying with friends, but after half an hour of hand-wringing and weeping he accepted Jayne's suggestion that he would be better employed sitting with the Duke of Granville.

Jayne escorted him to the parlour and made the introductions, and if Sir Francis found it odd that the duke wouldn't look at her, he didn't show it. She'd been unable to tease a word out of His Grace since their falling-out of the previous evening. Mercifully, Peter was more than willing to assume the role of valet, and Granville was well presented and comfortably seated in the parlour by the time Sir Francis appeared. Jayne took her leave of them with a curtsey, saying she would have refreshments sent, then closed the door behind her with a thankful sigh. She was accustomed to Sir Henry's boisterous demands for kisses of reconciliation after a disagreement, and found the strained, uncomfortable silence His Grace preferred wearisome.

When she returned to the chamber, she found Molly in tears at Alice's bedside over the added strain of having another guest in the house. Cook had told her she needed money for supplies, but the coin chest hadn't been replenished since Milady's seizure. What was she to do? Milady deserved better than to have her final hours disturbed by selfish men. Jayne begged her not to worry. She still had two crowns in her satchel which Cook could use.

Nevertheless, she was close to weeping herself. She hadn't slept for more than a couple of hours these last three nights and fatigue made her grief and anxiety worse. What would become of Alice's household after she died? Would Sir Francis take responsibility for them if Winterborne Stickland was already fully staffed? And what of the duke and Mister Adams? Who would take responsibility for them?

Towards noon, she moved to a desk in the corner of Alice's chamber and began penning a letter to her father.

My dearest Papa, I am desperately in need of your help . . .

The door opened so quietly that Jayne was unaware anyone had entered the room until Molly rose abruptly from her stool, causing it to tumble to the floor behind her. 'Oh, praise God, praise God!' she sobbed, holding out her hands. 'You've come!'

Startled, Jayne looked up from her writing and felt ready to sob herself. There surely was no more comforting presence than William, never mind that he was filthy with dust from the road and reeking of horse sweat. She rose to join her hands with his and Molly's. 'I feared my letter wouldn't reach you.'

'It found me yesterday outside Nottingham.' He glanced towards the bed. 'Am I too late?'

'No. Molly and I believe she's been waiting for you. We'll leave so that you may have time with her alone.'

He released their hands. 'Don't,' he said. 'You're her closest friends and your presence is as necessary to her as mine.' He knelt beside the bed and pressed a kiss to Alice's forehead. 'It's William, milady. I've ridden through the night to see you.'

He cradled his palm against her cheek and a flutter began in her eyelids.

'No boy had a kinder mother, no youth a better teacher, no man a more loyal protector. If love could be painted, it would bear your face, milady. I owe you more than I can say.'

Jayne couldn't tell how long Alice's eyes remained open or whether they truly moved from William to her to Molly, but there was no doubting the soft sigh of contentment that escaped her mouth or the sweet smile that settled on her lips. Jayne would have thought her still alive had not William, who had seen so many deaths, closed her lids with gentle fingers and bent his head in respect for a soul departed.

Molly wanted to fasten the shutters to signal a passing in the house, but William asked her to leave them open. 'Alice loved light, and Francis should be able to see her when he makes his farewells.'

Jayne, who had knelt to make her own farewells to this remarkable woman, rose to stand beside him, pressing her thumb and forefinger to the bridge of her nose to hold back her tears. 'He's in the parlour,' she said.

William placed a comforting hand on her shoulder. 'I know. I entered through the kitchen and discovered Cook in a bother over the number of guests in the house.'

Molly took up a brush and drew it gently through Alice's grey hair. 'Sir Francis came this morning,' she said through her own tears, 'but the others came yesterday. They're eating us out of house and home.'

'Would one of them be a strange little man in a nightgown who tells me he's valet to His Grace the Duke of Granville and insists on rummaging through Cook's cupboards?'

'I'm afraid so,' said Jayne. 'His master is with Francis.' She described the events of the previous day, finishing with the duke's pained silence after she reprimanded him. 'He hasn't wanted to speak with me since, but I can't in good conscience abandon him and Mister Adams. They're both terribly undernourished and quite unfit to make the journey back to Berkshire.'

William glanced towards the desk and the letter she'd been writing. 'What were you planning to do with them?'

'Beg Papa and Mama to take them in,' she said with a sigh. 'Granville will be rude to them but I couldn't think of anything else to do.'

He folded her hands in his. 'Your parents have no obligation to do anything for him and neither do you. I'll ask Francis to offer him rooms at Winterborne Stickland.'

'He's been shockingly neglected, William. He needs more care than an unwed man can give him.'

'Francis's household will look after him well enough.' He waited while Molly brought colour to Alice's cheeks with a dusting of rouge. 'Will you be kind enough to fetch Sir Francis, Molly? We shouldn't keep him from his mother longer than is necessary.'

Molly dabbed at her eyes with the hem of her apron. 'The household would like to take their leave of her, too, William. May I send them up when Sir Francis has finished?'

'Of course,' he said, opening the door for her. He waited for Molly to descend the stairs before speaking with Jayne again. 'I have no desire to meet the duke, so will leave as soon as I've secured Francis's promise to accommodate him. Once they've departed, send word to me at my house in Durngate Street and I will return. Are you comfortable with that?'

She shook her head.

'Don't make this difficult for me, Jayne,' he said harshly. 'I owe him nothing. Whatever troubles he has, he has brought on himself.'

'I don't dispute that,' she answered, 'but you asked if I was comfortable with your decision, and I am not. For myself, I would take the opportunity to satisfy my curiosity.'

_____

She made her way to the kitchen rather than stay with William and Francis, only to be caught at the door by Peter, who begged her to attend upon His Grace.

'Mister Adams has told him his grandson is here, ma'am, and he's most keen to see him. You will know better than I how to effect such a meeting.'

Stifling yet more sighs, Jayne followed him to the parlour where Mister Adams, still dressed in his nightshirt, was searching the drawers in Alice's bureau. She moved to his side and took a gentle hold of his wrists. 'It's not seemly to go through the possessions of one who has passed, sir . . . nor to remain in sleep attire in a house of death. You know this, for you have been His Grace's faithful valet for a long time now.' She drew him towards Peter. 'Allow Peter to assist you into something more befitting a sad occasion.' She waited until they were in the hall, then curtseyed to the duke. 'You wished to see me, my lord?'

'You have more patience than my daughter. Maria would have slapped his face and screamed at him.'

'And does that cure him of his confusion?'

He shook his head. 'He's so terrified of her he crouches in a corner whenever she enters the room, and begs me daily to remove him from her house.' He nodded to a chair in front of him. 'Sit down, Mistress Swift, and allow me to express my condolences. You must be deeply grieved by Lady Stickland's passing.'

She lowered herself to the seat and answered honestly. 'Not as grieved as I would have been had she suffered a lingering death, my lord. She was taken by shaking palsy twelve months ago and was deeply afeared she would be confined to bed, unable to speak or feed herself. To suffer a seizure and die peacefully in her sleep is the kinder end, I think.'

'Was my grandson with her?'

Jayne nodded.

'Is he still there?'

She nodded again.

'Will you bring him to me?'

Jayne chose a tactful response. 'Do you think it wise to request a meeting now, my lord? Alice was his mother in all but name from the day of his birth, and her death is as painful to him as it is to Sir Francis. He needs time to mourn before you demand acknowledgement for yourself.'

His Grace took a kerchief from his sleeve and held it to his eyes. 'You think me mean-spirited and selfish, and rightly so.

I behaved badly towards you last night and can only excuse my rudeness on finding you to be more honest than I expected. A dishonest woman would have said what I wanted to hear, but you did not. Will you forgive me, my dear?'

Jayne's sympathies were not so lacking in scepticism that she couldn't see when she was being used. 'I forgive you readily, my lord, but I doubt my father will. Sir Henry went to great trouble to have Sir Edward Hamway imprisoned for violent assault and attempted theft, and it will not amuse him to hear that so immoral a man is now telling lies about him.'

Surprised, Granville crumpled the kerchief inside his fist. 'Is that true?'

A shadow moved across the doorway before Jayne could reply. 'You really shouldn't doubt my future wife, sire,' said William, showing himself. 'Even George Goring, the most disreputable general in the King's army, tired of Hamway's deceits eventually and sent him home in disgrace.' He stepped into the room and bent his neck. 'Your servant, my lord. I am Colonel William Harrier.'

The duke's shock was greater than it should have been, since he knew already that William was in the house. He gazed at him wide-eyed, sucking at air, and Jayne became concerned that his breaths were too shallow and fast. Anxiety was the most likely cause, but she worried that his heart wasn't strong enough for so much emotion. She moved to his side. 'Sit tall and try to take longer and slower breaths, sire,' she said, taking his hand in hers. 'It will help if you breathe in through your nose and exhale through your mouth. We will do it together. Inhale when I squeeze your fingers and release when I let go.'

He calmed enough after a minute or two to raise his gaze again to William's face. 'You have the likeness of my father,' he said. 'He died when I was twenty and I have the clearest memory of him.' A tremor began in his lips. 'I have been most remiss in my duty to you, William. Will you forgive me?'

'There's nothing to forgive, sire. I've learnt more by making my own way in life than I could ever have done if I'd been forced to accept the constraints of being your grandson.'

The old man released Jayne's hand and pressed the kerchief to his eyes again. 'Are you aware that I petitioned the King to allow the dukedom to pass through my daughter to my other grandson?'

'I am, and have always wished you success in the matter.'

'Most men would be angered to have a rightful title removed.'

'Only those who feel the need for them.'

'Your cousin and his mother want nothing else.' The duke stared at William over the hovering kerchief. 'But you have more the bearing of a Granville than your cousin. My daughter encourages him in arrogance and laziness, and his single contribution to the King's cause was to surrender my estate in Somerset without a shot being fired. He spent the rest of the war in Oxford, doing nothing, and is now betrothed to a simpering miss who is even more shallow-minded than he is.'

William shrugged. 'What can I say except that he sounds eminently suitable to be your heir, sire?'

Jayne watched blotches of distress rise up the old man's neck and into his cheeks, and guessed it would be seconds only before he began struggling for breath again. 'Anxiety isn't good for you, my lord, so I beg you to find a less troubling subject to discuss.' She stooped to smile at him. 'I recommend humour. You showed such a fine sense of fun yesterday at the inn that May quite fell in love with you, and since William is similar—for he's a great tease also—I warrant you'll discover more about each other through laughter than confrontation.'

He raised a gnarled finger to stroke her cheek. 'Does he deserve you, my dear?'

Jayne's eyes filled with amusement at this second blatant attempt to use her. 'It's not my place to say, sire. You must find that out for yourself.'

Word of Alice's death spread quickly, and visitors came to the front door to pay their respects. Sir Francis, alarmed at having to receive Puritans, begged Jayne to stand with him, and she did so gladly in order to give William time alone with his grandfather. Nevertheless, it was an hour and a half before the queue came to an end, and she worried that was overly long for two men who held opposite views on everything.

Resigned to finding Granville hurt and William gone when she and Sir Francis entered the parlour, she smiled in relief to see them sitting side by side with their legs stretched in front of them. Together, with their heads canted at the same angle, they laughed to hear her say she was glad to be done with Puritan pleasantries, and she wondered if they were aware of the similarities between them.

'It's a dour religion indeed,' said William, rising to his feet and offering her the chair.

His Grace chuckled. 'So dour that William tells me Lady Alice hid Shakespeare's plays inside her Bible as a means of making the interminable hours of prayer more endurable.'

Sir Francis moved to the mantelpiece and thrust the toe of his boot morosely against the raised edge of the hearth. 'They're expecting her to be buried in one of the Dorchester graveyards. An elder told me he's already chosen the Bible readings, and I guarantee we'll listen to more warnings of God's judgement than promises of a better life in the hereafter. Is that what she wanted?'

'No,' Jayne assured him, refusing the chair in preference to standing. 'When she knew her time was limited by shaking palsy, she told me that her heart never left the Church of England. Her wish was that you take her home to Winterborne Stickland and bury her next to your father in your own graveyard with an Anglican priest saying Anglican prayers. Will you do that for her, sir? You'll find the instruction in the top drawer of her bureau.'

His demeanour brightened immediately. 'Most readily,' he said. 'I feared I would have to leave her here.'

Jayne shook her head. 'She was too fond of laughing to believe she'd rest easily amongst people of a more solemn frame of mind. She said Puritans were only happy when they were resisting the pull of Satan.' She paused for a moment, wondering if William would agree with the lie she was about to tell. 'She made one other request of me, Sir Francis, though she didn't memorialise it in writing. She asked that William and I offer each of her servants employment at Winterborne Houghton. As her heir, the choice of hiring them should be yours, but since William and I are well acquainted with all of them, Alice thought they would be more comfortable working for us. Does that meet with your approval?'

His relief was obvious. 'Certainly. I have maids enough, and William has none. If he's willing to take them on, I can be shed of responsibility for them. Are you in agreement, William?'

William was smiling indulgently at Jayne, clearly aware that she'd invented the request. 'By all means, for the same idea had occurred to me, though I question whether Alice considered the poor state of the servants' quarters at Winterborne Houghton before she made the plea.'

Jayne had an answer ready. 'She didn't expect to die so soon. She spoke many times of her hopes of attending our wedding and seeing the house restored.' She turned to Sir Francis again. 'You'll do us a great kindness if you allow the maids to remain here until after our marriage in the autumn, sir. I will ensure they maintain the property in good order and have money to feed themselves.'

William answered before Sir Francis could. 'That won't be necessary, Jayne. I spoke to them while you and Francis were outside, and they've agreed to take up residence in Winterborne Houghton after Alice's funeral.' He reached for her hands. 'His Grace would like to accept your invitation to visit Swyre for a few days, so I plan to ride with you both and ask Sir Henry to advance the date of our wedding.' He lifted her fingers to his lips. 'Three weeks must pass for the banns to be read, but there's no prettier time to be married than the first week of June.'

It was another two hours before Jayne was able to talk with him in private, and by then her nerves were in shreds at the speed with which events were moving. With William's assistance, Sir Francis had secured the services of a funeral undertaker who was able to supply a coffin and an open-topped wagon to transport Alice's body and her servants to Winterborne Stickland, where they would stay until after Alice's interment. And when the time came for the wagon to leave, the driver had little trouble negoti-ating a path through the much-thinned crowds of the previous days. The church bells had fallen silent at midnight and the people of Dorchester had taken this as a signal to return to sobriety and work, for even peace, it seemed, could not be celebrated indefinitely.

Only Granville and Mister Adams remained in Alice's house, and Peter was waiting with His Grace's coach some thirty yards up the street to allow Alice's wagon to pass. William beckoned him forward. 'You remember your instructions?' he called, drawing Jayne clear as the horses pulled alongside.

'Yes, sir. We're to follow the Bridport highway and wait at the King's Head tavern until you join us.'

William took Jayne's arm and turned her towards him. 'I'm conscious that one of us needs to ride ahead to alert your parents to unexpected guests, and, since my horse is stabled here in Dorchester, it would make more sense for me to do it. Are you agreeable to that?'

She regarded him with disfavour. 'Do you expect me to be?'

'No,' he said with a smothered laugh, 'which is why I instructed the coachman to wait for me at the King's Head. I guessed you'd be bent on riding astride once you retrieved your mare rather than travelling demurely in the carriage.'

'Not as bent as I am on having a conversation with you before we reach Swyre, William. Do you have any idea how Mama will react to being told she has to plan a wedding feast in three weeks when you assured her less than a month ago that it couldn't happen before the autumn?'

'I thought she'd be more put out by having the duke and Mister Adams imposed upon her.'

Jayne shook her head. 'We'll be lucky to escape with our lives when she learns that all her careful planning for the autumn has been wasted. Whatever possessed you to come up with such an idea?'

This time his laugh was loud enough to be heard by others. 'I thought it inspired,' he said. 'I can't think of anything more enticing than marrying you in three weeks' time. I'd do it today if the law allowed us.'

Jayne saw a matron frown at them. 'You should be mourning Alice, not making light of our wedding,' she admonished. 'And I suggest you find a less flippant answer for Mama or she'll assume our urgency to wed is because I'm carrying your child.'

William sobered abruptly. 'That wouldn't do at all,' he agreed. 'Your father would horsewhip me from the house. Will the truth satisfy Lady Margaret?'

'It depends what it is.'

'Your penchant for involving me in your charitable enterprises, Jayne. I don't say I share all your sympathies—Samuel Morecott being one—but I'm willing to accommodate them if it makes you happy.' Humour returned to his eyes. 'Making you mistress of Winterborne Houghton, and allowing you to give houseroom to whomever you please, seemed the perfect solution to my sudden—and *deeply* unexpected—acquisition of a grandfather in need of care. By rights, Lady Margaret should pity me rather than chastise me, since Andrew tells me you plagued her with stray dogs throughout your childhood.'

A smile twitched at the corner of Jayne's mouth. 'She'll pity me more,' she warned. 'Alice told her at Christmas that half the windows at Winterborne Houghton were broken and the inside was dripping with damp. Molly and the maids might be able to endure such conditions, but your grandfather won't. He'll die sooner there than at the hands of your aunt in Berkshire.'

'Are you suggesting we return him to her?'

She sighed. 'What alternative is there? He can't stay at Swyre until Winterborne Houghton is ready. It wouldn't be fair on Mama.'

William gave his ear a thoughtful scratch. 'It won't do, I'm afraid. I've already given him my pledge not to send him and Mister Adams back to Berkshire. Your wretched insistence on pointing out his frailty plucked at my conscience.'

Jayne stared at him in exasperation. 'You can't make Mama responsible for that. If you've had a sudden attack of guilt, you must provide a solution yourself.'

'I thought I had,' said William plaintively. 'You've captured His Grace's heart, Jayne, and he's set on living with you at Winterborne Houghton. As indeed is Mister Adams, who mistakes you for an angel.' He laughed and trapped her hand between both of his before she could rap his knuckles. 'I'll not tease any more,' he promised, 'though I find your lack of faith in me a little hurtful. The house is two-thirds towards completion. I've had a dozen men working there for five months under Francis's supervision, and he tells me the roof and windows are now secure, with every broken tile and pane replaced. The damp is cured, the reception rooms and bedchambers on the first floor have been completed, and two anterooms to the kitchen have been set aside as a hospital. In addition, Molly assures me that she and the other maids will care for His Grace and Mister Adams until you can join them in three weeks' time. Will that do?'

She entwined her fingers with his, wondering that amongst all his other concerns, he'd remembered his promise to make her a hospital. 'You haven't mentioned furniture.'

'Francis has instructed carriers to remove everything from Alice's house tomorrow and transport it to Winterborne Houghton, which means there will be beds, tables and chairs for most of the rooms. He wants us to think of it as her wedding present to us.' He touched a finger to her lips. 'I trust it will suffice for the moment.'

Her eyes softened as she kissed his palm. 'You truly are the most irritating man,' she said.

1646–1649

Following a further two years of war, incited
by a treaty between the King and Scotland,
King Charles is tried, convicted, and executed for
treason on 30 January 1649.

TWENTY-SEVEN

Winterborne Houghton, Dorset, 30 January 1649

JAYNE THOUGHT LIFE HAD A habit of turning in circles as she and Ruth sat together on the terrace of Winterborne Houghton, watching Isaac, now an accomplished rider, put his pony through its paces on the grass beyond. Nearly four years had passed since the day Sir Edward Hamway had attempted to steal her father's cattle, but she was still able to picture the event in her mind. The main difference between then and now was that there was no sea for her and Ruth to enjoy, but the antics of Granville and Mister Adams were as entertaining. Mister Adams, a favourite of Isaac's because they took the same childish pleasure in everything, capered about the flagstones, mimicking the turns and steps of the pony, while Granville, using canes to support himself, performed his daily exercise of walking up and down the terrace to increase his strength and balance.

Other memories intruded as Jayne looked past Isaac to the parkland beyond, for so much had happened in the two and a half years since William had brought her to Winterborne Houghton. She always remembered that day with a smile, for it had been the morning after their wedding and William had been unusually nervous when he'd asked her to walk on foot from the highway. Their path had taken them along a rutted driveway, unsuitable for a carriage, and then onto ground overgrown with wild saplings, brambles and furze. So untamed was the land that Jayne's heart had begun to sink at what to expect of the house, and her astonishment had been all the greater, therefore, when the trees thinned and she found herself looking at the most beautiful building she had ever seen.

Constructed in stone and brick during Elizabeth's reign, and rising elegantly above a stone-flagged terrace, it took the form of a recumbent 'E', with three elegantly gabled projections, one in the centre and one at either end. Each projection was adorned with pretty mullioned windows, but these were small compared to the immense floor-to-ceiling windows in the recessed walls. Her gasp of wonder had caused William to sigh in relief before twirling her in his arms and asking if she was happy with her new home, and all she could think to answer was that her father would be mortified to know there was a prettier house in Dorset than Swyre.

If those were indeed Sir Henry's feelings, he had hidden them well on his and Lady Margaret's regular visits to Winterborne Houghton. With the war ongoing through the King's refusal to accept Parliament's terms, and his promise to the Scots to impose Presbyterianism on England in return for being restored to his throne by a Scottish army, Jayne's parents had come often to support her during William's absences. Lady Margaret assisted her in the managing of the household, while Sir Henry devoted his time to entertaining Granville.

Mercifully, Dorset had seen none of the fighting after Lady Bankes surrendered Corfe Castle to Parliament in August 1646, but the skirmishes were said to be ferocious along the Scottish borders and in the few parts of England where the King was still revered. The continued conflict meant William's hope of resigning his commission had come to nought, and instead of allowing him to live the life of a country farmer, Sir Thomas Fairfax had promoted him to lieutenant general.

Ironically, the person who had taken most pride in William's advancement was Granville. It mattered not who reared a child, he was fond of saying, blood would always out. Jayne had been often tempted to answer that his other grandson had the same blood, but in truth the subject was best avoided. Lady Maria had brought her son on an unannounced visit to Winterborne Houghton within three weeks of Jayne's arrival in the house, and their behaviour had been both discourteous and unpleasant.

At the time, Jayne had been shocked by Lady Maria's hatred of her, but now she remembered the silly woman with amusement. Lady Maria's greatest fury had been directed at the magnificent furnishings William had ordered brought from the upper floors of his house in Dorchester. There were paintings and tapestries from France, Holland and Italy, along with gilded timepieces, ornate armoires, lavishly padded chairs and finely wrought tables, all of which were collected together in the salon awaiting Jayne's decision on where to place them. For reasons best known to herself, Lady Maria had decided the items had once belonged to her father, and she derided Granville for his foolishness in gifting his possessions to a man who didn't deserve them.

While her son had contented himself with sneering at Alice's humbler furniture and paintings, Lady Maria had flounced about the room, hissing insults. Winterborne Houghton had nothing to recommend it. The house had been cheap and gaudy when Ralph had lived in it, and under Mistress Swift's management could only get worse. She had classed William as a common thief and swindler, her father as a confused old man without the ability to make decisions and Jayne as a low-born temptress who had used her wiles to seduce them both.

Mister Adams, frightened out of his remaining wits, had clutched Jayne's hand and cowered behind her skirts, but this only incensed Lady Maria further. Was there any man Mistress Swift wasn't prepared to seduce in her ambitions to be a duchess? It was bad enough that she'd stolen the affections of Milady's own coachman and groom; must she steal those of His Grace's senile valet also? Jayne, ignoring her, had asked Granville if he required her to stay. Upon receiving a firm shake of the head, she led Mister Adams from the room. Shortly afterwards, Lady Maria and her son departed, never to return, and the duke's only comment on the matter was that, if Jayne were wise, she would regard his daughter's display of jealousy as a form of flattery. For herself, Jayne thought it more likely that anger at losing control of her father was the cause, but she only ever shared that opinion with William.

Because his duties kept him close to the Scottish border, William's visits were few and far between, but Jayne didn't begrudge his absences, since they were always followed by unexpected and never-to-be-forgotten reunions. These were Jayne's sweetest memories, for he invariably arrived alone, usually at night, and the first anyone else knew of his presence was when he wandered into the kitchen to tease the maids and sample whatever Cook was preparing for breakfast.

His greatest pleasure was to spend time with his son. Born on 9 May 1647, the anniversary of Alice's death, he had been christened Elias Henry Granville Harrier, and no child had a more doting, if sadly intermittent, father than William. He felt his absences more strongly each time he returned, for, as the little boy grew, he became shyer of the uniformed stranger who arrived without warning and was gone again within days. The most constant man in Elias's life was Granville and, while Jayne found His Grace's forbearance of the toddler's demands for attention touching, she was suspicious of his motives, guessing he realised how much easier it would be to influence the son than the father.

She watched Granville now, determinedly taking his daily steps with Elias strutting happily beside him, and she thought what a pity it was that Alice had died without knowing she had helped forge William into a man his grandfather could admire. Jayne was never sure if William reciprocated His Grace's admiration or merely tolerated the old man's presence in his house, but he was invariably courteous to Granville, deferring to him whenever he thought the situation demanded it. On Jayne's advice, Granville refrained from speaking about the dukedom, having accepted her argument that William would inherit the title whether he wanted it or not and a wise grandfather would allow him to make up his own mind when that time came. This reasoning appealed to Granville. He held the view that William had been at the heart of soldiering and political intrigue too long to be content with the quiet life of a country gentleman and took it as a certainty that he would exploit his status in due course in order to exercise influence.

With sudden exuberance, Elias ran to wrap his arms about his mother's legs and rest his cheek on her lap, and Jayne bent to kiss him, wishing William was there to share the moment. Granville might be right to say he'd tire of being a country gentleman eventually, but at present his single ambition was to leave soldiering behind and enjoy a peaceful life with his wife and son. In every letter he wrote, he spoke of his desire to be home, raising Elias in the way Alice had raised him and supporting Jayne's work as a physician.

On Richard's advice, Jayne had delayed her hospital project for a year to be assured of a safe pregnancy. Nevertheless, she had refused to be treated as an invalid and had used the time to oversee the finishing of the house before setting the labourers to cutting back the trees and shrubs along the driveway and clearing the parkland of furze and wild saplings. Since most had been hired in Dorchester, William had given them cottages on the estate for the duration of the restoration, but shortly before Elias's birth, they had entreated Jayne to ask him to make their positions permanent and allow their families to join them.

He had travelled south a month later to meet his new son, and Jayne had relayed the hired men's request, reminding him he needed farmhands for the land. She told him she found no fault in any of them. They worked hard and willingly at whatever she asked them to do and all had confessed to preferring the freedom of Winterborne Houghton to the harsh religious strictures of Puritan Dorchester. In addition, several claimed to have wives who were skilled at nursing and midwifery. William had groaned and said she'd recommend a one-legged gnome as long as he had a wife with a talent for bandaging, but His Grace had chuckled and advised him not to look a gift horse in the mouth.

Thereafter, simply by treating her own people and their families, word of the hospital had spread around the neighbouring estates. Jayne's greatest supporter was Emmeline, who became a frequent visitor two months after her marriage to Sir Francis in August 1647. She was as shy as he was and every bit as tongue-tied as Alice had described, but her unstinting praise of Jayne's abilities in her letters to friends sent word of the hospital to Blandford and beyond. In addition, many of Jayne's patients from the west of the county continued to call on her services, either by travelling to Winterborne Houghton or begging her by letter to visit them, and this last service had been made easier when Ruth and Isaac came to live with her.

They had visited in the spring of 1648, and their joy to be at Winterborne Houghton led to the stay becoming permanent. Ruth's quiet serenity and womanly love of embroidery endeared her to Granville, while Isaac's willingness to play with Elias meant the toddler had a boy to emulate rather than an old man. For Jayne, the arrangement gave her the freedom to work in her hospital and visit patients in their homes, knowing that someone she trusted was supervising her son; and Ruth took pleasure from being useful, confessing that life in her parents' house was restrictive and lonely compared with the bustling excitement of Winterborne Houghton.

Jayne didn't doubt that Andrew's ability to write to her without Joseph and Elizabeth intercepting his letters, and his occasional visits whenever he was given leave to spend time in Dorset, added to Ruth's delight in being there, and Jayne did all in her power to support their growing attachment to each other. In one of her regular letters to Richard, she had asked his advice on how to counter any arguments her father might raise on the matter of first cousins marrying, and Richard had suggested appealing to Sir Henry's pockets. The chances of a still or damaged birth were slight, and there was no better way of consolidating a family's wealth than by uniting the offspring of brothers.

Jayne's single regret about living in Winterborne Houghton was that it was so distant from Richard's house in Bridport. Had she still been in Swyre, she could have ridden the Bridport highway in half an hour and discussed the matter with him in person. Instead, she had to make do with letters until the many descriptions she sent him of cases and remedies, and how a hospital managed entirely by women was gaining credibility amongst all classes of people—including men—persuaded him to make the journey himself.

He had arrived during the last week of August 1648, and his only concession to age was to come in a hired carriage rather than on horseback. Jayne remembered her joy on seeing him, for he was quite unchanged despite his advancing years. Indeed, his mind remained so sharp that, unlike Granville, he had recognised within a day that her lightness of manner was masking a deep anxiety. He had urged her to confide in him, and Jayne would have done so, had she not invited Francis and Emmeline to lunch. Instead, she was obliged to play hostess and give carefree answers to her guests' many questions about William.

The last she had heard from him was some three weeks earlier, when he'd been ordered to join his regiment with Cromwell's to confront an army of twenty thousand Scots. He'd referred to the matter in the drollest of tones—*Don't concern yourself for us, dear wife. I'm told their commander, the Duke of Hamilton, is as pretty as Prince Maurice and as poor a leader*—but a subsequent letter from Andrew had painted a different picture. *We number but a third of the Scottish force and must march a hundred miles to meet them in battle. This time, I fear we may be beaten. Pray for us, sister, and comfort Ruth if the worst should happen.*

Jayne had kept the contents of the letters to herself, unwilling to impose her anxiety on anyone else, but her sense of foreboding had increased as each day passed. She had clung to the notion that no news was better than bad news, and her heart had lurched with dread, therefore, when her lunch party was interrupted by a voice from the dining-room door. She turned to see her brother Philip, covered in dust from the road, and with a heavy sigh rose from her chair to greet him.

'That's a poor welcome for a weary brother who's covered thirty miles in an hour and a half to bring you word of your husband,' he said with a grin, limping into the room and bowing to her guests. 'Your Grace, sirs, ladies, forgive my intrusion but our brother Andrew reached Swyre from Ashbourne in Derbyshire some two hours since and begged me to carry a message posthaste to Jayne.' He took hold of her hands. 'Andrew wants you to know he was wrong, sister. Twenty thousand Scots were no match for eight thousand Englishmen. The Duke of Hamilton was routed at Preston Moor in Lancashire and then fled with the remnants of his sorry army to Derbyshire, where he was taken prisoner five days ago.'

Jayne took a moment to compose herself. 'And what of William?'

'He was ordered to escort Hamilton to London to face charges of treason for inciting a second civil war.' Philip released her hands to reach into his pocket. 'He had time to pen you a note before he left and promises to write again as soon as he is able.'

He passed her a scruffy piece of paper which was folded but not sealed. She spread it open on her palm and read the lines that were written on it.

'What does it say?' demanded His Grace.

Jayne's eyes welled with tears of joy. '"The war is over and my duty done. Have you room in your house for a weary soldier who dreams of a peaceful life?"' She raised her head. 'Is he right? Can we now hope for peace?'

Richard's answer had been prescient. 'Not unless the King bows to Parliament's will,' he said. 'The fighting may be over but the arguments will continue. There's no easy solution to the problem he presents.'

And so it had proved. Parliament had split into two camps. The timid favoured continued negotiations to keep the King on his throne, while those weary of his continued obstinacy favoured putting him on trial for treason for rousing the Scots to wage war on England. This latter faction was led by Oliver Cromwell, and with so much uncertainty regarding the King's fate, William's longed-for return had been delayed once again. Towards the end of November, he had written that arrears of pay and Parliament's continued refusal to indict the King were inciting rebellion amongst the troops. In every rank, voices were demanding why they'd been asked to fight if victory went unrewarded. The regiments billeted in and around London were particularly restless and he feared it wouldn't be long before they marched on Parliament. Meanwhile, Sir Thomas Fairfax had placed London under martial law.

*I can't say how or when this will end, Jayne. Our soldiers
feel their grievances strongly because they've received
neither pay nor gratitude from Parliament since their
defeat of Hamilton, and they're stating loudly that six
years of unremitting war has merely replaced one form
of tyranny with another. Know that my greatest wish is
to be at Winterborne Houghton, but I am duty-bound to
remain with those who have fought so gallantly under
my command.*

Christmas and the New Year came and went, followed by
a letter from William in the first week of January to say that
Parliament had finally passed an ordinance to set up a High Court
of Justice to try the King for treason. The date proposed for the
commencement of the trial was 20 January 1649.

*Tension within the army is very high. Some side with
Fairfax, who is against the trial out of fear the King will
be portrayed as a martyr; others with Cromwell, who
considers it a necessary evil if the country is to find peace.
Each is petitioning me to lend him my support, and
I'm deeply torn between the two. Will you stand by me
whichever choice I make, Jayne? I fear I'm as likely to be
on the wrong side of history as on the right.*

Jayne had answered that she would defend him whatever
the outcome, but she received no reply to her letter. Francis had
ridden to Winterborne Houghton on 25 January to report that
Emmeline's father had heard from an acquaintance in London
that the King's trial had started on 20 January. In view of the

secrecy surrounding it, the acquaintance couldn't say how it was progressing, but Francis had warned Jayne and Granville to expect trouble. Rioting was expected whichever verdict was delivered, and Sir Thomas Fairfax was poised to impose martial law across the country.

Jayne wondered now if thoughts of martial law were causing her to imagine the sound of rattling bridles and cantering hooves. But no. What had begun as a far-off drumming grew louder in the still air, and she and Ruth watched together as a column of mounted men emerged from the trees that lined the first half of the driveway. The leading riders slowed to a trot to take the bend that would bring them to the front door and, though they were yet too distant to make out faces, Jayne was certain that neither William nor Andrew was amongst them.

Granville paused in his pacing to lean heavily on his canes. 'We're about to come under military control,' he said.

'Do you wish Isaac to ride to the stable for Peter and Harold?' asked Ruth. 'If they alert the farmhands, we'll have a good twenty to assist us.'

Fighting a renewed sense of foreboding, Jayne lifted Elias onto her lap. 'We're better off alone,' she said as calmly as she could. 'The code of the New Model Army forbids its soldiers from imposing themselves on women who lack protection. We'll wait here and present as helpless a tableau as we can.'

She encouraged them all to continue what they were doing and listened for the sound of the latch on the door to the terrace being raised. She watched out of the corner of her eye as Molly escorted an officer through it, and gave a relieved smile when she saw that it was John Metcalfe. He walked forward and bent over her hand.

'You look well, Lady Harrier, and this must be Elias. He bears a strong resemblance to his father.' He turned to Ruth and then Granville. 'Ma'am. My lord. I am Major John Metcalfe of Lyme Regis and serve under General Sir William Harrier.'

Granville used his canes to move closer. 'What brings you here and how do you know my status?'

John looked uncomfortable. 'I have a message for Lady Harrier which I would prefer to deliver in private, sire. Sir William advised me that it might not be suitable for every ear.'

Jayne set Elias on the ground and urged him to run to Mister Adams. 'If it's His Grace's Royalist allegiance or Mistress Morecott's sex that's worrying you, John, let me assure you there's nothing you can say that will shock them. Should we assume the trial has ended?'

He nodded. 'Three days ago, milady.'

'And the verdict?'

John cast an uneasy glance at Granville. 'Guilty, milady. The death warrant was signed by fifty-seven men, one of whom was General Cromwell. Your husband and brother remain with him in London until after the execution, but I and the men who accompany me—all from Dorset, Devon or Somerset—have been given leave to return to our homes. Sir William interceded on our behalf when we explained our reluctance to be present at the King's death.'

'How long before that happens?'

John looked past once more her to Granville. 'Knowing His Grace's allegiance, I'd rather not say, milady.'

'But you will,' said Granville firmly. 'Speak.'

John made a gesture of apology. 'Today, sire . . . the thirtieth day of January . . . and the hour—two after noon—is imminent.'

The duke's horrified gasp suggested Jayne had been wrong to think he wouldn't be shocked. She rose to her feet and guided him to her place on the bench. 'Breathe deeply, my lord. You expected no less.'

'But not without warning, and not that my grandson would choose to witness it,' he muttered, allowing her to lower him to the seat. 'What sort of man stands with murderers?'

John stood stiffly to attention. 'With respect, sire, you're in no position to judge. Like most, you have sat in comfort while men have died on the battlefields. If Lady Harrier, who has seen the bloodshed at close quarters, condemns her husband for trying to end it, I will listen to her, but not to you who have been shielded from it.'

Granville studied him for a long moment. 'My grandson is never so discourteous, Major Metcalfe.'

'My apologies, sire, but Sir William deserves your praise and not your calumny. He is a man of principle who has fought long and hard on the side of the people, and the King's continued attempts to set his subjects—be they English, Welsh, Irish or Scottish—against each other angers him. The terms offered His Majesty over the last seven years have been fair and just, yet he has rejected them all, preferring that his country destroy itself than cede any portion of his power.'

'If you feel so strongly, why have you not stayed to watch the execution?'

'Because I am a Puritan, sire, as are the men who travel with me. We follow the path of righteousness and fear God will judge us harshly if we assist in putting a lawful sovereign to death.' He turned to Jayne. 'Your husband is the truest of friends, milady. He negotiated the release of every soldier in his regiment whose conscience troubles him in this matter, and, despite his own qualms, refuses to abandon General Cromwell in his time of need. Your brother, as aide to General Cromwell, does likewise. Whatever is said of this affair afterwards, know that those closest to you have acted with honour.'

Jayne took both his hands in hers. 'Thank you, John. Your words are most comforting. Now hasten home to Ann and give her my kind regards.' She released him to Molly. 'May God go with you and those who accompany you.'

He bowed. 'You and yours also, milady.'

Jayne waited until Molly had escorted him back into the house. 'Had I cared less for him and his wife, I would have accused him and his comrades of cowardice,' she murmured. 'Like Pontius Pilate they wash their hands of responsibility for the one action that might give us peace.'

Ruth nodded. 'They'll not benefit by it,' she said. 'Pontius Pilate is as reviled as those who demanded Jesus' death.'

'The Harrier and Swift names will be as reviled,' Granville muttered grimly. 'Jayne's husband and brother made poor choices when they decided to support murderers.'

TWENTY-EIGHT

JAYNE WAITED UNTIL ALL IN the house were abed then crept down to the kitchen, where she lit candles and stoked the fire. The hearth was so deep and wide that this room, despite its large size, was always the warmest in the house, and she sat at the long oak table to work at her hospital notes. But try as she might to fix her attention on her writing, she kept breaking off to listen for the sound of the front door opening.

If necessary, she would sit there every night until William returned, because she refused to let him enter a darkened house alone and unwelcomed. Granville's hurt and angry reaction would be voiced by others, since every Royalist would seize on 'murder' and 'martyrdom' as easily as he had, and Jayne was determined that William should know from the moment he stepped inside his home that his wife's promise to defend him had not been made idly.

The hour-candle told her it was close to midnight when a sudden draught set every flame flickering. She heard the scrape of boots on flagstones, the jingle of metal as spurs were unbuckled and discarded, and the rattle of a sword-belt being laid across a chair, and she rose to her feet when William appeared at the end of the corridor and turned towards the light.

'Are the smiles for me?' he asked, treading on soft feet towards her.

She held out her hands. 'Always,' she said. 'You inhabit my head far more than a man should. I was remembering the first time I saw you, in Alice's kitchen with your sober clothes and pointed hat, and thinking that Papa would never have allowed me to leave Swyre again if I'd confessed to a liking for a Puritan footman in Dorchester.'

He reached across the table to caress her fingers. 'And I was so fearful of seeing you again, I begged Alice not to pursue a friendship with you.'

'What was to fear?'

He urged her to sit and pulled out a chair for himself. 'A woman who defied convention even more courageously than she did. I thought it safer to keep you out of sight and out of mind.'

'Did it work?'

He made an attempt at humour, but it was clear to Jayne that his mood was too sombre for flippancy. 'It might have done had Prince Maurice not given me reason to be jealous.'

She smiled in acknowledgement of the attempt, but also to hide her concern at his appearance. They were sitting opposite each other, as they'd done across the desk in his house in Dorchester, and she was shocked by how pale and drawn he looked. His pallor was accentuated by dark stubble around his jaw and deep shadows beneath his eyes, yet she knew it couldn't be weariness from the journey that had drained him, for he'd ridden twice as far on his visits home from the north. 'Cook has prepared a mutton stew for tomorrow,' she said, 'and though my talents are vastly inferior to hers, I'm sure I can warm it for you now. There's also a keg of ale, newly broached, which I'm more than capable of drawing. Will you allow me to do that for you?'

He shook his head. 'I have no appetite for eating or drinking, Jayne.'

'Nonetheless, as your physician, I insist you try,' she said firmly, rising and moving to the pantry, where she found the stew still in its cauldron. She hung it from a hook above the fire and kept her back to him by busily stoking the embers. 'Am I right to think the King died bravely and you're now questioning your support for Cromwell?'

His sigh was heartfelt. 'He spoke his last words in a steady voice and then knelt to accept his fate without a tremor. A great groan rose from the crowd when the axe fell, and I found myself groaning with them. It wasn't meant to end this way, Jayne. Fairfax was right to say he'll be viewed as a martyr.'

She filled a tankard from the keg, and placed it on the table in front of him before resuming her seat. His longed-for home-coming would be sad indeed if she couldn't lift his melancholy mood. 'You'd be ill-advised to repeat that word in front of Ruth,' she said lightly. 'On the twentieth occasion that Granville used it, she lost patience with him and said no man who clung so hard to earthly power as the King could ever be considered a martyr. Granville was quite startled because he'd never seen her angry before. Her face was so purple that he quite forgot my red one.'

William digested this in silence for a moment. 'It was never my intention to make you bear the brunt of his disappointment, Jayne. I asked John to speak privately with you and leave me to make the explanations to Granville.'

'We were together on the terrace when John arrived, and he had no choice but to tell Granville as well.' She rested her chin on her hands and smiled mischievously at him. 'You've no reason to apologise, husband. I was thoroughly exhilarated to be your champion, as was Ruth, though I don't remember Granville mentioning disappointment. If I'm wrong, Molly will correct me tomorrow, for your grandfather's voice is as loud as Sir Henry's, and there wasn't a single slur amongst the many he produced that she didn't hear.'

She was rewarded by a small glimmer of humour at the corners of his eyes. 'Were they bad?'

'Unremittingly dreadful,' she answered with a laugh. 'I've never met a man so determined to be unreasonable. Our quarrel lasted a good hour, until I warned him I would never speak to him again if he mentioned murder or martyrdom one more time.'

William reached for the tankard and took a swallow of ale. 'Was that enough to silence him?'

She leant forward to wipe froth from his lips. 'Of course not,' she said, sucking her finger, 'but it helped that our beautiful son smacked his hand for shouting at me, and that Mister Adams called him a "mean old man". Also, that Ruth asked if he thought the King entirely guiltless in the matter of the war, and that Isaac quoted verses from Exodus which say each man must pay as his judges determine.' Her eyes danced. 'But Molly's intervention made the greatest impact.'

'What did she do?'

'Brought our entire household onto the terrace and said that if His Grace wished to retain a pleasant relationship with them, he should cease insulting their master and mistress. They took grave exception to hearing Miss Jayne described as a "jumped-up squire's daughter" and an "ignorant woman", and Sir William as a "cowardly murderer" and "Cromwell's lickspittle", since it was their considered opinion that there were no braver or more independent-minded people in Dorset than Sir William and Lady Harrier.'

William took another, larger swallow of ale, and Jayne was gratified to see colour begin to return to his cheeks. 'You're teasing me.'

'Not at all,' she assured him. 'Molly sent word to Peter and Harold to round up our fieldhands, and when they aligned themselves beside the household, Granville discovered himself to be quite outnumbered. I don't say he's reconciled to the execution, nor ever will be, but he has a better understanding of why you supported Cromwell after the men nominated Harold to speak for them.'

Creases formed about his eyes as he took another swallow of ale. 'What did he say?'

'That the outside workers owed everything to you, who had given them a position, and nothing to the King, whose war had taken the lives of their fathers, brothers and friends. In their opinion, the King's head was a small price to pay for an end to division, and all had prayed that enough brave men would see the matter through. They had learnt from Molly that their own master was one such man, and they wished His Grace to know they were proud to be in your service.'

'That doesn't sound like Harold. Are you sure you're not putting words into his mouth?'

'A few, perhaps, but only to take out the "ums" and "aarrs". I can quote his final sentence verbatim.' Jayne made an attempt at Harold's Berkshire burr. '"Ah'll tell you this, Milor, yer gran'son showed a deal more courage than tha scurvy troop of clodhoppers what churned up our driveway in their 'aste to inform Miss Jayne they was running away.'" She laughed again. 'Mister Adams, Isaac and Elias thought it such a worthy speech they clapped prodigiously and then capered about Granville until he joined them in applauding the magnificent loyalty of your workers.'

William didn't believe her. 'The workers barely know me.'

'Not true. You've been their favourite subject of gossip since they discovered how many tales Alice's servants can tell about you. Molly has been at your side since you were a boy, so she has more than most. There's not a person in Winterborne Houghton, including Granville, who isn't as well acquainted with you as you are yourself.'

He groaned. A happy sound. 'Are the stories kind or unkind?'

'Invariably kind . . . except for the one about the day you wet your britches because you were enamoured of a neighbour's daughter and refused to leave her side for anything as mundane as using a pisspot. They all love that tale.'

He gave the beginnings of a laugh. 'I was seven, and she was twelve.'

'Indeed, and Molly's always sure to make that clear. It wouldn't do at all to have our people thinking it was a recent event.'

William looked past her towards the fire. 'I don't deserve you, Jayne.'

'Almost certainly not,' she agreed, 'but you have me, nonetheless.'

'No, I truly mean I don't deserve you.' He surged to his feet. 'Nothing I've ever done merits being burnt to death in my own kitchen.'

Jayne turned to see stew pouring down the sides of the cauldron. 'Oh, dear Lord!' she said, leaping from her chair and flapping her skirt at the thick miasma of burning fat and gravy that was rising from the embers. 'What should I do?'

William rounded the table and used a curved poker to remove the pot from its hook and place it on the flagstones before stamping on the sizzling embers. 'You have to be the worst cook in Dorset,' he murmured, putting his arm about her waist and drawing her close.

'I know,' she agreed, resting her head on his shoulder. 'It's a mercy Molly trained you so well as a footman.'

He kissed her hair. 'I'm beginning to think you preferred me as a footman.'

'It's only natural,' she said. 'I'm descended from Eve and we share a taste for forbidden fruit.' She nodded to the charred meat around the lip of the cauldron. 'You do realise we'll have to eat that. It's burnt to a crisp, but Cook will chase me about the kitchen with a rolling pin if we waste it.'

His arm tightened about her. 'Are you afraid of her?'

'Infinitely so. I made the mistake of suggesting her broth might be improved with a little salt, and I'd have felt the weight of the rolling pin across my buttocks if Molly hadn't stepped between us. You should have warned me she doesn't take kindly to criticism.'

Laughter ruffled her curls. 'I forgot. It's more than twenty years since Alice or I dared try.'

'Then I trust you're happy to make penance by eating the blackened remains.'

'Is this your way of encouraging me to eat whether I want to or not?'

'If it were, I wouldn't admit to it,' she said, turning to plant a kiss on his mouth. 'Mama tells me a wife must retain a little mystery if she wants to keep her husband's interest.'

'And what does your father tell you?'

She raised her hands to cradle his face between her palms. 'That only the bravest and most admirable of Harriers can ever hope to catch a Swift.'

Newport Community
Learning & Libraries

ACKNOWLEDGEMENTS

WITH SPECIAL THANKS TO Roger Holehouse for his insights on the siege of Lyme; Tim Goodwin for his excellent history: *Dorset in the Civil War*; and the editorial and design teams at Allen & Unwin in Australia and the UK, whose help and support in the making of this book have been invaluable—Annette Barlow, Ali Lavau, Christa Munns and Clara Finlay in Sydney; and Sarah Hodgson and Kate Ballard in London.

If you too enjoyed *The Swift and the Harrier*, read on for Minette's illuminating answers to our reading group questions...

What was your inspiration in writing about the English Civil War?

The divisions caused in Parliament and the country by the EU referendum. The same divisions happened in the 17th century, when the choice lay between accountable government through Parliament and unaccountable government through Charles I, who refused to accept any curtailing of his power.

What came first for you – the plot or the characters?

The characters. I needed a neutral witness to the war and found that person in Jayne Swift, a trained physician from a Royalist family. Being neutral, she's willing to treat the sick and injured from both sides, and this allows the reader to see the conflict through her eyes. In addition, I needed a character of firm conviction who could exemplify why allegiances were so strongly felt. I found that person in William Harrier, who becomes an intermittent – though somewhat enigmatic – support for Jayne in times of difficulty.

This novel has a decidedly feminist bent, drawing attention as it does to the often crucial role of women during the English Civil War, something that until relatively recently has been under-discussed in historical fiction. Was Jayne inspired by anyone particular? And what inspired you to give her a medical background?

She follows the strong-minded pattern of Jane Austen's heroines! It's always fascinated me that when women began to be published in the late 18th/early 19th century, they depicted their heroines as insightful, free-thinking and clever. Prior to this, chronicles/histories were written by men at the behest of wealthier men who wanted their legacies preserved, and women had no place in them. All this changed when women were widely published. The blanket of anonymity was ripped away, and fully-formed, proactive female characters emerged. Jayne Swift predates Elizabeth Bennett by 150 years, but women like her certainly existed. Alice Leevers famously practised medicine in the 16th century when it was against the law for women to do so; while, a century later, Elizabeth Moore and Mary Rose successfully petitioned the Archbishop of Canterbury to grant them licences to call themselves 'doctor', which, until then, was a right enjoyed only by men.

———————————————————●———————————————————

Your previous historical fiction novel, The Last Hours, *was also centred around a female protagonist and set in the West Country, but 300 years earlier than the drama of* The Swift and the Harrier. *What particularly draws you to setting your dramas in tumultuous times and is it important to you have to a female protagonist?*

The history of both periods is fascinating. The Black Death in the 14th century brought an end to 300 years of serfdom (slavery), and the Civil War heralded the beginnings of democracy and constitutional monarchy. These were huge social changes, during which hundreds of thousands lost their lives. To set stories in the midst of such upheaval is both challenging and exciting. I have greater freedom to explore the *mores* of the times if I write through women, because, being marginalised, they have more to criticise than men.

———————————●———————————

The love story between Jayne and William is beautifully understated and comes secondary to the main thrust of the plot, which is something to which many of your readers have responded really well; we love Jayne's assertiveness and refusal to conform to societal expectation. Was it important to you to illustrate for contemporary readers the importance of asserting themselves, regardless of prevailing expectations?

I can never predict what readers will take from a book, but I always hope my characters are well-drawn enough to allow readers to identify with them!

———————————●———————————

The novel is incredibly well-researched, brilliantly illuminating readers about not only everyday life for the masses during the English Civil War but also about the struggles between Royalists and Parliamentarians, and within that the role of religion. Did you enjoy the research part of the creative process? Do you have any tips for aspiring writers keen to cast a light on a particular period of history that interests them?

I love researching history because it explains so much about the present day. My best tip for aspiring writers is to Google Amazon for books about a period that interests them. The best non-fiction books are often out of print, but Amazon acts as a distribution hub for antiquarian bookshops across the country, and there's nothing more exciting than receiving a dog-eared tome from a shop 300 miles away. You feel the history even before you start reading.

—————•—————

Would you like to resume Jayne's story in a sequel to this novel?

She's certainly hard to forget!

—————•—————

Which historical fiction authors have had the most influence on your own writing, and why?

Daphne du Maurier. She was a consummate storyteller, and her histories, set in Cornwall, remain as clear to me now as when I first read them. As a teenager, I also loved the books of D.K. Broster and Georgette Heyer.

————————●————————

Is there a particular author or novel who inspired you to become a writer?

Too many to mention, but Daphne du Maurier's *Rebecca*, Graham Greene's *The Power and the Glory*, Harper Lee's *To Kill a Mocking Bird* and James Baldwin's *Giovanni's Room* made the most impact on me when I was growing up.

————————●————————

You were a phenomenally successful author of crime fiction and thrillers for many years – what inspired you to try your hand at historical fiction?

I thrive on change, and the two genres are not so different. There are as many criminals in history as there are in crime fiction!